This book is for my own mistress of crafts,
Jennifer Armstrong

Maggie
Darling

Maggie Darling

A Modern Romance

James Howard Kunstler

Atlantic Monthly Press
New York

Published simultaneously in Canada
Printed in the United States of America

FIRST EDITION

Library of Congress Cataloging-in-Publication Data

Kunstler, James Howard.
    Maggie Darling: a novel / by James Howard Kunstler.
        p. cm.
    ISBN 0-87113-910-3
        1. Women millionaires—Fiction.   2. New York (N.Y.)—Fiction.
    3. Married women—Fiction.   4. Food writers—Fiction.   5. Celebrities—
    Fiction.   6. Connecticut—Fiction.   7. Adultery—Fiction.   I. Title.
    PS3561.U55M34 2004
    813'.54—dc22   2003060103

Atlantic Monthly Press
841 Broadway
New York, NY 10003

04 05 06 07 08   10 9 8 7 6 5 4 3 2 1

"Everything has been figured out, except how to live."
—Jean-Paul Sartre

~ Part One ~

Kenneth Departs

I

〜 The House of Yule 〜

"Never has there been such a Christmas!" Kenneth Darling proclaimed for at least the third time since his wife, Maggie, the goddess of hearth and home, descended from the rooms above, scrubbed, perfumed, and engarbed in a confection of antique red velvet (by Marc Fatuli) that was cut so as to display a bosom as lush and pink as two blushing pears made of marzipan. To Kenneth, Maggie's breasts seemed to precede her into a room like a pair of mysterious envoys from a faraway royal domain where sweetness reigned. He now swept across the room on a surge of desire and nostalgia this eve of the great holiday and took his place beside this wife of twenty-five Christmases.

They made a handsome portrait in the oval mirror that hung above the Federal inlaid mahogany serpentine-front sideboard. As Maggie lit the tapers in a favorite pair of spruce-green, petal-and-loop glass candlesticks deployed amid the gilt pinecones, holly boughs, silver bells, and other trappings of the season, Kenneth's manicured hand crept down her décolletage. He buried his nose in the wisps of sweet-smelling silver-blond hair behind her ear and whispered, "Never has there been such a Christmas."

"Are you stoned?" Maggie inquired.

"I've had a dram or two."

"Nothing more?"

"A teeny-weeny toke, perhaps," Kenneth whispered.

"Smoking pot again, are we?"

"Is that the royal or the editorial 'we'?"

"The matrimonial," Maggie said without irony.

"Ooo. You really know how to hurt a guy."

This was how it went with them typically. En garde, thrust and parry, touché. Maggie was getting good and goddamn sick of it. The wordplay aside, Kenneth's pot smoking irritated her only moderately in and of itself, though she would have been severely annoyed had she known the truth, namely that Kenneth was working on a snootful of cocaine as well as the pot and two pony glasses of straight Norse vodka. He was lit up like the antique pearlescent star at the top of their eighteen-foot Christmas tree, and the first guest had yet to arrive.

For a few years now, Kenneth had been on relatively good behavior. Maggie sometimes essayed to think he had "matured." Back in '96, hadn't they spent nearly a million dollars in legal fees clearing up that little incident when he drove his German automobile through a radar trap on the Merritt Parkway at 127 miles per hour—it handled like a dream—and was so whacked out on blow that he left a two-ounce plastic baggie of the stuff right out on the passenger seat for one Officer Wilsey to see? Not that Kenneth couldn't afford to pay for his error. Lawyers loved to see him coming the way kitchenware purveyors rubbed their hands at the sight of Maggie.

The nineties had been stupendous years for Kenneth. Starting out in the stuffy old bond house of Throop, Cravath, Herndon, and Hobbs, he had learned the trick of packaging any old thing as a salable security: odd lots of mortgages, clumps of credit card debt, you name it. From there it could be abstracted further into options and futures, all of it oozing profit. When Kenneth was a boy he and his prep school buddies had played a variation of Monopoly in which absolutely everything on the board was for sale, not just the real estate from Baltic Avenue to Boardwalk, but also Chance, Community Chest, Go, the jail, even the manufacturer's logo in the center. Everything was a commodity. You could even buy the tokens each player used to travel around the board—the top hat, the race car, et cetera—and charge exorbitant rent for their use. These boys had grown up and entered their fathers' world of brokerage and had begotten the Wall Street of the eighties and nineties. That was how Kenneth Darling parlayed a very modest one-million-dollar trust fund into a two-hundred-million-dollar fortune—and he was a small fish, a guppy.

Maggie's feelings about Kenneth were so complicated these days that she would not have known where to begin even with the help of Fairfield County's most telepathic headshrinker—not that she needed one. Crude as it was, she rather enjoyed feeling Kenneth's paw down her dress, for she was a woman of a certain age, and it was reassuring to know that she was desired by her husband, who by any objective standards of measurement was still a prize catch. Kenneth competed in triathlons. It was his chief avocation. At age fifty-two he had the body of a Dartmouth sophomore—a better body than the indolent beer-swilling Dartmouth sophomore he had actually been years ago. Six foot two, 177 pounds, Kenneth had pectoral muscles like Kansas City strip steaks, shoulders that looked padded under the Versace suit but were all solid deltoid meat, and a hard rippling belly that a Mexican washerwoman could scrub soapy linens on. True, he had lost his hair—at least the sandy strands on top—but what remained on the sides curled about his ears and neck to contrast nicely with his perpetually tanned skin, and his well-shaped head made up for its baldness as an elegant old house by the sea makes up for its faded paint with classic architectural proportions. His face had the same carpentered precision. Had he not been a minor Wall Street wizard with $200 million, he might well have appeared in gentlemen's clothing advertisements. Add a pair of horn-rimmed spectacles and you would have an impression of intellect, not entirely a false one either, for Kenneth read novels.

Beyond all the good bone structure and rigorously trained gristle, however, stood the matter of his character, revealed already in part by the monkeyshines with drugs. There was also his tendency for a kind of perverse willfulness that Maggie called "Kenneth's passive-aggressive streak." He injured by omission rather than by commission. He forgot things: an anniversary, thank-you notes, the party at the Museum of Modern Art where he was supposed to meet Maggie after work. He called it absentmindedness. He was one of those people who say they have no sense of time and yet never show up early, only late. Maggie considered his behavior the foul excrescence of some long-buried rage, probably against his mother, Georgia, the bitch. He almost never finished a project outside the office, and Maggie wondered how many things he left dangling there, despite the fabulous stream of income. Of the nine triathlons Kenneth had entered since his coke rehab in 1996, he had dropped out on the final miles in eight of them, variously on account of "cramps," "dehydration," "dizziness," and other vague complaints. In the early years of their marriage, this nonsense about not finishing things nearly drove Maggie crazy. (Maggie always finished what she started and had never missed an appointment in her life.) Back then, they worked on things together—rehabilitating the original orchard, for instance. These days, Kenneth simply paid somebody to do things: refinishing his sailboat, buying Christmas presents, driving Hooper, their son, down to his Swarthmore registration.

Lately, they might have dwelt on separate planets. Kenneth, more than ever, had his Wall Street bastion at Throop, Cravath, his exercise regime, his lunching clubs, and his sailboat. Maggie no longer had Hooper to look after. Now she had her career. In her published books on cookery and party giving, she turned her natural mode of living into a national object lesson on the domestic arts. Not the old dishpan hands, "Hints from Heloise" suburban drudgery of her mom's day, but a new, glittering, upper-crust vision of the American hearth and home. To succeed at this was quite a feat in an age when many educated females wrote off homemaking as a sucker's game invented by the enemy, men, to keep women down. Apparently, a residual desire to provide something more spiritually fortifying than microwaved veal stew and canned entertainment still lurked deep, even in educated hearts. And, of course, more and more Americans, including those with good incomes, lived in soulless, artificial places that they despised, in homes that mocked their ideals about a good life, surrounded by laborsaving gadgets that eliminated all the shared material enactments of marriage, until couples stayed together mainly because they liked the same TV shows.

Maggie's evocation of the American home was an antidote to all this, and she was making a fortune writing books about it. Nothing like Kenneth's millions, but to date a good $7.8 million in net profits. In short, she could easily take care of herself now, and nearly in the manner to which she was accustomed. It was something she and Kenneth didn't talk about openly—for money, among those who have a lot of it, is considered a squalid topic—but Maggie's recent success had changed the equation of their union.

"Let's have a quickie, darling," Kenneth breathed warmly in her ear, his left hand still rummaging in her bodice, his right hand on the velvet overlaying her Junoesque belly.

"You must be insane," Maggie said, not pugnaciously but with a deep rueful exhalation. Kenneth was an avid lover, perhaps to a fault. But could there be a worse moment?

At once footsteps resounded on the ancient pine floors as servants swarmed into the hall seemingly from every opening. Kenneth extracted his hand and jerked himself around looking nonplussed. One of the waitresses hired for the night noticed his loss of poise and giggled. She was a Sarah Lawrence freshperson. Meanwhile, a chunky brunette with laughing eyes, dressed in a chef's white tunic, marched up to Maggie carrying a clipboard. This was Nina Stegman, Maggie's assistant. Aide-de-camp was more like it. Tonight, she was in charge of a Christmas Eve Feast for Two Hundred, as the affair would eventually be recorded in one of Maggie's books on holiday entertaining. Maggie, blushing, smoothed her velvet gown and adjusted her emerald drops.

"I'll see to the barman," Kenneth said and made himself scarce.

"The last of the capons will be finished at seven sharp," Nina reported, "but the left oven on the big Garland is acting weird."

"Weird?"

"It'll shoot up to five hundred for no reason."

"Damn! The thermostat's shot again," Maggie said decisively. "It happened on Thanksgiving in '93 and incinerated three acorn-fed pheasants I'd mail-ordered from Michigan. You'll have to regulate it manually. Here's what you do. Take a wooden spoon and jam it in the door so it stays open a crack to let the heat out. Keep close tabs on the thermometer inside. It takes vigilance but it'll work in a pinch."

"Roger," Nina said, in her jocular military manner. She loved high-pressure situations, as did Maggie, and for much the same reason: both were highly competent individuals who relished the chance to shine in an emergency. "Did you want to use the hollowed-out hubbard squashes for the stuffing?"

"No, the footed Targee silver bowls. You know, those acanthus-leaf things."

"Oh dear, I thought I'd put the parsnip puree in those."

"No, the Staffordshire luster."

"Roger. And the yams in the Meissen basins."

"Check," Maggie said as Nina scribbled away. "Okay then, hors d'oeuvres—endive and codfish gunk?

"Done."

"Empanadas?"

"Baked and resting. Will brisk as needed."

"How about the mango salsa."

"Just spooned it into radicchio cups."

"Do they sit okay on the tray?"

"The weight of the salsa flattens out the bottoms."

"Shrewd. How about the minisoufflés?"

"Capons out, soufflés in."

"Angels on horseback?"

"All saddled up and ready to ride."

"Crab sticks?"

"An anytimer. The first guest."

"Do I look all right?"

Nina lowered her pen, eyes narrowing. Maggie adored her assistant's brutal honesty.

"Something's a little odd here," Nina said, wedging the clipboard under her arm and fussing with Maggie's left shoulder strap.

Maggie was tempted to tell Nina that Kenneth had been feeling her up a moment ago—a perverse impulse to brag—but something stopped her.

"There, that's better," Nina said. "The house looks gorgeous." She kissed Maggie on the cheek and bustled back toward the kitchen.

A photographer materialized, burdened with Nikons. This would be Reggie Chang, who had worked with Maggie on her last three books. Maggie was his favorite subject. He could just point and shoot.

It was impossible to get a bad picture of her. Reggie had never seen anything like it. He worked with thousand-dollar-an-hour models all the time, and even these ethereal creatures could look like goons and harpies once in a while. But Maggie, never. She had some supernatural ability to appear winning, intelligent, and perfectly natural in every shot. The camera not only loved her, it seemed to owe her some huge debt. Each contact sheet was flawless. And the oddest thing was, until her rise as an author and tastemaker, Maggie had never modeled professionally for so much as a toothpaste ad.

On top of the professional pleasures of photographing Maggie came the side benefits. For example, tonight's lavish affair. Reggie loved parties and Maggie's were simply the best. Perhaps a little short on film stars and the Soho art-noir crowd, but with plenty of celebrities of the more elevated sort. And always with that deeply specific sense of occasion. A Maggie Darling Fourth of July made you glad to be an American no matter which knucklehead occupied the White House or what country we were bombing. And a Maggie Darling Christmas made Reggie feel as though the blood in his veins went back to Ethelred the Everready of the Saxons. There wasn't a time Reggie came to Maggie's house when she failed to feed him magnificently. Her kitchen made Lutèce look like a Greek luncheonette. Reggie couldn't figure out how she did it—and he wasn't the only one. After a day of shooting, he'd sit at the big scrubbed pine table sipping a kir while, out of what seemed like nothing more than a few scraps, Maggie whipped together fettucine with lobster chunks in ginger cream, or some such. He had seen her do it! Not Nina Stegman or some factotum. She blew his mind.

Reggie was more than half in love with Maggie Darling. Driving out of Manhattan in his sporty red Miata, he wondered endlessly what possible circumstances might induce her to pose in the nude for him. These thoughts led to sexual fantasies that embarrassed even Reggie in the privacy of his own skull, they were so hopelessly adolescent. For instance: Maggie bent over an arugula patch, dressed only in clogs and gardening gloves, presenting her bare buttery posterior as she glanced over her shoulder at the lens . . . things like that. Yet, no matter how bestial the tableau, Reggie could not imagine Maggie looking other than winning, intelligent, and perfectly natural. To him, she was no less than what her books (and his photos) made her out to be: the quintessential American woman.

Reggie never let on about the depth of his feelings. The fact that Maggie was twelve years older than he made her seem that much less obtainable, though the older-woman angle also increased her allure. Lastly, there was Kenneth. Reggie thought of him as Hercules Unchained with a bottomless bank account. Next to Kenneth, Reggie felt like a fat little laughing Buddha of the type sold in cheap Chinatown giftshops.

"I'm so glad you're here," said Maggie, greeting him with a kiss.

Melting in her hearthlike glow, Reggie said, "I shot a roll of the house from outside. With the snowflakes swirling around it looks like one of those liquid-filled paperweights that you shake."

"It's snowing out!"

"Why, yes."

"I had no idea." Maggie bit her lip, imagining her guests' automobiles fishtailing into highway guardrails and ditches, nobody showing up, all the food and work wasted—but she immediately dismissed the thought as though it were a misbehaving employee.

"Say, that's a snazzy outfit, Reg," she said, forcing herself to focus on something immediate and real.

It was a shawl-collared dinner jacket of crushed velour, in deep holly green.

"Ralph Lauren, fifteen hundred bucks," Reggie said. He knew she'd ask.

"Very nice. Say, do you mind following me around while I see to things?"

And so Reggie tagged after her like a paparazzo, snapping his shots as Maggie made a final inspection tour of the premises before the big rush.

2
꧁ Air Kisses ꧂

It is true that Maggie Darling had acquired a great many material treasures over the years, but nothing—not her meticulously collected trove of antique furniture, the fabulously equipped kitchen, or any of the various gardens, borders, arbors, orchards, nutteries, and groves that she had painstakingly carved out of their thirty-acre spread—quite matched the pleasure that Maggie got from her ballroom. The seventy-by-forty-foot party shack had been the last operating cow barn in Upper Stepney. It was built in 1817 by an extraordinary figure named Ezra Stiles who invented an improved Argand lamp, wrote hundreds of popular Methodist hymns, and fathered his last child at the age of seventy. Maggie and Kenneth bought the building for fifty thousand dollars, then paid another hundred thousand to disassemble it timber by timber, move it to their spread in West Rumford, and reassemble it on a site adjoining the existing conservatory. It cost them yet another hundred grand to wire, plumb, refinish, and trim it out just so.

Maggie now descended the single stone step from the moist, fragrant conservatory into the ballroom—Reggie Chang followed at a respectful distance snapping pictures. Entering the enormous space always took her breath away, but especially before a bash, when it was not cluttered up with people. A maid bustled about lighting candles in the wall sconces. The two bartenders, Felix and Jesus, were busy cutting limes. Kenneth was nowhere to be seen.

At the far end of the room, disposed against an immense arched window twenty-four feet high by twenty feet wide, composed entirely of six-inch glass panes, stood the eighteen-foot-high Christmas tree. Upon it hung hundreds of Venetian glass balls, a wing squadron of Florentine papier-mâché cherubs, yards of honest cranberry ropes, and countless tiny brilliant electric lights. The inside surfaces of the barn were left unpainted. The timbers, soaring up into the half-open lofts, retained their natural burnt umber patina of age. The carpenters had added lovely scrolled brackets at the junction of every post and beam. The old lofts had been reconfigured into a horseshoe-shaped upper gallery, open at the end where the big tree stood against the enormous window. Along this eight-foot-wide gallery, sofas, soft chairs, and tables were arrayed, where guests could repose and look down upon the action below. A section of the gallery at the side, center, served as a musicians' balcony, and members of a six-piece chamber orchestra now milled around up there, unpacking their instruments and adjusting their chairs.

Downstairs, a hardwood dance floor was framed by flagstones. The whole floor was heated by a complicated system of hot water pipes running in a grid below so that even on a cold winter night one could walk around the vast room barefoot in perfect comfort. Round café-style tables naped in pale pink damask stood on the flagstones around the dance floor. Opposite the musicians' balcony stood a fieldstone fireplace so large that Maggie could stand inside it in flat shoes. Tonight, of course, a Yule log blazed on a bed of glowing embers.

Maggie asked Felix for a sherry, and she stood contemplating the room in the evening's last still moment, effectively ignoring the whir and snap of Reggie's camera. The still moment was a bit of a ritual for her before a big bash. This was the time when she tried to tell herself to let go, to relax, to cease trying to control things around her. Even as she entertained these therapeutic thoughts, her eye fixed on the swags of pine roping that scalloped the rail of the gallery above, and Maggie wished that she had decorated the fastening points with sprigs of holly rather than red ribbon. In fact, it was not easy for Maggie to turn off her mind. Though the sherry produced a thrilling buzz, especially on an empty stomach, it also perversely brought a thousand and one worrisome details bubbling into Maggie's forebrain. She had to hold on to a thick wooden post to keep herself from racing into the kitchen, where, she imagined, Nina had unaccountably burned every victual on the menu. Reggie's strobe flashed as his camera caught Maggie staring dreamily at the tree, the anarchy of her thoughts completely concealed from his lens. Then the Mosleys (of ABC Television) stepped into the ballroom and the Christmas Feast for Two Hundred was under way.

The Mosleys were always the first ones to arrive at a Maggie Darling affair because Paul was the longtime producer of the *Good Morning America* show and his schedule had him up at three-thirty every morning and in bed by nine at night. They were soon joined by Leonard and Hattie Moile of the powerhouse Manhattan law firm Moile, Moile, and Schlange, which handled the legal work of Throop, Cravath. The Moiles lived in Cross River, just a stone's throw over the Westchester county line.

There were air kisses. A waiter materialized bearing flutes of pink Dom Ruinart; all happily hoisted except Leonard Moile, who limped to the bar for a Scotch.

"Your house is so gorgeous," said Eva Mosley, "that I don't see how in good conscience I can ever have company again."

"I gave up entertaining years ago because of Maggie," Hattie Moile said. "Honestly, darling, this is carrying perfection to the last limit."

Maggie wanted to jump out of her skin. Her still moment was shattered. She hated this phase of a party, when the early arrivals showered her with inevitable compliments in their nervousness at being the first ones there. She loved to see people having a good time, but she couldn't stand being the object of attention. She knew she was a good hostess—she was a professional. It depressed her to hear how inadequate others felt. It made her feel like a freak, as though paying attention to details and having standards were pathological symptoms of a loathsome disease. Hattie Moile, for instance, was a superb cook. So what if she was so disorganized that supper at their house rarely appeared on the table before ten-thirty (as though they were Spaniards). And Eva Mosley grew fabulous hybrid roses, even if she kept the cheapest imaginable plastic furniture on her bluestone terrace. "You can take the girl out of Woolworths," Maggie's mother always said, "but you can't take Woolworths out of the girl . . ."

The musicians tuned their strings overhead, lending more discordant overtones to Maggie's racing thoughts. She glanced at the huge window beyond the tree and saw snowflakes whirling under the eaves. In her imagination, more cars crashed on the slick country roads. Then, she felt a queer sensation, as of a bubble bursting in her head. Suddenly the stone floor seemed to give way, and the room wheeled as pangs of terror rifled through her.

"Excuse me a moment," she said and, managing a cracked smile, hurried out through the conservatory to the powder room off the library, locking the door behind her. She barely recognized the glamorous creature she saw in the mirror. She felt, at that moment, like a mental patient. Her heart pounded in her chest like a galumphing beast. Her breath came in short, shallow huffs. Rivulets of sweat ran down her side and disappeared damply into her bra strap. She started to shake like a malaria victim.

Maggie ran the cold water and stoppered the sink, then patted her forehead with a wet guest towel. She did not want to disturb her eye makeup, minimal as it was. When the sink was full, she plunged her hands in the icy water up to her elbows. Maggie had discovered this trick of hydrotherapy in college, about the same time that she first began to experience anxiety attacks—coincidentally, about the same time she first met Kenneth.

As her arms grew numb, her pulse and breathing slowly returned to normal. She pulled the stopper from the sink and shook the excess water off her forearms. It was over. Everything would be all right. These anxiety attacks had become a ritual before any large affair. The exquisite terror of them had nearly ceased to terrify her after all these years. They had become something more like a religious obligation. By the time she emerged from the powder room, the musicians had begun playing and guests were trooping in by the carload. The faces seemed to have leaped directly off television screens and magazine covers into Maggie's broad foyer, all crying "Merry Christmas!" and shaking snowflakes out of their hair.

Here, for instance, came Nate Blankenship, owner of the New York Mets, all six foot eight of him, a Chrysler Building of a man, and his wife, Holly, an obelisk of a woman. Behind them was Lula Baron, the powerful editor at Knopf, towing in her wake like a waterskiing sheepdog the beloved but beleaguered novelist Harry Pearce, who was between wives and rehabs. Next came Hal Whitten, the menswear designer who had rediscovered the vest. Taking off her ankle-length nutria coat beside him stood the long, languid S curve of model and MTV personality Kathy Clevenger, all legs and lips. Here was Tony Provenzano the award-winning playwright (*Flesh to Spirit*) and his longtime companion, the actress Julie Petard. Now Lucius Milstein, the young painter; Clare Fanning, the *New Yorker* columnist; Earl Wise of Odeon Records; Connie McQuillan of *People* magazine; Fedo Prado, principal dancer with the NYC Ballet; Duff Woodcock, executive chef of the Four Seasons; Connecticut senator Dick Pierson and wife Tina (they lived practically up the street in Rumford Center); Janet Higgenbotham of the Metropolitan Opera, her highly acoustic bosom exploding out of a red moiré dirndl—in short, more celebrities than you could shake a gutta-percha cane at. Even the faces that one could not instantly connect with celebrity seemed to glow with distinction and achievement.

Uh-oh. Crossing Maggie's threshold like a rodent entering the world's loveliest cheesebox scurried the furtive figure of Lawrence Hayward, arbitrageur supreme, limping like Shakespeare's Richard III ("War wound," he always said of his shorter left leg—but he was too young for World War II and too old for Vietnam and had been nowhere near Korea, so what could one say?). Lawrence ("Call me Larry and you're dead on Wall Street") Hayward (rumored to be an Anglicized version of Havaarti) had materialized in New York from Cleveland (of all places) in the mid-1970s, having built an empire of suburban car washes, drugstores, and overnight dry cleaners. On Wall Street he proceeded to pile up a second-layer fortune—now estimated to be $27 billion—buying and selling enormous quantities of stock at tiny margins at absolutely the right moment. It was really the stupidest kind of scam imaginable, Maggie thought, and almost certainly rife with illegality, the way a Roquefort cheese is veined with blue mold. "But if it's so stupid, then why can't everyone else do it?" Kenneth always asked Maggie when she started in on Hayward, and he would answer the question himself: "Because the truth is, Lawrence Hayward is a genius." This, after all, was the reason Hayward was there: Kenneth wanted him to come. He was a baleful presence at Christmastime, Maggie decided, watching Hayward hand over his funereal black vicuña cloak to one of the college kids. He was Jacob Marley in fresher clothes. His face had the same sunken, half-starved, vole-eyed, semi-mummified look of John D. Rockefeller at ninety—except Hayward was fifty-seven. They said he subsisted entirely on celery sticks and rice crackers. She would make it a point to observe what he ate tonight.

The hired help swarmed through the rooms hoisting trays of hot and cold hors d'oeuvres: the wild boar empanadas, the angels on horseback, the endive with codfish gunk, the crab sticks, the crudités (she saw Hayward snatch a celery stick, by God!), the Gorgonzola tartlets, the figs and prosciutto, the salmon beignets, the mustard-glazed boneless miniribs, the drunken prawns, the delicate seafood-sausage tidbits, and the darling little pigs in blankets—this final item a tribute to Maggie's dad, Frank Hadjuk, of Bethlehem, Pennsylvania, gone now almost ten years to the night. She carefully wiped a tear from the corner of her eye, thinking of him, a million miles and a million years away from her present situation in the world.

She rode the tide of guests into the ballroom, as though she were flotsam on some enchanted sea. The musicians in the balcony above played one of Dowling's stately sixteenth-century galliards. It was barely audible over the vivid thrum of conversation. Waiters plied the enormous room refilling champagne flutes. At last Maggie sensed that the evening had achieved a certain momentum that no disaster short of a conflagration could halt. The party was like a great improbable engine, a steam-powered carriage on wheels, a mass of fascinating machinery, valves, shafts, pistons, whistles, and bells, which, once rolling, could run to the ends of the earth at full throttle. Maggie felt the familiar palpable sensation of release, as of a two-ton office safe being lifted off her shoulders, that comprised the very essence of what she lived for. Her lips crept upward until her face quietly beamed and she was able, at last, to admire what she had accomplished.

3
⤙ Cruise Control ⤚

Maggie began to work the room like a honeybee visiting blossoms in her garden. She had a gift for swiftly engaging other minds, knowing, to some degree, what stirred and animated her friends, and quick to reach the heart of things without any nervous preliminaries. With strangers she had a sort of policy: focus on them, draw out a thing or two about their hopes and dreams in the first minute, be genuinely interested in what they say—you might learn something, she sincerely believed—and always remember that every individual is a universe. This policy she almost completely violated when she turned around in the vicinity of the great holiday tree and found herself confronted with Lawrence Hayward. He seemed to flinch as their eyes met.

Attempting to recover his poise, Hayward took her hand and bestowed a European-style air kiss on it. "Charmed to meet the renowned lady of the house," he said. The whole gesture was so pompous and fraudulent that Maggie wanted to smack him in the head. The violence of this sudden urge amazed her. But then a waiter swerved by with a tray of angels on horseback, and she was seized by a yet more vicious impulse.

"Won't you try one, Lawrence?" she said, snatching a plump oyster enrobed in bacon off the silver tray, and dangling it before him.

"No, thank you," he said, recoiling with a weird little wave of his long waxy fingers.

"You can't be worried about cholesterol?"

"Never liked seafood," Hayward muttered.

"Come on now, open. Wider."

Hayward drew back, like Quasimodo in that scene on the pillory when Esmaralda attempts to give him water and he, at first, shrinks from her. Maggie adroitly penetrated Hayward's defenses, though, and deposited the plump tidbit in his mouth.

"That's a good boy," she said.

Hayward's discomfort thrilled her. His face turned a perfect shade of verdigris, as though Maggie had just antiqued him. He chewed the oyster perhaps three times before swallowing it, as a man might chew and swallow some incriminating wad of paper just when the FBI agents arrive. His ensuing smile seemed wan and unpersuasive. Just then, Maggie caught the eye of Guido Pasquelini, curator of the Met's medieval collection. She told Hayward to try the wild boar empanadas and buzzed away on her rounds.

4
⟶ A Dark Vision ⟵

It was while listening to Pasquelini discourse on Christmas traditions of the Veronese that Maggie happened to spy Kenneth across the ballroom before the great hearth. He and Charlie Duckworth, a colleague from Throop, Cravath, stood on either side of a young woman, name unknown. A slender, long-necked thing, she was pale as a swan in her strapless black dress (Ungaro?). Just then, an alarming thing happened. Maggie thought she saw Kenneth pat her on the bottom. Did that really happen? she wondered. Pasquelini jabbered on, something about little nut cakes and a procession through the streets. Did Kenneth do what she thought she saw him do? It was hard to really know, because the next moment, a clump of guests drifted between them, making further surveillance impossible. No, Maggie told herself decisively, no such thing happened. It was some trick of the light and the eye. And so resolved, she helped herself to a flute of champagne as a waiter glided by.

Maggie squelched her impulse to visit the kitchen just before dinner was served. Nothing would bolster Nina's confidence more than to be left completely in charge without interference from the boss. When the victuals did appear, they arrived on the buffet tables brilliantly and piping hot, each platter, bowl, basin, and salver garnished impeccably, with curlicues of steam wafting up into the rafters.

At Maggie and Kenneth's table sat PBS anchorman Jim Nealon and his wife, Dory Dean, editor of the *New York Times* Wednesday Style section; Henry Cravath, surviving founder of Throop, Cravath, and his wife, Betsy; Harold Hamish, Maggie's editor; Joyce Munger, the ruthless but charming literary agent (known in the business as "the White Whale"); Red Oldham, dean of the New York restaurant critics; Brian Sharpe, the interior decorator with a record twelve *House and Garden* covers, and his boyfriend/assistant Tony Sargent; and Dick and Tina Pierson (ten years earlier, the senator had been West Rumford town supervisor while Maggie and his wife took turns heading the PTA).

"Who was that young thing standing with you and Charlie Duckworth a little while ago?" Maggie asked her husband quietly.

"Who?" Kenneth seemed to have trouble hearing.

"The black strapless number. With Charlie."

"Oh. Some girl he's going with."

Well, Charlie had been divorced two years, it was true.

5
ᓫᐣ A Perfect Angel ᓫᐣ

Any other time of year, saxophones might have struck up a Gershwin tune, but tonight, after the waiters swooped in to clear the supper dishes, the Fairfield Conservatory Fiddle-Di-Diddlers, as the ensemble called themselves, began to play a series of eighteenth-century English country dances: "Dick's Maggot," "The Maid Peeped Out," "Rufty Tufty," "The Waters of Holland," tunes evocative of an old-world Yuletide, while Fedo Prado and three members of the corps de ballet demonstrated some authentic dance steps of the era. Soon, they had a dozen of the younger and more elastic guests going at it in the center of the room. Leaning against the wall beneath the musicians' balcony, Maggie found Denny Sherlock following the action. Sherlock worked in Throop, Cravath's takeover department. He could take a perfectly good, profitable company and suck out its assets quicker than Count Dracula could drain a young countess's blood supply. An avid amateur cook, he was always grilling Maggie for information and ideas.

"Say, Maggie, how do you keep those little seafood sausages from falling apart?" he asked.

"I cheat a little," Maggie answered briskly. "Cornstarch." They had to speak right into each other's ears to hear, the music and conversation was so loud. Meanwhile, a colossal chocolate cake in the traditional Yule log shape—decorated with meringue mushrooms and sprigs of candy holly—was carried out by a pair of strapping Yale boys and placed triumphantly on the buffet to a chorus of admiring "oohs" and "aahs." Maggie stood on tiptoe to ask Sherlock, "Who's that young thing with Charlie Duckworth?"

Sherlock craned around the room until he spotted the couple. "Laura Wilkie," he reported. "She's an analyst."

"Gosh, she's awfully young for a shrink."

"No, an analyst with us. Tells us what's hot and what's not. Princeton. Smart."

"Ah. How long?"

"She came on in, oh, September."

"Really? How long has Charlie been going out with her?"

"Hey, it's news to me they're going out. Good for old Charlie." Maggie, flushing, held out her champagne flute to a passing waiter for a refill.

The musicians concluded "The Waters of Holland," and a ripple of excitement passed through the big room. Frederick Swann, the English rock star (he recorded for Earl Wise's label), took stage, so to speak, at the center of the dance floor. All chatter ceased until the only sounds in the room were a few coughs and the crackling of the hearth. Without any introduction, and accompanied only by someone in the balcony playing a small lap harmonium, Swann sang an early American song of such compelling and stately beauty that women around the room goggled at him in a transport and not a few of the men became lightheaded. Togged out in a sort of dueling blouse, black leather pants, and an embroidered red silk vest, Swann's nimbus of long frizzy blond hair framed his head like an angel's halo in a Florentine fresco. Swann was capable of bravura vocal feats à la Ray Charles—indeed, he was usually accused of imitating the master—but tonight he sang in a pure ringing tenor that startled those familiar with his usual work:

> *My days have been so wondrous free*
> *The little birds that fly*
> *With careless ease from tree to tree*
> *Were but as blest as I*
> *Were but as blest as I*

Ask gliding waters if a tear of mine
Increased their stream
And ask the breathing gales
If ever I lent a sigh to them
I lent a sigh to them.

Swann sang the verses twice and bowed deeply. The harmonium above played a lilting coda, and an eerie silence followed as the astonished guests joined in applause that rose to cheers and whistles. Then Swann faded back into the admiring crowd. The Fiddle-Di-Diddlers struck up "Maiden Lane," and Maggie, as amazed as anyone, floated out of the ballroom to the kitchen.

6
ꞈ In Camera but Not Obscura ꞈ

Nina and her four assistants already had the counters and stoves wiped down. A ziggurat of plastic tubs and hampers filled with leftovers remained on the big scrubbed pine table awaiting storage. Maggie decorked two bottles of Veuve Cliquot La Grande Dame and poured the champagne into a set of etched amethyst flip glasses for the kitchen crew.

"Everything was absolutely splendid," she told Nina. "I'm so proud of you. Of all of you." Maggie hugged the sturdy Nina. The gang made short work of the two bottles. When Maggie emerged back into the party, she was tipsy. She couldn't remember the last time she drank too much. It might have been as long ago as the seventies—perhaps the night Nixon flew away for good in his helicopter. On her way back to the ballroom, in the library, she came upon Earl Wise and Frederick Swann huddled with Ed Parrot of Paramount and Antonio Zarillas, the rising filmmaker widely expected to snare an Oscar nomination for *The Book of Moonlight* starring Jack Nicholson. The four men ceased their obvious and rather shameful business schmoozing as Maggie crossed the room to them. Wise introduced her to Swann.

"You are a very great lady," Swann said in a caressing voice that was a good stage Mayfair. Maggie wondered about his upbringing, having assumed, perhaps wrongly, that he was some kind of Southwark lumpen prole. It occurred to her that Swann was a very capable actor, besides being a soul crooner, and that, in fact, the huddle she had interrupted had something to do with a possible career move. As he spoke, Swann's eyes roved up and down Maggie like a pair of busy hands until she had the peculiar sensation of standing before him absolutely naked. She touched her neckline to reassure herself that her gown was still actually there.

"You sang like an angel," she said. "Such a lovely song. I'd never heard it before."

"Well, 'tis American, you know," Swann said, thumbs in his vest pockets, assuming at once an unlikely, but entirely charming, donnish air. "Perhaps the first composition by a native American—the music, at least. Fellow named Francis Hopkinson penned it in 1759. He was one of those lads who could do everything: painter, writer, solicitor, a real man of parts. Signed your Declaration of Independence too, the impudent rascal . . ."

It happened that Maggie's eye caught something moving in the background, as the human eye will even in a crowded room. Across the library and halfway down the hall that led to the ballroom was the bathroom where Maggie had had her anxiety attack. From it now emerged the young woman in the black strapless gown, Laura Wilkie, who had been standing between Charlie Duckworth and Kenneth before supper. Laura Wilkie carefully closed the door behind her and, smoothing her dress, vanished down the hall.

". . . The words, however, are by the English poet Thomas Parnell, from his 'Love and Innocence' . . ." Swann continued.

Meanwhile, Lucius Milstein waddled into view. He tried the bathroom door but, finding it locked, waited outside. Maggie felt an impulse to go down and inform him that the room was unoccupied, but seconds later the door opened. A familiar bald head thrust out and glanced down the far end of the hall toward the ballroom. Maggie instinctively drew back behind Swann, barely peeking past his brawny shoulder. The bald head swiveled to glance up into the library, the face revealing itself to be Kenneth's. He emerged fully then and, straightening his necktie, strode out of sight toward the ballroom.

". . . I collect musical antiques," Swann went on. "I should love to do an album of them someday, but I suspect Earl would sooner sign K. D. Lang to do an album of Canadian birdcalls. Are you, uh, quite all right, Mrs. Darling?"

In fact, Maggie had gone white and she appeared to wobble.

"I'm fine," she lied, "but I've just remembered something terribly urgent in the kitchen. Would you gentlemen excuse me?"

Maggie backed out of the library and made her way unsteadily to the kitchen, groping for the backs of chairs, tabletops, and newel posts along the way, like an old person expecting to fall down. Her head swam. Her thoughts seemed to swirl in a thick, opaque, boiling sauce, like béchamel.

Nina and the other cooks had gone. Two Yale boys and the Sarah Lawrence girl sat at the big table smoking cigarettes and drinking champagne. They got up and skulked away when Maggie appeared. Ignoring them, she emptied a quart of milk into a saucepan, spooned in cocoa powder and sugar, added a splash of vanilla extract, and stirred the mixture just short of boiling. Next, she filled a large stainless-steel thermos bottle, grabbed two mugs, snatched her canvas field jacket off a peg near the door, and slipped out into the night.

7
↶ Out in the Cold ↷

A light snow still fell, but the wind had died down, lending the darkness a soft calming presence, like death at its most gentle and poetic. Perhaps two inches carpeted the ground and cloaked the yew hedges that lined the driveway. Maggie stumbled forward toward the west meadow, which had been set up as a parking lot for the occasion. Two more Yale boys stood there in hooded, insulated jumpsuits—provided by Maggie, of course—slapping their sides, stoically fending off the interminable boredom of their assignment.

"I've brought you something warm," she said gravely, pouring them each a mug of cocoa, and herself some in the thermos cup.

"Why, jeez, thanks, yeah thanks, Ms. Darling," they said.

"What are your names?"

"I'm Roger and this is Mark."

"What do you want to do in life, Roger?"

"International law."

"How about you, Mark?"

"Just regular law. You know, a lawyer."

"Divorce?"

"Sure, why not?" Mark chortled. "Hey, this hot chocolate's awesome."

Through an awkward pause in which the young men couldn't think what to say to their employer, who was herself apparently lost in thought, a Christmas carol could be heard thrumming inside the house. Janet Higgenbotham's piercing soprano carried above the other voices.

The great arched window of the ballroom glowed like an amber tombstone in the distance.

"Sounds like some party in there," Roger observed.

"Oh, it's been a most amusing night," Maggie said. The leaden irony, which went right over the boys' heads, choked Maggie like a wad of underchewed beef. The next moment car headlights cut through the gateposts of the fieldstone wall that hid the house from the prying eyes of passing motorists. The car proved to be a familiar black Saab, one that belonged to Kenneth once upon a time. It pulled into the meadow, stopping beside the three standing figures. Maggie's son Hooper rolled down the window.

"What are you doing out here, Mom?"

"Entertaining the troops."

"We decided not to go to Belize after all," Hooper said.

"I'm so glad you're home," Maggie said, riven by emotion. She reached inside the window and hugged Hooper's beautiful blond head. Her tears left one whole side of his face damp.

"Gosh, get a hold of yourself, Mom," he said. Just then, Maggie noticed a girl in the passenger seat. "Oh, this is Alison," Hooper inserted, offhandedly. "Alison, my famous mom."

"Nice to meet you, Maggie," the young woman said with a flip of her hair. It was hard to see her face in the lights of the dashboard. She seemed pretty in an undergraduate way, but Maggie detected the gleam of metal in one nostril and her lower lip.

"Thought we'd camp out in the orchard cottage," Hooper said, referring to the guest house. Maggie seemed distracted. "That all right, Mom?"

Maggie knew that Hooper had brought girls there before. But in the past he'd always sneaked them in. She didn't like the idea of giving the two of them explicit permission to sleep together on the premises, but she could not bring herself to object. She had been sleeping with Kenneth in his parents' pool house when she was younger than Hooper, for goodness sake. To thwart them seemed ethically insupportable and grotesquely prudish. Yet she hated the idea. It tinged all the rue she was feeling with rage.

"You'll have to make the bed," she said dryly.

"No problem, Maggie," Alison said.

"Quit calling me Maggie," she snapped. "Do you think we're best friends or something?"

"I'm sorry, Mrs. Darling."

"Don't call me that either," Maggie retorted, her voice cracking. "Aw, hell."

Roger and Mark inched away clutching their mugs.

"What should I call you?" Alison asked.

"I don't know," Maggie said, dissolving in tears.

"Are you okay, Mom?"

"Party's a disaster," was all Maggie could say. "Complete fiasco."

"We'll just go down to the orchard house, Mom. We won't even peek into the party."

"Get some food," Maggie said between sobs. "Kitchen's loaded."

"Okay."

"And sleep tight," she said and then reached in and hugged his head again, desperately, saying, "I love you so much."

"I know, Mom. Hey, parties come and parties go. You know that better than anyone. It'll be all right. You'll see."

"I'm sorry you're having such a tough time," Alison added.

"You're sweet," Maggie said, suddenly adoring the girl. "Be good to my boy."

"Merry Christmas, Mom. We'll see you in the morning bright."

The car swerved out of the meadow and down a snow-covered lane behind the enormous house. Maggie stood in the darkness bawling, she knew not how long, but a duration sufficient to clear her mind.

8

✑ The Little Cookie ✑

At one-thirty in the morning, the last guest had gone, the ballroom was cleared and swept, all the glasses and plates and platters and party things had been washed and stowed back in the enormous pantry, the help had been paid in crisp bills and set free. The house stood cocooned in winter stillness, except for the reassuring tick of the Aaron Willard arched-hood grandfather clock (circa 1790) in the upstairs hall. Kenneth sat on the chair in front of Maggie's vanity heaving sighs of exhaustion. One sock dangled stupidly half off his right foot.

"Come to bed," said Maggie, who sat propped up against the cherrywood headboard perusing a rival's new book of Tuscan-inspired recipes, busily annotating the pages with a felt-tipped pen.

"I'm so tired," Kenneth moaned.

Maggie patted the mattress briskly. "Come on now."

Kenneth pulled his tuxedo shirt over his head like a lacrosse jersey, without undoing the studs, wadded it up, and flung the thing in the direction of his closet. It landed on the carpet with a mild thud. This sort of slovenliness usually drove Maggie up a wall, but she said nothing. Next Kenneth stood up and dropped his pants and underpants and, stepping forward, left them mashed together in an unappetizing heap. His triathlete's face sagged, and despite the meaty pectorals, bulging deltoids, and rippling abdominals, he looked middle-aged. Maggie drew the quilt open, inviting Kenneth into his customary side of the bed. He crawled in, flopped this way and that, pounded his pillow, and finally settled on his back, pulling the quilt up to his chin.

"Must be all those drugs," Maggie remarked.

"Oh, I wasn't so bad tonight, Mags," Kenneth replied, eyes closed. "Didn't put a lampshade on my head."

"No, you didn't put a lampshade on your head." She carefully placed her book on the night table and slid down off the great raft of pillows so that her head lay on Kenneth's meaty chest.

"I'm tired, Mags," Kenneth said, code words meant to signal that he was not especially interested in sex at this time.

"You just relax now," Maggie said.

"Hey, at least turn off the light, babe."

"In a minute."

She pecked a trail of perfunctory kisses down his sternum to his navel and then a little below, where her sensitive nose picked up what she suspected: a telltale aroma of bluefish and cumin, a combination that uncannily simulated the natural perfume of female sexual equipment. In fact, Maggie once made such a dish of bluefish in cumin seed—baked in parchment paper with cilantro and lime—and she and Nina had turned to each other with exactly the same thought. They ended up making a joke about it. Bluefish à la puta they had named the dish. And here it was now, all over Kenneth's groin. She recalled the scene in the library earlier: the girl exiting the powder room, then Kenneth slinking out moments later. He wanted to be caught! Maggie was sure of it as she resurfaced now above the quilt.

"How long have you been banging Laura Wilkie?"

Kenneth's eyelids rolled up like windowshades in a cartoon. "Who?" he asked.

"Laura Wilkie."

"Who's Laura Wilkie?"

"I see. You're going to pretend that you don't know who I'm talking about. The little cookie in the black strapless thing that Charlie Duckworth's supposedly going with."

"Her? You think I'm banging her?"

"She works for Throop, Cravath, doesn't she?"

"Not in my department."

"How come you pretended not to know her name?"

"I am not 'banging' this Laura Wilkie creature."

"Kenneth, you are really such a lousy liar, I don't see how you can even make a living on Wall Street. I can smell her all over you."

"I was dancing, for God's sake. I got sweaty."

"That's not sweat, you bastard. It's bluefish and cumin!"

"Huh . . . ?"

"Pussy, you dolt. I can smell her all over you!"

"Oh, please . . . Can we talk about this in the morning?"

"No. You're not going to be here in the morning."

"Ha!" Kenneth said with a little snort and closed his eyes again as though challenging her. Maggie rose to her knees, put both hands together as though clasped in prayer, and brought them down as hard as she could on Kenneth's solar plexus. Springlike, his body catapulted weirdly off the bed, as though he had been launched like a missile, and then he was crawling rapidly around on the carpet emitting the most peculiar shrill noise, just like the pigs they had seen being slaughtered for market in northern Spain years ago. For several moments, Maggie worried that she had actually stopped Kenneth's heart. But then he stopped squealing and commenced gasping for breath, and she understood that she had simply succeeded in knocking the wind out of him. A few more moments and he was merely breathing hard and coughing. He even managed to mutter "You bitch!" between breaths, and she knew he was perfectly all right.

In the interval she grabbed the fireplace poker out of its brass stand.

"I saw you come out of the bathroom ten seconds after Laura Wilkie came out, you lying, stupid sonofabitch," Maggie growled. "Out," she demanded. "Out of the house!" When Kenneth failed to move, she whacked him across the buttocks with the poker. The blow seemed to propel him to his feet, and he took an apelike stance, as though to menace Maggie physically. She let him have it again, this time on the shins.

"Ow! You crazy bitch!"

"Out! Out of my house!"

"This is my house too."

"Not anymore," Maggie barked. "You threw it away for a five-minute standing fuck in a toilet."

She brandished the poker overhead again. This time Kenneth lunged for the fireplace tool stand and seized the little brass broom. "Come on, Mags," he said, taunting her like one of the characters out of the rumble scene in *West Side Story*. "Come on. Try and hit me again."

"Moron," she said, scurrying across the great bed until she seized the telephone receiver and punched the numbers 9–1–1 on the keypad. "Hello," she said pleasantly. "This is Maggie Darling at 1803 Kettle Hill Road in West Rumford. My husband is about to beat me up with a fireplace tool. Would you come over right away? Thanks, so much." She hung up. "They'll be here in about seven minutes," she smiled.

"Oh, that was really brilliant, Maggie. Just the kind of publicity you need, I'm sure—"

"Put on your pants and pack a bag, buster."

Kenneth pitched the brass shovel into a corner in disgust. It bounced off his StairMaster exercise machine. Before he could get his Gucci loafers back on, two Connecticut state police cars pulled into the long driveway. Their sirens were off, but the revolving gumball roof lights made a creepy flickering blue fantasia out of the winter landscape. Maggie flew downstairs in a red tartan flannel robe to let in the two troopers. Kenneth followed moments later, sheepishly toting a leather-trimmed canvas overnighter. He walked past the policemen and out the front door, which they had failed to close behind them.

"Just a minute, sir," one of them called out, and Kenneth turned around.

"He didn't actually strike me," Maggie said. "He only threatened to."

"Ha!" Kenneth barked.

"Well, technically you don't have to actually strike a person to commit assault, ma'am," said the first trooper. "Do you intend to press charges?"

"Oh, certainly not," Maggie said. "Just get him out of here."

"Uh, sir, your wife wants you to leave the premises."

"Really? What do you suppose I'm doing out here in the snow at two o'clock in the morning with a suitcase in my hand."

"I don't know, sir," the trooper said, apparently immune to sarcasm. "But we'll just stick around until you leave, if you don't mind."

"What if I do mind?"

"We only say that to be polite, sir. If you don't remove yourself right away, we'll have to arrest you and take you in and all. You won't like it. Even well-off people like yourself, their lawyers really don't like gettin' called this time of night, especially Christmas Eve, and, well, I'd just get going, I was you."

"Have yourself a merry little Christmas, Maggie," Kenneth said, and then, shaking his head as if utterly baffled, he headed for the garage where his BMW waited in all its Teutonic grandeur. Soon, his red and orange taillights disappeared through the gateposts. Maggie made coffee for the troopers and carved them each huge slices of the chocolate *bûche de Noël*. Of course, it was an excuse for them to wait around and see whether Kenneth intended to return. But he did not. Maggie knew that they would never dwell together again under this roof. And when the troopers departed at last around three o'clock Christmas morning, Maggie trudged back upstairs to the bedroom and cried her heart out.

~ Part Two ~

Alone, Nearly

I
⤸ The Dreadful Light ⤸

Maggie woke up at eight-fifteen on Christmas morning with the sense of having undergone a full-blown personal transformation, something like a biological metamorphosis. She was not the sort who rose out of sleep like a scuba diver slowly circling up to the surface from the aqueous depths, but rather she snapped immediately to consciousness like someone stepping out of a matinee right into blaring daylight. Blinking at the stark Christmas sunshine that reflected off the new-fallen snow onto her bedroom ceiling, she apprehended the vacancy in bed beside her and at once recalled a series of mental snapshots from the night before: Kenneth patting Laura Wilkie's behind; Laurie Wilkie skulking out of the bathroom followed closely by Kenneth; Kenneth squealing in pain on the bedroom carpet; Kenneth standing in the snow clutching his gladstone bag; finally the soothing cup of chamomile tea that she sipped while watching the cops as they ate their cake. Only the tears shed over these events were not recalled—but neither is the pain of a root canal recalled the morning after a session at the endodontist's, though one certainly remembers being there.

Girded though she was against the snares of emotion, Maggie did feel strangely brittle this morning, as if she might crack like a Nankin vase at the slightest provocation. There was something tragic about the block of harsh sunlight on the ceiling, something in its brilliance that evoked youthful sickrooms and loss—for instance, her bout with chickenpox in October 1959, the fever and delirium, her throat on fire, her father, Frank, with his high Magyar cheekbones and wheat shock of hair, hovering with storybooks and iced juice. (Frank was always the caretaker in the household, not her mother, Irene, who begrudged children their illnesses, even went so far as to accuse them of malingering, until they threw up or broke out in a rash, and then Irene was too disgusted and frightened to go near them.) The block of sunshine on the ceiling had confused little Maggie in her fever. She kept asking Frank to "change the channel." The worst illness she had suffered in thirty-seven years since then was a hangover. Birthing Hooper was a breeze, compared to what most women go through. She delivered exactly on her due date, at ten in the morning, after precisely seventy minutes of labor, and was back in their first home—the spacious apartment in a brownstone on a quiet street in Chelsea—baking genoise for company thirty-six hours later, a display of efficiency that appalled kith and kin alike.

Staring into the light on the ceiling, Maggie attempted an inventory of her losses. Her father, now dead, was surely lost. Hooper, not quite lost, was mainly absent. Irene was not absent enough. Maggie understood that she and Kenneth had lost each other years ago and that the final crisis was only a formal verification of that loss. The hole this left in her life wasn't so much a matter of who would take care of her, but rather whom she would now care for. Even if she had ceased to love Kenneth, he was, at least, the one who sampled her chocolate hazelnut waffles, sniffed her floribunda roses, gloried in her antique linen sheets, and basked in the glow of her hearth. He was the one who was there. He'd been easily tolerated. But, gosh, wasn't that exactly the problem? Strange too, she thought, how she had enjoyed his body long after she had consigned his hopes, dreams, thoughts, opinions, feelings, and peccadilloes—in short, his soul—to the burn slot of her personal estimation.

The notion that her sex life with Kenneth was over, and the somewhat hysterical leap that her sex life altogether might be over, pitched Maggie into a spasm of grief that left her momentarily breathless. She sat up suddenly in bed and gasped, holding herself crosswise until, becoming sensible of her full breasts, she cupped them as in a gesture of offering to an imagined lover. Wouldn't another desire her,

she wondered? Who was this someone, and might she meet him before it was too late? She shuddered at the idea, but it also propelled
her into a general consideration of what lay ahead in her life. And
being, above all, a practical person, she decided that what lay ahead
was breakfast.

2

✌ The Giftee ✌

An unnatural stillness seemed to grip the house as Maggie, now dressed in a khaki Armando Tuzzi jumpsuit, moved through the finely appointed rooms until she reached the sunny east parlor, where a smaller auxiliary Christmas tree—the so-called real family tree—stood handsomely between the baby grand piano and a fine reverse serpentine slant-front mahogany desk that she and Kenneth had picked up at Sotheby's a year earlier. Presents lay heaped under the tree. Rummaging beneath the fragrant boughs hung with gingerbread people and clove-studded orange pomanders, Maggie located all the packages tagged "For Maggie, with Love and XXX, From Kenneth." They were easy to find since they were all wrapped in the same kind of paper— this year it was a strange sort of high-tech matte black paper tied with gold Mylar ribbon. It was Kenneth's custom to assign holiday gift-buying duties to a professional shopper, a creature who could only exist in a world where expressing personal sentiment was considered just another burdensome chore better assigned to menials, like taking out the garbage. In theory, this shopper was supposed to become familiar with the personal desires and aversions of the "giftee," as the questionnaire put it. But, unfortunately, Kenneth also assigned the chore of filling out the questionnaire to an underling, who, as regarded Maggie, had not the dimmest idea how to answer queries such as the following:

Home decor preferences (mark one):
1. Traditional
2. Modern
3. Antique
4. Retro
5. Other

So, every year, Maggie received from Kenneth all sorts of things incongruent with her personal predilections: a lava lamp, an inflatable six-foot-tall rubber pencil, an automatic bread making machine that extruded loafs shaped like artillery shells with the texture of Styrofoam insulation, a biography of Gurdjieff, a martini shaker shaped like a zeppelin, articles of clothing by the egregious Lazlo Bluth, a Madonna record, a Dunhill cigarette lighter, a diamond and sapphire brooch in the shape of a jaguar just like one owned by the late Wallis Simpson, a paddleball racquet, and so on, things she had absolutely no use for.

Maggie assembled this year's nine packages in a neat pile beside her favorite wing chair, fetched her silver Montblanc pen and a sheaf of Christmas gift tags, and wrote out nine new tags to replace the ones on the packages. "From Kenneth to my dearest dumpling, Laura," she penned in her fine broad-nibbed hand, "From Kenneth to Lovebucket," "From Kenneth to darling Fuckbones," and so on in that vein until the job was complete. Then she packed the gifts in a shopping bag and placed them in the front hall closet. At last, it was off to the kitchen, her refuge against all the gales of life.

Maggie could see the orchard cottage from the big window over the sink. The little white guest house with the cut-out hearts on its green shutters stood a short distance down a formal alley of antique roses on a direct axis with the window—planned that way, of course. The rose bushes stood uniformed, like sentries, in their protective winter wrappings of burlap. The cottage lay nestled among a dozen or so apple, pear, and quince trees that Maggie had planted herself when Hooper was a toddler. Their black limbs were sleeved with snow. Hooper's sporty Saab sat parked to the left, wearing its own white cap. The thought that her baby boy was old enough to drive cars and sleep with girls thrilled and appalled her equally. Thinking of the two of them down there snuggled moistly under quilts in the cast-iron bed—which she had found in a Danbury garage sale for twenty-five dollars and lovingly repainted— Maggie tried, by sheer force of will, to compose a cheerful attitude, one untainted by jealousy, peevishness, or middle-aged gall. Well, she told herself, at least here was someone to make breakfast for. She wondered if the girl—one of those suburban names: Heather? Margot? Melissa?— liked to cook. So few young women did these days. The editorial assistants at Trice and Wanker apparently subsisted on take-out sushi and diet soda. What kind of families would they raise? In the event that Hooper, God help him, actually got hitched to this Heather-Margot-Melissa—and it was hardly beyond the realm of possibility, since Maggie had married Kenneth, after all, a week after his graduation—then perhaps the object lessons couldn't begin soon enough.

Galvanized by the task, Maggie went into balletic motion, seizing items from the stainless-steel refrigerator, snatching bowls, pans, and implements from their various racks and shelves, flipping on the radio to fill the huge sunny kitchen with the oratorios of Christmas morn, cracking eggs and whisking batter—all the while apprehending in little illuminating flashes how wonderful it might be to finally be free of Kenneth. In short order she produced a great stack of cornmeal pumpkin pancakes with a dozen links of her own champagne sage breakfast sausages. While these things warmed in the oven, she rolled out a stick of butter on her marble pastry slab, and cut out patties with a little star-shaped cookie cutter. These she arrayed cunningly on a scallop-shaped plate and garnished with a narcissus blossom from the forced bulbs blooming on the windowsill. Finally, she poured heated maple syrup into a crystal cruet. Soon, she had the breakfast arranged on a large tray along with a thermal carafe of coffee. She slipped on her gum boots and a down vest in the mudroom and carried the tray down to the orchard cottage, delighting in the powdery, featherlight new snow and the bracing air.

With perhaps five paces to go, however, she detected sounds of passion within the little building. For a moment she stood numbly in place trying to distinguish between her son's striving moans and the girl's odd, higher-pitched birdlike hoots. But then, in terror of being discovered, she shrank back to the kitchen and returned the corncakes and sausage to the oven. After what she considered a decent interval—ten minutes—she called the cottage on the intercom phone.

"Yunh?" Hooper answered breathlessly.

"Merry Christmas," Maggie chirped. "Are you guys alert?"

"Sort of."

"I'm coming down with breakfast now."

"Uh, gee—"

"Don't worry. I'll leave it out on the porch."

"Great—"

Maggie recomposed the tray, brought it down again, set it on a wicker table near the door this time, and retreated once more to the kitchen. Sipping her own cup of steaming Kenya arabica and nervously nibbling a corncake, Maggie observed the cottage from the kitchen window. As the seconds ticked by, the tray remained out on the little porch, its steaming contents rapidly refrigerating in the nineteen-degree air. She snatched the phone angrily off the wall.

"It's sitting out there getting ice cold," she said.

"Give us a minute, Mom, huh?"

"Hooper, darling. At least do me the honor of bringing it inside now so I won't feel that I wasted an hour of my time making it for you."

"Sure, Mom."

"Bon appétit."

As she hung up, the doorbell rang.

3
⌒ Déjà Vu All Over Again ⌒

Maggie flung open the heavy, hand-carved American chestnut door (circa 1820) and there stood Kenneth in his costume of the previous night: a wilted tuxedo. She was most surprised by her own shock at seeing him there.

"Feeling more reasonable?" he asked.

"What a question!"

"Well, you were pretty angry last night."

"I'm still pretty angry."

Kenneth flinched slightly, as though expecting a blow.

"Maggie, can we please have a discussion?"

"You're sure starting out on the wrong foot, buster. Am I feeling more reasonable? What's the assumption there? That I've got PMS? That I'm being inappropriate? That you're okay and I'm not? I'm reacting to something you did, you shit heel!"

"I'm sorry you're upset—"

"No you're not. You're sorry you got caught."

"How can I apologize?"

"You can't."

"I don't want to lose you," Kenneth blurted, suddenly blubbering, his athlete's shoulders jouncing up and down with each sob. Maggie had never seen him shed a tear before, not even at his father's funeral, and the sight unnerved her.

"Oh, for God's sake, come in so I can shut the door."

Kenneth shuffled across the threshold.

"Go into the library. I'll bring you a cup of coffee."

Kenneth nodded through his tears and moved blunderingly, like a great wounded beast, toward the room in question. In the kitchen Maggie considered dumping a shot of cognac in Kenneth's coffee, but the prospect of what it might do to such an obviously unstable person stopped her. When she entered the library, he was merely snuffling.

"Aren't you going to ask me where I spent the night?" he asked.

"Kenneth, you're a very wealthy man. You have a fine car in perfect working order and a wallet full of platinum credit cards. This is a civilized part of the world. If you couldn't find a decent hotel, then you're just a hopeless case."

"I drove up to Hanover and back," he said, ignoring her scorn. Hanover, New Hampshire, home of the Dartmouth Indians, was his old college town.

"How intrepid of you. Must have been exhausting."

Kenneth nodded, his mouth set tightly as though holding in more tears, his eyes rheumy and red as a cocker spaniel's.

"I . . . I thought that maybe if I went back there I could find part of myself that I somehow lost over the years."

"And what did you discover?" Maggie asked.

"I want us to be the way we used to be," Kenneth said.

"We'll never be twenty years old again."

"No. I mean, I wish we could . . . try and start over. I can change, I swear—"

"Wait a minute. What was it that you lost and went up there to find?"

"My sense of proportion. Priorities. Values."

"Sounds kind of metaphysical—"

"I don't want to lose our life together, Maggie. It means everything to me."

"You should have thought about it before you stuck your thingy in that strumpet."

"Won't you ever forgive me?"

Maggie sipped her coffee, ruminating before she said, "I understand that even good people sometimes misbehave, and that life is full of strange surprises. If you had banged some girl in a hotel, jeez, even if you'd had a lengthy affair off-premises and then ended it, I might have forgiven you." She puffed out her cheeks. "The part that kills me is you doing it under our roof, with people crawling all over the house. What if it had been Hattie Moile who saw you? The humiliation! Or Connie McQuillan, for God's sake, with her pipeline to *People* magazine! Inside a week I'd be an international butt of ridicule."

"Nobody *saw* anything," Kenneth said, an irritated, dismissive note creeping into his voice.

"Really? You weren't patting Laura Wilkie's little behind right in the middle of the ballroom? Don't bother denying it. I saw it—let's hope fifty other people didn't. You know, the thing that really gets me is that you couldn't have waited five measly little minutes in the bathroom before venturing out. It's as though you were determined to get caught."

Kenneth moved to the edge of his chair, looking about furtively from one place on the carpet to the next, as though searching for something he'd dropped, his jaw muscles twitching and his eyes darting here and there.

"Remember the party," he said, "when I walked into that room and caught you with Rudy Swinnington."

"What *are* you talking about?"

"At the Sigma Chi house."

"Oh, for goodness sake, that was more than twenty-five years ago, before we were even dating. Is that what you drove all the way up to New Hampshire to rediscover?"

"But that's exactly the point. I didn't know you, yet I forgave you. I called you up three days later and asked you out, after I saw you acting like a goddamn floozy with the biggest sex maniac in my fraternity."

"You probably called because you thought I was an easy lay."

"Aha!" Kenneth crowed, as though he had successfully led the prosecution's star witness to the edge of a cliff. "Tell me, since I never asked you before, did you fuck old Rudy that night?"

"I don't even remember."

"Oh God."

"I'm surprised you didn't ask Rudy yourself."

"You just don't get it, do you, Maggie?"

"I didn't even know you then, you jerk, so what does it matter?"

"Because you," Kenneth declared, peering down along his index finger as though it were a rapier, "are guilty of having a double standard."

"Kenneth, how do you make so much money? Is it that easy, what you do?"

"What do you mean?" he said, with sneering condescension.

"I mean, you don't think very logically. Are you just a good guesser with all those stocks and derivatives? It must take something besides . . . intelligence."

"Don't start in on what I do. It's made *everything* possible for you."

"I might have been just as successful on my own. And sooner too. Because for so many years I did what I'm good at just for us, never think-ing I could market myself."

"You won't be able to keep this up on your own, you know."

"Kenneth, between the books, the videos, the catering company, and the product endorsements, I earned two and a half million dollars this year alone."

"If you think you can maintain yourself in the style you're ac-customed to on that, you're out of your mind," he retorted, adding "Ha!" for emphasis.

"I can and I will, and if necessary, I'll make more money."

"Not here. Not in this house."

"I suppose you're going to take it away from me."

"Maggie, I've got what they call deep pockets. I can reach down in there and pull out so many goddamn lawyers that your life will seem like a perpetual ABA convention. You will be doing Chinese fire drills in the superior court until you are old and bent and gray and too weak to so much as soft-boil an egg."

"Thank you for answering my question."

"Pardon me?" Kenneth said. "What question?"

"How you get by on Wall Street. Apparently you substitute hate-fulness for brains."

Suddenly, he was upon her, springing athletically from his position on the loveseat to hers on the wingchair, from which he dragged her down to the pale apricot carpet. Working with a peculiar combination of brute force, tenderness, and manual dexterity, he quickly peeled Maggie out of her Tuzzi jumpsuit and managed, as well, to pull his own trousers down. Then he grasped the back of her head with one large hand, as though it were a muskmelon, and covered her mouth with his. Maggie punched him ineffectively in the ribs but did not scream for help, aware that the only rescuer within shouting distance was Hooper. She was more horrified at the thought of him barging into the oedipal spectacle of his mother being violated by his father—a scene, Maggie thought, that might turn the boy either homosexual or catatonic—than of herself being violated in the first place. But as Kenneth, all unwashed reek and sinewy limbs, seized one substantial breast, and prehensily nibbled her lips, Maggie gaspingly recalled those moans and hoots that Hooper and the girl had emitted in their throes of youthful passion, and she felt herself yielding to an irresistible tide of mammalian carnality that seemed to reduce all of them to so much living flesh and hair hurtling helplessly through time. Moments later they were both completely naked—Maggie actually assisting Kenneth out of his shirt—enacting one classic position after another (well rehearsed after twenty-five years of marriage)—in an upward-reaching fugue of fuckery that culminated with Maggie bowed backward in a near headstand and Kenneth yogically arched above, as though he were copulating with a wheelbarrow, and then they collapsed in a heap on the floor.

They lay motionless for several minutes, Maggie on her back, Kenneth on his belly, touching only at the forearm.

"I knew we'd get over this," Kenneth said.

"You are as thick as lentil soup," Maggie replied.

Kenneth looked confused. Sensing that her remark was not a compliment he said, "Come on, you enjoyed that. Deny it and you insult your own sensibilities."

"I got swept up in an old habit. It doesn't speak well for me. I'm ashamed of myself. But it doesn't change things between us."

"We've always had fights and made up after."

"That wasn't making up," Maggie said. "That was farewell."

"Aw, you can't mean it."

"But I do."

Maggie sat up, searched the vicinity for her underwear, and began reassembling herself. The jumpsuit hung from a Tiffany dragonfly floor lamp like a dead paratrooper in a tree. Finally, buttoned back in, she fetched the shopping bag of Christmas presents from the closet and stood it beside Kenneth's head, saying, "These are for you."

Kenneth peered into the bag at all the little boxes in their black matte wrapping. "Gee, thanks," he said, all puzzlement and gloom. "Did you open the ones I got for you?"

"These *are* the ones you got for me, you idiot. Give them to your little cookie."

Kenneth glanced in the bag again and made a face.

"If you drive me away, you'll miss me," he said.

"I can't wait to find out."

"You've been waiting for an excuse to dump me, haven't you?"

"What does that make Laura Wilkie? A little test you decided to spring on me?"

"She was a mistake, Maggie, a mistake!"

"That's right. And a bigger one than you bargained for. You see, what I don't like, Kenneth, is the idea that you are in any way the aggrieved party here, that something unfair is being done to you for no good reason. You screwed another woman under our roof on Christmas Eve with all our friends around. That's what this is about. And that's why you will shortly pack a few suits and socks and underthings and find another place to stay. You and your lawyers don't frighten me. I am going upstairs now to bathe you out of me. When I'm done, I expect you to be gone. Or else we go back to square one with the police. Am I clear?"

"Shrew."

"Keep it up and you'll lose those precious minutes I've allotted you to pack your things."

She left him supine on the carpet. There was a telephone in the master bath in case of any further shenanigans, and the sturdy door was furnished with a brass dead bolt. What more harm could he do now? Maggie wondered. If he set the house on fire, Maggie thought, she would climb out the bathroom window onto the porch roof and escape. These things occurred to her. As the large tiled bath filled, Maggie heard dresser drawers slamming shut and muffled exclamations of a word that sounded like "Christ!" She had just slid into the hot, capacious, welcoming tub when a knock resounded at the bathroom door.

"I'm leaving now."

"Splendid."

"Do you have to be such a wiseass in our last moments together?"

"I'm commending you for a job well done."

"What? Our marriage?"

"No, packing your stuff quickly."

"This is good-bye, then."

"Okay. Good-bye, Kenneth."

"Just tell me one thing. Did you fuck Rudy Swinnington that night or not?"

"I'm reaching for the phone."

"Answer me!"

"In a moment I'll dial the troopers."

"You haven't heard the last from me."

"I suppose not. But from now on, don't come over unless you call first."

"I loved you with all my heart," Kenneth barked. Maggie knew it couldn't possibly be true, but it brought tears to her eyes anyway as the years suddenly trailed before her in a psychic blue sky like the tail of the kite that was her life. Minutes later, she heard the immaculate motorcar purr to life outside and bear Kenneth forevermore into her past.

4
∽ The Horror of Family ∽

Punch-drunk with emotion, Maggie floated out of the bathroom around noon. She put on a black cotton turtleneck and a drab gray jumper (no makeup whatsoever) and glided into the hall in a cocoon of shock, feeling only the urge to cook something simple and monstrously hearty. Mashed potatoes and turnips came to mind, a childhood favorite, teased into great fluffy cirques and dotted with tarns of golden liquid butter. She had just descended the stairs when the doorbell sounded again. It was an old-fashioned electric bell from the thirties, really ringy. Maggie liked it because it could be heard from any of the house's remote rooms and outposts, especially during noisy social gatherings, but at close range it was shrill, and Maggie reacted as if she'd stuck her finger in a light socket.

"Is that you again!" she hollered at the door. No reply. This time, she vowed, she would kick Kenneth in the balls, no questions asked. As an insurance measure, she seized an umbrella from a brass stand by the door. It was a Swilby and Tuttham bumbershoot, the finest in the world, bought in London a year ago for 120 pounds sterling, exceedingly sturdy, with a nickel-silver tip that would make a nice impression on Kenneth's soft tissues, in case he blocked her kick. When Maggie flung open the door, there stood Kenneth's mother, Georgia, all four feet eleven inches of her, in a scarlet Chanel suit and matching hat (trimmed with green sprigs of holly) that might have appeared festive on someone who did not look exactly like the ancient Mexican mummy displayed on the fourth floor of the Museum of Natural History.

"Merry Christmas, my dearest girl!" Georgia screeched, throwing her hands up like a crippled cheerleader. Her visits, which had stabilized at about five per year, always began on this note of nearly hysterical affection before swerving off into carping and criticism. The sight of her mother-in-law propelled Maggie out of her comfortable cocoon of shock into an orbit of panic, which only worsened when she saw her own mother and stepfather's black Mercedes turn through the distant gateposts and roll ominously up the driveway.

"Expecting rain?" Georgia asked.

Maggie blinked, chucked the umbrella back in the stand, and bent to peck Georgia's heavily rouged and powdered cheek. "We've had some trouble around here," Maggie said.

"What sort of trouble?"

"Uh, rumors of a prowler. Yes, a prowler."

"Prowlers?" Georgia said as though the word had five syllables. "In my day prowlers did their prowling at night. What is the world coming to?"

"I wish I knew."

Behind Georgia loomed Maggie's mom, Irene, and her husband Charlie Moss. Charlie Moss was a second-generation New York City slumlord who extracted his wealth from hundreds of decrepit buildings in Manhattan and the Bronx the way strip mining companies extracted coal from the hollows of Appalachia. Irene met Charlie three years after she divorced Frank Hedjuk, moving, with little Maggie in tow, from Factorsville, Pennsylvania, to the great metropolis of Gotham—a lifelong dream—where Irene found work as an usher at the Morosco Theater. She had struck up a chat with Charlie during the intermission of *How to Succeed in Business Without Really Trying,* while his first wife was off in the powder room. "How do you like the play, sir?" Irene asked with her winning smile, sizing up his beautifully tailored glen plaid suit and gold cuff links. "Story of my life," Charlie said with a humorous snort, and inside of two minutes Irene had conveyed her telephone number, her marital status, and the nature of her availability. After that, Charlie didn't have a chance. Eight months later, in October of 1962, Irene (now the second Mrs. Charlie Moss) and Maggie moved from their one-bedroom flat on Ninety-second Sreet, in the shadow of the old Knickerbocker brewery (where the whole neighborhood stank of hops), into a fourteen-room duplex on Sutton Place. By this time, Frank Hedjuk had spiraled into the alcoholism that would kill him, and it was Charlie Moss whom Maggie Hedjuk had to thank for her years at the Brearly School and Smith College.

"Why, Maggie," Irene remarked over Georgia's humped shoulders, "what a dreary costume for the day of days." This was the quintessential Irene.

"It's a very special Christmas," Maggie averred in a sort of growl.

In the interval since Kenneth's assault, Maggie had completely forgotten that the whole parental gang was scheduled to pay its usual holiday afternoon call. Aside from the fact that enough ill feeling existed between both wings of the family, as well as between the generations, to sink any clan gathering, there was the problem of breaking the news about Kenneth. Now, panic filling her brain like one of those gelatinous blobs in a lava lamp, Maggie's mind sought refuge in the question of what she might feed everybody.

5
∽ The Empty Chair ∽

The three aged parents settled around the great kitchen table sipping rum toddies while Maggie prestidigitated a Christmas luncheon out of the odds and ends at hand. An hors d'oeuvre loaf of Maggie's own veal and fig pâté, ringed by slices of her sourdough bread, occupied a silver platter at the center. The rum toddies were designed to get the old folks tanked rapidly. The warmth and sweetness disguised their kick.

"Where's my big boy?" Georgia asked in her crowlike voice.

Maggie deftly ignored her, ducking into the walk-in fridge to snare a carton of eggs, some red peppers, two heads of limestone lettuce, and one of radicchio. Back at her station in the kitchen, she grabbed the phone and dialed the orchard cottage.

"Yunh . . . ?" Hooper answered.

"Are we up yet, darling?"

"More or less."

"Your grandmothers are here. And Charlie, too. We are going to have lunch. I do expect you'll join us. Pronto, if possible. Catch my meaning? Bye."

"Where is our little Hooper?" Georgia inquired. "Where is everybody?"

Maggie refreshed Georgia's drink. Soon she had a batch of cheddar scones baking in the oven and heaps of red peppers, onions, and potatoes sautéing on the stove. Charlie ranted about the underclass, setting forth well-rehearsed positions that Maggie had heard perhaps sixty-three times before. It was nearly all Charlie ever talked about, and loudly, too, and it was one of the reasons she did not invite Irene and Charlie to her annual Christmas Eve extravaganza. Another was Irene's humiliating habit of asking everybody what things cost: their jewelry, their clothes, their summer houses, their children's college tuition. It drove Maggie crazy. Luckily, Charlie had Danny, a married son from his first marriage and a third-generation slumlord, who conveniently threw a party of his own every Christmas Eve, where, thank God, Charlie and Irene were the star attractions.

"They're like monkeys," Charlie now declared of the African-Americans who occupied many of his apartments. "They piss in the stairwells. They break the fixtures, the lights, the toilets. They don't care. They live there, you see, but they don't care. Someone, please, tell me why a person would piss in the hall where they live? I don't care how much you hate your landlord or whitey or whatever. I don't live there. Sure, I own it, but it's not like they're pissing on me. They're pissing on themselves. They're like monkeys. If I gave out free bananas I could rent every last miserable unit."

"Miserable." Maggie said, tossing a steel colander noisily into the sink. "That's the operative word, right Charlie?"

"Aren't we testy," Irene observed.

"Excuse me," Charlie said. "Affordable housing. And the reason it's affordable is that it's less desirable. That is the way the world works, and the way it has always worked."

"I blame Eleanor Roosevelt," Georgia exclaimed and then, holding her eighteenth-century etched flip glass in Maggie's direction, said, "Pour me another, dearie."

A certain clattering in the mudroom preceded the entrance of Hooper and Alison.

"Good God! It's that prowler again!" Georgia cried.

"What prowler?" Irene said.

"The daytime prowler," Georgia said. "Have you ever heard of such a thing?"

"I never have."

By now Charlie was on his feet, poised as though awaiting an enemy invasion, but the two youngsters slouched in giggling and Charlie visibly deflated. Hooper sported the popular headgear of his generation, a baseball cap worn backward so as to display the interesting plastic adjustment strap. Alison's gold nose ring glinted in the afternoon light.

"Where's Dad?"

"I sent him out for something," Maggie said. "Everybody, this is Heather, Hooper's friend."

"Alison," the girl corrected her with a friendly giggle. Maggie wondered if the two of them were stoned but decided it was more likely the transports of love that made them so goofy. They both reeked of sex, a rich, zooey stink. The aroma embarrassed and frightened Maggie, dredging up jagged reminders of the Laura Wilkie incident. Her hand shook as she broke a dozen eggs into a steel bowl.

"Aren't you going to offer us a beverage, Mom?"

"Of course," Maggie said with a catch in her voice. "Help yourselves. It's on the stove."

"Heather," Irene inquired, "whatever possessed you to pierce your nose?"

"Just a little fashion experiment," the girl answered guilelessly, ignoring the mistaken name.

"What if the fashions change, dear?"

"I'll just take it out and the hole will eventually close."

"But it could leave a spot. A spot on your nose."

"Then she'll have plastic surgery, Grandma," Hooper said, hacking off an inch-thick slab of pâté. "They take a little laser and it's over in a second."

"But why disfigure yourself in the first place?" Charlie said.

"In my day, you only saw that sort of thing in the *National Geographic*," Georgia said.

"Your colored don't even do this to themselves. It's only the white kids. Ever notice?" Charlie said. "What is it with them? What is it with you, Heather?"

"Charlie, chill out. Her own parents aren't as tough on her as you guys are," Hooper said. "And it's Alison, everybody, not Heather. Think you can remember?" Maggie rather admired the way her son stood up to the elders.

"Did you ever hear of showers, young man?" Irene asked.

"Sure. Why?"

"Why?" Irene echoed him. "You smell like a gym bag."

Hooper and Alison swapped a glance and he made a face.

"This is a decadent generation," Charlie said. "I thought the sixties were bad, but now I don't know if today's not worse. You see those whaddayacallem groups on the MTV? The rapsters? They're like monkeys. And the white kids want to be like them. What I want to know is, why is it mandatory to wear a hat backwards or sideways? What's wrong with wearing it the way it was designed to be worn, with the peak in the front?"

"It's just a style thing," Hooper said.

"Style, schmyle," Irene said, using one of the Yiddishisms she borrowed from Charlie. "At least he could take it off in the house!"

Hooper took it off and hung it from the pot rack above the table. "Happy, Grandma?"

"Will everybody please stop picking on everybody!" Maggie said. "Alison, be a dear and help me set the table. You'll find everything you need in the pantry."

"Sure."

"Where the hell is that boy of mine?" Georgia asked.

"Yeah, where is Dad?"

"God, there are so many sets of plates in here!" Alison said. "Which ones should I use?"

"The pearlescent hobnail ones. And the pale-blue damask napkins," Maggie said, beginning to cook a frittata in an enormous copper sauté pan. "And use the good silver. Hooper, go show her."

"Where in hell is your help, Maggie," Georgia croaked.

"It's Christmas, for goodness sake, Georgia," Maggie said, pulling the sheet of scones from the oven. "They're in their own homes with their loved ones."

"And where in hell did you send my son, anyway? To Philadelphia?"

Maggie directed Alison toward the dining room, where the young woman began distributing plates and silverware as though she were dealing a poker hand. She was quite unsure about the placement of forks in relation to knives and spoons, having grown up in a household where each member individually prepared his or her own meals in a microwave oven whenever the mood struck and then ate in front of the television.

"Okay, everybody," Maggie said. "Luncheon is served." Maggie brought the frittata in on an enormous blue and white Canton platter. It was cut into manageable wedges. The scones followed in a silver wire basket. There was a green salad dressed in lemon juice with hazelnut oil, and a salver of Maggie's own pickled onions, grown on the premises and doused in her own sherry vinegar. When Maggie observed how Alison had set the table, her heart sank.

"Are we going to start without Kenneth?" Irene asked. His empty chair was suddenly the most conspicuous place at the table.

"I think we should," Maggie said quietly. "It's apt to be a long time before he returns."

Georgia, who had fairly wobbled into the dining room, now threw down her napkin, saying, "Where in hell is he? What did you send him out for? This is altogether irregular!"

"Yeah, Mom, what's going on?"

"Well," Maggie began, a lump the size of a damson plum massing in her larynx, "I sent him away."

"We know that!" Georgia crowed. "I want to know where and what for!"

"He did a bad thing and I asked him to leave."

"Did you say 'a bad thing'?"

"A very bad thing," Maggie replied.

"You asked him to leave?"

"I told him to pack his bags, yes, and go."

At this Alison burst into tears.

"You threw my boy out?"

"I did." Daintily, Maggie speared a chunk of potato and ate it. The others set their forks down.

"Did you call a lawyer?" Irene asked dryly. Then her voice rose an octave: "Charlie, call Bob Markowitz! This minute." He was their lawyer.

"I'm not going to call Bob on Christmas," Charlie said.

"He's Jewish! What does he care about Christmas?"

"I'm Jewish and I care about it," Charlie said.

"Okay, fine. Then I'll call him."

"Uh, Mother—"

"This is an emergency," Irene said.

"This is not *that* kind of emergency," Charlie said. "And Bob Markowitz isn't a goddamn plumber, so just sit down."

"This is so sad! I'm sorry, excuse me," Alison sobbed, and ran, weeping, from the room.

Hooper rose from his seat but did not follow her. "This is too weird," he muttered.

"Did he hit you?" Irene asked in the manner of a private investigator.

"As a matter of fact, I hit him," Maggie said.

"You hit my son!" Georgia screeched. "You trashy thing!"

"What did he do to you, Mom?"

"I'd rather not say."

"You hit my son and had the gall to throw him out of his own house! Where's the phone. I want a phone."

"Don't let her use the phone, Maggie," Irene said. "She'll call a lawyer. She'll call a whole squadron of lawyers and a judge too!"

"I'm calling my chauffeur, you tramp."

"There's a phone right around the corner in the library," Maggie said, splitting a scone.

Georgia struggled in her chair. "Help me up, goddamnit!"

"Sure, Grandma," Hooper said and led her from the room.

"You watch," Irene said. "She'll call the FBI. They're connected, all these old Connecticut biddies. Everybody knows everybody clear up to the top."

"Mother, please!"

"How can you sit there and eat?"

"I'm hungry. And life must go on."

"This is a helluva note," Charlie said, glancing around the room at the sideboards and the paintings on the wall, as though he were taking an inventory of Maggie's and Kenneth's joint possessions. "A helluva note! Sheesh."

"I have called the beeper service and Humberto will be here to pick me up in five minutes," Georgia declared. "How could you snooker me into this . . . this meal! After what you've done!"

"Kenneth did it to himself, Georgia. And, you know, he could have called you and told you not to come over today. That's what a considerate man your son is."

"*You* might have called us!" Irene chimed in. "Did we need to drive all the way up here from the city for this? You might have considered our feelings too."

"In the rush of things I just forgot," Maggie admitted. She now put down the scone, her appetite finally quashed.

"I suppose you think you're going to soak my boy," Georgia said.

"She's not just going to soak him, you old bat, she's going to take him to the cleaners and have him Martinized," Irene retorted. Then, to Maggie: "What was it anyway, honey? Adultery. Did he have a bimbo?"

"You're the bimbo," Georgia shrieked at Irene. "And you," she turned to Maggie, "are nothing more than a gold-digging scullery maid." The blasts of a car horn resounded from without. "Hooper! Help me to my car."

"Sure, Grandma,"

When she was gone, Irene said, "Well, are you going to tell us about it?"

Maggie sighed and said tonelessly, "He did it here, right under our roof."

"With a girl?"

"Of course with a girl," Maggie said. "Kenneth is not homosexual."

"You never know these days," her mother said.

"Oh, for Christ's sake, Irene. Ken's as straight as a Doberman pinscher," said Charlie, who was the only person who ever called Kenneth "Ken."

"Why are you defending him?"

"I'm not defending him."

"Of course you are."

"Look, there's no point in slinging mud," Charlie said. "Saying the guy's a pansy—"

"Don't be so naive," Irene said, her eyes narrowing like gunports in an armored war vehicle. "There's gonna be plenty of mud slung around before this thing is over."

"Believe it or not, I really don't want to talk about this now," Maggie said, pushing fragments of frittata to and fro on her plate.

"Well, we're only trying help," Irene said.

"I'm sure, Mother, but I wouldn't mind being alone just now."

"As you please," Irene said coolly. "Charlie, let's go."

Charlie snagged a couple of scones for the drive back. Irene departed under a cloud of wrath mingled with Chanel No. 5 and with barely a word of farewell. Charlie kissed Maggie paternally and whispered in her ear, "If you need anything, *anything,* call me at the office." Then they were gone and she was alone with Hooper.

6
⤷ The Good Son ⤶

He helped with the dishes. There were not enough to run the big restaurant-grade dishwasher, so they did them by hand, Hooper drying. Hooper, of course, asked what was going on between his father and mother, and Maggie gave him an edited, sanitized version of the Laura Wilkie incident. Hooper absorbed it thoughtfully and, after an awkward pause, said, "Maybe sometime you'll be able to forgive him."

"Maybe," Maggie said, without conviction. She couldn't stand another quarrel today, not even a difference of opinion.

"Anyway, I'll be around for a while," Hooper said.

"Oh?"

"I'm taking a break from school."

"A break? You're dropping out?"

"I'm taking a semester off. I know this guy who graduated ahead of me who's got this, like, internship at MTV. He says there might be something for me there too."

"Would you live in the city?"

"I thought we might commute from here. Hey, under the circumstances it'd probably be good for you to have us around."

"Us?"

"Yeah, Alison and me."

"She's dropping out too?"

"Well, we're, like, a unit, Mom."

"And what's she going to do?"

"She has this friend who works for Calvin Klein. We need some real-life experience in the real world, Mom. That's not such a bad thing." He put one large, sodden hand on her shoulder and gently took her chin between his thumb and index finger and made her look at him. "Don't worry," he added. "We won't get in your way."

"She doesn't even know how to set a table," Maggie said as she broke down and blubbered.

"She'll learn, Mom. You'll teach her." Hooper let his mother bawl on his shoulder. "I'd better go see about Alison," he eventually said. "Her family's a mess. She had this image of ours being this absolutely perfect all-American unit, like the way it is in your books. I think this pulled the rug out from under her a little, psychologically."

"Tell her she's welcome to stay and that I apologize for all this . . . unpleasantness," Maggie said. "Do you mind if we postpone presents until tomorrow?"

"Naw. Get a good night's sleep."

"Thanks. I'll try. You turned out well, Hooper. I'm glad you're going to stay around for a while." He tossed the dishtowel manfully onto the counter, pecked her on the cheek, and departed.

Maggie was determined to make the day after Christmas as normal as possible. Normality, she decided, would be her refuge against the pitiless storms of life. So she drew up a to-do list, posted it on the refrigerator door, and retreated to her bedroom.

It made her sick to be there. Kenneth had left drawers open and a lot of miscellaneous crap on the surfaces of things. Maggie collected the items—an ivory box full of cuff links and collar stays, his cummerbund, some paperback books, a nasal spray, a travel alarm, sunglasses—and put them in a couple of shoe boxes. She felt as though she were collecting the effects of a dead person. After that, she moved the furniture around the room so that it bore no resemblance to the place where she and *this person* had shared an intimate life for so many years. But that didn't help much either. The room still bore a kind of psychic stench that only two fresh coats of paint and a complete redecoration job might eradicate. So she took her reading (Austen's *Mansfield Park,* Menendez y Vega's *Cuisine of the Andes,* and the latest biography of Vita Sackville-West) into the north guest room, as she called it, which was decorated in the manner of a timberland adventure, with Hudson Bay trade blankets on the double bed, a fishing creel casually hung off the birchwood armoire, snowshoes leaning in the corner, a stuffed muskellunge grinning on the wall, and other trappings of the North Woods. In bed, at last, the day's traumas and rigors began to loosen their grip, and she drifted off into an exotic world of Andean recipes: blue potatoes in groundnut sauce; loin of llama with pigeon peas; salad of cactus pads and squash blossoms . . .

7
∽ Nearly Sisters ∽

Sometime before midnight, the phone rang. Maggie held the opinion that people who phoned after ten o'clock were a lower life-form, but she was not the kind of person who could lie there and ignore a ringing phone, even if the caller was apt to be the unspeakable pig who had until lately shared her bed.

"Do you have any idea what time it is," she barked into the handset, which had been cunningly embedded in a little section of birch log.

"Maggie, never mind that. It's me, Lindy." This was Lindy Hagan, formerly Lindy Katz, Maggie's roommate at Smith. Lindy was married to Buddy Hagan, the extremely successful producer (*A Woman Scorned, Dreadnought, A Kind and Restless Heart, Second Chance*), and lived in Los Angeles. Lindy and Maggie had not talked in perhaps a year. Once they'd been as close as sisters. Closer, really, for there were no sibling resentments. Lindy had an actress's husky voice, though she hadn't worked professionally since the eighties.

"I have to get out of here," she said without any small talk. Lindy's manic edge—the quality that always made her so fascinating to be around—seemed more like sheer panic now. "I hate everyone and everything in L.A., okay, and I can't handle being here another day. Not another second."

"What on earth is going on?"

"So I find out last week that Buddy is gay, okay—"

Maggie sat up and gasped. Buddy Hagan, gay? A series of snapshots flashed through her mind: Buddy Hagan waxing a surfboard on the beach at East Hampton, 1983 (the summer that she and Kenneth had the old windmill house on Rum Road), all the media wives, art groupies, and starlet wanna-bes tripping over one another to get a look at him; Buddy in his tuxedo at the Academy Awards with his face as golden as the statuette's, hoisting his Best Picture Oscar in triumph; Buddy relaxing under a linden tree in the Place Dauphine in Paris one Easter in the nineties when the four of them took the Concorde over on a lark. She never would have suspected . . .

"Did you catch him in the act?"

"Are you kidding? I'd be a fugitive on a murder warrant in Paraguay by now. No, no, no, no, no. He announced it, just like that. We're at Bagatelle on Melrose, okay? Little pink tables. Fresh poppies. Nicholson is sitting across the room. Geffen, Katzenberg, Whoopie Goldberg, George Clooney. Julia Roberts. The Boss and Patti. It's like goddamn *Entertainment Tonight* in there, which I realize is very shrewd on Buddy's part because he knows I won't throw a shit fit in front of this crowd, okay? 'There's something I'd like to share with you,' he goes. You like that part? 'Share with me'? Ha! You get the close shot? The rugged face, the slitty Clint Eastwood eyes, the Ralph Lauren western casual wear. Is this too much? So I go, 'Share away, pal,' which, okay, sounds a little snotty, but I'm not into this New Age, kiss-my-crystal, sugar-coat-the-bad-news bullshit, which I can see coming about thirty miles away, only me, dumb bunny, I think he's lost another twenty mil or something on some stupid development deal that's gone into turnaround for the third time. Only he goes, 'I've become acquainted with a side of myself that lay buried for years.' This sounds like dialogue from one of his shitty movies, okay? 'Speak English,' I go. 'Okay,' he goes. 'I'm bisexual.' Okay, reaction shot— me with my jaw bouncing off the tablecloth. Got it? So I go, 'Am I supposed to congratulate you, like this is some kind of achievement in life?' 'No,' he goes, 'I just want you to know, because I'm being blackmailed by someone, and I'd rather share it with you myself than have you see it on the news.' Tell me something, Maggie, what is it with men and their pricks? Why do they have to stick them in every hole—?"

"What on earth did you say to him?" Maggie asked, refusing to be sidetracked by cosmic questions.

"Well, I go, 'How long has this been going on?' What I'm thinking right now is about maybe gouging both his eyes out with my demitasse spoon, okay. And he goes, 'Some time now.' And I go, 'Is he the only one, this blackmailer?' And he goes, 'No, there've been others.' So I go, 'Can we leave or do I throw up right here in the persimmon clafouti?' So, like nine minutes later we're in the car driving over Mulholland, and I go, 'Will you take an AIDS test?' and he goes, 'Don't be silly.' And I'm thinking, if he wasn't behind the wheel I'd ram my nail file into his brain stem, okay? Just put him out of his misery right there. So the next day I go into Dr. Eugene Brill's office for an AIDS test. That was ten days ago. The results come back tomorrow." At this, Lindy broke down sobbing.

Maggie tried to comfort her over the line, inserting phrases between sobs like "poor thing" and "poor Lindy" and "there there." She wished she could rock Lindy in her arms and felt that all her words were inadequate.

"I thought I could handle it, but I can't," Lindy sobbed.

"Get on the first plane out of there tomorrow morning," Maggie said, as though she were giving directions to Nina for a catering job. "And I'll be at Kennedy Airport to meet you."

"Oh, I was hoping you'd say that. Dear, dear Maggie!"

"Where's Buddy now?"

"Who cares? The Sunset Marquis, for all I know, playing kiss the lizard with a valet parking attendant. I threw him out of the house the night he broke the news." Lindy resumed weeping.

"Don't worry, everything's going to be all right," Maggie said.

"Not if I have AIDS," Lindy shrieked. "I'll get covered with sores, okay, and my brain will turn to potato kugel, and I'll go blind and deaf and have fungus growing out of my—"

"Lindy! Lindy! Lindy! Darling! You're going to be here with someone who loves you. That's the only thing that matters. What time is it in L.A.? Nine o'clock? Start packing pronto. It'll make you tired. Bring a lot of things for a long stay. Remember, it's winter here. Call me as soon as you know your ETA."

"Maggie, you're so . . . you're the perfect friend," Lindy said, sniffling now.

"Funny," Maggie said, "that's what I always thought about you."

"I didn't ask you a thing about your life. I'm such a self-involved piece of shit."

"Look, you're the one who's in a jam. You get the attention now. That's how it works. Pack up, knock back a vodka, and get some sleep. We'll talk tomorrow."

A chill slowly spread from her center down her arms and legs as she replaced the phone. Scrunching down under the fresh sheets and the wool blankets, she thought, How easily we are reassured, like little children waking from a nightmare. Mommy or Daddy need only be there, invincible, omniscient, eternal. With a stabbing sensation in her stomach, she remembered the very first moment she became aware of mortality. It was during that same childhood illness she'd remembered upon awakening and seeing the sunlight on the ceiling. "Will you die someday, Daddy?" she'd asked during one of the respites from her delirium.

"Oh, that's way, way off. Can't see it from here."

"And Mommy too?"

"Oh, maybe in a thousand years."

"And me?"

"No, not you, honeybear. God made you special."

"Does that mean I don't get to go to heaven?"

"Y'see that's just it, this is heaven. You're already there. That's the biggest secret of all. This world, and everything in it, was made just for you. Nothing can ever hurt you here."

"But I'm so sick, Daddy."

"Oh it's just God's way of making sure you'll appreciate things more when you feel good. Now try and get some sleep."

Frank had switched off the lamp, whose base was a painted carousel horse he had carved himself. Maggie remembered feeling so sad when he left her in the dark because she knew she wasn't that special, and even at eight years old, she knew what the darkness really meant.

⤳ Part Three ⤳

Multiple Incivilities

I

🖚 A Rake in His Lair 🖚

The offices of Trice and Wanker, book publishers, occupied the former
Vanderhorne mansion, an impressive Richardsonian heap of red sand-
stone, at Forty-seventh and Madison Avenue. Harold Hamish, Maggie
Darling's editor, could be found in the third-floor corner office, formerly
the bedroom of Horace Vanderhorne (1832–1911), plutocrat, empire
builder, and swindler. The large, elegant room was paneled with wainscoting plundered from a cardinal's palace in Brugge, and Mr. Hamish
used the very desk upon which old Horace had schemed to manipulate
the stock of the Albany and Susquehanna Railroad to corner the gold
market (causing the panic of 1869) and later to secure the vice presidency
for his crony Chester A. Arthur in 1880.

    All the dark wood gave the room an air of masculine solidity,
and Hamish himself seemed a perfect accessory there. He was dressed
this morning in one of his trademark cashmere turtleneck sweaters,
charcoal gray, under a herringbone tweed jacket, with taupe moleskin
trousers and cordovan riding boots. He often wore boots to the office
straight off his morning ride in Central Park, and the room smelled
vaguely of horses. Hamish, sixty-one, combed his thinning silver and
brown hair straight back. He disapproved of the baldy's combover tech-
nique that other men his age favored. A very robust mustache—"a
modified Nietzsche," he called it—decorated his somewhat thin upper
lip, and its points hung down like fangs, lending him a carnivorous look
not inconsistent with his reputation in the literature business. It was said
of Hal Hamish that he ate authors for breakfast, critics for lunch, and

picked his teeth with poets, but like most folklore this was gross over-simplification. He only chewed up (and spit out) authors who failed him, either in volume of sales, diligence to their craft, or flaws of character like alcoholism. Critics, he often observed, were put on earth to be squashed like bugs. Poets—let's be fair, he would say—should be pitied for pursuing a vocation that offered no hope of material rewards, though he published a few as a sop to the college professors.

In Maggie Darling, on the other hand, Hamish had everything he could ask for: steady productivity and a motherlode of material, looks that middle-aged women (i.e., most book buyers) would sell their souls for, and a supernatural flair for promotion. He also admired her settled domestic life and he liked to quote Flaubert on the subject: "If you want to be a maniac in your writing, you must be regular in your habits." That is why Maggie's startling announcement of impending divorce rocked him like a body blow.

Seated to the side of his desk in a wine-red leather club chair, wearing a handsome Ralph Lauren faux military tunic and a matching ankle-length navy skirt, Maggie related the salient details of the Laura Wilkie incident during the Christmas Eve extravaganza, including how she'd tossed Kenneth out after all the guests had gone. She omitted the part about Kenneth's return Christmas morning and the sordid business that had ensued—it still confused and shamed her. Hamish listened attentively with his boots up on the desk—actually resting upon a manuscript of the latest novel by Nobel Prize winner Diego Sangay, peering intently over his tortoiseshell half-glasses in a doctorish way.

He had always wanted to like Kenneth, without quite succeeding, though Hamish was reflective enough to consider that jealousy might be the obstacle. He admired Kenneth's dedication to fitness, his taste in clothing, his ability to make enormous sums of money. It was not so easy, he learned, to get inside the fellow's skull. They shared a proclivity for sports. Hamish leaned toward the blood variety involving guns, rods, and animals, while Kenneth favored activities that called for large and expensive pieces of equipment, for instance, yachting. One year, following the birth of Maggie's second book (*Feasts for All Occasions*), Hamish had taken Kenneth trout fishing in the Catskills. Kenneth showed no skill with the rod. They had some lively, if superficial, conversation on the drive up, mostly on the subject of women. Yet Kenneth adroitly avoided tendering any intimate details of his life with Maggie. This frustrated Hamish. Hamish himself was full of juicy morsels about former wives, lady authors, lesbian celebrities, creamy editorial assistants, and select female personae from the performing arts. As they approached the Tappan Zee Bridge on the return, Kenneth fell silent and Hamish found himself nervously holding forth in a way that later embarrassed him. Finally, he could not decide whether Kenneth was just naturally reticent or if there was some central vacancy there. The upshot: they did not become boon companions.

Yet even while this news from Maggie electrified him with its vague scent of personal opportunity, Hamish felt sorry for Kenneth Darling this bright winter morning. The way he saw it, Kenneth had just blown a great thing with the most desirable woman in America.

"Men are baboons," Hamish declared solemnly while Maggie rifled her handbag for a Kleenex. "We pretend that there is a moral dimension to life and howl when someone violates our inflated sense of honor, yet there comes along the first little kitty cat and off we prance, our ensanguined organs foremost. Pardon the mixed metaphor." Hamish sounded a bit like a middle-period Orson Welles this morning. "I have but one rule where women are concerned," he added. "Don't let the little head do the thinking for the big head."

Maggie managed a rueful little laugh through her tears.

"You're such a fraud, Hal" she said. "Why, before you even left Clarissa, you were running split sessions between ———"—Maggie cited a much-ballyhooed young authoress of a sensational first novel— "and ———"—she dandled the name of a sexually voracious, slightly over-the-hill movie actress then in New York doing a Broadway play— "and ———"—she dredged up a beautiful but foul-mouthed so-called performance artist, then composing her memoirs of the 1990s downtown art scene under Hamish's tutelage.

"I hadn't thought of that minx in ages," Hamish reacted, wincing theatrically. He appeared to take the recitation as a backhanded tribute to his virility. "Ye Gods, what a nightmare!"

"Which one?"

"The whole horrifying cavalcade, actually. How in hell do you remember all these tramps when I can barely remember what I had for breakfast?"

"But you never eat breakfast."

"Maybe I should start. Probably improves the memory. If only Clarissa could have cooked the way you do, things might have turned out—uh, well. There are few secrets between us, aren't there, Maggie?"

"I'm grateful that you're always there when I need you."

"I'd do anything to make you feel better."

"Take me to lunch at the Four Seasons."

"Done."

They walked the five blocks up Madison. A gray velvet sky gave the busy avenue the intimate feel of a low-ceilinged room. Along the way, an impressive number of pedestrians gawked at Maggie, apparently recognizing her from the books and videos, and one Junior Leaguish woman, a perfect stranger in a camel hair coat, pearl earrings, and a helmet of gleaming gold hair, actually accosted her by the arm and said, "Hi, Maggie. Love your balsamic duck. It's become my main company dish."

Maggie was a bit startled by the attention and more surprised at the way it bolstered her spirits. The idea that fame held compensations had always seemed a little indecent to her. But the strange woman's unalloyed good cheer made the world seem, at least temporarily, a better place. Meanwhile, Hamish beamed at Maggie's side, as though he were walking the town's most magnificent show dog up the avenue.

2

∽ A Rumpus in the Grill Room ∽

At the restaurant, they settled into a banquette in the Grill Room. Familiar faces grinned or glowered in every corner: two former cabinet secretaries (state and commerce); a movie actor renowned for his durable good looks and short stature; his powerful agent; a TV network president; the playboy scion of an Italian automobile fortune; the prime minister of Denmark; a deputy mayor; and enough CEOs to fill an issue of *Fortune* magazine, not to mention several other book biz people of Hamish's rank who were huddled with their best-selling authors. The room's graceful geometry and restful lighting affected Maggie like a calming drug. She ordered shrimp and corn cakes with ginger cilantro sauce and a salad of julienned root vegetables. Hamish ordered the hearty ragout of venison with herbed polenta.

"I want to tell you about my next book," Maggie said as the waiter delivered their drinks—she, pale Madeira, he, a single-malt Scotch whisky, neat.

"Your diligence amazes me," Hamish said, "under the circumstances."

"I have a large establishment to run, and Kenneth will have his slimy lawyers pulling every string in the superior court to drag out even a temporary separation agreement. Besides, I have a point to prove. I want to carry on without him and his filthy lucre. Which brings me to the next point. Joyce is apt to ask for a shockingly large advance."

"I'd say the money boys at Trice and Wanker understand your value to the firm, both present and future," Hamish said with a wink. "What's the book idea?"

Maggie smoothed the linen tablecloth. "Housekeeping," she said.

Hamish drew back in his seat, gazed ruminatively at a distant chandelier, glanced back at Maggie, sipped his whisky, and said, "Houskeeping?"

"That's right."

"You mean as in cleaning up the house."

"Cleaning, redecorating, refurbishing, yes."

Hamish fidgeted in his seat, glanced at various points on the ceiling, and pronounced, "It's brilliant." The photographic opportunities came to him now in a rush: Maggie on tiptoes with a feather duster, Maggie hanging wallpaper, Maggie somewhat dishabille, on all fours, scrubbing pine planks with a wire brush, the deep cleft between her freckled full breasts exposed by the camera . . . He knocked back the rest of his drink in one gulp and sucked air in noisily over his teeth. "Clarissa was a bust in the housekeeping department," he remarked when the whisky fumes cleared his windpipe. "Couldn't make a bed to save her life. Wouldn't have known the front end of a vacuum cleaner from the ass end of a hair dryer."

Maggie had always wondered why they'd never been invited to Hamish's apartment during the Clarissa years. The four of them would meet for dinner in the city, of course, but always in restaurants.

"My boy Hooper found himself a girl who has no idea how to set a table," she said. "It's remarkable. I believe a lot of modern women are absolutely lost when it comes to the fundamentals. Even some of the bright ones—"

"Madame," a waiter announced, cradling a bottle of Perrier-Jouët, two flutes, and an ice bucket. "From the gentleman behind you." Maggie turned 180 degrees to see Frederick Swann at a table not ten yards away, the singer's lean, earnest, smiling face enveloped in its nimbus of golden Renaissance curls. He was seated with Earl Wise, chief of Odeon Records, the Hungarian film director Franz Tesla (*Last Train to Graz, This Rotten Earth*), and two young women of actressy demeanor.

As Maggie's eyes met his, Swann made a little writing gesture in the air, as though he were wielding a pen. "Ahem. Madame?" the waiter said and proffered a folded message:

> My Dear Ms. Darling,
> Never have I passed a Christmas Eve more agreeable than the gala in your lovely country home. You are a goddess. I shall be recording here in New York the next several months. Might we manage to meet discreetly so that I can admire you at leisure? I am at the Royalton, registered under the name Sir Humphrey Davy.
>
> Humbly,
> Swann

Maggie visibly blanched as she read the note, then turned a palpable scarlet, swiveled again in her seat, smiled at Swann, and silently mouthed the words *thank you.* Swann smiled boyishly in return.

"What was that all about?" Hamish inquired.

"He had a good time at my party Christmas Eve."

"Let me see the note."

"No," Maggie giggled, thrusting it inside her tunic.

"It's a mash note, isn't it."

"Not at all. It's a thank you."

"No secrets, Maggie," Hamish said. Though waggling a finger at her in a kidding way, he was plainly unamused.

"Getting back to housekeeping—"

"Don't make a fool of yourself with that young man. You could be his mother."

"What a sweet thing to say."

"I don't want to see you get hurt."

"You're jealous!"

"You're damn right I am," Hamish said, refilling his champagne glass. "He's got more hair than I do. And the sonofabitch will still be prancing around up here in the fresh air thirty years from now when I'm in the bone orchard pushing up daisies— What in the hell?"

A commotion seemed to erupt around the captain's station near the restaurant's entrance, harsh words foreign to this serene setting that had silenced the buzz of table conversation. A glass broke. All heads turned to see four figures in paramilitary drag and ski masks rush into the room. They carried automatic machine pistols low at their sides so the weapons were not immediately conspicuous. The quartet posted themselves at equal intervals around the large room with soldierlike precision. Once in position, the figure in the middle hoisted his gun overhead.

"Yo! Can I have your attention please?" he said.

As soon as he said that, of course, all the restaurant patrons exclaimed loudly.

"Shut up! Of course this is a robbery. Listen carefully. Mens, put your wallets and your watches on the table please. If you got one of them plastic Casios, keep the motherfucker. Women, put your handbags and jewelry on the table. There will be no further instructions. Do it right and nobody gets hurt."

Three of the figures pulled nylon sacks out of their camouflage jumpsuits and began circulating from table to table, scooping up booty. Maggie carefully removed the rhinestone drops from her earlobes, though they were worth less than fifty dollars. These days, one didn't dare wear real jewelry on the streets of New York. She was rifling her handbag when one of the robbers arrived at the table.

"Just give it up lady," he said, raking Hamish's billfold and Rolex into his sack. "All of it."

"I'm keeping my car keys. They're of no use to you."

"Who said?"

"Look, it's parked way down on Forty-third Street."

"What kind of wheels it is?"

"Nineteen ninety-eight Ford Fiesta," she lied.

"What's a nice lady like you drivin' a piece of shit like that for?"

"It was my husband's idea."

"Oh, yeah?" he turned to Hamish. "Well, you a cheap motherfucker—"

"Yo!" the leader barked from the center. "Shut the fuck up over there."

The robber took the handbag and the earrings and moved on, leaving Maggie her keys. Shortly, the gang reassembled at center.

"The Businessmen's Lunch Posse would like to thank y'all for your cooperation," the leader said. "Remain seated and nobody will get hurt. Have a nice day." He fired a dozen rounds into the ceiling as punctuation and the quartet departed while everyone's stunned attention was focused overhead on the falling ceiling debris. The entire operation took under ninety seconds. When the patrons realized that the robbers had indeed gone, the room swelled with astonished voices and a good deal of nervous laughter too. To Maggie, whose ears still rang from the gunfire, it seemed eerily as if a party had resumed.

"Were you trying to get us killed?" Hamish asked.

"Hal, I absolutely have to be at Kennedy Airport at three-thirty to pick up a dear friend who is in the midst of personal crisis of the gravest kind."

"Maggie, you do not try to reason with armed robbers."

"All right. Next time I won't say a word."

"Next time! If there *is* a next time, I'm moving to Switzerland."

A waiter brought out their meal at that moment, apologizing on behalf of the management for the terrible inconvenience of the robbery and saying that their lunch was on the house. Then the police arrived. The patrons were asked to remain until an officer came around to interview them. In the meantime, Maggie dug into her shrimp and corn cakes while Hamish, still smoldering, barely pushed the food around on his plate.

"I'm going to buy a pistol," he announced gloomily.

"Oh, I see. Trying to reason with them is stupid, but pulling a pistol on four men with machine guns is smart."

Hamish glared at Maggie as though from the entrance to some dark bunker where all the entitlements of manhood were stored.

"Can I taste your venison?" Maggie asked and went prospecting on his plate without waiting for an answer. "Hmmm. Fabulous! They have a way with game here."

The two set off for Hamish's office barely fifteen minutes later. His mood improved along the way, and upon arrival he began spouting a play-by-play of the brazen robbery for every editor and coffee girl on the third floor. While he held forth, Maggie called in to report her credit cards stolen. Finally, she got Hamish to extract a hundred dollars from petty cash to cover the parking lot bill at the airport and the bridge tolls home.

3
∾ A Most Soulful Reunion ∾

Lindy Hagan emerged from the jetway looking wan but beautiful in black silk cords by Stephano Guglianni tucked into bloodred Luchese cowboy boots and a black cowl-necked cashmere sweater by Deiter Hunsbacher. In one hand she carried a burnished leather satchel of a type that Ernest Hemingway might have lugged through the Spanish civil war, and over her other arm hung a black wool riding cape. Anxiety clouded her heart-shaped face as she scanned the large, busy concourse, until Maggie shouted, "Here, Lindy! Over here!" and then both of them erupted in a fit of squealing and hopping up and down that had the other travelers turning their heads.

The squealing fit was a throwback to their years at Smith College. It had been their signature greeting, whenever they reunited after a Christmas break or a summer vacation. (There was even a brief period of infantile regression in the fall of their sophomore year when they squealed every time they crossed paths on a quad.) Since people began recognizing her in public, Maggie had avoided anything that might make herself conspicuous, but the sight of Lindy projected her instantly back to those wonderful college days when the world was new and they were a pair of gorgeous nobodies with a golden future before them.

When they were done hopping and squealing, Maggie squeezed Lindy and, feeling her ribs through the cashmere sweater, exclaimed, "Darling, you're practically a skeleton!" Lindy appeared to take this as a compliment, for she'd ridden the diet roller coaster much of her life.

"God help me around you then," Lindy said, with a hint of her trademark lopsided smile, as she led the way to the luggage carousel. "You'll be force-feeding me strudels and foie gras and God-knows-what *chazzerai*, and I'll be as big as a mobile home in a week!"

"Don't worry. We have enough exercise equipment at home to open a spa."

"Can you get the Foodstuf line of products here in the East?" Lindy asked. "They make these simply fabulous nutrition-free foods. Mayonnaise, crackers, cottage cheese, this frozen shit that tastes just like ice cream—I think they hang some extra carbon atoms on the molecules so they're too big to be absorbed through your stomach lining."

"What happens to it in your body?"

"It just passes through, like the Lexington Avenue express. Nobody eats real food in L.A. anymore—ah, here are my things."

In the car—a one-year-old luxury-equipped Toyota Land Cruiser—Maggie began to spin the incredible tale of the holdup at the Four Seasons as Lindy listened in rapt astonishment. The Van Wyck Expressway ran through the grittier neighborhoods of Queens—Ozone Park, Jamaica, Richmond Hill—where the shop fronts proclaimed their wares and services in a dozen different alphabets. On every other corner, it seemed, groups of hump-shouldered men stood around fifty-gallon steel drums warming their hands over burning rubbish. The expressway itself, especially the median strip with its beleaguered plantings of yew and juniper, was littered with a stupendous amount of windblown plastic trash. These images of squalor and disorder streaked by in strange contrast to the recording of Handel's stately Water Music playing on the Toyota's splendid stereo system.

"It's great to be back in the real world," Lindy said quietly.

Just after turning off the Van Wyck onto the Whitestone Expressway, they observed two figures in hooded sweatshirts drop a concrete block from an overpass a quarter mile ahead. The block struck the roof of an Oldsmobile, then bounced off the car's trunk onto the road. The Oldsmobile fishtailed wildly for several hundred yards before the driver regained control. Maggie swerved to avoid hitting the concrete block, which had come to rest in her lane, and in swerving almost careened into a white Jeep racing to pass on her right. The Jeep's driver blared his horn. They could feel vibrations from the rap music roaring out of his speakers. Maggie swerved back into the left lane. Lindy wheeled around in her seat to see the two hooded figures on the overpass running away.

Emitting little gerbil-like squeaks of fright, Maggie struggled to steer while Lindy sank back in numb disbelief. Seconds later, they were soaring up the approach ramp onto the Whitestone Bridge. Lindy opened the window, stuck her head out, and shrieked. Maggie opened hers and did the same. All it took was a glance between them to establish that this was a variation on the squealing game. They shrieked their way across the entire bridge, the sodden gray wintry expanse of Long Island Sound below. At the tollbooth on the other side, Maggie implored the toll taker to call the police about the boys on the overpass, but he only retorted in some foreign gibberish and angrily waved them on. Lindy dove into her leather satchel and extracted a bottle of Stolichnaya vodka that already had a pretty good dent in it. She gulped down a martini's worth before passing the bottle to Maggie who, with still-trembling hands, gratefully took a healthy swig.

"I think they're trying to kill people out of sheer boredom now," Lindy said as the claustrophobic streets of bombed-out tenements in the Bronx gave way to the more open, strip-mall ambience of lower Westchester. "That could easily have been the end of us."

"The most unspeakable things happen every day in New York," Maggie said. "Babies left to die in gym bags. Homeless people set afire just for the fun of it. Schoolgirls killed by stray bullets. Girlfriends dissected by their ex-lovers. The sheer volume of mayhem boggles the mind. Funny, though," she halted in reflection, "it's just a story in the newspaper until something happens to you."

"We tolerate the intolerable in this fucking country," Lindy said, fairly spitting out the words. "What's happening to us, Maggie? What's happening to America?"

"I don't know," Maggie said with sigh. "The future is what's happening, I guess."

"If this is the future, then maybe I'd be better off dead."

"Oh, darling, don't say that. There's so much to live for, even with all the bad people and terrible things in the world."

4
∽ Home at Last ∽

Silence enveloped them as they crossed the state line into Connecticut and left the last ragged edges of the wounded metropolis behind. Large fluffy snowflakes began to bounce off the windshield. Maggie turned off the Merritt Parkway at the Wilton exit and proceeded north toward Rumford along a series of increasingly rural county roads. Large old houses could occasionally be glimpsed through the woods, their distant lights aglow in the gathering purple twilight, nestled securely in the gentle snow-mantled landscape like children tucked in warm beds.

"It's like being home again, the metaphorical home that the heart ever yearns for," Lindy said softly, though the Connecticut countryside was far different from the raucous suburb of Great Neck, Long Island, where she grew up. "This is what I dreamed about all those nights alone in bed after Buddy moved out. The *not-L.A.* world. The world of real snow and real, old houses and pumpkin soup and autumn leaves and children skating on ponds and families with dogs and long walks on country lanes all bundled up in sweaters and mufflers." She paused to gulp from the vodka bottle and proffered it to Maggie, who was slightly woozy from the first snort. "I guess it all boils down to a return to basic values," Lindy continued histrionically. "In L.A. nothing matters and anything goes. I want to purge all that from the depths of my soul and be clean again."

"Dear heart, I'm afraid there's something I must tell you," Maggie said carefully, as though defusing a bomb. "It doesn't alter a thing between us or your staying here, but it's been extremely upsetting."

"Oh, Maggie, I'm so sorry. I'm such a hateful self-absorbed pig," Lindy said, tears leaving sooty mascara trails down her gaunt cheeks. "I'm so ashamed of myself. Please forgive me. Here I am acting like the only person in the world who's got problems. I'm disgusting. You should let me die."

"Lindy! How on earth did your ego get so tattered?"

"I guess that's what happens when your husband turns gay on you. I must have been repulsive to him."

"You are not repulsive. You're lovely and sweet and clever and talented and fine."

"That's somebody else you once knew."

"Lindy, you've never looked more beautiful. Maybe you're going through a rough patch and struggling to figure out what's important, but I can't stand to hear you run yourself down."

"I was his wife, okay? And now he hates girls. Connect the dots."

"I'm sure it's nothing you did. You don't catch homosexuality like the flu. Poor Buddy's probably been all torn up and confused inside since his first pimple in high school."

"Do me a favor, okay? Don't go feeling sorry for the bastard. I might die fifty years before my time because of him. My nana lived to be ninety-eight years old, okay? I'm genetically programmed for the long haul. And now . . . this! This fucking disease!" At this, Lindy's tears escalated into outright bawling.

"Oh, dear heart, oh poor Lindy, we don't know that yet—"

"Look, here I go again! You start to tell me [snuffle] something important about your life and [snuffle] all of sudden the spotlight's back on me and my stupid problems. I'm such a hopeless egomaniac. If I had a gun, I'd shoot myself."

"Did you have a therapist in L.A.?"

"Maggie, if there's a single human being in L.A. who doesn't have a therapist, they'd have to put him in a raree-show. L.A. is an endless chain of therapy."

"Maybe you ought to see somebody here."

"Lenny—uh, Dr. Gorshak, my shrink—gave me a whole list

of names in your area. Who's your shrink, by the way. Maybe he's on the list."

"Haven't been going for quite a few years."

"Why not?"

"I don't know. I wasn't miserable. I was coping with life well enough, though at times I was far from happy. The house was an enormous distraction. And the garden was an even more colossal project. The catering company took a lot of energy, of course. Then the books happened and the videos. I really didn't have time for therapy."

"I've been seeing Gorshak three times a week for years."

"Do you think he's helped you?"

"Oh, absolutely. Incredibly. If nothing else, I haven't been fat since 1992. I'm much more together. I mean, you might not know it because of this mess I'm in. But thinking you may die a horrible premature death is not exactly conducive to good mental hygiene, okay? It's really set me back."

They drove past the quaint village center of West Rumford with its general store, Olde Post Road Inn (now a bed and breakfast), Unitarian church, post office, liquor store, pizzeria, garden center, and French auberge (a dreadful place run by a vile Luxembourgoise who was once caught pouring bleach into Blodgett Brook in order to bring up trout for his kitchen).

"It's so darling!" Lindy exclaimed. "So *Our Town!*"

Maggie turned onto winding Kettle Hill Road—which they had fought aggressively and successfully to keep unpaved for fifteen years—and then turned through the familiar brick gateposts to her own long gravel driveway.

"Stop the car!" Lindy said.

"Huh?"

"I want to get the full effect."

Little daylight remained. Just enough to make out the snow-capped sentinels of the bundled rosebushes, the various outbuildings, trellises, arbors, fruit trees, and other features of the extensive grounds. The handsome old white clapboard house stood sheltered in its grove of towering sycamores, planted the same year as Cornwallis's surrender at Yorktown. The house itself was even older, pre–Revolutionary War, though Maggie's rehab of the interior had been a veritable gut job clear down to the bare beams. Electric Christmas candles still glowed at every window and an evergreen wreath five feet in diameter hung across the second-floor Palladian window.

"This," Lindy intoned, "is a picture I could happily carry in my head to the grave."

"Dear heart, please! Stop being so morbid."

"It's perfect, though. It's everything that L.A. isn't." Lindy resumed weeping, softly this time, into a wad of tissue paper. Maggie proceeded down the driveway. Hooper's Saab sat in the oval turnaround and Maggie explained that he was home for the holidays.

"He's driving already!" Lindy exclaimed. She remembered him as a towheaded twelve-year-old riding a surf skimmer on the beach at Malibu one spring when the Darlings flew out to visit. (In truth Maggie went to attend a party, where the guests included Michael Caine, Harrison Ford, and Gene Hackman.)

"And screwing girls," Maggie added grumpily.

"He must be quite the hunk now," Lindy remarked, "if he's anything like his old man. Oh, God! There I go again! In all this time I haven't even asked you how Kenneth is. I'm so embarrassed. My egotism is simply mortifying. How can you ever forgive me?"

"Well, I'm afraid there is some news about Kenneth, actually."

Lindy seized Maggie's upper arm. "He's okay, isn't he? I know about this absolute *genius* of a cardiologist—"

"No, no, no, he's perfectly all right—physically. It's just that I, uh, threw him out of the house on Christmas Eve. Kenneth doesn't live here anymore."

5
∽ The Fateful Call ∽

Lindy fairly reeled into the house, punchy with shock, despair, psychic dislocation, self-loathing, anxiety, hunger, travel fatigue, and the effects of roughly five ounces of 100-proof vodka. Florence, one of the maids, had readied the Shaker guest room—so named for its austere furnishings—and Maggie installed Lindy there directly for a nap. The fateful phone call to Lindy's Los Angeles doctor had been set in advance for seven o'clock Eastern time.

Hooper and Alison were deconstructing a take-out pizza in a remote part of the house called the game room because it contained a Ping-Pong table. Its chief attraction, however, was a television projection system Kenneth had acquired in order to watch the Olympics at nearly life-size scale—only now, MTV blared on it. Ghetto youths in hooded sweatshirts were extemporizing in rhyme about the need to kill policemen. The room stank of cigarettes. An aluminum pie tin full of butts sat on the carpet to the side of the pizza box.

"Hi, Mom."

"Hi, Maggie."

"Hi, gang," Maggie replied listlessly. "Turn it down some, huh? Someone's trying to sleep upstairs."

"Huh? Is Dad back?"

"No. Aunt Lindy."

"Really? What's she doing here?"

"Don't ask."

Back in Maggie's kitchen, the Center of the Universe, messages galore waited, from Nina concerning the Founders' Day brunch that Maggie's company, Good Taste, was catering on Saturday for the Hartford Arboretum; from Harold Hamish saying he would be quoted in the *Times* tomorrow about their luncheon adventure; from Della Montaigne of *Good Morning America* about a February guest shot; from Hattie Moile and various other concerned friends inquiring carefully and confidentially about rumors of a split with Kenneth; from employees, purveyors, antique brokers, manufacturers of cooking equipment, sundry pests soliciting services and charitable causes, and two hangers-up whom Maggie suspected might be Kenneth. Reviewing all the messages gave her a headache.

At quarter to seven, she made a pot of her favorite gunpowder tea and brought up a tray with some edibles to the sewing room. Little sewing actually got done here—there were seamstresses for that. Rather it served as an intimate refuge, a place where Maggie retreated those evenings when Kenneth was being insufferable, particularly during his cocaine years. Here she perused seed catalogs on winter evenings, plotted revisions and additions to the gardens, composed recipes on a laptop computer, wrote notes to far-flung correspondents, including a clutch of literary personages and admirers from around the world.

The small chamber, hardly seven by nine, contained a chaise lounge draped with brocaded throws, a smallish padded armchair, a darling little Hepplewhite scrivener's desk, and a great deal of tactilely satisfying bric-a-brac: ceramic glove forms, onyx and malachite eggs, vermeil snuff boxes, the gold and jade finial that once adorned a mandarin's hat, a jeweler's brass magnifying loupe, and a silver Newport tankard filled with thirteen Bakelite fountain pens (twenty-five bucks for the lot at the East Rowney auction). Botanical prints adorned the walls. Most significantly, the room did not have any windows. This was hardly the fatal flaw it might seem, for rather than inducing claustrophobia, it lent an ambience of the securest coziness, completely blotting out the wide world and all its agencies of harm and woe. The little room reminded Maggie of a train compartment—some of her fondest memories were of the overnight trips to summer camp in a Pullman—and here Maggie liked to imagine that she was crossing the Alps at night or that she might throw open the door to discover Istanbul suddenly at her feet.

It was to this refuge, this luxurious bunker, that Maggie led a still somewhat groggy Lindy to place the fateful call to Los Angeles at seven o'clock sharp.

"I don't know if I can go through with it," she said.

"Be brave, dear heart."

Lindy huddled at the edge of the chaise staring at the telephone. Maggie poured Lindy a cup of tea, which she ignored. Instead she methodically ate all the lemon fingers, madeleines, and hazelnut meringues that accompanied the tea, one after another, with bulimic determination.

"Would you like me to dial for you?" Maggie asked.

"Wait a minute."

"It's seven."

"He's not going anywhere. Don't *utz* me. I'm not so anxious to find out if I'm gonna be dead next Christmas, okay? I prefer not knowing for ten more seconds. Did you ever wish you were a cow?"

"I beg your pardon?"

"You know, you drive out in the country and the cows stare blankly at you as you drive by."

"Yes?"

"They don't have a single thought in their heads, those cows. Not a shred of a thought. They don't think about tomorrow—hell, they don't think about five minutes from now. Or yesterday. Or five minutes ago. They're not tortured by regrets. They don't worry about money, about making deals, about whether some asshole director is going twenty million over budget, about what's for dinner, about their husbands turning gay. I'd like to be a cow. If I die from this shit, that's what I'm coming back as. Okay, I think I'm ready to make the call—"

But as Lindy reached for the handset, the phone rang and she recoiled, as from a rampant cobra. Maggie picked it up, holding an index finger aloft to signal that she would deal with the caller swiftly. Lindy rolled her eyes.

"Hello."

"Maggie Darling?"

"Speaking."

"Lawrence Hayward here. Say, that was quite a shindig you put on Christmas Eve."

"Glad you enjoyed yourself—"

"You're good with food. Anyone ever tell you that?"

"A few, here and there. Listen—"

"Never meant much to me before. Think I might have missed out. Say, where can you get something to eat around here?"

"Huh . . . ? Where are you exactly?"

"In my apartment. Fifth Avenue and Eighty-first. Can you just fire me a recommendation? Thought I'd try eating, you know, some better food for a change."

"Oh. Well. Try Civita on Seventy-sixth off Madison."

"What should I order?"

"*Coniglio in salmi*'. Listen—"

"What the heck is it? Some kind of spaghetti?"

"Jugged hare. You'll like it. Lawrence, I can't talk just now. Forgive me, but I left something on the stove—"

"'Course, 'course. Nothing to forgive. Well, thanks for the tip. Bye."

Maggie stared at the phone as though it were some strange artifact from another planet.

"Excuse me a moment," Lindy said. She vanished down the hall and returned shortly cradling her vodka bottle. "I'm not a lush, okay? But this is extraordinarily stressful, wouldn't you agree?"

"Oh, certainly."

"Got any valium?"

"Lindy! You can't mix downers and alcohol!"

"Of course you can. Grow up."

"Well, I'm sorry, I haven't got any."

Lindy knocked back a bracer, gasped, washed it down with some tepid tea, and snatched the phone up, hitting the keys with her long-nailed thumb.

"This is Lindy Hagan calling Dr. Eugene Brill. About my test results. What test? Listen, honey, just tell him it's me, he'll know what this is about. Huh? Well, it's really rather personal. I don't care if you're a nurse, I don't want to discuss it with you. Just shut up and tell the doctor who's calling, okay? Why, you little bitch!" Lindy lowered the phone into her lap.

"What happened?" Maggie asked.

"She hung up on me."

"You were a bit rough on her."

"Hey, whose side are you on?"

"Yours, of course."

"Did you hear anything she said to me?"

"No."

"Then how dare you assume that I was the only one being rude?"

"Lindy, I realize this is difficult for you—"

"I'll show you difficult!" She redialed rapidly. "Hang up on me again, little missy, and you'll be emptying bedpans in the back wards of Canoga Park State Hospital tomorrow. This is Lindy Hagan. Yes, *Missus* Buddy Hagan. That's right, the producer. Sure I'll hold."

Lindy poured another snort into her now empty teacup. Her hand shook so violently that the bottle clattered against the china.

"Ah, is that you, Dr. Brill? Yes, I'm just fine, thank you. A little concerned about whether I'm going to be around this time next year— ha ha. What? Sure, I'll hold."

Maggie crossed and recrossed her legs, nibbling a knuckle as she watched Lindy nervously twine her dark hair into a slick frayed cord.

"Ah, you're back," Lindy said. "No kidding? I didn't know you dabbled in real estate. It sounds like a pretty good buy to me. What? Pico and Crenshaw. Well, it's not very close to the freeway, is it? How the fuck would I know the comparables, Dr. Brill? Yes, I'll hold."

"What on earth are you two talking about?" Maggie whispered.

"Some broker's trying to sell him on a six-unit in mid-Wilshire. There's a very hot restaurant on the ground floor: Urkh M'ghurkh. Mongolian. Investment property."

"I can't believe he's treating you this way."

"Hey, I don't want him to hang up on me."

"It's atrocious."

"It's California. See why I love it there? Motherfucking doctor makes three million a year treating movie stars' sore throats and it's not enough money, okay? He needs more— Uh yes, I'm here, Dr. Brill. No. Well, actually I'm in Connecticut. At a friend's. No, he's not with me. I haven't seen the bastard since he broke the news. No, I don't think that's too expensive for Benedict Canyon. Well, if it's a complete tear-down, of course. Say, Dr. Brill, I wonder if you happen to have my test results handy. No, it was an . . . uh, uh, uh, an AIDS test, remember? Yeah, I'll hold."

"You should call the state medical ethics board," Maggie stage-whispered.

"You don't have to whisper, Maggie!" Lindy shouted. "We're on fucking hold again!"

Maggie retreated into the padded chair, drawing her heels up on the seat under her skirt. Lindy poured herself another vodka.

"Yes, I'm still here, Dr. Brill. What? You're opening the envelope? What the fuck is this? Oscar night? Sorry. Yes, I want to hear the results. Okay. I'll stop cursing, I swear. Say that again. I am—?"

Maggie seized both sides of her own face, making deep indentations in her cheeks.

"—How reliable is this test? Hmmmm. I suppose that's reassuring. I mean, it's great news. What? Well, I'm glad you're glad, but I assure you nobody's gladder than me. No, I won't be returning to L.A. anytime soon. Well, I don't consider it a shame. I'm hardly in a state of mind to consider dating. In fact, Dr. Brill, I wouldn't go out with you if you were the last straight man left on the planet, you moneygrubbing little prick. Yeah, good-bye, asshole."

Lindy flung down the phone.

"Are you going to be all right?" Maggie asked.

Lindy was able to nod before her eyes rolled up into her skull and she spiraled off the edge of the chaise lounge onto the creamy carpet.

⊷ Part Four ⊷

A Virtuoso at Work

I
⤳ Rescued from the Void ⤳

During the months of January and February that year, the Businessmen's Lunch Posse struck five more Manhattan eateries, but not just at lunchtime. They swept into Le Cirque, the Post House, Aureole, and Lutèce in broad daylight but hit La Grenouille at night, where an indignant young sous-chef ran out of the kitchen with a cleaver aloft, naively intending to "defend the establishment's honor"—as it was later reported by his coworkers—only to be blown away in a shit storm of nine-millimeter slugs.

The detectives on the case, in this time of dwindling city services, were able to deduce little beyond the perpetrators' ethnic persuasion, basic modus operandi, and unfailing good taste in victims. The posse members, for their part, grew more brazen about sampling the cuisine wherever they struck, snatching tidbits of ginger carpaccio off a plate here, grilled monkfish there, and offering instant reviews—"Yo, this shit is fine as a motherfucker!"—as they made their rapid and disciplined exit to the van waiting outside.

"Shorn Like Lambs!" one tabloid newspaper put it after the Lutèce caper, quoting a Brooklyn community organizer who gleefully referred to the gang's exploits as "New York's newest, most politically inventive growth industry." It became necessary for restaurants to hire private armed security guards, and those who couldn't afford it watched over empty dining rooms, cried over spoiled produce, and ultimately saw their businesses die.

Yet, life as it was practiced on Kettle Hill Farm in West Rumford, Connecticut, 56.3 miles from the Plaza Hotel, took on a merrier air than it had known in many years. To Maggie's happy surprise, Hooper and Alison both actually found intern positions at MTV and Calvin Klein, respectively, and began a regimen of commuting into the city as soon as the holidays, with all their bothersome festivities, drew to a close.

Lindy Hagan, with a clean bill of health, a future to consider, and a somewhat battered worldview, did not return to California. Instead, she took a place in the household as a sort of psychological reclamation project for Maggie, with most encouraging early results. She put on ten pounds, and in the right places too, for Maggie maintained a rigorous schedule of daily workouts. In turn, she helped Maggie and Nina with the business of Good Taste and seemed to relish her simple duties—as an improving patient relishes the little victories of occupational therapy in one of the better sanitariums. Hardly a whiz in the kitchen, Lindy could be counted on for rudimentary production tasks like baking muffins in quantity, deveining snow peas, and filling cored cherry tomatoes with curried crabmeat. Altogether, the household fell into an easy and amiable rhythm that fostered a general striving toward brighter futures for all concerned.

Kenneth Darling remained absent and incommunicado. A few preliminary letters arrived from his attorney, full of threats and promises of withering legal battles to come. Maggie's lawyer reassured her that they represented little more than bluster, though, and said that behind all the tough talk her husband could easily be viewed for the pitiful helpless wiggling white worm that he was.

It was a Thursday afternoon in late January, during an odd interval with no one else in the house, when Maggie herself stumbled psychologically. Lindy was in Westport enjoying a session with her new psychiatrist, Dr. Irwin Klein (author of *The No-Fail High Self-Esteem Diet*). Nina was off solo, handling a simple afternoon tea for thirty at the Ridgefield Historical Society, the kids were at work in the city, the maids done for the day and gone. There were no photo shoots, no editorial wrangles, no product endorsement sessions, no dinner guests, not even any phone calls from the environmental charities about their tiresome rain forests and interminable whales. For the first time in weeks, Maggie was completely alone.

James Howard Kunstler 99

Gazing out the kitchen window at the sleeping garden and the windblown snow and the long, blue shadows, she felt herself slipping helplessly into that silent void between all the thousandfold chores and obligations of her life. The void frightened her and the stillness of the snowy landscape amplified her fear into a kind of free-falling despair. She longed at that moment to be enfolded in a man's strong arms to keep from pitching into that void, and it occurred to her more than fleetingly, for the first time in weeks, that there was absolutely no man in her life. She suddenly craved one, craved all the brawn and musk and stupidity and courage of a man.

This longing, this physical hunger for enfoldment, resolved into a clear picture of Maggie's predicament, like a reflection on the surface of a pond once the wind dies down, and her fear and despair clarified into a thrall of simple loneliness. She looked out at the wintry garden beds and saw her future in the cold blue barren snowdrifts. And, as sometimes happens in those odd moments when our little lives call out to the vast looming void where the true spirit of the world dwells, the void answered—Jung would have called it an instance of *synchronicity*—this time, happily, in the very longed-for form of a man's voice.

"Swann here," the voice seemed to sing at the distant end of the phone wire.

"Uh—" Maggie struggled for words as the fearful void reeled back in her consciousness. "Um, yes? Maggie Darling, speaking."

"Frederick Swann. Remember me, Mrs. Darling?"

Suddenly, Maggie was combing her thick silver-blond hair with her fingers. "Frederick Swann the . . . performer?"

"Oh, I like that. Hadn't thought of myself quite that way before. Mrs. Darling, I wish to scold you. Three weeks have passed since our chance encounter and you have not answered my note. I am bereft."

A pregnant interval ensued before Maggie burst out laughing. "Don't you . . . have groupies?" she struggled to say.

"Oh, I see. You imagine that I'm hip-deep in adolescent kitty cats. Well, I suppose I could be, but that is not to my taste, Mrs. Darling. You are more to my taste."

"I'm . . . very flattered, Frederick."

"Swann. Swanny to my intimates."

"You *are* very swanlike."

"I take that as a compliment."

"It was intended to be."

"Yet if anyone is swanlike, it is you, Mrs. Darling—and conversely, 'liked by Swann.'"

"I hardly know what to say."

"Say you'll have supper with me tonight."

"It's rather short notice, isn't it?"

"Yes. I should not like to give you any time to reflect on the proposition, because I'm afraid that you'll find any number of reasons to wrinkle your lovely nose and say no thank you. What do you say?"

"I say I'm too old for you." She laughed again.

"Nonsense," Swann retorted as though disposing of a little fluff of lint. "I suppose you'd like to argue the point, though."

"I don't like to argue about anything."

"Splendid. Then you'll dine with me tonight?"

"You are persistent."

"Oh, just please say you will."

"I . . . will," Maggie said impulsively, horrifying herself.

"Good. I'll send a car."

"Where do you propose to dine?" she said, falling helplessly into his cadence of speech.

"Why, here, of course. The Royalton. The car should arrive at your establishment at roughly seven o'clock. Dress for comfort. Any questions?"

"Yes. Do you know that I am a married woman?"

"I have intelligence, Mrs. Darling, that some time ago you showed your husband the door, that you are, these days, married as a matter of legal circumstance, and there it ends. Do I have this correctly?"

"That's a fair, if glib, summary. Who told you that?"

"Let's just say I made inquiries. The source is reliable. I'm thrilled by the prospect of our evening together. Till later, then, Mrs. Darling. Good afternoon."

2
∽ The Fetching ∽

Lindy returned from her headshrinking session at quarter to six and found Maggie upstairs in her bedroom amid heaps of separates. It was at once apparent to Lindy that Maggie had a date with someone. Though Lindy begged and pleaded with her, Maggie would not reveal the date's name until she was satisfied with her costume: a demure claret cashmere scoop-necked jersey worn with a simple black merino skirt, black tights, and Holly Borghese black velvet, gold-buckled slippers. Only then would she utter the words *Frederick Swann,* and when she did, it was as though Lindy had been thrown against the wall by a poltergeist.

"You're old enough to be his mother!" Lindy whispered, hoarse with amazement.

"Technically, perhaps," Maggie agreed, closing the clasp on a simple gold chain that dangled a jade heart just above the cleft between her breasts. "I made the same point to him, but he doesn't seem to care."

"Where did you meet him? How did you get to know him? What's he like? What about the other guys in his band? Oh, Maggie, you be careful, now."

"Well, what's the worst that could happen?"

Here they shared a knowing glance and commenced to hop up and down and squeal, until it was as though they were back in the college dormitory and all the men in their world were like so much delectable barbecue.

The car, owned by Odeon Records, came five minutes early. It was an immense vintage Bentley that had once belonged to the contralto

Olga Kathura, with a bar and a compact-disc player (nothing so vulgar as a television) in the passenger compartment and only one disc in evidence, Frederick Swann's latest, titled *The Bitter Wine of Loneliness*. The driver wore a snappy mauve and green uniform that looked as though it had once been used on a *Star Trek* episode. The bar included a mini-refrigerator that contained three bottles of Louis Roderer Cristal and one of Swedish vodka. Maggie's sense of thrift would not allow her to crack one of the champagne bottles, so she poured herself two fingers of vodka in a pony glass and listened to Swann's plaintive tunes all the way down the parkway.

3
∽ Tortured by Menials ∽

The employees of the Royalton Hotel dressed in a uniform of black slacks and plain black shirts buttoned at the throat, male and female alike. Maggie couldn't help imagining that the hotel had been taken over by the Vietcong. The decor featured darkly lacquered surfaces everywhere, furnished incongruously with chairs and sofas draped in baggy white slipcovers that looked as though they'd been borrowed from the porch of a beach house. It was all so arch, so determined to make a memorable style statement, that Maggie felt the distinct urge to bake sugar cookies and distribute them around the lobby as an antidote.

"Mr. Swann's suite?" she inquired discreetly at the desk.

"We don't have a Mr. Swann registered here," the desk clerk said with a straight face, as though greatly impressed with his own ability to keep secrets.

Maggie's sharp annoyance rather surprised her. "Oh, come on, I know he's here."

"Sorry, ma'am. Not according to the register."

She wanted to break something, specifically the invitingly slender neck of the young man behind the counter. Just then she recalled that day at the Four Seasons and the note passed by Swann—some name he was registered under, some figure from English history. She racked her brain.

"Do you have a Mr. Cromwell here?"

"No."

"A Mr. Carlyle?"

"Sorry."

"Newton?"

"No Newton."

She was about to inform the little maggot that Mr. Earl Wise of Odeon Records could probably straighten out the problem in a digital nanosecond—and reduce the maggot to a mere unemployment statistic—when a name popped into her head. "Have you a Humphrey Davy here?"

"A *Sir* Humphrey Davy. Yes. Suite 1004. Go right up. He's expecting you." The clerk smiled oleaginously and returned to his computer keyboard.

Swann was waiting down the hallway when the elevator discharged Maggie onto the tenth floor. Seeing him, lithe, golden, barefoot, and altogether luminous in a pair of artfully distressed blue jeans and a blousy white silk shirt, the annoyance at once drained out of her and she trembled slightly.

"I hope you like garlic," he said.

4
⌒ Spellbound ⌒

"My father was posted to Singapore when I was nine years old," Swann declaimed some minutes later, brandishing chopsticks from which dangled a morsel of some khaki-and-carmine-colored flesh that Maggie could not quite identify. The suite contained a well-equipped kitchen, done in the hotel's signature dark lacquered cabinetry and brushed chrome. "He was chargé d'affaires," Swann continued. "Our life there was an idyll out of E. M. Forster. More servants than one knew what to do with. Lots of lovely insects for a boy to play with. The Goliath beetles were my favorites, so large—about as big as a baby's shoe—that you could paint numbers on their shells in nail polish and race them about the courtyard. No need for batteries, either. More champagne?"

"Thank you."

Here Swann dropped the morsel of mystery meat into a long-handled wok where it sputtered and danced. Maggie observed intently, as she did in any kitchen not her own. He seemed comfortable with the procedure.

"Mind if I ask? What is that stuff?"

"'Tis an Asiatic conch, the cornet of Melaka. Sweet as milk-fed veal. I have it flown to me when I am recording, for it is reputed to be not only a creative tonic but an aphrodisiac. The whole operation sets me back a mere two hundred pounds—air freight, dry ice, the lot— which, I daresay, is little more than one casually drops at any decent bistro in this town—am I right?"

"I suppose—"

"Lest you think me extravagant."

Swann emptied a steel utility bowl of conch into the wok and began stir-frying.

"Where did you learn to cook?" Maggie asked.

"'Twas my parents' misfortune to be present at the royal cricket grounds on Boxing Day 1983, the afternoon that a band of Malay unionists ran amok in the grandstand. Among other atrocities, they lobbed a hand grenade into the governor-general's box. Mother was mortally wounded and—" Swann dabbed his sleeve at the corner of an eye "—died the following morning at hospital without regaining consciousness. Father was merely crippled, made a quadriplegic."

"How horrible."

Swann emptied a saucer of little chopped things into the wok. A steamy cloud redolent of lemon and jasmine blossoms wafted to the ceiling. Soon, he was ladling chunks of conch and its aromatic broth over rice-filled black ceramic bowls, which he carried to a small round table naped in wine-colored linen and set with a kind of modernistic silver service that looked more like miniature weapons of war than eating utensils. A single dark-petaled tulip stood there in a tubular chrome vase.

"Father and I returned to London," Swann continued at the table. "He'd lost everything, you see, for all we'd had as a family, really, were foreign office perquisites—our quarters in the embassy compound, cars, servants, the whole bloody kit. And all that remained was his civil service disability pension. So, there we were, just the two of us in a cramped basement flat in Fournier Street round the corner from the Spitalfields Market. 'Twas there I learned to cook and keep house, for father was quite helpless. I did not even attend school, since we could not afford a day nurse, and the only alternative would've been the soldiers' home, of which father had a morbid terror. So I stayed home with him all but a few hours of the day, feeding him, changing him, sponging him off."

"It sounds like the sheerest hell for a boy of—how old were you?"

"Twelve when Mum died. More champagne?"

"Thank you. By the way, this is delicious. You have a deft hand with the lemongrass. It can overpower a dish."

"I don't believe in conquering the senses by main force. Where was I?"

"Home with Dad."

"Ah, yes. I scrimped and saved and bought my first guitar, a twelve-string Hafenstoller. Father loathed the telly. I diverted him with little ditties I'd make up about characters in the neighborhood—the butcher's boy and Mrs. Cutglass, the landlady. The truth is, my own little life was nearly as circumscribed as Father's. The few hours I had to myself each week I spent skulking about the Guildhall Library, copying galliards and pavanes out of ancient quartos. More conch?"

"Thank you. How long did this go on? This . . . way of life?"

"It ended mercifully one week before my sixteenth birthday. Father, you see, had lost an eye, a kidney, his gall bladder, a portion of the liver, and half a lung in the grenade attack, in addition to the spinal injury, and one morning I threw open the curtains to discover that he had become an angel overnight. Within two weeks I'd joined my first band, Petrolbombs, as lead vocalist, and never looked back."

Maggie would not recall the ensuing events quite so clearly the next day, for one glass of champagne chased the next, and after devouring some heavenly confection made out of chocolate, puff pastry, brandied pears, and crème anglaise, she found herself smoking hashish out of a little bone pipe. This led to a sequence of amatory tableaux that came back to her only in hallucinatory fragments afterward: Swann bending to kiss her throat; her breasts heaving beneath the cashmere; his hand deftly popping the brassiere clasp between them, liberating them; her hands fumbling to unbutton his shirt; the crucifix of curly blond hair running from nipple to nipple across his chest and down his slender abdomen; her skirt dropping to the floor with an audible thud, and his long-fingered hands cupping her "little wet bottom," as he called it; his blue jeans coming away as though they had been made of crepe paper, and the surprisingly sudden appearance—since he did not wear underpants—of his enormous rampant organ, which compared to Kenneth's member the way a Genoa salami compares to a Coney Island red hot. And then in bed Swann was seemingly indefatigable, flipping her this way and that, rotating her to all compass points in a duet of penetration that went on, with a few breathless intervals, until pinkish gray light glowed in a slit between the draperies. Then she fell unconscious.

"I adore you Mrs. Darling," were the words that roused her later that morning. Though a hangover gripped her like the thought of a death in the family, she surrendered again to Swann's repeated amorous incursions, until it felt as though her brain had somehow taken up residence in that tractless region beneath her belly and all of life was reduced to a watery adventure down some yawing rapids of pleasure.

"In Singapore I had a nurse named Mrs. Gray," Swann murmured in the aftermath.

"Were you in love with her?"

"I have a distinct memory of her washing my willy in the bath, with rather more vigor than the task called for."

"In America we call that child abuse."

"I don't think I was harmed by it. Poor thing. It might have been all the fun she ever had."

Just then, Maggie's headache reasserted itself, like a large gong banging in a tiny room. Swann announced that he was late for the recording studio. He induced Maggie into the luxurious shower, where he massaged her temples under a stream of hot water, then had her one more time in a position the yoga masters call "two storks spearing carp," and shortly they were in the Odeon Records limousine plying down Ninth Avenue with a steaming thermos of espresso and a basket of warm almond croissants.

Swann hopped out at Fifty-first Street, saying, "I want to see you in Connecticut, Mrs. Darling, at your hearthside, very, very soon."

And Maggie, feeling stupefied with fatigue and infatuation, replied, "Yes. Certainly. Supper sometime. Soon. I cook too, you know . . ." Then he was gone and the rest of the trip north up the parkways and highways and little back roads dissolved into a blur of amazement.

5
∽ Reflection ∽

She slept again until afternoon, letting Nina, Lindy, and the crew handle a board members' luncheon for Medithrax Industries of Norwalk (makers of Zip-Flex, a medical adhesive designed to replace surgical sutures) and canceling a photo session with Reggie Chang for the new book, which Harold Hamish had deftly retitled *Keeping House*. When she awoke, she seemed to levitate about the rooms on a magnetic cushion of sexual energy. Every thought turned to Swann. Bake a lemon ginger tea cake—would Swann have eaten such things back in England? Polish a silver cinnamon-sugar shaker recently acquired at a Ridgefield junk shop—it rather looked like Swann's uncircumcised willy, only smaller. Send away to the gourmet seed company for their special slow-bolt cilantro—how winning that Swann had cooked her supper, and such a good one, too!

Every now and then, Kenneth entered her thoughts, the way a refrain in a minor key enters an otherwise sprightly concerto. But it was clear to Maggie that she had exited the arid wilderness of their marriage and entered a thrilling new mysterious lush frontier. She could accept the refrain in a minor key as a signifier of memory and experience, even relishing its piquancy as a counterpoint to the major key of Swann-Swann-Swann that suddenly resounded through her senses. It was midafternoon, the day after that amazing night at the Royalton, when Maggie arranged a dinner party at Kettle Hill Farm to present the astounding fact of her liaison to select members of the world at large. She was finished grieving for the marriage whose actual moment of death she had failed to recognize.

6
☙ The Guest List ❧

"Christy Chauvin! Are you out of your mind?" Lindy cried as she mulled over the guest list for an Intimate Supper for Eight in the Winter Garden, padding up and down the carpet of Maggie's redecorated bedroom—all the lingering scents and traces of Kenneth eradicated with a new rag-rolled paint job (Creamsicle with a coolish sea foam trim), and all new bedclothes and window dressings. Cynthia Wise, wife of Earl, maestro of Odeon Records, had recommended Christy Chauvin, a supermodel, as a supper guest. Ms. Chauvin had been writing a pop culture column for *Slate.com* since September. It was rumored that she actually composed it herself. "Not only is she drop-dead gorgeous but a goddamned intellectual. You're asking for trouble, Maggie," Lindy said.

"Does it occur to you that this might be a little test?"

Lindy appeared to weigh the idea a moment. "Maggie, let me explain something about the real world to you, okay? Human beings are opportunistic. Men are like dogs and women are . . . not much better. Place temptation in their path and they will behave badly. This is not hypothesis. This is fact. One does not go around testing this proposition."

"I've invited her."

"She goes out with that schmuck actor, what's-his-face."

"Arlie Hodge. She dumped him last week."

"Great. She'll be all over your Swann like a cheap suit."

"I can't wait to find out. Besides, an intimate supper needs a little frisson. I like the way a great beauty puts people on edge. They eat more."

"Groovy," Lindy said. "I've gained ten pounds since I arrived."

"All muscle," Maggie said. "Those workouts are paying off. You look fabulous."

"So who's on this list for me?" Lindy said. "Hmmm. Obviously not Earl Wise. Reggie Chang?"

"Reggie's there for . . . solidity. He's the cornstarch in the blanc-mange. He's normal. A flat-out nice person."

"Meaning, not my type. Too nice, too normal."

"That's not what I meant."

"No, it's true. I require . . . an *extravaganza* of a man. So this Lawrence Hayward must be my ticket. Seems as though I know the name from CNN. Corporate big shot? Help me out here, Maggie."

"Wall Street. One of the five richest men in America. Multiple billions. Divorced three years. Lonely."

"Somehow I don't get a snapshot here."

"Think of a rodent."

"Oh, lovely. And what does that make me? A wedge of Emmentaler."

"I just thought it might be interesting for you." Maggie giggled girlishly. "The guy has been calling me three times a week lately. He's in Milan—where can he get something to eat? He's in London, hungry. He's in São Paulo. It's as though I've become his personal international dining-out adviser."

"Well, obviously he sees that Kenneth is out of the picture. He spies an opportunity."

"No, I think it's something else. I think this sorry little creature is peering out of the shell where he has spent a dreary, if lucrative, life. He glimpses sight, sound, and wonderful, wonderful tastes beyond the gray boundaries of his gray world. He's reaching out toward sensation. I find it strangely moving. Anyway, you don't have to . . . make yourself available to him."

"Multiple billions. Jesus. It gives me the shivers."

7
↬ Bon Appétit ↫

She'd planned cocktails for seven-thirty in the library by the fireside. Reggie Chang arrived ten minutes early and shot a roll of Maggie in the kitchen with a white chef's tunic on over her black, long-sleeved, waterwashed crepe de chine dress (off-the-rack, Bendel) and in the conservatory with the table set for eight among the tree ferns, orchids, and blazing votives. The photos were intended for Maggie's planned volume *Easy Feasts*. It was a bit of a sham since there would be no hint in the book of Nina and an assistant who were really preparing the meal or of the Yale anthropology major (female, in a tux) who was engaged to serve for the evening. Maggie understood that her readers expected a degree of fantasy in her books, though—if anyone could be Maggie Darling, then there would be no need for Maggie.

Christy Chauvin turned up at 7:35, virtually on time, a fact that rather impressed Maggie, who was prepared to dislike the brainy model despite her own rationale for inviting her. Reggie, too, was pleasantly surprised that Christy allowed him to shoot half a roll of her, since she was customarily paid $5,000 an hour for regular work. But in a Southern voice only slightly evocative of magnolia and perspiration, Christy said, "Why don't we just keep the agency out of this."

The Wises arrived at quarter to eight with excuses about trouble on the Merritt Parkway and Lawrence Hayward minutes behind them with no explanation for his tardiness and the whole world of Wall Street seemingly on his shoulders. Hayward looked fleshier than he had at Christmastime, and as the Yalie began passing little tidbits of smoked trout mousse in puff pastry on a silver tray around the room he perked up noticeably—at the tidbits, not the Yalie, though she was a fine-boned example of her type. Swann, to Maggie's mounting panic and embarrassment, did not show up until ten after eight—more rumors of trouble on the Merritt Parkway; some kind of shooting incident, police cars all over, more he couldn't say—but the force of his physical radiance and effortless charm sent the other personalities into vectors of interaction. He soon had the library abuzz as though twice the number of people were in the room, and at quarter to nine the company removed to the conservatory for supper.

They began with lobster and blue corn tamales on pools of *chilpotle* cream. More champagne went around (a Bollinger Grand Annee, no great shakes, but decent). The table was round, like a clock. Maggie sat at six o'clock with Swann to her left at seven and Lawrence Hayward to her right at five. Christy Chauvin was deployed at noon, that is, directly opposite Maggie so that Maggie could observe her body language vis-à-vis Swann. Lindy occupied the place at Hayward's right, say three o'clock, next to Earl Wise at one, with Cynthia Wise and Reggie Chang at about nine and ten respectively. Maggie always made the point in her books that male and female dinner guests ought to be seated alternately.

"I've been following your column on *Slate.com*," Lindy declared to the whole table as much as to Christy Chauvin. (In fact, she had only read one piece on the Web that afternoon.) "I hear you write the damn thing yourself?"

"Well, of course I do," Christy said.

"What are these black flecks in the sauce?" Hayward asked Maggie.

"Shiitake mushrooms, dear," Maggie said, instantly regretting the *dear*. She'd meant it to be reassuring, but it struck her as being either patronizing or overly affectionate, she wasn't sure which. Hayward seemed not to notice. He was momentarily lost in a transport of new flavors.

"I don't think we're moving in the direction of one sex," Lindy said.

"Gee, that wasn't my point at all in the column," Christy said. "In fact, just the opposite."

"There is a fish which inhabits the upper reaches of the Brahma-putra that is said to change its sex from male to female and back again as the population demands," Swann said.

"The population of fish, you mean?" Cynthia Wise put in.

"It couldn't be the people," Maggie said.

"The headwaters are in Tibet," Swann said. "The human popu-lation is insignificant."

"What about the ones in the middle?" Reggie Chang asked.

"The people or the fish?" Maggie asked.

"The fish," Reggie said. "The ones changing from sex to sex."

"They must be very confused," Lawrence Hayward said.

"'Tis a rapid transformation," Swann said.

"Do fish have penises and vaginas?" asked Cynthia, always the amateur clinician.

"They have ovaries," Maggie said brightly. "That's how they make caviar."

"It's an awful lot of equipment to be growing and getting rid of and growing again," Earl said. "Seems biologically profligate."

"'Tis not gotten rid of," Swann said. "The organism is born with both sets. One or the other shrinks to vestigial form, while the set of organs in demand swells to dominance."

Maggie noted that Christy Chauvin wore a look of refined skep-ticism, as though Swann might possibly be making all this up.

"I thought your point in the article was that we'd all be gay in a hundred years," Lindy said.

"God, no," Christy said. "In a hundred years we'd more likely be cyborgs."

"Is that anything like a troglodyte?" Cynthia asked.

"It's a machine. A man-machine," Hayward said as though his dreams were haunted by them.

"Anyway, I don't think we'll all be gay," Lindy said. "It's like a disease, this gay thing, infecting our culture, infecting families."

Cynthia Wise coughed conspicuously behind her hand.

"Great champagne, Maggie," Earl said. "Such tiny bubbles."

"Well, nobody here's gay, are we?" Lindy asked.

There was a conspicuous effort by some not to glance around the table.

"Count me out," Hayward said with an arid chuckle. "I mean, since you asked."

In attempting to look away from Hayward, the Wises found themselves both glancing inadvertently at Reggie Chang.

"Hey, I like girls!" he said, defensively. "Always have."

"We didn't mean—" Earl and Cynthia both said at once.

"Because, you see, my husband is among the infected," Lindy interrupted, a strange reddish inner glow emanating from her face, as though the accumulated rage inside her was fissioning into heat and light, and then tears literally squirted from her eyes. "The sonofabitch turned faggot on me and wrecked my life, and I'm sick of reading about how great homos are and how normal it is, because it's a fucking sickness."

The rest of the company seemed as breathless as Lindy, except Christy Chauvin, who said, "Life is often tragic. Under the best circumstances life is difficult for everybody."

"What's that supposed to mean?" Lindy said.

"That misfortune visits all of us at one time or another."

"How would you know?" Lindy practically shrieked.

"I have an older brother who was born without arms or legs," Christy said, as evenly as if she were a Sotheby's executive describing an antique chair. "There was a certain sleeping pill in the 1960s that caused the most severe birth defects. Today Richard is a vice president of Angelus Electronics in the artificial intelligence division. He has a wife and a healthy normal child of his own. Anytime my own thoughts turn to the futility of existence, I think of him."

The table was, of course, silenced. The dozens of burning votives deployed around the conservatory audibly hissed.

"I'm so ashamed of myself," Lindy cried. "I'm such an asshole!" Racked by sobs, she kicked back her seat and seemed to stagger from the room.

"Almost bought Angelus a year ago," Hayward remarked. "Greatly undervalued."

As Lindy reeled out of the conservatory, the Yalie materialized with three bottles of 1989 Pomerol (L'Evangile) and cleared the first-course dishes. Swann got up and went about the table quickly filling wineglasses.

"There is a custom in the Gironde that when any member of a supper party receives a bad mussel, and eats it, everyone at the table must take a full glass of the *vin d'hôte* in sympathy. Cheers everybody!"

Swann threw back his leonine head and drained his glass. The others followed his instructions like common sailors quaffing their rations of grog, without a word, except Earl Wise, who said, "Ahhhhh," when he was done.

The meal itself, of course, had a momentum of its own. The Yalie returned with plates of venison scallops slow-braised in port with sage accompanied by truffled orzo and pencil-size asparagus, the first of the year from down south.

"Mortification is a great clarifier," Christy observed, and the warm humid room (like her native Savannah) rang with relieved laughter. The Yalie refilled their glasses. Swann toasted Maggie with extravagant praise that, in a most subtle and yet unmistakable way, conveyed his erotic admiration for her as well, and conversation resumed as though nothing more than a naughty child had disturbed its brilliance.

Maggie concluded, between the mesclun, pear, and walnut salad and the dessert of homemade petits fours and jam tarts (a nod to Swann), that Christy Chauvin had conducted herself more than admirably, downright impeccably, especially vis-à-vis Swann. The Englishman, for his part, and notwithstanding his skillful patter, seemed entirely consumed with Maggie (his hand having worked its way under her skirts to caress her sleekly waxed thighs and the furry mound between them) and regarded the stunning supermodel with no more attention than he showed the others. Lindy's horrifying breakdown was all but forgotten until the company made for the door and their various waiting limousines at eleven o'clock and Christy whispered in Maggie's ear, "Please tell your friend to call me sometime if she wants to talk. And thanks so much for a lovely home-cooked meal."

"You ate like a champ."

"Anorexia ain't us," Christy quipped. "I think we'll be fast friends, Maggie." And then she was gone into the night, with Earl, Cynthia, and Reggie fast behind. Hayward lingered awhile, and Maggie was not clear why. It was obvious that she was with Swann. The two of them were draped over each other like Siamese twins. Hayward asked to see the kitchen, so they went in there where the colossus of Wall Street goggled at the hanging pots and cooking implements like a boy in a hobby shop. Nina and the staff were long gone.

"You actually know how to use all this stuff?" he asked.

"I do."

Hayward threw open the massive stainless-steel door of the Sub-Zero refrigerator. "Mind if I, uh . . . for the road?"

"Of course not."

He seized a handful of petits fours and jammed them into the pocket of his silver-gray suit jacket.

"Oh, let me give you a napkin, at least—"

"Don't bother. I throw these suits out," he said, beeping his chauffeur.

At the door moments later Hayward hesitated a moment, saying, "Let me buy you a meal sometime in the city, Maggie. I'm getting to know some good places." He seemed oblivious to the fact of Swann. Swann looked amused.

"Thanks. You're very kind," Maggie said and watched Hayward duck into the back of an enormous limo the same color as his suit. When at last the two-hundred-year-old front door latch clicked shut, Swann was upon her hungrily, as if there had been no lobster tamales or venison. She had no opportunity to even look in on the forlorn Lindy. Swann gathered Maggie into his arms and carried her upstairs to the bedroom, where he went to work upon her with the determination of a Consolidated Edison jackhammer operator cleaving relentlessly through an obdurate layer of New York bedrock. His ability to recover from a completed act and recommence service astounded Maggie, though she understood her own experience to be extremely limited, having been a college bride.

8

∽ Night Sounds ∽

"I'm leaving for Venice a week from Tuesday," Swann announced in the exhausted aftermath of their third coupling. For an instant, all the warmth of Maggie's perfervid flesh ran cold and salmon seemed to leap up the fluids of her spine leaving icy sparks where they broke the surface. Swann added, "And I hope I can persuade you to come with me."

"Dearest boy," Maggie said, melting again. But then the cool light of her own intellect reimposed itself and the damp sensation returned to her exposed skin; she drew up the covers over the pale moons of her breasts. "I have so many obligations," she said. "I don't know."

"Come for a week. I implore you. I beg you."

"Isn't it funny, I've never been to Venice."

"How is that possible?"

"We could only travel to places where my husband could take his morning run. He said Venice was . . . too cluttered."

"Oh, but Venice is divine. You must come. Come. Please come."

"There's so much to keep up with here. The gardens. My books. I'll have to think, look at my calendar, check with Nina—why must you go?"

"I'm to star in a movie," Swann said.

"A movie!"

"Oh, Maggie, I want so much to be an actor. I'm sure I can be a good one. A worthy one."

"I'm sure you can, darling."

"I am bombarded by scripts and hounded by directors. The scripts are all abysmal and the directors imbeciles—until now. I have scheduled a meeting with Franz Tesla, the director of *This Rotten Earth*. Do you know the film, Maggie?"

"Why, of course. Post-communist Budapest. The geese dead of industrial pollution. The boy with the broken balloon. So sad but . . . I don't know . . . uplifting in a way. Say, didn't it win some big prize?"

"Many. The Palm d'Or at Cannes; also a Best Foreign Film nomination at your Oscars—though not the blasted statue itself. There was a Swedish prize and something from Argentina as well."

"How thrilling for you, darling. Can you tell me about the script? What's the story?"

"Well, the title is *Starvation*. 'Tis about vampires."

"Really?" Maggie said, her enthusiasm slipping a few microns.

"I play the main character, of course. Vampire-in-chief," Swann said, laughing at himself. "All right, I see what you think, Maggie Darling, for I can read you like a menu through a hotel window. I know this sounds like idiotic rubbish on its face. But it's a start in films, and I do so want to be an actor, and the script's tolerably intelligent, and with this Tesla I feel that I am truly in able hands. Will you come for a week, even a few days, to see me off on this . . . this new career?"

"Yes. I'll come," Maggie said. Hearing the word from her own mouth sent her into such a hungry transport of carnal desire that she had Swann one more time, rising to a rapid summation after a few mere strokes of his raw but ready engine. Afterward, they slipped into a jungly realm of sleep.

When she woke up, it was still night. The digital clock registered 3:38. Swann didn't snore so much as purr. Somewhere outside the bedroom she detected a muffled sound that might have been sobbing. Her heart sank as she recalled Lindy's outburst at supper and imagined her old friend's humiliation at her own behavior. There was a rhythmic, gasping aspect to the sound like someone struggling for breath that alarmed Maggie and caused her to sit halfway up in bed. There was a note of choking, too. But then the gasping, sobbing, and choking ceased and the house resounded once again with the silence of its great age overlaid by the cybernetic workings of its expensive mechanical systems. Maggie lay back, struck by the sexual perfumes that saturated the sheets. Swann purred on. She felt an urge to go to Lindy but wondered if it would only make Lindy feel worse to think she had awakened Maggie at such an ungodly hour. Staring into the darkness, worried and unable to find the leafy path back to slumber, Maggie heard a door creak open. She pictured Lindy in search of a stiff drink downstairs and thought, under the circumstances, they might have one together. Imagine Maggie's surprise, then, after throwing on her plush red and black buffalo-checked robe and stealing quietly out of the bedroom, to discover Hooper in the hallway at the head of the stairs.

"What's going on?" she whispered.

"Just came up to use the bathroom, Mom."

"What's wrong with the one out in the cottage?"

"I wanted to soak in the big tub."

"Oh."

"There's just that dinky shower down there."

"That shower is *not* dinky. It's fully tiled, with the finest Swedish Skara showerhead, twenty-seven pinholes to the square inch."

"I mean, compared to the tub up here."

"Well, it's apples and oranges," Maggie said, growing irritated. The scent of sex hung between them like an unwhispered secret. It disconcerted Maggie to imagine what Hooper thought about her sleeping with Swann. She was equally troubled by her awareness that Hooper was perpetually drenched with the scent of Alison and that there were so many pheremones ricocheting about the hallway that merely standing there with the grown child of her womb seemed dangerously indecent.

"Well, then go use the tub," Maggie said. It was at the other end of the hall, next to the North Woods guest room.

"I think I'll just get going, since I woke you up and all," Hooper mumbled.

"Hey, I'm up, you might as well."

"I'll come back in the morning or something."

"Whatever you want to do is all right with me," Maggie said with a sigh. "I'm going back to bed." Something about the sound of the word *bed* agitated her further, and when she leaned forward to peck him good night on the cheek, she felt momentarily like a character out of the old Greek theater. It wasn't until she shed her robe and crawled back next to the slumbering Swann that it even occurred to her that there might be any connection between the muffled sobs and gasps issuing from Lindy's room and Hooper's presence in the hall. The possibilities this connection raised seemed unspeakable.

Instead, she reached for the television remote and the wireless headphones that remained from the Kenneth years, when her chronic exasperation over his exploits had caused frequent spells of insomnia and she would sometimes divert herself with old movies. CNN was on. She caught the tail end of a report on the Russo-Chinese skirmishes around Blagoveshchensk. Commercials for home security systems and a tummy muscle tightener were followed by a story about a sniping on the Merritt Parkway that killed one driver with a gunshot to the head and left five others dead and seven badly injured when the shooting victim's car jumped the median and smashed into three other cars. Trying to sound competent, the spokesman for the Connecticut state police nevertheless revealed that the authorities didn't have a clue besides the caliber of the bullet.

"This is obviously a sick individual," the police spokesman said, as though anointing the culprit with infamy might drive him out of his dark hiding place into the bright circle of celebrity glory awaiting him.

Part Five

Hugger-Mugger

I

⟿ Casting Call ⟿

Basilisk Pictures's Boeing 747 was outfitted like a South Beach hotel in the high Art Deco mode, all melon and sea foam pastels and gleaming chrome. An aircraft that normally carried 238 frequent fliers had been redesigned in this case to accommodate a maximum of thirty passengers. The usual mummy-in-a-casket seats were replaced by overstuffed leather loungers and sofas in various configurations around coffee and dining tables, and at the center of the "main salon," as it was called, stood an Art Deco billiard table. Most remarkable, according to Buddy Torkleson, Basilisk's chief of production, the plane contained a hydraulic gyrostabilizer, which not only kept the cabin level as the plane banked and turned but also absorbed all the turbulence so there was barely any sensation of motion once the craft reached cruising altitude. Explaining the whole thing to Maggie, Torkleson said, "Think of a capsule suspended in a semiliquid gel inside a flying tube."

Besides the main salon there was a formal dining room, a complete kitchen, a gym with ten Nautilus workout machines, a sauna, and six staterooms with full-size beds and private baths. The magnificent aircraft had originally been commissioned by the emir of Qatif, a gambling addict who wagered away the drilling rights to his little oil kingdom at the Circus of Nero blackjack table in Las Vegas. The plane, too, had been swallowed up in the black hole of his indebtedness but it later resurfaced, since the Circus of Nero hotel and casino happened to be subsidiaries of Behemoth Communications, which also owned Basilisk Pictures.

The cast of *Starvation* and its top crew members had boarded at Kennedy around 6 P.M. and were scheduled to arrive at Venice's Marco Polo Airport at 7:40 A.M. Italy time. The passengers, besides Maggie Darling, Frederick Swann, director Franz Tesla, and producer Buddy Torkleson, included the featured players Sir Nigel McClewe, fifty-seven, lately winner of the Best Supporting Actor Oscar for his role as the anthropophagous maniac in *House of the Nine Lamps;* Regina Hargrave, another British veteran of stage and screen, age unknown but rumored to be at least fifty-three; Steve Eddy, twenty-two, a TV teen heartthrob from the weekly series *Westwood,* who had successfully transitioned into feature films; Lisa Sorrell, twenty, who made a splash playing Dustin Hoffman's daughter in *Little Tree* and a teenage prostitute in *Strip Mall;* Dawn Vickers, twenty-eight, considered to be "brilliant but a project"— meaning she was a temperamental bitch with box-office charisma—and Teddy Dane, forty-six, a dwarf who had knocked around television and movies since graduating from Yale, where the great Robert Brustein had once dared to cast him as Hamlet. Along with these players were Giovanni Scarpone, the production designer; Celia Danklow, costume designer; Stefan Wedekind, the first assistant director; and Ladislaus Pilis, the director of photography in every Franz Tesla picture from *Sausage and Kisses* to *This Rotten Earth.*

As soon as they reached cruising altitude, Tesla announced that there would be a screening of *Last Train to Graz* in order to familiarize the cast with his directing style. A flight attendant came around with a cart, which, oddly, dispensed only mineral water—at least a dozen different varieties, but nothing else.

"Have you no wine on board?" Swann asked less with indignation than incredulity.

The attendant squirmed and looked helpless.

"I say, Franz," Swann called across the cabin, "can't one have a real drink?"

"No. No drinks," Tesla said. "A glass of wine is one hundred sixty calories. You are all too physically robust for this film. Mineral water only."

"Oh, bloody fucking Christ, here we go," Regina Hargrave was heard to mutter.

"Most extraordinary," said Nigel McClewe.

"No one ever accused me of being too robust," Teddy Dane said.

"Uh, Franz," Swann persisted, "what about those not actually on-screen? Mrs. Darling, for example."

"They must suffer with the rest of us," Tesla replied. "It would hardly be fair to the ones being asked to sacrifice. Houselights down please."

The film was shown on a large rear projection screen. The stunning opening shot, so often dissected in college seminars, took the viewer from an overhead of the sprawling Graz ceramic works, through a skylight in the factory roof, down among the mob of rioting workers, and finally straight into the mouth of the wounded Andrei gasping on a forklift. Tesla stopped the action frequently to remark on his directorial decisions. He took pains to point out where and how the actors had failed to carry out his instructions and how important it was to do so. "The fillum [film, he meant] exists only in the mind of the director until the instant the camera captures the image. The actor is a mere instrument. You, you Lisa Sorrell," he said, shining a flashlight in the ingenue's foxlike face, "you are a paintbrush, do you understand?"

"Uh-huh," the actress said, nodding vacantly.

"Call me a fucking paintbrush, I'm outa here," Dawn Vickers could be heard to mutter in the darkness.

"Very well. We have a nice parachute for you, mademoiselle. I think you find the North Atlantic a bit cold for your taste this time of year."

"Can't we at least have some peanuts?" Steve Eddy asked with a whiny edge.

"Mineral water only," Tesla shouted. "Now, pay attention. You see this shot at police headquarters with Eva, the party functionary . . ."

So it continued. The film, which normally ran one hour and forty minutes, took three hours and ten minutes with Tesla's didactic interruptions.

When it was over, the director sent the performers to their staterooms to get some sleep. With a good deal of grumbling and millions of dollars in salaries at stake, they did as they were told. Maggie now very clearly understood her mission in the days ahead: to feed Swann and the rest of the cast when the despotic Tesla was not around. Toward that end, after a session of ravenous copulation with Swann at 32,000 feet, Maggie snuck out of their stateroom to investigate the airplane's galley.

Back down the corridor another movie flickered on the screen in the main salon, though only Tesla seemed to be watching it now. Maggie stole into the galley, closed a sliding panel door behind her, and threw a light switch. A butcher block workstation stood in the middle of a room about a third the size of her kitchen in Connecticut, but it was ingeniously equipped. Cooking tonight was out of the question, she realized, no matter what materials lay at hand. The noise and smells would certainly alarm the authorities. The aft wall of the kitchen comprised a bank of refrigerators below waist level and dry storage above. The refrigerators contained only cases of mineral water and fresh flowers. The cabinets above, however, were stocked with a bonanza of snacks, including English shortbread, mixed nuts, Japanese rice crackers, assorted *biscotti,* ballotines of Belgian chocolate, and enough liquor to hose down the Fairfield County Historical Society. Maggie stuffed her aqua Basilisk-issue terry-cloth robe with boxes of goodies and grabbed a fifth of Courvoisier VSOP by the neck. She killed the lights and tiptoed back down the corridor. Loud snoring could be heard above the movie sound track in the main salon. She was reaching for the doorknob to their room when the adjoining door opened and Regina Hargrave's head appeared.

"What's up?" Regina whispered. "We're fucking famished!"

"We?"

Steve Eddy's head popped out above Regina's.

With an impish smile, Maggie hoisted the cognac bottle.

"You are a very saint," Regina gasped.

Maggie pulled back the folds of her robe, displaying the snacks.

"She's no saint," Steve Eddy croaked. "She's God."

An irritable harrumphing snort resounded up the corridor.

"Tesla!" Maggie whispered.

Regina indicated in sign language that they would follow Maggie into her cabin. Maggie turned the door handle and they all piled in. The two stars were stark naked. Their bodies looked eerily familiar, however, and indeed Maggie had seen them before in the nude scenes of their movies.

"What's this . . . ?" Swann said, awakening.

"Just us, love," Regina said, climbing into bed beside him. Steve Eddy crawled in on her other side, forming a sandwich with the veteran actress in the middle. Maggie sat on the end of the bed and leaned forward so that all the goodies spilled out of her robe onto the bedspread.

Regina had already seized the cognac. Steve Eddy scarfed down chocolate bonbons with methodical precision while Swann devoured a box of shortbread. Maggie gorged on the sweet-salty rice treats. The bottle went round and round. They ate like that for perhaps ten full minutes, with no exchange more elaborate than a groan or an "mmmmm" or an "ahhhhh." As her hunger abated, like a wolf sent scurrying from a country garden, Maggie reflected on how strange and magical it was to be six miles above the Sargasso Sea with the present company in a state of undress.

"I love your movies," she blurted out to Regina, feeling instantly like any crass, moronic fan.

"Well, I love your cookbooks," Regina said, and at once they were both giggling. "But I tell you, this fucking food nonsense will not continue," Regina whispered, sounding very much like the imperious monarch she'd played the previous year in Kevin Costner's historical epic *Catherine the Great.*

"Darn straight. I'm a growing boy," Steve Eddy said.

"What a nice way to become acquainted with the great Swann," Regina said, caressing his Apollonian face and hoisting herself to it until her magnificent bosom was exposed and their lips touched. Eddy ignored the developing scene and determinedly started in on a fresh box of coconut crisps. Maggie goggled in wonder and horror as Swann appeared to yield to Regina. His right hand came up and seemed as though it were about to cup her dangling breast, but instead he gave her a little slap on the shoulder, saying, "Not tonight, dear, I have a headache," a famous exit line from one of Regina's early comedies, *The Great Cosgrove.*

"Clever fellow," she teased him, evidently intoxicated.

"Ahem," Maggie said, clearing her throat.

"Remember the sixties, love?" Regina said to Maggie as she sank back into the pillows, not bothering to cover her famous mammaries, which joggled like plates of aspic when Regina spoke. "What a mad era."

"I remember them," Maggie said, "but probably not the way you do."

Regina shot her a hostile glance but just as quickly broke up laughing again, seeming to recognize the ironic truth in Maggie's reply. "Well, I'm sure they don't remember the sixties," Regina said, rolling her eyes at the two men.

"Mine are but a small boy's memories," Swann said, nibbling a sweet biscuit. "Lawns and cricket bats."

"I was dead then," Steve Eddy said.

"Dead?"

"Not born yet. Same as being dead."

"He's very philosophical," Regina said. "Makes up for what he lacks—"

She had finally succeeded in wresting Steve Eddy's attention from the snacks.

"—for what he lacks in experience," she concluded. "Well then, let's shove off, love."

Maggie watched the boy climb out of the bed with a remarkable feline economy of movement. A moment later, the two stars were gone. The bed was full of crumbs and Maggie made Swann get up while she shook the bottom sheet out. Then they were recumbent again.

"Thanks for the provisions, Mum," Swann said, brushing her cheek with his hand.

"Mum?"

"Mind if I call you that?"

In fact, she did, but he was so sweet she could not bring herself to say so.

"These movie people, they live on another planet, don't they?" she said instead, feeling exhaustion pull her down like an ocean undertow. Somewhere in the distance an engine droned.

"You think this is strange? Wait till you see Venice," Swann said.

2

⤚ The Water Palace ⤙

Venice was a dream from the moment the limousine discharged them
at the Tronchetto and they piled into the mahogany launch on the Grand
Canal. It wasn't the architecture that got Maggie—many of the city's
grandest buildings evinced an oriental preoccupation with repetitious
detail that did not appeal to her Western mind—but the *arrangement*
of the buildings, the compactness and intimacy of them along the backward S of Venice's watery main street, and most of all, the way the town
visibly brimmed with life, as though the whole place were a stage set
for an enormous never-ending opera. The day itself was gray and cool
with a kind of continuous spittle issuing from the leaden sky that did
not quite add up to rain. It was when they passed underneath the Rialto
Bridge that Maggie noticed something else about Venice: the wonderful absence of automobiles. She felt like some long-suffering victim of
a chronic disease magically freed of symptoms. At the same time, an
emotional rumble gathered deep inside her, and not until they came
around the curve at Rio Nuovo did she identify it as an upwelling of long-
repressed rage at Kenneth for having deprived her of Venice all those
years. Finally, as they passed under the Accademia Bridge, the tumult of
emotion spilled out of her and tears streamed down her cheeks as she
gazed up at the beautiful Swann, his golden curls swept back in a clammy
breeze that stank of fish and sewage.

    The launch turned down a narrow side canal near Longhena's
Santa Maria della Salute and one of the boatmen leaped onto the
fondamenta with a line.

"Swann's quarters," Tesla announced. Another boatman wrangled their luggage ashore. "You have an hour to get comfortable," Tesla barked. "Costume fittings at eleven. Blocking at three. We send the boat for you."

"What about lunch?" Dawn Vickers asked.

Tesla laughed, the agile boatmen leaped back on board, and the handsome boat puttered away. Meanwhile, a mulish elderly male servant threw open the door to a dark palazzo and took up the smallest items of their luggage. Swann turned to regard the ancient structure with its rotted stone dog heads snarling down blindly from the elaborate lintel above the entrance.

"Here stood the fortification of Narses the Eunuch, the emperor Justinian's victorious general in the wars against the Goths," Swann declaimed. "The building and the facade you see today were completed in 1611 by the salt merchant Pedrocchino Guaio. In 1926, 'twas purchased by the American socialite and art patroness Babe Hathaway, who turned the courtyard into an artificial jungle populated by monkeys and declawed ocelots. Tales of her decadent soirees still reverberate through Venetian society. At one unfortunate gala, for example, she had a score of boys painted gold to resemble naked torch-bearing statues. One died of toxic dermal asphyxiation on the spot and the rest soon became palsied imbeciles. Babe's bottomless bank reserves shut up the families and the magistrates. There were also innumerable gifts for public works between the world wars. Miss Hathaway—she never married, though the list of her famous lovers, including Mussolini, would clog a Rolodex—committed suicide here in 1939. The note she left said that she had tasted everything life had to offer except old age, an ignominious dish she preferred to forgo. Thus she went out, with a generous dose of morphine, among the potted palms and bromeliads, surrounded by her beloved pets."

"Swann, are you making this up?"

"The idea."

"How do you know all this?"

"I bought the bloody heap three years ago," he said and they went inside.

3
⤳ A New Life ⤳

Swann went off to his fittings and blockings, conveying the secret message that the cast were all invited for a hearty supper whenever Tesla released them from their duties or nine o'clock that evening, whichever came first. Meanwhile Maggie had the run of the city. She couldn't remember feeling so free and fulfilled since the day that Hooper entered nursery school. Actually, all that seemed another lifetime—not just Hooper's childhood but Connecticut, Kettle Hill Farm, and the rest of her alleged real life. Though a self-confessed control freak, she was determined to refrain from checking in with the crew back home as long as possible—certainly not on her first day in Venice. So, after inspecting the kitchen—fabulously up-to-date—and the pantry—full service for twenty—she left the palazzo for a quiet little café off the Campo San Angelo to reflect on the amazing path that fortune had taken her down since the fateful Christmas Eve party when she threw Kenneth out into the snowy darkness.

Here she was, a woman on the shady side of forty-five, widely admired, successful in business, financially secure, physically radiant, desired by a man with the look of an angel and the libido of a Shropshire ram; and she was in Venice, no less, consorting with *stars of the silver screen,* supported by a Hollywood strike force of technicians and factotums. Even Tesla's insane diktats about food worked to her advantage: she was truly in a position to rescue her new friends. It was too much. She wanted to sing out Rogers and Hart right there in the café. But the extremity of her own high spirits rather alarmed her—or perhaps it was the poor night's sleep on the airplane or the syrupy Italian coffee jangling her nerves. In any case, she resorted to the palliative that rarely failed to clarify her mind: she began making lists. She devised a menu for that evening's secret banquet. She made a shopping list. And she wrote out a game plan for getting things done. She liked the way her sense of organization made her feel so in charge, so forthrightly American.

4
∽ A Plague of Doubts ∽

She had no trouble finding the open-air seafood market behind the Ponte Rialto. There she bought mussels, divine little brown and white clams, the *gamberoni* or giant Adriatic prawns, and a great mass of monkfish fillets. She found the Venetians to be very patient with her phrase-book grasp of the language. They directed her to the strada Nuova for other foodstuffs, and she rode a *vaporetto* to the Ca' d'Oro one stop over. Here were all the purveyors of sausage, cheese, pork, poultry, fruits and vegetables, herbs and spices, condiments, bread and pastries, each in his own little establishment. A nice man in the wine shop offered his teenage son to help Maggie lug her accumulated provisions a block over to the Grand Canal, where water taxis waited. The teen, a slight youth outfitted in short pants, a round-collared shirt, and a V-necked sweater, was anxious to practice his excellent school English, and he stayed aboard to help Maggie find her way back to Swann's palazzo. He told Maggie it was his dream to move to America. She told him that America had become a gigantic dreary *tronchetto,* from sea to shining sea, and he would be much happier remaining in Venice. She tipped the boy and boatman the equivalent of twenty dollars apiece, grateful to have gotten home so swiftly with all her purchases. The boy protested that the tip was extravagant, and the boatman told him to shut his foolish little mouth, which resembled the pudendum of a goat, and that was the end of it.

Maggie napped until five o'clock—she *never* indulged in naps at home—in a bedroom whose ceiling had been decorated with angels and clouds by Tiepolo. Then it was off to the kitchen to play. Swann had equipped it down to the last citrus stripper, and the armamentarium of cookery was arranged in a way that Maggie the professional recognized as impeccably rational. The counters and workstation were all built into salvaged seventeenth-century cabinetry, with excellent overhead halogen lighting on dimmer switches. Fresh oregano, chives, thyme, chervil, parsley, and three kinds of basil grew in deep stone windowboxes along a south-facing window. There was even a small but powerful stereo with a good supply of discs—though none by Swann. Maggie put on Scarlatti and went happily to work. The mulish old butler, Teo, and a sturdy uniformed maid, Adelina, who might have been any age between forty and sixty, looked in regularly to ask if everything was *bene*. Both were apparently astounded to find the *consorte della Inglese* slaving over a hot stove, and old Teo seemed so anxious and perplexed that Maggie sent him out to the local *alimentari* for a bottle of Marsala just to give him something to do.

By eight o'clock, Maggie had constructed a salsa Bolognese, the stock for a *zuppa di pesce,* a large spinach *torta,* a terrine of roasted vegetables, a terrine of polenta and chicken livers, a green lasagna, and two tiramisus. Then it was up to the bath with a bottle of Brunello di Montalcino (the 1986 Soldera) for a contemplative soaking. The tub was a massive sleigh-shaped thing with a gold dolphin for a faucet. Maggie's legs ached and she realized she'd been on her feet since the middle of the day. As the steaming bath drained her discomfort away and the wine began to assert itself, Maggie wondered if it were really possible to make a life with Swann. He seemed, at this moment, a figment she'd dreamed up in a traffic jam on I-95, something to get her mind off the insistent annoyances of real life. Assuming that he was real, that she was really here in Venice, that they were together—as in *a couple*—was there a . . . well, was there a future in this? Was he a prospective mate? What in hell was she doing?

She sat bolt upright as panic seized her. A flurry of half-formed anxieties flew before her field of consciousness the way partridges explode out of the brush on an autumn walk through the woods. What would become of the farm? The gardens? Hooper? Nina and the staff?

What about her book and television obligations? Where would they live? Would they marry? Was she insane? She ran cold water over her wrists—which helped a little—except it chilled down the whole tub. Finally she lunged for the wine bottle on the bathside table, poured a goblet, and gulped it down. Soon, the partridges of worry flew over her mental horizon and disappeared.

5
ᔧ Home Is So Far Away ᔧ

It was quarter to nine when she came back downstairs in a simple black jumper over a white cotton tee. Adelina had set the dining table in the glass-roofed courtyard where Babe Hathaway's little jungle of palms, bananas, and live monkeys had long ago been replaced by a dozen potted ficus trees. Maggie explained the menu and the service routine to Teo and Adelina, then returned to the kitchen to arrange antipasti on a huge old hammered brass tray while Teo opened wine bottles to breathe them out. By nine-thirty, neither Swann nor the others had materialized. Though she was vaguely anxious, she understood that she could not reasonably expect punctuality under the circumstances. So, she retired to an enormous salon on the second floor that Swann had designated the drawing room but was only minimally furnished with a Bosendorfer grand piano, a lute, and some ancient Queen Anne sofas and overstuffed chairs in plain baggy cotton slips. She lugged the wine bottle and goblet with her, along with her current reading: *Cutting and Grafting the Modern Apple* by Alfred Pollard. The subject and the wine—two thirds of the bottle by now consumed—conspired to remind her of the multitudinous tasks and chores that awaited her in her garden back home: setting out the seedlings; pruning, feeding, dividing, and transplanting the perennials; double-digging the beds; repairing the greenhouse, the chicken house, the toolshed, and the bee scapes; dusting and spraying . . . Thank God for Bob DiPietro, her ever reliable chief gardener and his crew of four yeomen. It was one of the fictions of Maggie's public persona—as portrayed in her books and on videos—that she could manage the many acres of immaculately groomed gardens without ample help. She hadn't meant to project a dishonest persona. She hoped her smarter readers would understand that *The Maggie Darling Country Life,* like any show, entailed some stagecraft with a full complement of stagehands. Actually, leaving out Bob and the crew had started as an aesthetic decision on Reggie Chang's part. They cluttered up the photographs, he said. This would change with the next book, *Keeping House,* Maggie decided. From now on the last page of every Maggie Darling book would include a group shot of all the backstage helpers. She had gone no further in her reveries when the book on grafting slipped out of her hands and she sank into the brocaded cushions into sleep.

6
∽ The Intruder ∽

In her dreams, Maggie was in an enormous closet where hatboxes tumbled off a high shelf, bouncing off her head and shoulders and crashing onto the floor. The commotion was transformed into the sound of footsteps and voices below, and she realized, now fully awake, that Swann had finally arrived. She had an ache in her neck from the hard cushions and a rough taste in her mouth, so she gargled a mouthful of wine, ran her fingers through her hair, and descended to meet her guests.

"I could eat a fucking Belgian cart horse," Regina Hargrave snarled. "Oooh, Christ, it smells divine in here!"

"Feed me! Feed me!" said Steve Eddy in the weird nasal voice he was cultivating for his character in *Starvation,* Reuthner, the feckless young Swiss engineer–turned–vampire-in-training. Maggie noticed that he was now holding hands with tiny Lisa Sorrell, who either was stoned or had developed a thousand-mile stare from two days of nutritional deficit. Regina introduced Maggie to four actors of various gender identities who had flown in from England that morning. Swann stepped forward and gave Maggie a husbandly kiss. "Tesla's been a beast all day," he said. "Nothing but that damned mineral water and a few soda biscuits. Nigel's about to chuck it."

"I *am* about to chuck it," Nigel said. "And to think that Merchant and Ivory wanted me for Herbert Asquith in *Sissinghurst.* Oh, this is Horst," he said, indicating at his elbow a sinewy young man with dyed orange hair and a sniveling facial expression that might have been acquired at birth. "My catch o' the day," Nigel explained with a salacious wink.

"I am zecond costume assistant," Horst said. "Nice plaze you haff here."

Maggie was abashed to realize that she'd literally overlooked Teddy Dane, who bumped against her hip in the crowded vestibule. "I'm very grateful you invited us over, Mrs. Darling," the diminutive veteran actor said in a voice like deep plush velvet. "This is a very old-fashioned city, really, and all the restaurants have closed for the night, even if we'd dared try to sneak into one."

"Tesla's spies are everywhere," Swann said.

Dawn Vickers followed her nose straight to the kitchen zombie-like and went to work on the antipasto. The rest of the gang followed. The kitchen soon rang with cries of delectation, laughter, and clanking wine goblets as the Tesla-induced gloom dissipated. The cast devoured the antipasto like army ants—eating even the garnish—before Maggie could shoo them into the courtyard for the main event. The courses came out in no particular order, given the late hour and the condition of the guests. In a little while they were all drunk. Dawn Vickers engaged in a belching competition with the doll-like Lisa Sorrell. Steve Eddy brought out a bag of Afghani high-test weed. As he was lighting the first reefer a thunderous pounding echoed through the old palazzo. Someone at the front door? Swann signaled Teo to see about it. The table fell silent except for Regina Hargrave, who was braying at a story Teddy Dane told about working on a recent Schwarzenegger epic. Nigel McClewe reached over to clamp his hand over Regina's mouth. Then there was some shouting from a distance—the harsh Magyar voice of the despised Tesla.

"I know they are in here," he cried. "And I smell cooking!"

The actors gaped at one another while Teo could be heard attempting to placate the director. Swann brought his index finger across his lips. "Sssssshh." He then stood, took off every stitch of clothing, and strode out of the room like a naked deity who had somehow fallen from a Tiepolo ceiling and come to life.

"Why Franz," Swann's voice echoed melodically off the stone walls, "to what do we owe the pleasure of this unexpected call?"

"I know they are here, Swann. Don't try to protect them, and don't try to deceive me."

"Why, dear boy, I believe you've had too much too drink."

"That is not your affair," Tesla cried. "You stink of garlic!"

"Mrs. Darling fried me a friendly tidbit, I confess. I'd offer you the leftovers, but frankly, Franz, we were screwing our brains out when you came by, and as soon as I can persuade you to leave we shall resume—that is, if the spell hasn't been broken."

Maggie shrank in mortification, but it was all the others could do not to howl. Regina stuffed a napkin into her mouth. Dawn Vickers held a loaf of bread in one hand and stabbed it repeatedly with a fork. Steve Eddy fumbled with a joint he was rolling and spilled marijuana all over his plate.

"You think this is frivolity, Mr. Swann?" Tesla ranted. "This is craft. This is art. And you are tools. Tools do not think for themselves."

"I say, old chap, look here at my tool. It has a mind of its own and it wants to get back to what it was doing just a little while ago. I presume to speak for it, since it lacks that ability, but I assure you, sir, that you trespass on its sense of decorum."

Two of the English boys made silent masks of hilarity at each another.

"I have news for you."

"What's that, Franz?"

"Mine is bigger."

"You don't say?"

"Look for yourself."

"A contest is hardly necessary, Franz."

"No, look. Here it is."

Tears streamed down Regina Hargrave's cheeks.

"I shudder at its sight," Swann declared. "Why, 'tis more gorgon than organ."

"Just so you know."

"Well then, what do you propose we do at this hour, Franz? Duel?"

Regina Hargrave's explosive laughter finally propelled the napkin out of her mouth like wadding shot from a cannon.

"I heard that! Who is that up there? I demand to know!"

Swann had to physically seize Tesla's shoulders to restrain him.

"'Tis Mrs. Darling, my lady friend, Franz. Upon my honor. Be a good chap and sod off now, will you please? It's midnight. And for goodness sake, man, put that thing back in your trousers."

"I hear your whispers of mockery," Tesla shouted to the unseen others within. "All will be punished! All will suffer!"

The enormous ancient door slammed as Tesla walked out zipping his fly. An interval of suffocating silence followed, then an eruption of laughter and even some applause when Swann reentered the candlelit courtyard room.

"How big was it?" Regina blurted out.

"'Twas not so long as a Brompton banger nor so broad as a Butzbach bratwurst—" Swann began.

"But 'tis enough," Nigel McClewe chimed in, having played Mercutio many times in repertory as a youth. "'Twill serve."

The director's immoderate intrusion was quickly forgotten and an ambient good cheer restored. But the cast had a 6 A.M. call, and at the urging of the consummate professional Teddy Dane, the party adjourned at a quarter to one in the morning.

When the last guest was gone, Maggie and Swann retired to the glorious bedchamber upstairs, the angels aloft seeming to swim before their eyes. Swann averred that he had achieved such an unprecedented state of exhaustion that lovemaking was out of the question. Maggie was in complete accord. What bothered her was when he pecked her on the cheek saying, "'Night, Mum."

7
⤷ Making Movie Magic ⤶

She prepared a big English breakfast for Swann at the crack of dawn. He said, "Thanks, Mum," and little else, as he was preoccupied with studying his script and all the last-minute rewrites. Maggie could not bring herself to inform him that, notwithstanding the traumas of his childhood, she didn't relish a dual role in his life as lover and mother. But promptly at six the water taxi arrived to convey them to the set on the Piazza San Marco, and there could be no discussion.

Tesla was shooting out of sequence, standard procedure in the movie business; the interiors would be completed the following month in Toronto. Today's work happened to be the movie's climax. The setting is eighteenth-century Venice. Salario (Swann), chief of the ancient "guild of vampires," having vanquished his nemesis, the nobleman-cum-necromancer Grimaldi (McClewe), is cornered by an angry mob of carnival maskers near the *campanile*. Among them is Grimaldi's protégée, Nicola (Dawn Vickers), a vampire initiate who is determined to hunt down her former lover Salario for the glory of God, the honor of the Venetian Republic, the dawning Age of Reason, and the satisfaction of revenge. The shot at hand involves the mob overrunning the stately procession of the doge (Teddy Dane). In the ensuing melee, Salario escapes down the Rio Canonica with Nicola in hot pursuit, wooden stake and mallet at the ready.

The piazza was strewn with the equipment of moviemaking, a dozen trailers serving as mobile production offices, costume shops, and dressing rooms for the principal actors. Lighting scaffolds stood among anacondas of cable and humming electronic generators. Camera cranes loomed at five different positions. Technicians swarmed everywhere laying dolly track and adjusting light levels. An Adriatic morning fog made the time of day indeterminate, though, in fact, Tesla was shooting day for night. An army of extras queued up to a gauntlet of costume assistants who fussed with their outfits and accessories. Trying to imagine the cost of all this made Maggie's head swim.

In his own trailer, Swann was besieged by two dressing assistants, a wig wrangler, and the makeup chief. Regina Hargrave, already in costume as Nicola's mother, the dissolute marchioness della Fabrizio, wandered in clutching a cardboard cup of herbal tea against the morning chill.

"What do you think of our little showbiz world?" she asked Maggie.

"It's such a spectacle in and of itself," Maggie said. "Nevermind the movie."

"Yes, nevermind the movie," Regina said, her husky voice dripping disdain. "Have you read the script, by the way?"

"Only little snippets here and there."

"Well, it's the sheerest drivel. I think it was written by Mr. Torkleson's nine-year-old son. A word of advice, darling. Your first day on a movie set will be the most exciting day of your life. Your second day is apt to be the most boring. Don't let it get you down."

Someone was calling Regina's name on a bullhorn outside.

"Ta," she said and departed.

8
⤺ The Battle of Wills ⤻

The scene involving the doge's procession and the mob took all morning, though it would run no more than forty seconds in the final cut. It
required thirteen takes. The complexity of the operation awed Maggie.
It made a major catering job like a society wedding or a Christmas feast
for two hundred seem like a stroll down a country road. When something went wrong it was rarely a major problem such as the doge's litter-
bearers missing their cue or the twenty-seven horses misbehaving.
Rather, a fuse would blow in a generator, or a gaffer would trip over a
cable. On take 11, one of the mob extras had failed to put out his cigarette before the cameras rolled. Tesla had behaved with stoical forbear-
ance until then, but the cigarette set him off. He stalked across the damp
square to the offending extra, shouting, "You think we are doing Noël
Coward here? You are trying to appear sophisticated? You are not just
a member of the rabble? You are special? Cosmopolitan? A little bored
with life? Jaded?" Tesla's voice grew louder as he closed in. The extra,
meanwhile, had ditched the butt. He seemed astounded that Tesla kept
coming at him, and before he knew it Tesla had him by the sleeves, tossing him out of the security of the mob and over beside the wheels of a
crane. When the extra went down on the slippery pavement, Tesla commenced kicking him savagely like an old-time commissar beating up a
factory worker caught trying to pilfer a cotter pin. Tesla kicked and
kicked until it appeared that he had injured his own foot and the poor
extra had subsided in either resignation or unconsciousness. Tesla finally limped back to the directorial chair in stark silence while a couple

of grips dragged the battered extra behind a trailer. Ten minutes later during take number 12, a cloud of San Marco's famous pigeons decided to fly back and forth in front of camera two. Take 13 was distinguished, it seemed to Maggie, only by the fact that nothing went wrong.

Tesla's PA called a lunch break—for the crew only. The cast was told to assemble for rehearsal in a kind of artificial *piazzetta* formed between three trailers and a crane near the *campanile*. Along with the usual ration of mineral water, Tesla had provided trays of raw vegetables and fresh fruit. None of the principals complained—apparently regarding this as an improvement. But then Dawn Vickers appeared with a plate heaped with farfalle *rustica,* veal and portobello mushrooms, and assorted morsels of antipasto, all from the tent of the caterer that was serving the crew. The dark-eyed beauty, famed for her lopsided grin, took a chair between Nigel McClewe and Steve Eddy exactly opposite the director and attacked the contents of her plate with a dramatic gusto that looked, to Maggie, a little bit deliberately provocative.

"Who gave you permission to stuff yourself like a pig, Dawn?" Tesla asked, pronouncing her name more like "Down."

Looking right at Tesla, Dawn merely shrugged her shoulders and continued eating.

"See here, Franz—" Swann tried to interject.

"When I want your opinion, Frederick, I'll let you know. Dawn, let us speak adult to adult, yes? Who is the director here?"

She pointed at Tesla with her fork.

"Ah, so you understand that someone is the authority here."

Dawn nodded.

"Yet, when that authority issues instructions, you disobey?"

Dawn speared a marinated artichoke heart, regarded it happily for a moment, and popped it into her mouth. Then she nodded her head in agreement.

"So, I understand this to be deliberate insubordination?"

She speared a little ball of fresh mozzarella. The others followed back and forth as though seated in the grandstand at Wimbledon. Dawn nodded again, swallowed, and dabbed her lips with a napkin.

"How would you like it if I fire you from this fillum, Dawn?"

"I've been fired before," Dawn finally replied. "The first time, the director was a cokehead—you know, out of control. He's dead now. The second time it was a prick like you, but just a plain old lowbrow American prick. He didn't have your artistic pretensions. Anyway the movie was a complete piece of shit. *Burnout?* Did you see it? And he hasn't worked in features since—not that I take credit for that."

"I am to be insulted and intimidated now, yes?" Tesla said, his voice still level, with even a note of grim amusement in it. "I see. You ruin the careers of mortal men, like Medusa, turning them to stone?"

"Gosh, I'm not that bad," Dawn said, downing a forkful of veal.

"Well, then, perhaps the two million dollars of your salary has some meaning. I appeal to strictly your mercenary sense."

"It's two point two five, actually."

"Whatever. I fire you, you lose it. Pphhhttt."

"See, the thing is, Franz, I've made nine major feature films in the past seven years. I live rather frugally by the standards of my . . . *ahem* . . . my peers. I've got this little twenty-five-hundred-square-foot cottage in Santa Monica. It's darn comfortable, don't get me wrong, but it's not gonna turn up in *Architectural Digest,* if you know what I mean. I drive one of those Jap Jeep knockoffs. The thing is, I've got over ten million stashed in the bank. I don't ever have to do a lick of work again in my life if I don't want to. A chimpanzee could invest this nut and get me eight percent a year. As it is, of course, I do a lot better than that, but don't get me started on investment strategies. Anyway, bottom line: you do what you have to, poopsie. I ain't starving anymore."

Tesla got up and shambled across the circle of chairs until he loomed over Dawn.

"I suppose you want a bite?" she cracked.

Tesla seized her plate with both hands and dumped the contents over her head. Dawn merely sat there, letting the veal slide down the side of her face, doing a sort of Jack Benny. One could see that her reputation for comedy was well earned. Less generally known was the set of skills she had begun to acquire while filming the futuristic thriller *Kill Zone* with Kurt Russell and Chuck Norris back in '98. There'd been damn little to do on location out there in the Utah desert, but Fox was paying for an instructor in the obscure Korean martial art known as Twan Po, which figured in the plot, and it turned out that Dawn had a gift for it. The little cult gave out headbands rather than belts, as in karate and its offshoots, and Dawn had diligently worked her way up the grades to the black headband in the years since. Nevertheless, it came as a surprise to everyone when Dawn suddenly whirled into a weird dancelike motion and, in under a minute, delivered at least thirty kicks, jabs, and other assorted blows to Tesla's glandular soft spots, leaving the director gulping and gasping on the ancient paving stones of San Marco like some primordial mudfish. Then she dumped the platter of fruit over his head, letting the syrupy juices dribble off the edge and splatter on his cheek as he moaned and vomited.

"Hey guys, what's up?" a voice full of banal California sunshine could be heard to say. The others now gaped as Buddy Torkleson came around the trailer and stopped short. Taking in the scene, he looked rather disturbed in his frat boy casuals. "Jeez, uh, he's not having a spell or anything, is he? You all right there, Franz? Jeez, whadja . . . ?"

Production assistants suddenly materialized from all directions.

"Think I'll go grab a bite," Teddy Dane said.

"Quite so," Swann agreed.

"Might have been a bad piece of calamari," Steve Eddy told Torkleson as the PAs tried to hoist Tesla to his feet.

"I'll have it tested," the baffled Torkleson said as the rest of the principal actors and a stunned Maggie made for the caterer's tent on the other side of the square.

9
∽ Delicate Persuasion ∽

Production was suspended while Torkleson huddled with the recuperating Tesla in trailer number 2. When Tesla emerged at two-thirty, he had the pale look of someone who had been drained by a vampire, not only of blood but of his very soul. When filming resumed at five o'clock—a shot of Swann, as Salario, leaping on wires over the Bridge of Sighs—Tesla was a man transformed. He performed his duties with robotic efficiency, but his inner spark seemed extinguished.

Dawn Vickers received an extremely apologetic and polite visit from Torkleson at her suite in the Hotel Europa. Though packing her bags as the meeting began, she was persuaded to remain in the cast; her current release, *Death Frolic,* was doing so well ($32 million its first weekend) that she had donned a mantle of box-office invincibility. Tesla, Torkleson assured her bluntly, had been *whipped into line.* "These foreign guys, they get ideas in their heads," the producer added genially. "One more complaint and this Hungarian mutt is out on his ass," the producer said with the full authority of Basilisk Productions behind him. To underscore his sincerity he opened a lizard skin attaché containing bricks of hundred-dollar bills that amounted to half a million dollars. "Some walking-around money, Dawn. Just take it. A little bonus. Don't even tell your accountant. Keep the goshdarn attaché."

Thus, a typical Hollywood personality conflict was typically resolved.

10
∽ Apprehensions ∽

That night, following a quiet hearty supper of osso buco at a little place on a back street of the Giudecca, Swann serenaded Maggie in the drawing room with his lute. This naturally led to the bed chamber and a session of *amore*. But Maggie's efforts felt perfunctory in Swann's service and at the sweaty conclusion he whispered, "'Night, Mum," in her ear before falling instantaneously asleep. In the ambient light thrown up through a window that opened onto the courtyard, the angels on the ceiling seemed lost amid their clouds the way Maggie felt lost in the fluffy cuckoo-land of showbiz. The illusions that she and Swann had any prospect of a real life together all sloughed off her like the protective layer of her very skin, leaving her in raw agony for hours until darkness swallowed her in a pall of shame and confusion.

11
⟿ Sweet Betrayal ⟾

Regina understood it too perfectly. Maggie's second morning on the set of *Starvation* was interminable agony, made all the more so by the truth Maggie barely concealed from herself: that her run with Swann was over, that she had a personal duty to the now elusive thing she'd once called *a life of her own,* and that she didn't have the slightest idea how to end it with Swann.

It drizzled on and off and they were able to shoot only one minor scene before noon: some business with Salario (Swann) and his mind slave Reuthner (Steve Eddy) on the Rio del Mondo Nuovo. The petty technical mishaps that attended every take allowed Maggie, for the first time, to feel some sympathy for the defanged and emasculated Tesla, who, in the mere expectation of a large paycheck, now slumped in his chair quietly enduring everything. After lunch with the cast (Nigel McClewe working obviously and obscenely to seduce the naive Steve Eddy), she told Swann that she was going to the nearby island of Murano for the afternoon to visit the renowned glass blowers in their studios there.

Off the set she felt for a while that she could breathe again, but then the drizzle turned to punishingly cold, hard rain. Her head ached, she felt empty, and just shy of Murano she asked the pilot of the motor launch to turn around and take her back to the palazzo. It was really with a sense of astonished relief that she entered the bedroom and found Swann entwined in the still sleek, caramel-colored legs of Regina Hargrave.

Neither of them seemed to hear Maggie come in. The very ab-normality of her recent life enabled her to stand there in thrall watch-

ing the incredible spectacle—and not without a certain entitled exhila-
ration. For not only was it an extraordinary artistic performance, but
out of it emanated the clear light of liberation from what she now saw
was a mortifying and monstrous episode of self-betrayal.

"Oh God, oh shit, oh fuck," Regina exclaimed in seamless segue
with the rhythmic conclusion of her orgasmic gaspings, as her eyes
popped open to discover Maggie in the doorway. Swann, who was on
top, kept ramming away until Regina literally slapped his forehead, at
which point he gaped first at Regina with a look of bestial stupidity and
then, following her glance, with a look of childlike horror at Maggie.

Knees wobbling but hopes soaring, she crossed the chamber to a
little coral-colored slipcovered armchair and demurely sat down. For
perhaps only the second time in ten years she wished she had a cigarette,
if only to savor more intensely this gratifying moment.

"What can I say?" she asked with a sigh, trying not to appear pleased.

"I am a disgusting cad!" Swann cried, assuming a position of
contrition, sitting with his head in his hands at the end of the bed like a
Rodin statue.

"And I am a whore without equal," Regina said, drawing the
bedsheet up only so far as her belly.

"How will you ever forgive me?" Swann maundered.

"She'll never forgive you, you ponce," Regina said. "I wouldn't."

"This is rather awkward," Maggie averred. "What if I just bustled
around and packed some things?"

"Oh, God," Swann sobbed. "What have I done."

"Let me explain some basics, Swanny," Regina began. "We film
stars—and by extension, you musical stars, or whatever you are now,
some hybrid, I suppose—we performers in the public eye are special
and we have tacit permission from society to behave in special ways,
as the ancient demigods once did. We act out the fantasies of the mul-
titudes. They expect it of us. Ordinary self-restraints don't apply to
us. These days we literally get away with murder. Do you see what
I'm driving at, Swanny? We're just doing our bit. Oh, Maggie, dear
darling Maggie Darling, whom I admire so very much, you mustn't
take this at all personally. We're just doing what we're supposed to."

Swann flew off the bed and flung himself at Maggie's feet.

"Oh, my dearest Mum. Please don't leave me."

"Does he call you Mum, too?" Regina asked, lighting a cigarette.

"Yes," Maggie said, released from all feelings of embarrassment and regret. "Say, may I have one of those?"

"Certainly. Forgive my manners. These days smoking is so outré. Nobody else smokes."

Maggie maneuvered around the groveling Swann to take a cigarette from the proffered pack. Regina flicked the lighter for her.

"He lost his mother in some dreadful act of terrorism," Maggie said, exhaling a plume of smoke.

Swann's sobs turned to a racked heaving.

"Oh, what rubbish." Regina climbed out of bed and strode majestically across the room to where Swann lay curled. Maggie was dying to know what she did to preserve her superlative figure. Plastic surgery? Implants? Hormones? All that and step aerobics, too, no doubt. "Did you tell her that sob story, you absurd quiff?" Regina said, kicking Swann on the buttock, just hard enough to elicit a little howl between his heaving sobs. "For your information, his progenitors are alive and well in West Wycombe. Papa is a veterinary surgeon and she that carried and bore him"—Regina paused for dramatic effect—"raises hybrid primroses for the Royal Garden Society. Did he give you the whole script—the racing beetles, the Malay bombing, the paralyzed father, the gruesome apartment in Spitalfields?"

"Why, yes."

"All lies. You shabby boy."

"I'm sorry," Swann moaned. "I'm *so* sorry."

"Oh, be still."

"You've been lovers before, haven't you?" Maggie said, the ineluctable truth finally dawning on her.

Regina laughed, though not cruelly. "Dear, dear Maggie. How do you think he got this part? Would you like me to call the airport for you?"

"That would be very kind of you, Regina," Maggie said, stepping over Swann to collect her lotions and unguents on the nearby vanity. "I'll get my things together in the meantime."

ᔌ Part Six ᔌ

Domestic Complications

I
∽ Party Pooper ∽

It was a pity that she had to find out about it in the newspaper. It was seven in the evening at Kennedy Airport when Maggie settled into the back of the hired limo with the *New York Times*. She'd been out of the country five days altogether and had seen and read no news of America during her *Venetian interlude,* so she devoured the paper greedily as the car sped north toward Connecticut through the spring darkness. The Chinese and Russians were still at it along the Amur. Pacific Northwest separatists ("Treeheads") had blown up a National Forest Service administrative building in Washington State near the Grand Coulee Dam. Ted Turner was attempting a hostile takeover of the eponymous broadcasting company he had sold to Time Warner several years earlier. (An attractive fellow, that Ted, Maggie noted, and lately available, too.) National unemployment statistics topped 12 percent. The Morgan Chase–Fleet-Citibank megaconglomerate was about to be gobbled up by the ultraconglomerate *Deutschehauseurobank,* which had acquired Argentina in a default action a few months earlier. The Businessmen's Lunch Posse had brazenly robbed Le Cote Basque and Zoe in a single afternoon. A headline in the Metro section reported "No Suspects in Parkway Snipings."

Maggie held the newspaper closer and adjusted the gooseneck reading lamp. The lone fatality in a second Merritt Parkway sniping that injured five people was Robert DiPietro, fifty-seven, of Botsford; DiPietro had finally been disconnected from life support after two days in Stamford's St. Cecilia's Hospital. Maggie lurched forward in her seat

groping for something to hold on to. The world spun and lights in the
opposite lane seemed to skewer through her. She knew she was hyper-
ventilating and tried to calm herself by counting each breath, but she
could not escape the knowledge that her chief gardener and dear friend
Bob DiPietro was dead. Murdered! Another statistic in America's slow-
motion holocaust. Rage and terror rifled through her like alternating
currents of electricity. The car was one of those stupid stretch vehicles—
it was all she could get on a moment's notice—and a window separated
the driver from the passenger's compartment. She wanted desperately
to talk to someone but at the same time was terrified of appearing so
obviously distraught. There were telephones positioned at either side
of the rear seat and she lunged for one, punching the keypad while she
gasped.

"Yo, wussup?" a deep male voice answered.

"Sorry, I must have the wrong number."

She punched in the number again.

"Yo, wussup?"

"Is this 645-5527?"

"I don' know what dis numbah is."

"Well, who are you?"

"Def Trip."

"What?"

"D. T. Big D. Mistah D. Yo, who dis is?"

"Wait a minute," Maggie said. "Is this the Darling residence?"

"It's aw'ite," the voice said. "Ain't my dream crib, 'zackly."

"Oh for God's sake . . . !"

She slammed the phone down and wept from Throggs Neck to
Greenwich. Computer technology had succeeded in taking the phone
company to Soviet levels of service in recent years. She tried to call Nina
at home and got an answering machine. Ditto Harold Hamish. Ditto
Hattie Moile and Eva Mosley. She considered calling her mother and
decided not to. Finally, with a feeling of disgust overtaking her rage and
sorrow, she merely slumped and quietly gnawed her nails, gazing out the
window as rain made the passing lights streaky and surreal, trying to
imagine her summer world without Bob. Impossible . . .

Eventually, the limousine threaded its way through the maze of familiar little country roads that led to Kettle Hill Farm, and Maggie thrilled, as always, to the long approach through the stone gates to the beautiful house. She arrived to find the driveway clogged with vehicles, though—a huge white Mercedes, a preposterous gold-flaked Chevy Suburban elevated on ultrahigh shocks, and Hooper's Saab—and her spirits collapsed all over again as she stepped out of the limo. Sinister drumbeats emanated so loudly from the east wing that her rib cage vibrated. She asked the driver, a tall Sikh in a turban, to follow her inside with the baggage and stick around for a few minutes. The house reeked of marijuana. She followed the smell into the game room, where a quartet of young black men was drinking cognac, eating pizza, and enjoying a video on the giant TV screen. They paid no attention to Maggie, even when she cleared her throat, so she strode between them and the screen.

"Yo, wussup?" the largest of the four asked with an edge of indignation.

"How do you turn this thing off?" Maggie asked.

"Yo, we 'bout to come on."

"Yeeeeeah."

"Turn it off!"

"Dis our flavor of de month, yo."

"Who dis bitch is?" a lank, shirtless youth asked the huge one.

"Flavah, flavah, be doin' me a favah," chanted another in a sideways baseball cap.

"New York Mets done put on the waiver," chimed in a fourth, who wore candy-red eyeglasses that gave him a demonically intellectual veneer.

"Where's my son?" Maggie said.

They glanced at one another, clueless.

The video that had commenced seemed to depict a jail riot. Prisoners and guards ricocheted around the screen spewing blood, while nubile women slithered in cages above the action to electronic squeals and percussive gunshots.

Maggie struggled to reach the cord behind the gigantic television and, finding it, ripped it out of the wall by main force. The horrible video stopped. Silence engulfed the room like a shock wave before an explosion. Maggie decisively turned up a wall dimmer switch and the halogen spots shot up full. The interlopers shielded their eyes. The one in the sideways baseball cap dropped a slice of pizza gooey-side-down on the carpet.

"Who the hell are you, and what are you doing in my house," Maggie demanded in a low, authoritative tone of voice that successfully galvanized their attention.

"We Chill Az Def," Huge said, as if anyone should have been able to understand this fact. "Who you is?"

"Oh, hi Mom," Hooper said, tripping in from the kitchen carrying a six-pack of Dutch beer and a giant bag of Famous Amos cookies. His hair hung down in weird, stiff ringlets, as though it had been styled with mud.

"Yo, H-Man. Dis yo' moms?"

"Who the hell are these people?" Maggie said.

"They're a group. Well, I mean, like, a band. They're rap artists."

"You know marijuana is still illegal in the state of Connecticut."

The rappers laughed and slapped one another's hands.

"This is not a drug den. Out. Out! Get up and get out!"

They continued to share bewildered glances. Hooper, too, made faces of a helpless sort. When the quartet failed to move, Maggie stepped up to the huge one and kicked him on the shin.

"Yeow!"

"Out!"

"Uh, Mom—"

"All of you. Out of this house."

"Uh, maybe you fellas could go back into the city," Hooper suggested.

"I can't believe dis yo' moms, Hoop. I thought you said she down?"

"Oh, I'm down," Maggie retorted.

"Hey, you s'posed to be the boss party bitch," Huge said, making huge childlike hand gestures of disbelief.

"What'd you call me?" Maggie said.

"Boss party bitch," Huge said, shrugging cartoonishly in his over-size NY Jets jersey and looking to his associates and Hooper for affir-mation. "Ain't that right?"

"Uh, Mom, that's just a kind of jargon. It doesn't mean—"

"Out. Out! Out!!" Maggie shrieked, her cries transforming her into something like a furious predatory bird, all beak and talons.

"It's okay, fellas. I'll see you in studio C tomorrow, three o'clock. Ain't no bullshit—"

Maggie's head seemed to revolve on steel bearings until she fas-tened Hooper in her gaze. "What did you say?" she asked.

"Just keepin' it real," he explained to his mother. "Representing."

"Representing . . . what?"

"My peeps," Hooper said timidly. The others cracked up.

"Do I have to call the troopers?" Maggie yelled.

"You's a muthafuckin' lousy host-*tess,* know dat?" No-shirt re-marked from his place on the sofa.

"You got dat shit right," Huge muttered.

For an exceedingly painful and elongated moment nobody spoke or moved. Faraway in the house, a thermostat tripped a motor in a re-frigerator. An old clock ticked in a hallway.

"Dis place is boring as shit," Huge finally declared. "'Mawn, le's book."

Sideways hat got up first, swept a giant baggie of weed off the coffee table, and stuffed it into the pocket of his unbelievably strange pants—which hung so low that most of his boxer shorts were visible. Red Eyeglasses stuffed two Heinekens in the cargo pockets of his cam-ouflage pants. No-shirt popped up from the sofa as though elasticized.

"Remember, studio C. Forty-ninth Street entrance. Lots of booty-hooty!" Hooper called cheerfully after Chill Az Def as they swaggered out of the room. Last out of the room, Huge snatched up the cognac bottle by its neck.

"That better not be one of my bottles, pal," Maggie shouted after him.

"Yeah, yeah," was all Huge said.

"It's okay, Mom. They brought their own refreshments," Hooper said. "This'll probably come as a shock to you, but they have the number one single and number one album in America right now. Those guys are all millionaires."

"This might come as a shock to you, Hooper, but I don't ever want to come home to a scene like this again."

"It's because their black, right?"

"No. It's because they're goons, they're answering the goddamned telephone instead of you, they're stinking up my house with dope, dropping pizza on the rug"—her voice climbed back into shrieking range—"and because Bob DiPietro was shot on the Merritt Parkway three days ago and he's dead . . . he's DEAD!" She dissolved into tears, shaking, and slumped against the wall with her face in her hands.

The luxury cars could be heard firing up outside and pulling out with as much gunning of engines as possible.

The Sikh limo driver suddenly emerged from the shadowy hallway around a corner, his grave face showing complete self-possession. Both Maggie and Hooper flinched to see him.

"You are a very brave lady," he said. "Yet, I observe all these goings-on with preparedness," he added in the stiffly formal parlance of the eternal foreigner, hoisting an impressive chrome Colt .45 automatic pistol out of his Gore-Tex windbreaker.

"Yikes!" Hooper recoiled further.

"Why you make so much monkey business in your mother's house?" the Sikh asked Hooper.

"It's just . . . entertainment," he said.

"To you Americans everything is entertainment now. Even the end of your world."

"Thank you . . . for protecting us," Maggie said.

The Sikh replaced the large gun in his waistband.

"No problem," he said. "You pay now? Two hundred."

"Yes. Sure." Maggie collected herself sufficiently to rummage through her shoulder bag and handed him some crumpled fifties, including an extra one as a gratuity. He gave her his card in exchange. "Upwardly Mobile Limousine, Prandath Singh, prop.," it read.

"Whosoever would anger the gods, they shall have their fannies kicked," he remarked obliquely, and a moment later he was gone too, just like that.

"Bob's dead?" Hooper ventured after the front door shut distantly. Bob DiPietro had been almost an uncle to Hooper over the years.

"What the hell planet do you live on?"

"I'm at work all the time. It's so weird you should come home the one time all week I'm actually here."

"Where's Alison?"

"In the city. She's going round the clock, too. We're, like, workaholics."

"Where's Aunt Lindy?"

"I don't know. Out. I heard about the sniper. But I had no idea Bob was the one that got shot."

"What's this world coming to?" Maggie said, collapsing in her son's surprisingly strong arms.

"I don't know, Mom. Maybe things have to kind of fall apart before they can come together again."

"Your hair is disgusting."

"I'm sorry. It's just a fashion experiment. You're back early from Venice."

"Didn't work out," she sobbed some more.

"I heard you were with Frederick Swann."

"Where'd you hear that?"

"Down at MTV. I work there now."

"Oh . . . ?"

"There's this show, *Gossip Nation.* You and him were on it. Still photos from some airport in Italy."

"Oh, God . . ."

"You looked okay, Mom. Don't worry. But I don't think the two of you are right for each other."

Maggie surprised herself by laughing, her head a dripping cavern of acid and rue.

"Do you know how absurd life is becoming?" she moaned.

"Oh, Mom, it's always been completely absurd to me."

"What . . . ? I tried so hard to make things normal for you."

Hooper stroked her hair.

"Maybe things were a little too normal. Mom, what were you doing with Frederick Swann in Italy, anyway?"

"I don't know," Maggie resumed bawling. "I have to go collapse right now before I have a nervous breakdown. We'll talk in the morning."

"Hey, I'm glad you're back, Mom. Sorry about the . . . uh—"

She held up a hand signaling that she could not endure another word of explanation.

"This place misses you when you're not around," Hooper could not help saying.

2

∽ Normality Please ∽

She almost missed the funeral. A DiPietro family friend answered the phone the next morning and directed her to Our Lady of the Holy Vessel in Danbury. She arrived only in time to join the motor procession to the Holy Names Cemetery. Bob's widow, Emily, a surgical nurse, who worked up to her elbows in gore every day at Danbury General, was in such a state of shock she had to be supported by her son Gene and a cousin. Maggie had resolved to continue Bob's salary a full year, and she asked the priest to find a way to let Emily know, so at least they wouldn't feel financially devastated. There was an insurance policy, the priest said, but the salary would be a great comfort in the meantime, he assured Maggie. Then they left Bob under the earth that he had so lovingly cultivated over the years.

After that, anything for normality, Maggie thought. Anything! She returned from the funeral to find Nina in the house's nerve center preparing cherry tomatoes stuffed with a caper tapenade for a board luncheon at Yale's Medievalists Society the next day. Maggie begged to be put to work at the most mind-numbing chores, and Nina's superlative antennae sensed Maggie's state of mind precisely. She instructed Maggie to pipe pastry puffs full of cream cheese flavored with curried crabmeat, and for an hour not another word passed between them. They were merely listening to the radio when, of all things, Swann's angelic tenor floated over the airwaves doing one of his preposterous pseudobaroque rock arias. Maggie crumpled into both tears and laughter—tears over her broken heart and laughter over the object of her broken heart. Then she was finally ready to sit down over coffee and tell Nina all about it. Nina had been married to a member of a folk-rock band in the seventies—she understood the species and the lifestyle. (Her ex now ran a whale-watching boat out of South Wellfleet on Cape Cod.) Maggie spared her no details of the fiasco in Venice, not even the humiliating denouement.

"I think Miss Regina did you a favor," Nina said.

"I had the weird feeling that she was giving me an out. On a silver platter, so to speak. All brisked and garnished."

"Exactly."

"And what's even odder is that I was absolutely elated to catch them together, as though, my God, what a lucky break!"

"You didn't have to worry about his feelings afterward."

"Well, he'd seemed so devoted."

"Poor puppy."

"I was both thrilled and crushed. Strange, isn't it?"

"No, it's normal under the circumstances. Just say to yourself, Thank God I'm normal."

"You know, after Kenneth . . . left, I didn't think there would ever be another man—"

"How absurd."

"No, really. And then Swann swept into my life like . . . like a force of nature. He activated something in me, something I barely remembered about . . . about desire. I don't regret a moment of it. If I'd stayed in Venice another day, I might have regretted the whole sordid affair. Do you think I've made myself ridiculous?"

"You've had a Maggie Darling Romance. If you don't mind my saying so, after twenty-odd years of Kenneth, I think you deserved a fling. Despite *People* magazine, the world will forget it a month from—"

"Oh no! It was in *People*?!"

"Just a little squib on a back page. Not even a picture."

"Well goddamn that Connie McQuillan after all."

"You can't hide these things, Maggie."

"Nina, are there any normal men left in the world?"

"I don't know," she said. "I've about given up looking."

"Oh, God. And you're, what, seven years younger than me?"

"Yeah, but I've been married twice, plus, let's see, four very serious live-in lovers over the years, plus fill-ins between. I've been man-free almost two years now, and you know something? I like it very very much. No caretaking, no nurturing, and no goddamned sharing—oh, that's the best part. Of course, I'd give it up in a second if the right one came along."

"The right one," Maggie echoed her and moved on to stringing sugar snap peas. "The right one."

"Isn't human nature pitiful?" Nina said.

3
⤳ Job Interview ⤳

The gardens were a wreck. Winter had taken its usual toll in snapped limbs and murdered roses, and during the spring, with Maggie so distracted and often absent, the little inhabitants of the many beds, groves, arbors, and nooks had risen and run riot like peasant rabble under a neglectful queen. Strolling through the wreckage made her weep again as she noticed all the personal touches left by Bob DiPietro over the years and the memories they stirred: the espaliered pears against the sunny south-facing wall; the water lily garden in the north pond; the granite curbs around the herb beds in the medicinal garden; the four-hundred-year-old oak that Bob had saved through skillful tree surgery; the purple martin mansion he had crafted the first winter he worked for them. Little emotional snapshots of the years came with each memory, mainly of Hooper as a little boy carrying on his perpetual play war against Bob and the crew—they were Indians, Romans, Nazis, or Russians depending on what movie Hooper had seen that week. Bob had been a wonderful cook in his own right, renowned for his rosemary lemon pound cake. "Oh, Bob," she murmured with a catch in her throat, "how will I ever replace you?"

The question assumed practical urgency very shortly, for Maggie soon realized that she didn't even have surnames for the guys on Bob's crew, an ever changing cast of casual laborers she knew only as Spud, Rory, Jose, Leroy, Theron, Moose, Big Eddie, Tom-o, Vidge, Mickey, Duane, and, no joke, Dummy, among others over the years; she had no means of contacting them directly. Bob had acted as a subcontractor, paying the crew himself, and Maggie did not want to bother his widow with such trivia.

Rather than advertise in the newspapers, she simply put out the word through her extensive personal grapevine that an excellent position as chief gardener at Kettle Hill Farm was available. It was testimony to that grapevine's efficiency that calls began coming in within a couple of hours. In the three days following her return, Maggie personally interviewed a dozen candidates. It was exhausting. They ranged from the clearly unqualified—a landscaper who installed bark mulch and junipers on suburban corporate "campuses"—to the unpleasant— a diesel dyke named "Jinx" who smoked small black cheroots and spat in the primroses. The rest were in between but not really suitable. She didn't want to hire someone merely temporarily, either, or train anybody from scratch or even halfway from scratch. Then, along came the final candidate in the batch, one Walter Fayerwether.

Something about him seemed not quite right at first: perhaps the fact that he seemed *too* right, the very picture of a sturdy Connecticut yeoman, six foot one in faded khakis, rubber L. L. Bean moccasins, a frayed blue button-down shirt that matched his eyes, blond hair gone mostly gray yet worn in a kind of youthful 1965 collegiate brush cut, steel-rimmed glasses that gave him a bookish air, and extraordinarily graceful long-fingered hands with fingernails so clean they looked as though they'd never touched raw earth. He'd pulled up in a gray Volvo at least ten years old. Aside from the paint having lost its lustre, it seemed immaculately cared for. When she introduced herself, he gave no sign of recognizing her famous name—neither, for that matter, had most of the others, but they'd been so obviously . . . well, blue-collar. This one seemed different.

"Let's walk the gardens," she suggested, and they headed down the brick path that led through the pear orchard. "How do you keep your hands so immaculate, Mr. Fayerwether?" Maggie asked directly. She surprised herself by having automatically addressed him so formally. There was something about him that seemed to require it, even though, these days, everyone from janitor to president called one another by first names.

"I soak them in a mixture of warmed beeswax and lanolin twice a week," he said. His voice had a rustic creak to it, like the door of an old barn opening.

"Really. I'll have to try that."

"Works real well."

"Ah, my favorites," Maggie said, stooping to inspect a white cottage tulip streaked with red. "Union Jacks!"

"Uh, Mrs. Darling."

"Mr. Fayerwether?"

"This specimen is a Sanguine Earl of Blowditch."

"I really ought to know my own tulips."

"Of course. I don't mean to be argumentative."

She regarded the bloom and then regarded Fayerwether looming just to the side of a rather harsh spring sun.

"All right. What makes you so sure?"

"The Sanguine Earl has yellow stamens. In the Jacks they're red."

"How do you know all this?"

"I understand you're looking for a knowledgeable gardener?"

"Yes."

"It's knowledge."

Maggie stood up abruptly. Fayerwether seemed a little flustered. They walked on.

"Place is a terrible mess," Maggie said as they strolled past the antique rose beds. "Just look at all these fractured canes."

"We had a rough winter."

"You can say that again," she muttered. "How're you on vegetables?"

"Pretty adequate."

"Herbs?"

"Same."

"I grow twenty-three varieties of basil alone."

"I can handle the pressure," he said, and she wondered if he was patronizing her.

"You sound mighty sure of yourself."

"I know my way around a garden, Mrs. Darling."

"Hmmmph."

They continued past the still mostly dormant perennial beds.

"You know my previous gardener was shot on the parkway."

"I heard. Tragic. Terrible. I wouldn't be using the parkway, though."

"I don't know what made me say that. It was quite a blow."

"All this mindless violence can make a person pretty angry," Fayerwether said. "Especially when it touches us directly."

"You sound like a psychologist, Mr. Fayerwether."

"I'm an art historian, actually."

"You mean, like freelance?"

"No. I taught at Yale."

Taken aback, Maggie reflected a moment. There *had* been something a little off about him.

"My my," she said. "I take it you're . . . no longer there."

"About five years ago I had to find something else."

"May I ask what happened?"

"I left a tenured job at a college in Illinois in '85 for the position at Yale. It was tenure-track and I was given assurances. Then along came political correctness. It was my misfortune to be a middle-aged white male at absolutely the wrong time and the wrong place," he said with chuckle.

"What about other colleges?"

"They're not hiring guys of my age and ethnic persuasion. I don't mean to complain. It's just how things are."

"Do you regret leaving that tenured job back in—what was it?"

"Illinois. No. The town itself was little more than a Kmart between the sorghum fields. I'm originally from the Hudson Valley and I missed the East."

"Kettle Hill Farm would require your complete attention, Mr. Fayerwether. It's not part-time. You couldn't have other clients."

"As it happens, my only other client just now is the Trost estate in Middle Stepney. And it's been sold, finally."

"Have you been there since . . ." she couldn't say it.

"Yes, I've been there since just after the Trosts' plane was shot down over Bermuda two years ago. The gardens were extensive and it all would've gone to hell. Before that, of course, I was at the Litchfield Arboretum, as I mentioned over the phone."

"Still, you're rather an advanced amateur, isn't that so?"

"No more than you are, Mrs. Darling," he said.

Maggie resumed walking, leading the way to the wisteria pergola that connected the medicinal herb garden to the swimming pool.

"Can you manage a crew? Bob, er, my previous gardener took care of it all, payroll, workman's comp. You know, like a chief contractor."

"Yes, I can do it like that," he said.

They walked in silence the rest of the way back to his car. He seemed comfortable with silence. She liked that. In fact, she had already decided to hire him when she held out her hand to shake and said she would call him the next day after reviewing all the candidates and making up her mind. Goddamnit, she thought, he was so handsome. And human nature was so pitiful.

4
ᕼ The Alien Monster ᕼ

She awoke to something like the sound of a kitty cat going through a brush chipper, a shrieking and clattering that alarmed her so frightfully at first that she leaped up, seized the fireplace poker from its stand, and took a defensive posture behind the chaise lounge in the corner of her bedroom. She half expected to be assaulted any second by some heinous, giant devil bat of the kind one sees on the cover of supermarket tabloids, but then the noise became the tearful shouts of a young woman pounding and kicking a door and rattling the doorknob.

"Open up this minute you fucking cowards!" she shrieked.

Maggie now recognized the distorted voice as Alison's. She ventured out into the hallway. At the far end, Alison pounded on the door to the Shaker bedroom with the flat of her hand. Her voice achieved a note in an upper register so piercing that Maggie worried about the valuable glass ewer in a niche beside the stairwell.

"I know you're in there," Alison shrieked.

Maggie hurried down to her and tried to calm her, but Alison more or less batted her way out of the attempted embrace.

"He's been fucking her for weeks!" Alison shrieked.

"Who has?"

"Your asshole son!"

"Hooper?"

"Is there another one?"

Suddenly the door was thrown open and Alison, off-balance as

she swatted at it, nearly crumpled onto Lindy, who stood there in her
flannel robe looking dazed and hurt.

"You wicked slut!" Alison growled. "Cradle robber."

"Is he really in there?" Maggie asked her old friend.

"This is so unfair," Lindy said, her mouth twitching at the cor-
ners like a dam cracking before a reservoir of emotion. "I can't believe
you'd think—"

"Hooper!" Alison wailed.

A figure larger than Lindy stirred behind her in the darkness.
Then he came forward, a handsome Latin-looking young man in boxer
shorts, with hooded eyes, a tattoo of a snarling black cat on his left shoulder, a gold chain featuring a small gold skull pendant with ruby eyes,
and luxuriant black hair, which was just now being gathered into a
queue with a rubber band. He was very handsome, Maggie could not
help but observe. Model handsome. And obviously a lot younger than
Lindy. Perhaps half her age. Maggie frankly didn't know what to feel,
except a kind of peculiar wary admiration.

"You're not Hooper," Alison said, suddenly conversational.

"I yam Javier," the young man said, scratching his ripply
abdominals.

"Satisfied?" Lindy glanced first at Alison and then at Maggie
with the glow of a true martyr. Her eyes brimmed with tears as she
gently closed the door in their faces. Blubbering was audible within.

"I'm so humiliated," Alison said. Maggie tried to gather the distraught girl into her arms, but she slipped away and hurried down the
hallway to the stairs. Maggie followed her as far as the balustrade. She
imagined Alison and Hooper locked in conjugal combat in the orchard
cottage like grown people, a spectacle that made her instantly ill. It
wasn't until she returned to her own bedroom that she realized Hooper
couldn't be in the cottage—why else had Alison been in the big house
looking for him? Yet his Saab was there in the driveway. Where *was*
Hooper? Life was getting so horribly complicated, it was worse than
nauseating.

In a little while a car came up the driveway. Maggie flew to the
window wondering, What now? Roving plunderers? Serial killers

from Norwalk? Her world seemed to be under an alien invasion. It turned out to be a Danbury Red Top cab. A shadowy female figure hurried past the yew hedges burdened with duffel bags and clutches. Alison! She was leaving! The driver got out and helped her load the trunk and then they were off. So, Maggie thought, massaging her throbbing temples, Hooper had gone and wrecked his first serious relationship. Attempting to picture his face, she came up with something that was more Kenneth than Hooper, and it shocked her. She suddenly wanted a drink. On her way to the kitchen to fetch a glass of sherry, she noticed a dim light flickering under the door of the bath beside the North Woods guest room. She padded past the Shaker bedroom, from which could be heard the grunts and creaking springs of ardor as Lindy went at it with her new paramour. What was life coming to on Kettle Hill Farm? A few short months ago it had seemed all stuffed turkeys and crafts, wholesome things, parties and dinners with dear friends and notables, brilliant conversations, lovely days in a garden not run riot, stability, fruitfulness, order, bounty . . . *ugh!* She shuddered recalling the moment that Laura Wilkie flitted from the fateful powder room on Christmas Eve, shattering her world like a blown-glass Christmas tree ornament.

She knocked on the door to the bathroom. There was a muffled groan, male, she thought. Hooper? Who else but?

"Hooper," she whispered. "It's Mom."

He responded with another, weaker groan, resonant of illness and tragedy. At once she entered the unlocked room to find Hooper supine in the tub with a candle flickering on the edge of the sink and a nearly empty Scotch bottle bobbing in the water between his surprisingly hairy legs.

"You're drunk!" she said.

"You're crazy," he muttered.

"You're absolutely pickled!"

"Yeah, well, t'morrow I'll be sober an' you'll still be crazy," he maundered and then hooted at his own joke.

Maggie shrieked more than once. There was clattering in the room next door, and shortly Lindy and Javier appeared in the doorway.

"It's okay, we're here, okay?" Lindy said, trying to assume command, though clearly horrified herself.

"Do joo know thees man?" Javier asked cocking a thumb at the tub.

"Of course I do. He's my son," Maggie said, trying to control the hysteria that struggled in her like a monster.

"Hey, lookit. Iss my ol' Aunt Lindy," Hooper said, his head lolling against the tiles. "See ya gotta new boyfriend. Wassyer name, boyfriend?"

"I yam Javier."

"Put'er there, man." Hooper held his hand out limply as though to slap five. In the flickering candlelight, a set of scratches was visible on his wrist. They were seeping rather than bleeding, but now the monster burst out of Maggie and she wailed uncontrollably. The commotion only put Hooper to sleep. His arm slid back into the tepid water leaving smoky wisps of blood suspended in the water, while the years seemed to drain from his face as the small muscles relaxed. Despite a mat of chest hair, he looked like a ten-year-old boy again.

"Maggie, just calm down," Lindy said. "Get him out of the tub, Javi."

"He tried to kill himself!" Maggie wailed.

"They're just scratches."

"Because of you!"

"Don't be ridiculous."

"You've been fucking my son!"

"How could I be fucking Hooper when I've been fucking Javier?"

Meanwhile, Javier had extracted Hooper from the tub and had him over one of his exceedingly broad Toltec shoulders like a sack of *masa harina*. Lindy directed him into the North Woods room where Hooper was deposited on the massive peeled-log bed. Maggie immediately saw to the wounds on his wrists, which, it was now rather obvious, looked as though they had been inflicted by a slightly annoyed tabby cat. Bandages were clearly unnecessary but she tied a couple of cotton guest towels around them so he wouldn't stain the 520-threads-per-inch percale sheets. She hoped that he would not throw up on them, either.

"Thank you for helping, Javier," she said politely, taking in the tattoo and the skull pendant. Back in college, she recalled, Lindy had been more disposed to men in Brooks Brothers button-downs.

"No problem," he said diffidently and went back to bed.

"I wasn't doing what you think," Lindy whispered moments later in the hallway as they prepared to retire to their rooms. "Really, Maggie. The idea. Disgusting."

"Where did you find this new guy?"

"Javier? He . . . he was waiting to see Doctor Klein."

"He goes to your shrink?"

"Well, yes. Obviously."

"That doesn't sound very macho."

"What a racist thing to say, Maggie!"

"Excuse me. He just doesn't seem the type to visit a shrink."

"Because he's Hispanic, right? This is a new low for you."

"A new low?" Maggie echoed back emptily.

"Yeah. Who just flew back from a fling in Venice with a guy young enough to be her own child?"

"It's not the same, Lindy, and you know it."

"Because he was British, I suppose, and a big fucking rock star, right?"

Maggie felt ashamed and exhausted and utterly disarmed.

"I think all this New England country-living bullshit is melting your brain," Lindy said bitterly and left Maggie alone in the hallway, shivering.

5

↬ Farewell ↫

Sherry wasn't potent enough. Maggie brought out a single-malt Scotch instead, a Glenpuladrule, knocking back a first shot like a customer in one of those old Third Avenue bars with the steam tables full of corned beef and cabbage and then pouring herself two more fingers to sip slowly in a fluted flip glass. The clock over the sink said quarter to four. When the phone on the kitchen table rang, she regarded it like a small UFO full of malice from another world. But rather than dash it against the wall or continue to listen to it ring, she reached for the handset, being, after all, just a little curious to know what kind of goddamned idiot would call at this hour.

"Swann here."

She couldn't help laughing. All the tension and horror of the night was transformed alchemically, it seemed, into a lucid recognition of life's absurdity.

"Sounds as if you've forgiven me," Swann ventured.

"No, I was just wondering what sort of goddamned idiot would call at this hour of the night." She cracked up again. "Now I know."

"What time is it there?"

"Going on four A.M."

"Zounds! I miscalculated."

"Anyway, I hardly forgive you, you toffee-glazed priapic piece of English shit."

"I'm awfully sorry."

"How's Regina?"

"Did you really want to chat?"

"Sure. I'm sitting here in the kitchen getting bombed on seventy-dollar whisky because my son tried to slit his wrists tonight."

"Good heavens! Whatever for?"

"I don't want to talk about it. How's Regina?"

"She's moved on to Teddy Dane."

"I guess she's just mad for experience."

"No, the thing is he's really a lovely chap."

"Well, yes . . ."

"And I think it's true love."

"What was it we had, Swanny?"

"Oh, my dear Mrs. Darling. I am so unworthy of you."

"That's a nice way of putting it."

"But, you see, I was paralyzed with worry. How could the two of us make a life together? In hotel rooms and strange cities? It seemed quite hopeless and impossible, and I couldn't bring myself to discuss it openly."

"I was having the same thoughts, dear boy."

"You were?"

"I couldn't find the words to tell you it wasn't going to work out. I wasn't cut out to be a groupie. If it's any consolation, I would've had to come home in any case."

"It's small consolation. I find myself consumed with desire for you. Yet I shall never have you again. Shall I?"

"That's right."

"You mean, right I shall or shall not."

"Not. Never again."

"I ask because I have to return to New York in a month to mix the album."

"New York is full of pert young things."

"I take it you will be unavailable."

"Your grasp of subtext is unerring."

"Well, then."

"Oh, before you go, how's the film going?"

"It's a heap of rubbish. Tesla's gone utterly Hollywood. Most of the scenes now end with explosions. If it doesn't ruin my career I shall feel extremely fortunate. By the way, you know, I don't think Regina cared for me one jot."

"How could you tell?"

"Because she was in another man's bed before nightfall."

"Well that's a pretty good sign right there. Say, how's that young Steve Eddy?"

"Nigel debauched him utterly. I predict he will never recover."

"I predict that you will recover, Swanny."

"Do you think so?"

"You can always sing in a saloon somewhere."

"Quite right. But how about yourself, Mrs. Darling?"

"I can always make sandwiches somewhere."

"What a bloody good sport you are."

"That's me to the very core. A good sport."

"Good-bye, my dearest Maggie Darling."

"Good-bye you wretched boy."

❧ Part Seven ❧

Lost and Found

I

⤳ The Absent *Objet* ⤳

Things were missing. The first thing Maggie noticed—by its absence, that is—was the ruby ewer that lived in the niche by the stairwell. She'd come across the piece the summer of 1989 at a tag sale in Maine among a clutter of cheap china sauceboats, cheaper plastic teacups, and other unwanted effluvia of some deceased spinster's dissolving household. A Sotheby's employee later appraised the ruby ewer at $1,200, the monetary value being quite beside Maggie's love of its sheer excellence as a wrought object. Now it was gone. Her mind leaped to certain obvious culprits—so obvious that the leap instantaneously provoked overwhelming pangs of shame and guilt for the very leaping. For example, Quinona the laundress, a twenty-year-old single mother from Norwalk who was sometimes ferried to Kettle Hill Farm by obvious male gangbangers. Or Javier. She tried to tell herself it was only the tattoo that prompted her suspicions, but a harsher voice nagging inside insisted she was a racist bitch. So had similar thoughts about Florence, the day maid. Her very suspicions disgusted her so much that she couldn't bear to think of the ruby ewer at all anymore, however excellent it was.

But then her silver Lincoln and Foss coffee urn turned up missing the morning that Reggie Chang drove up from the city with a crew of stylists and assistants to begin shooting the photos for *Keeping House*.

"Someone's pinching things around here," Maggie whispered to Nina while the assistants set up the props for a vignette in which Maggie would be shown cleaning a crystal chandelier with baking soda and a toothbrush.

"Who's pinching whom?" Nina whispered back.

"No. Stuff's missing."

Nina visibly stiffened and the air seemed suddenly heated between them.

"Are you accusing me?"

"Would I mention it if I suspected it was you?"

"I really don't know."

"Oh, come on, Nina. I trust you absolutely—"

Reggie interrupted: "We're ready for you, Maggie." Nina marched back to the kitchen where she was testing recipes for the summer catering season. They never did get a chance to clear up the misunderstanding, since Nina departed at four o'clock while Maggie was demonstrating a method for regilding old picture frames in her crafts room.

Around five, while the crew rearranged furniture for some shots of Maggie dusting a valance in her second-floor boudoir, she happened to glance out a window and see Walter Fayerwether's Volvo motoring up the driveway. When it pulled up to the boxwood border a blond woman stepped out—a rather young blond woman, not more than twenty-five, it appeared from a distance, and rather shapely, too, in perfect blue jeans and a clingy short-sleeved, scoop-necked magenta top. Shocking, Maggie thought, wondering at the same instant why she was shocked. But her meditation was cut short when the young thing reached back inside the car and honked the horn—three vigorous blasts. Moments later, Walter himself appeared through the arbor, all loose joints and smiles, waving at the girl. To Maggie, the tableau smacked of a magazine advertisement for country casuals, by way of a porn movie. Walter gave the blonde a little smooch and a familiar squeeze. The two of them hopped into the Volvo and drove off.

"Maggie, the stepladder's in place," Reggie said, as the Volvo turned through the gateposts.

2
↜ Rummage ↝

The assistants began packing up the light stands and other paraphernalia around seven. Nina was gone for the day, Lindy was God knows where, Hooper was down in the Utopia of MTV, she assumed. The prospect of an evening absolutely alone unnerved Maggie.

"Could I induce you to stick around for dinner?" she asked Reggie as he headed out the door.

"Twist my arm."

She did.

"What's on the menu?" he asked.

"Oh, I dunno. I'll have to rummage."

"Rummage, did you say? My favorite dish!"

So they repaired to the kitchen. Ever alert to thematic menu ideas, Maggie took the idea of rummaging seriously and got under way by shaking up two Bacardi cocktails, which she served in a couple of 1840 pale green Feniger flutes. Among the many and various contents of the fridge she descried a seven-pound free-range stewing hen, which she plunked into her largest Romertopf clay vessel, along with a cup of Meyer's dark rum, a fistful of hand-ground Jamaican jerk seasonings, a drift of cilantro, a heap of Vidalia onions, and a shag of dried tangerine peel. By the time the ensemble went into the oven it was eight-fifteen, with two hours' cooking time to go.

They switched to Cuba Libres while the hen stewed, and Maggie constructed a sort of Caribbean tiramisu for two out of sliced mango, overripe figs, day-old orange tea cake, and a simple syrup laced with sixteen-year-old Puerto Rican *añejo*. Reggie was good company, she mused, a fundamentally decent person, bright but no overweening genius, full of interesting information beyond gossip, obviously talented, respected in his field, and sufficiently solvent to own a 2,500-square-foot loft studio in Tribeca and keep a sporty little Mazda Miata privately garaged. One had to admire any artistic soul who could make a decent living, she reflected. For a certain kind of normal woman, he might even be described as a catch. Why did she never see him with a date? He was always solo. She'd suspected the obvious, but hadn't Reggie declared himself heterosexual at Maggie's very table some weeks ago? His production assistants were hardly unattractive—one of them, Rene, had done her share of modeling. Yet there was not the slightest sign of . . . activity. No sexual joking. No touching. What was Reggie's problem? she wondered.

They sat at the table with the rum bottle, a six-pack of Diet Cokes, a dish of lime wedges, and a hunk of pork and prune pâté between them, hacking away at the pâté with decreasing decorum as the hen stewed and the hour grew late. For Maggie, this was the point where things grew blurry in recollection. It seemed that Lindy came home, but not through the kitchen. Maggie heard a car, the front door opening, Lindy giggling, and a man's voice (Javier?); they went directly upstairs without even a howdy-do. Maggie must have expressed some irritation. Reggie had it all coolly analyzed. Lindy, he explained, was treating her the way adolescents treat their parents: Maggie was *the enemy*. This had never been a feature of their relationship, Maggie insisted, pouring another drink. People change, Reggie said. He was so good to talk to. So wise and reassuring. There was something terrifically appealing—even sexy—about it. She'd never thought about Reggie that way before. His sex appeal was extremely understated, she concluded. She could also probably break him of the habit of wearing V-necked sweaters all the time. They made him appear softer and rounder than necessary. Emotionally, he seemed a tower of strength, especially compared, say, to a basket case like Kenneth or a hothouse flower like Swann. What could be more important between two adults than that sort of emotional and *moral* strength? she thought, in the rapturous vapors of yet another rum—for, in Reggie, the two seemed one and the same. Surely the hen was done by now. Well, it wasn't falling off the bone, the way she liked it, but they were just too goddamned ravenous. Besides, the room was beginning to rotate . . .

3
⇜ Things Just Happen ⇝

She woke up with a throbbing head, staring at Reggie's naked spine. She understood at once whose back she was looking at but had no recollection whatever as to how they had gotten from the kitchen table to her bed or what had transpired between them afterward. All that Maggie could discern amid the plangent emotional disorder in her skull was a vague notion that she had done something to further and unnecessarily complicate her existence. Reggie stirred. Maggie suppressed an impulse to bolt. He turned over and, sleepily murmuring a word that may have been *darling,* enfolded her in his arms, burying his head between her neck and shoulder. There was something both reassuringly familiar and shocking about the heat of his yielding fleshy body and the trace of his cologne.

"I'm afraid I'm going to be sick," she said, and Reggie opened his arms, liberating her. She flew to the bathroom and proceeded to lose the remaining contents of her stomach. When she was done being sick, she took four aspirins and staggered into the shower, letting the pulse-o-matic showerhead massage her neck and shoulders for such a long time that the water ran tepid—quite a feat considering the size of the heater tank that she and Kenneth had installed during the last renovation. When she could resort to no further delay, she emerged to find Reggie sitting propped up against the pillows looking drained, his eyes glassy and his mouth downturned like a ravaged soul in an Oriental woodcut.

"Aspirin?" she said.

Reggie nodded distantly. She fetched him some with a cup of water, then sat on the edge of the bed in her red-and-black-checked robe, toweling her hair to keep her hands occupied as he swallowed the pills.

"This is terrible," he said, after draining the glass.

Maggie sighed. In fact, she did not quite understand what he meant. It was regrettable, perhaps, that they'd fallen into bed together— at least this was the point of view she had adopted during the clarifying interlude in the shower—but it need hardly be considered catastrophic. Did it?

"We're grown-ups," Maggie said. "We'll get over it."

"That's what I mean," Reggie said.

"Oh, come on. It's not so bad."

"Oh, but it is. I'm hopelessly in love with you, Maggie. Have been for years. Couldn't bring myself to tell you."

She sighed again.

"Now we've had this," he went on, staring forward as if into some dreadful fate. "Our little moment."

"Don't say that."

"Why not? It's the truth, isn't it?" he said, finally turning his gaze on her. It was not an angry look but there was something relentless, almost implacable about it—something she understood would never be satisfied by anything she might possibly say. She began to cry and to hate herself for it, recognizing it as the universal feminine dodge it was.

"My life's been a little out of control lately, Reggie. Things have been . . . just happening to me."

She reached for his hand but he drew it away. Then he climbed out of bed and began to dress, finding his articles of clothing where they'd been strewn.

"I'm going home now," he said when he had donned his sweater.

She sat as if paralyzed, holding the damp towel while he left the room. For the longest time she remained there, breathlessly, as though she distrusted her very power to move through the world without breaking things.

4
↬ Down by the Borage ↫

She went about her own house now as though it were contested territory rigged with booby traps. Even the carpets seemed mined. The prospect of normality dimmed by the minute as she apprehended that the
photo shoot would certainly not continue today. What about tomorrow?—that was the question that tortured her as she took refuge in the
sewing room to avoid facing a painfully bright May morning. Even in
this refuge of refuges, however, something—perhaps the strong English
tea—kept her on the edge of panic and eventually drove her out of the
house into the fresh air of the garden, where she determined to dig out
and divide the perennials in the sunny bed beside the chicken coop.

She was thus laboring, in a pair of khaki shorts that displayed
her tanned legs to good effect and an old denim shirt (once Kenneth's)
tied by the tails at her midriff, when Walter Fayerwether happened
along on his way to the herb garden with a wheelbarrow full of granu-
lar lime. The lingering effects of all that rum caused her to startle.

"Excuse me," he said. "Didn't mean to frighten you."

She hesitated to catch her breath before saying, "That's all right.
I'm a little jumpy today."

"Haven't seen you around much," he said. The sun hung just
above his right shoulder and she had to shield her eyes to see him. He
loomed like some heroic proletarian figure in a 1930s WPA mural.

"I'm having a . . . a somewhat abnormal year," Maggie said.

"I hope everything's going all right."

"Oh, sure, fine."

"How about out here?" Walter said. "Satisfied with the work I'm doing?"

"Oh. Yes. Uh, well, there were a few things I thought we might discuss."

"Fire away."

"Yes, well . . ."

"I've got a few notes of my own. Let's walk and talk."

Maggie took half a clump of divided rudbeckia and wrapped the root bundle in wet burlap. Walter offered a hand to help her up. She was not sure whether the gesture was excessively gallant or merely polite. Not knowing the difference anymore rattled her nerves again and made her shudder despite the sunshine. She rubbed her own hands in the lush grass to get the dirt off and reached up to take one of his, which was remarkably soft, warm, and dry.

"You should wear gloves," he said.

"I forget."

They strolled awhile in silence past the fenced cutting garden with its trellis of sweet peas straining toward the sun.

"Bob used to get milfoil out of Candlewood Lake from a man up in Sherman. We kept it in a big heap beside the vegetable garden for mulching."

"That must be why I keep turning up fishing lures with the rototiller."

"Yes," Maggie chuckled. "We've got quite a collection."

"I'll get a load down later in the week."

They entered the arbor that led through the bosky dell that was Maggie's shade garden, a recent project only partially complete. The new gardener's stolid competence impressed her, and his botanical knowledge was encyclopedic. Just along the path they tread, he identified seven varieties of plantain lily by name. He made some diplomatic suggestions about changing things—quite a departure from the way Bob had simply discharged Maggie's every wish and whim—but he was also willing to follow instructions. He recorded many notes in a little leather-covered minder as they wended back up from a bracken-filled slough along the banks of Kettle Creek to the graveled apron of the herb garden, where two of his laborers were setting out new sage plants to replace the winterkills.

"While we're at it, let's yank those spike lavenders for salvia," Maggie said.

"I was thinking along the same lines."

"And we must move the lovage. The damn things reached seven and a half feet last year. Shaded out all my marjoram."

"How about sticking them in the border with the mulleins and hollyhocks?"

"Good idea. You know I'm losing patience with the borage. It's crowding the fennel horribly."

"I'd give all the anises their own bed," he ventured.

"It would make for a nice scent zone."

She was already beginning to feel better. From there they marched around the drying shed to the poppy beds. The big ragged plants drooped with fuzzy, silver-green flower buds the size of apricots. A few of the buds were beginning to crack open to reveal the vivid and fantastic red-petaled blossoms within.

"When we first came here in '81 this spot was an automobile graveyard."

"Hard to believe now."

"It was hard to believe then. We hauled thirty-eight junkers out. The family that occupied the place had reached, shall we say, a low point in their dynastic fortunes. We called them the pig people—I know it's elitist and all that, but honestly you've never seen such a low form of human life. They had dogs shitting in the house. It was shocking."

"There are a lot of people out there who aren't making it these days."

"Of course. I don't mean to be flippant. The country's going to hell, isn't it?"

"Well, I admire what you're trying to do here, Mrs. Darling."

Something like an electrical shock ran through Maggie. She was not sure for an instant whether he was being ironic. The warm air between them seemed positively charged with lucent emotion.

"I'm just trying to keep one little corner of the world in order," she said

They strolled along the border toward a velvet purple smudge of irises in the distance.

"I suppose I'll bump into Mr. Darling, one of these days," Fayerwether said, sending another jolt through Maggie.

"I suppose you don't read *People* magazine, Mr. Fayerwether."

"Once in a while when I'm standing in the supermarket check-out line. Why? Are you in it?"

"You know, it would be awfully nice to have nasturtiums boil-ing out of these borders right into the path, like at Giverny."

"I have to pick up a few things tonight at Safeway. Should I have a look?"

"Don't bother. It was weeks ago. Anyway, to answer your ques-tion, Mr. Darling has not been living here for some time now. You won't be seeing him around."

"Oh?"

"And is there a Mrs. Fayerwether?"

"That ended some time ago."

"I see."

"If there's nothing else, then maybe I'd better run along, Mrs. Darling. Get a few things done before lunch."

"Sure," she said, feeling a little cheated. Then he was gone and she was left in the bright spring sunshine with her ragged nerves and too many unaskable questions.

5
❧ An Old School Hero ❧

She was studying the blossoms on the quince tree beside the house when a woefully familiar German car turned into the lane and barreled toward her, finally pulling up short in a cloud of dust. A little breeze dispersed the dust and the face behind the wheel resolved familiarly, too.

"Maggie," he greeted her expansively through the open window, all teeth and tan.

"Hello, Kenneth."

"You're looking every inch the mistress of the manor."

"And you the very . . . lord of the flies."

"Oh, Maggie, must we start on such a footing?"

"'Mistress of the manor?'"

"I meant it as a compliment."

"Sorry. I'm a little on edge."

"Life's not getting you down, I hope?"

"We all sail on choppy seas, don't we?"

"You *are* in a mood."

"Surely you didn't come to take my emotional temperature."

"No, I was in the neighborhood and I simply dropped by to say hello, to let you know that I'm all right—not that I expect you to care—and to let you know that I have decided not to contest the terms of our separation."

Maggie paused to take this in.

"I'm sorry about my remark," she eventually said.

"No problem," he said, smiling relentlessly.

"Of course that's good news about the separation."

"I've had a lot of time to think these past months. I don't expect to be forgiven, of course. I don't even expect to be invited in for a Coca-Cola. But we have to get on with life, don't we? And recriminations just hold us back, don't they?"

"I suppose they do."

"Couldn't help noticing you in *People* magazine."

"Oh?" Something alerted Maggie to fortify herself.

"That English warbler? He was on the scene Christmas Eve, wasn't he?"

"I thought you said no recriminations, Kenneth?"

"Merely a point of information. Come on, Maggs, I'm setting you up for life, no strings attached. Can't we be friendly?"

"Probably not in the way you mean. Not pals."

It was Kenneth's turn to reflect a moment.

"I see I'm kind of poking at a hornet's nest with a sharp stick here," he said. "It's just my manner. I'm defective that way. I know some things about myself that I didn't six months ago. My eyes have been opened. What I meant to say in my crude, blundering way was that I was glad to see you went out and had a little fun. Frankly, I wasn't sure you were capable of it—oops. There I go again. See, I don't mean to be that way. It's this obnoxious manner of mine. You know, when you've spent forty-eight-odd years being a jerk it takes an effort to be a human being."

"It takes an effort in any case, whether you're a jerk or not—not that I'm saying you are."

"No, I am. I definitely am. Was. Er, let's say I'm working on becoming an ex-jerk. I'm out of the market, too, you know."

"I didn't know."

"In the active sense. Throop, Cravath and all that."

"You can certainly afford to coast for a while."

"Who's coasting? I've established a foundation over in Ridge-field. The Different Drummer Self-Awareness Center."

"Really?"

"You betcha."

"What goes on there? Drumming?"

"Don't knock drumming. It lowers blood pressure and raises serotonin levels—did you know that?"

"I hear it makes men feel better."

"But that's just one part of the program. We're a holistic wellness center. I've signed up a staff. Nutritionists, fitness trainers, hypnotherapist, massage therapist, aroma therapist, a tai chi instructor, a TM counselor, an herbalist. I bought the old Pulsifer estate on Round Pond. I'm having the time of my life and learning incredible things and getting in touch with my own issues and, well, kind of getting my shit together for maybe the first time. It's a gas."

"I'm glad to hear that, Kenneth."

"Just thought you might be interested. I've been able to look back on our years together as a fantastic learning experience. You were a great teacher, you know that?"

"I have some pedagogic impulses," Maggie admitted.

"You really taught me to be humble."

"I can't say I was trying to do that. Maybe some other things, like show up on time at a restaurant."

"Doesn't that take a kind of humility? The awareness that other people matter too?"

"I suppose."

"That's all I mean."

"Where does Laura Wilkie fit in?"

"What does she have to do with anything?" Kenneth asked darkly.

"Just wondering. Since you referred to my private life."

"Well, she's out of the picture," Kenneth said and then, as though he were talking to a foreign soldier at a border crossing who failed to understand him, snarled, "*out of the picture.*"

"Have you seen our son?" Maggie tactically changed the subject.

"What?" Kenneth seemed momentarily lost in thought.

"Hooper."

"What about him?"

"Have you seen him. He hasn't mentioned you in a long time."

"Isn't he in school?"

"No, Kenneth, he took the semester off. Haven't you talked to him?"

"No. He's pissed off at me for breaking up the family."

"Have you tried to talk to him?"

"I've called."

"Where? School? Didn't anyone inform you that he wasn't there?"

"I called that number at the apartment he was living in at Swarthmore. There's this changing cast of characters there. They don't seem to know anything about anyone anymore."

"Well, he's been living here since Christmas."

"Hmmm."

"Would you like me to tell him to call you? I will if you want."

"No, don't twist his arm. Only if he wants to. He's got to want to. What the hell's he doing here, anyway?"

"Working for MTV in the city."

"Really?" Kenneth said, brightening. "Probably a good way to meet girls, huh?"

"I wouldn't know—"

It was just at that moment that Walter Fayerwether stepped through the arbor to the driveway.

"Well, I'll be goddamned!" Kenneth exclaimed.

The gardener stopped short, while Kenneth stepped out of the car and appeared to elongate himself in order to appear larger than he was.

"Walter goddamn Fayerwether!" Kenneth said.

Fayerwether glanced at Maggie, as though appealing for some explanation.

"Are the two of you somehow acquainted?" she asked.

"I don't think so," Walter said.

"Uh, Walter Fayerwether, meet Kenneth Darling, my soon-to-be ex-husband."

"Meet! Hell, Maggie, we're old teammates!" At that, Kenneth moved toward Fayerwether and fairly engulfed him in a bear hug, rocking from one foot to the other. Walter seemed to endure it stoically.

"What team were you on together?"

"Lacrosse. Choate. Nineteen seventy," Kenneth said, finally letting go and stepping back. "You don't remember me, do you Walt?"

"Not exactly."

"I was a sophomore, you see."

"Seventy was my senior year," Fayerwether said.

"I was a mere benchwarmer. You were like one of the gods."

"It was just a game."

"So what the hell are you doing here on the ranch?" Kenneth said.

"Working."

"You work *here*?"

"That's right."

"For my wife?"

Fayerwether nodded.

"Isn't life a kick in the guts! What as?"

"I run the gardening crew."

"Shhhhhhh," Kenneth said. "That's supposed to be a big secret.
The hoi polloi think she does it all herself."

Maggie folded her arms.

"She treating you okay?" Kenneth went on.

"I think we're both satisfied," Fayerwether said.

"Hunh. Satisfied. Say, Maggs, what happened to what's-his-
name, the old gardener?"

"He was murdered on the Merritt Parkway."

"No!" Kenneth drew back and held a hand in front of his mouth.
"When did that happen?"

"Recently," Maggie said, with mounting irritation. "You have
time for *People* magazine but not the newspaper, huh?"

"Well, gosh, Maggie. I've had my hands full. And people, you
know, bring things to my attention. But this, this is shocking. He was a
darn nice fellow."

"There's a sniper operating on the Merritt Parkway," Maggie
informed him.

"What are they doing about it?"

"I have no idea. Following leads, I suppose. Apparently you don't
live on this planet anymore—"

Just then another car turned into the drive. It was Walter's Volvo, with the blonde behind the wheel.

"Ah, my lunch date's here," Walter said. "Nice meeting you, uh—"

"Kenneth. Kenny back then. Of course I'm big now."

"Everything okay here?" Walter asked Maggie.

"Oh, sure. Fine."

"See you then, Ken."

"You bet. And don't let old Maggs here push you around."

"I'll be back in three quarters of an hour," Walter said over his shoulder as he got into his car.

Kenneth and Maggie watched the car turn around and drive off.

"What the hell did he mean, 'Everything okay here?'" Kenneth said.

"What the hell did *you* mean, 'Don't let Maggs push you around'?"

"I was just joking. You know, like when you said, 'lord of the flies.' Ha ha. A quip. Everything okay? Somebody's gonna show that sonofabitch what's okay and what's not okay."

"Kenneth!"

"Oh Maggs, you should have seen him in prep school. Most arrogant bastard you ever laid eyes on. He used to smack us younger guys in the ass with his stick during wind sprints. You don't forget that kind of stuff. Hey, you check out that little cutie who picked him up?"

"I've got a one-thirty dentist appointment, Kenneth."

"Really? What's up? Root canal?"

"I don't think you need be concerned."

"Am I being obnoxious again?"

"Look, I'm really grateful that you've decided not to drag our divorce through the courts. It'll save everybody a lot of aggravation."

"And I'm pleased that you're grateful."

"Well, then, I'll be seeing you."

"Not if I see you first," Kenneth said, and then, making his hand into a pistol, pointed his finger at Maggie and fired a silent shot of farewell. Then he, too, motored away.

6
⤳ A New Friend ⤳

No sooner had Kenneth departed than Lindy appeared from inside the house with a lean and spidery man—not Javier—in tow. His youthful face was pale complected and his close-cropped black hair came to a distinct V low on the forehead. He could have used a shave. The overall impression was simian. His costume suggested that he came from some part of the world with very different ideas about country casual wear: a black polyester knit shirt with sparkly gold-thread accents, tight gray slacks, and pointy black ankle-high boots. No tattoos were visible but neither was much skin. He trailed sheepishly a few steps behind Lindy carrying a couple of shopping bags.

"Put those in the back," Lindy instructed him brusquely, popping the rear hatch of her Jeep Cherokee—an amenity Lindy had extracted with a $50,000 payment from her estranged husband, Buddy, in their ongoing divorce negotiations. Lindy's sunglasses and the scarf tied around her head gave her, too, a look from another time and place: Audrey Hepburn in a sixties thriller—only a bad print, in a run-down theater, with the houselights left on, and an odor in the room. "Maggie, this is my friend Ratko," Lindy said distractedly.

"How do you do?" Maggie said.

Ratko shrugged his shoulders and sniffled.

"He's an actor," Lindy said.

"Really?"

"They blew up his theater in Zagreb."

"How terrible."

"The world's a mess," Lindy said. "Have you noticed?"

"Of course I've noticed. What a thing to say."

"Excuse me. The Prozac hasn't kicked in. Get in the car, Ratko. I'm sorry, Maggie, it bums me out sometimes, the world situation. It's like there's this big drain out there and I can see us all whirling around it."

"Frankly, Lindy, I wonder if this Dr. Klein is helping you."

"What can *he* do about the world?"

"He could encourage you to not obsess about things you can't control and concentrate on things you *can* control."

"Like what?"

"Your own little life."

"I've tried self-absorption," Lindy said with a dismissive laugh. "Believe me, I'm much better off focusing on the real world."

"But one must have personal aims, goals."

"Oh, I see," Lindy recoiled. "Like something besides sponging off my friends, right? Ratko!" she snarled. "I thought I told you to get in the car!"

"No, Lindy, dearest, that's not what I mean—"

But Lindy retreated behind the wheel of her luxury sport-utility vehicle and slammed the door and peeled out of the driveway as though she were a lone heroine in a movie hurrying off to save the world from a horde of radioactive locusts.

7
ᶜᵔ Invitation ᶜᵔ

The house seemed eerily underinhabited for this hour of the day and season of the year. Quinona the maid was polishing the brass fireplace fender in the drawing room. But where was Nina? The monthly job manifest, kept on an enormous chalkboard in the kitchen, indicated that they were scheduled to cater the New Milford Museum of Crafts annual fund-raising luncheon three days hence. Ordinarily, Nina and at least two assistants would be preparing great bricks of country pâté and firkins of tapenade at this stage. A call to Nina's house incited only the answering machine. "It's me," Maggie told it. "Where are you? Please call." Then, having prepared herself a jam omelet (a comforting old childhood favorite, heavy on the fresh cracked pepper), Maggie fielded a blitz of incoming calls; about half of them the usual pests and solicitations for product endorsements; one interesting inquiry from a PBS television producer about the possibility of a Christmastime craft and cookie-making special; an interview request from a young man at the King Features newspaper syndicate; one proposal of marriage from an elderly lunatic in Palm Springs; and a personal reminder from Gerald Nance of the Metropolitan Museum of Art's Costume Institute that Maggie had been invited to the opening night party for a show featuring the garb of Napoleon's imperial court on loan from the Musée de l'Armee, and why hadn't she RSVP'd?

"We need you desperately to energize the room," Gerald put it in his winning way.

"Who else is coming?"

"The usual suspects," Gerald drawled, meaning the thin sugary crust of the buttery uppermost layer of New York wealth and privilege.

"Who's catering?"

"Humble Pie."

"They're never humble enough for me," Maggie said, "but I like their duck salad. Which room?"

"That damnable Temple of Dendur," Gerald said. "We've got it all tricked up with runways and miles of fairy lights. Can I depend on you?"

"Oh, all right."

"See you at seven."

It suddenly seemed a welcome opportunity to get out of the dreary house for the night. The prospect of being at large on her own exhilarated Maggie, though not so far back in her mind lurked the possibility that an appropriate and available man might present himself on such an occasion. Nance had barely signed off, and Maggie had begun mulling over what to wear, when Harold Hamish rang.

"Maggie, my Maggie," he began.

"Something's always wrong when you start that way."

"Okay," Hamish admitted. "The Chinaman's up and quit."

"Must you call him that?"

"Oh come on. Don't get that way with me. He's Chinese. He's a man. A man of China. Ergo, Chinaman. Anyway, he's bowed out, kissed off, walked, resigned from the job."

"Oh, dear . . ."

"You know, he's a very good photographer, this fella. The very best, I should say. What did you do to him?"

"Why do you suppose I did anything?"

"He was bawling on the phone."

"Oh, God . . ."

"Did you throw a shit fit or something?"

"Of course not. Have I ever?"

"Well he's all busted up. Gone loony. What's more, he says he's destroyed all the film he shot so far. Did you sleep with him?"

"Harold!"

"He sounded wracked with heartbreak. I've got a sixth sense for it."

"Well, if you must know, I did," she shocked herself into admitting.

"Good Christ, Maggie. I was afraid of this, with Kenneth out of the picture. Makes me want to assume in loco parentis just to protect you from yourself. By the by, I caught you in *People* magazine with the English crooner, you naughty girl."

"When I see Connie McQuillan, I'll personally wring her neck."

"They'll put you on page one of the *Post* if you do. Hey, what's up with the you and this crooner?"

"We're through."

"Who dumped whom?"

"I've never actually hung up on you before, have I, Harold?"

"I like to think we can be absolutely blunt and frank, like siblings. You've never gone huffy on me, either."

"I'm having a very hard day. Week. Month," Maggie said. "It's been a hell of a year so far."

"The thing is, we're already into the Chinaman for sixty grand, and if we have to sue him to recover, it'll probably cost us twenty grand."

"I feel dreadful about this. You have no idea. I've always been so comfortable around Reggie. He stayed for dinner. We got drunk. Things got out of hand."

"After Clarissa and I went off the deep end, I carried on like a goddamn schoolboy. Love makes us ridiculous, Maggie. Surely I've told you that before. Okay, look, I'll put out the word tomorrow and see if we can come up with somebody else. It's a damn shame. That Chinaman has a style, and it's become very much the Maggie Darling visual style. But I suppose a new look isn't the worst thing in the world. You might even cut your hair. Say, the green drake hatch is under way up north."

"Excuse me . . . ?"

"The green drake. It's a kind of fly that the trout like to eat."

"Sounds like a duck."

"It's a mayfly, actually."

"Oh. Well, that's nice."

"It occurs to me that fly-fishing for trout might be something you'd find relaxing and diverting."

"Hmmmmm. Maybe I would. It's very complicated, isn't it?"

"Hellishly. The knots alone would keep you in thrall for hours at a crack. It's a real Maggie Darling sport."

"Sounds rather up my alley."

"I've still got that place in Vermont."

"Have you?"

"I go every weekend this time of year."

"Is this an invitation, Harold?"

"Standing."

"It sounds interesting. And fraught."

"Fraught? How so?"

"I will not be seduced by you."

"I'm beginning to think that you have a smutty mind, Maggie. An old gaffer like me! The idea. Why I don't remember what love is. And I'm half sure I don't want to be reminded. Anyway, the invitation stands. Here's the phone number up there, if the spirit moves you."

She wrote it down.

"Harold, I didn't mean to insinuate that you are in any way a pig, like some men I could mention. You know how much I value you as a friend."

"Then do me a favor."

"What?"

"Call the Chinaman and get him back on board."

"He never answers his phone."

"Leave him a heartfelt message then. Ooop. I've got the dutchess of York waiting in the anteroom. See you soon I hope."

It was true that Reggie Chang never answered his phone, even when he was home. However, he had a perfectly good answering machine and it was his custom to selectively return calls. Knowing this, Maggie was more inclined to write a heartfelt letter, but she felt obliged by her friendships with both Harold and Reggie to do the more difficult thing and leave a message on his machine. She steeled herself and dialed.

"Hi, this is Reggie," the tape recited cheerfully. "Leave your name and number and I'll get back to you."

"I know I've hurt your feelings and I'm terribly, terribly sorry," Maggie began. "I feel so foolish saying this to a machine. If you're there, Reggie, please pick up. Anyway, I want to talk to you, or see you, or both, very soon. I, uh, I'm coming into town tonight to go to an opening at the Met. I'll call you when I'm in town. Really, we must talk. I feel so . . . Oh, I'll call again later."

She showered, threw on an uncomplicated black Donna Karan jersey with a rope of freshwater pearls, a few dabs of mascara, and a little spritz of L'Adventura, and hurried out of the deafeningly quiet house to her mighty Land Cruiser. On the way down to the city, she listened to a recording of Henry James's *Wings of the Dove,* hoping to elevate herself. But it was too hopelessly tedious and by New Canaan she switched to a tape of Blossom Dearie singing Cole Porter.

8
A Ruined Man

The Temple of Dendur, a midget Egyptian monument about the size of a railroad millionaire's mausoleum, was housed in its own large, austere room at the rear of the Metropolitan Museum's labyrinth of galleries, with one enormous slanting wall of glass panes facing the interior of Central Park, which at this time of year afforded a lovely crepuscular vision of lavender sky and tender green foliage, like a scene out of a Childe Hassam painting. The room itself, a bombastic space on its own terms, was decorated with potted orange trees strung with constellations of little white Christmas lights for the occasion. A series of temporary runways ran out from the granite podium supporting the little temple itself, upon which models in costumes of the Napoleonic era strutted to and fro through a blitzkrieg of throbbing laser beams and disco lights. The music was a raucous techno-pop that ricocheted off the hard surfaces of the room like razor blades shot out of a riot gun. Waiters dressed as hussars in frogged tunics and polyester bearskin hats circulated with trays of champagne and tempting little morsels. Half the faces in view were familiar from the party pages of *Vanity Fair* and the *New York Times* Sunday Style section. It was characteristic of this room to seem both ominously underpeopled and claustrophobic at the same time.

"Why, my dear Maggie Darling," exclaimed Lawrence Hayward, battling his way toward her through a knot of Trumps, Kravises, and Perlmans. Maggie was astonished to notice that Hayward, the once skeletal ascetic, had turned positively plump since his appearance at her supper table months earlier. His war-wound limp had turned into a kind of comfortable waddle. "How are you, you lovely creature?" he said.

"Very well, thank you, Lawrence," she said, watching as he snatched a nugget of *gougere* from the tray of a passing waiter.

"You know how to make these things?" he inquired.

"Piece of cake," she half hollered above the din.

"No, it's more like cheese pastry," Hayward said.

"I meant, we make them all the time."

"Perhaps someday you might instruct me in the art."

"You want to learn how to cook?"

"I'm developing an interest. And I owe it all to you."

"Really?"

"To that moment of . . . of revelation at your Christmas party when you placed a roasted oyster in my mouth. Until that moment I couldn't be bothered with anything beyond the animal mechanics of digestion. I feel as though you've opened a door in my life."

"Gosh. Imagine that," Maggie said, trying sincerely to think of Hayward as an improved human being, and having some trouble despite his poetical flourish.

"I saw you in *People* a while back," Hayward said.

"That vile rag!"

"Don't be offended. I didn't actually read the item. Closely. Say, where's the Englishman tonight?"

"Can we talk about something else?"

"We can talk about your ex-husband."

"He's not quite ex yet."

"Oh?" Hayward seemed surprised. "The two of you reconciling after all?"

"God, no. What made you think so?"

"Well, since Kenneth's gone kerblooie, I thought he might have come crawling back for a hot meal and a place to sleep."

"Pardon me. What do you mean *kerblooie*?

"Since he tanked."

"What do you mean 'tanked'?" Maggie asked, her interest turning into anxiety.

"Why, I mean lost it all."

"I saw him just this afternoon," Maggie said. "He's going through a transition, all right, but he didn't seem completely crazy. Any more than usual, that is. When he's not on drugs."

"I don't mean his *mind*," Hayward said, leaning close now to speak more directly into her ear as the musical number crescendoed in a cacophony of shrieking synthesizers. "I mean his *money*."

"Excuse me, did you say money?"

"Yes," Hayward said, as the music stopped. "He lost it all the past month."

"Lost all his money!" Maggie cried, and a score of heads, many of them famous and some of them beautifully coiffed, ratcheted in her direction. She seized Hayward by the elbow and literally steered him out of the room to the corridor between Dendur and the Chinese galleries. Hayward seemed not to mind being steered about. "What do you mean 'lost all his money'?" Maggie said, trying to suppress a rising hysteria.

"I'm sorry to be the bearer of bad tidings. Your, uh, husband got involved in some dubious derivatives—Malaysian mortgage options, Japanese synthetic petroleum bonds, and double-loaded pension fund share resale futures—and leveraged pretty much all he had on a bet that the yen would fall three quarters of a point against the deutsche mark. It wasn't a good bet."

"You mean he's wiped out?"

"Well, yeah. I think the SEC has paid him a few calls, too."

"What! Please, Lawrence. Be literal!"

"He could be subject to prosecution. Some of these trading instruments he created—they were a little iffy."

"Oh, God!" The blood drained out of Maggie's head and she had to lean against the marble wall, which was shockingly cold in its own right. The first horrible fantasy that assaulted her was a picture of bank officials and sheriff's deputies swooping down on Kettle Hill Farm armed with repossession notices. The house had been paid off years ago—but who was to say that Kenneth hadn't gone and somehow hocked it in this orgy of financial self-destruction? And what of the promised divorce settlement? She literally imagined a flock of thousand-dollar bills fluttering away into the blue sky like a mob of starlings.

"Are you all right, Maggie?"

"No. I need a drink."

"Want me to go in and grab one for you?"

"First I need some air," she gasped, glancing this way and that way like a cornered animal.

"You just hold on there a moment, Maggie Darling." Hayward reached for a slim cellular phone on his belt and punched a single button on the keypad. "Bring the car around to the front of the museum," he barked into it. Then, he placed his hand on the back of Maggie's waist and navigated her like a sleepwalker through the otherwise deserted galleries to the exit, where a guard let them out.

9
⤳ Gotham ⤳

"Drive around the park," Hayward told his chauffeur through an intercom; then he opened a veneered console revealing a minibar. "What's your poison?" he asked Maggie.

"Vodka, please."

"I, uh, don't have any. How about Scotch?"

"Okay. With some of that sparkling water."

A machine spat ice cubes into a crystal tumbler at the touch of a button. Hayward made a strong drink and presented it to Maggie as though he had concocted a terribly complicated cocktail, say a zombie or a Sazerac, and deserved to be praised. She knocked half of it back in a couple of gulps and gazed wanly out the window at the artificial pastoral of the park in murky twilight.

"Peanuts?" Hayward asked, producing some little foil pouches. "I get them on airplanes. They give them out, you know. For years and years I never ate them."

"Have you been collecting them?"

"Well, they were free."

"No thanks," Maggie said.

"They stay fresh a long time."

"I thought you said you never ate them."

"I used to never eat them. Lately I've gotten to appreciate them. They're good, and good for you. And I defy you to tell me what year any given bag is from. They're vacuum sealed."

Maggie sipped her drink as they drove up along the reservoir. Here and there, the campfires of the radical indigent flickered in the gathering darkness.

"Did I hear you say that you saw Kenneth recently?" Hayward tried a fresh tack.

"Just this afternoon," Maggie said quietly. "He came over to the house. He talked about opening some kind of therapy center over in Ridgefield."

"Therapy center?"

"I don't know. It all sounded very New Age, but I thought, Who am I to judge?"

"If you don't mind my saying so, Maggie, I think your husband could use some of his own medicine."

Maggie sighed. The Scotch was finally salving her nerves. "He said he was prepared to settle our separation. It was my impression that it was the main reason he came over. Why would he say that if he was . . . ruined?"

"When you've got nothing, you've got nothing to lose."

"Where does that leave me?" Maggie fairly whispered to herself.

They drove in silence toward the Harlem Meer. A crowd of perhaps a hundred came into view gathered around a blazing trash can by the lakeshore. The mellow bonking of Caribbean steel drums was audible against a background of hooting and laughter. The tragic cornices of 110th Street loomed darkly in the distance. Hayward nervously jingled the ice around in his glass.

"You know, I'm a very wealthy man," he said.

Maggie half expected to feel his hand on her thigh.

"I'm not looking for a sugar daddy, Lawrence."

"How about a friend?"

"It depends on what kind of friend."

"A friendly one," Hayward said, reaching for the Scotch bottle. "Recharge?"

"Thank you."

"I help my friends."

"Kenneth is your friend."

"Kenneth was a business associate," Hayward said. "He screwed me on those Malaysian mortgage options, by the way. Skinned me out of a cool fifteen million."

"Good gosh!" Maggie muttered.

"Oh, I can absorb a loss of that order. It won't affect my standard of living one iota. But it's a lot of money. I'm not so out of touch with normal life that I don't recognize that. I was once normal myself."

"Normal in what sense?"

"I got up in the morning. I went to an office. I worked like a dog. I drove around goddamned Cleveland all day and all night picking up bags of money at my car washes."

"That sounds like hard work," Maggie said, chuckling mordantly, "picking up bags of money."

"Do you have any idea how much five hundred dollars in quarters weighs?"

"No."

"It's like loading feed sacks onto a freight car. Take it from me. I did that, too, when I was sixteen in Logansport, Indiana."

"Is that where you're from?"

"Yes, ma'am. Cass County, Indiana."

"Were you poor?"

"Not at all. My father was a machinist. He made a good wage, even in the Depression, boring holes in engine blocks for the Lawnsman Mowing Machine Company. We lived in a nice little bungalow in a decent neighborhood. 'Course, if you wanted pocket money in those days, you had to work, and, believe me, I was happy to load feed sacks onto freight cars. It made me the man I am today."

Maggie turned fully to Hayward for the first time since they'd embarked in the car. He looked less like a rat now than a squirrel with cheek pouches puffed full of nuts. There was a light in his eyes, too, that could as easily have been a sparkle as a glint.

"Anyway, I just wanted you to know that you can depend on me if you find yourself in a jam," he said.

"That's very nice of you, Lawrence, but you're a married man."

"This has nothing to do with romance. This is friendship. If that doesn't work for you, let's call it business. You make a bit of money at these enterprises of yours, don't you?"

"Yes," she admitted. "Yes, I do."

"About how much?"

"I . . . I can't believe we're talking about this."

"Why? Do you think it's indecent? A lot of you Easterners do, you know. It's worse for you than pornography. Your boy Kenneth was like that—except when he was on drugs. That's how a fellow knew when he was on them. He loved to talk about money when he was stoned."

"You knew about the drugs?"

"Oh, sure. So what do you figure your net earnings amounted to last year?"

"Roughly two and a half million," Maggie said.

"A person could live on that," Hayward said.

"It does seem like a lot of money," she agreed.

"Of course, when you're used to a certain level of expenditure, it's surprising how things add up—clothes, foreign travel, the like."

"I have a staff. There are many regular ongoing expenses. But I'm hardly profligate."

"Then you have nothing to worry about."

"Frankly, Lawrence, I'm worried that Kenneth might have hocked the house."

"I doubt that he could have accomplished that without your knowledge and approval. How much do you figure it's worth?"

"We bought it for two-fifty in 1981. But it was a wreck back then. Now it's . . . it's been considerably improved."

"A million and a half?" Hayward ventured.

"At least."

"Look, as long as you're still legally married, with an interest in this property, he can't transfer the title on you. In the worst case, if he's collateralized it, you can pay off the lien, and if for any reason you need a loan without any strings attached, then you come to me and we'll arrange it."

Maggie's head seemed filled with helium. The lights in the apartment buildings along Central Park West, now visible through the scrim of trees, twinkled with promise, as the lamps of a village might denote reprieve to a lonely wanderer emerging from a wilderness.

"Why are you doing this for me?" she asked.

"Because I admire you. I'm grateful to you. You've made me feel better as a . . . a person. Is that so terrible?"

"No."

"Can't anyone have pure motives?"

Maggie couldn't help laughing heartily. A tremendous weight seemed to have been lifted off her. "I must tell you, Lawrence, you must be the least likely person in America to be considered motivated by purity and innocence."

"Just shows you what a cynical age we live in."

"Maybe so."

"Talk about the *People* magazine mentality . . ."

"I'm truly grateful to you, Lawrence," she said, "but of all the people to restore my faith in the human race, well, you're a humdinger."

Hayward leaned toward the intercom below the hand strap. "Dexter," he told the chauffeur, "you can take us back to the museum now."

"Wait. Would you mind terribly dropping me downtown?"

"No. Just say where."

"Vestry Street, between Hudson and Greenwich."

"Cancel that, Dexter. Head downtown, instead. *Way* downtown."

10

↪ Emergency ↩

The big sleek silver limo exited the park at Columbus Circle and turned south on Seventh Avenue.

"What's waiting downtown for you?" Hayward asked as they entered Times Square.

"A friend," Maggie said.

Hayward seemed content not to inquire further.

The Disney Corporation's efforts to sanitize the theater district had been overwhelmed in recent years by the sheer numbers of those whose livelihoods depended on vice. Prostitutes paraded luridly in front of a store selling Mickey Mouse merchandise, and drug dealers held open market at twenty-foot intervals up and down Forty-second Street, just like the old days. Farther down Seventh, Chelsea was crawling with young people in black outfits, the art mob lately removed from Soho. Sheridan Square in the West Village seemed rather depopulated by comparison, the new strains of AIDS II and III having taken their toll in recent outbreaks. When they crossed Canal Street, Maggie directed the chauffeur to Hudson and then down to Vestry, Reggie's street.

He lived in a four-story building that had begun its life as a patent-medicine distillery in the 1860s. From this modest structure issued many thousandscore pints of Craven's Sovereign Tonic, a ubiquitous provision on every Civil War battlefield (it had an alcohol content of 40 percent and tasted like chamomile-flavored whiskey). Since around 1900, the building had been a butter and egg jobber's warehouse, a speakeasy, a taxicab livery and dispatch office, a Greek restaurant, and finally a discotheque, before Reggie Chang acquired the property during a real estate downturn in the early 1990s. The first floor was currently occupied by The Happy Bean Cafe, a natural foods restaurant. Reggie's studio and home occupied the second floor—which had been Edgar Craven's office suite for thirty-eight years—and fronted the street with a marvelous copper-roofed bay window that stretched the full twenty-five-foot width of the building. The third- and fourth-floor lofts were rented respectively to a successful cabaret singer and a lady entomologist from the Museum of Natural History. The rental income exceeded the mortgage and taxes by several thousand dollars a year, so Reggie lived there for free and then some.

From the car, the flickering bluish light of a television played across the big second-floor bay window.

"May I use your phone?" Maggie asked Hayward.

"Certainly."

He flipped the mouthpiece open and punched the *on* button to get a dial tone for her. Reggie's answering machine picked up on the first ring, as usual. Maggie waited for the familiar greeting and electronic cue. "Reggie," she said. "It's me. Pick it up, will you? I'm downstairs, right outside on Vestry, in a car."

"That his machine?" Hayward asked.

"Reggie, please. I know you're home. I can see the TV glowing in your window. I'm coming up. I'm going to ring your doorbell in a minute and you'd better let me in."

"Do you want me to wait here?" Hayward asked.

"No, you go ahead. I'm liable to be here awhile."

"What if he's really not home?"

"I know he's there, Lawrence. I'll grab a cab after."

"Okay. Remember what I told you now, Maggie. You've got a friend."

"I appreciate it very much."

She felt an impulse to embrace him. It seemed natural enough, except that he was who he was. She took a chance. He possessed a solidity that was surprising and reassuring, and he wore a cologne faintly redolent of midwestern machine shops.

When the big car pulled away, she could make out sharp popping noises in the distance. It sounded a little bit like Chinese New Year. Though she didn't know it, this was the sound of gunfire across town on the Lower East Side, where armed, radical rent strikers and their squatter allies, holed up in a desecrated synagogue on Orchard Street, were exchanging fire with an NYPD SWAT team. Close by the Hudson River, Vestry Street itself was as tranquil as a country lane at this hour.

She entered the vestibule of Reggie's building and pressed the buzzer on the wall. He refused to buzz her in or even speak into the house phone. She was growing annoyed. There seemed nothing left to do but leave when a long-legged redhead in a bloodred patent-leather spring coat glided down the stairway and strode theatrically to the door. It was the cabaret singer, Lorna Dougal, Maggie realized. Though she had never actually met her, she owned several of the singer's recordings, and Reggie was always gossiping about her cavalcade of boyfriends.

Ms. Dougal lit up in a toothy, slightly cockeyed smile as she opened the door.

"Why, Maggie Darling," she exclaimed. "Of all people!"

"Why, Lorna Dougal," Maggie lilted back, as the tension of the preceding hours suddenly yielded to this happy little accident of minor celebritydom.

"I was just readin' one of your books in the tub."

"Which one?"

"*Fifteen-Minute Feasts.*"

"I was listening to your *Live at the Oak Room* CD just the other day in the car. If they still made them out of vinyl, I would have worn out the grooves by now."

"Oh, I'm such a fan of yours," Lorna gushed, her renowned Southern charm evidently as authentic offstage as on. "Reggie never stops talkin' about you."

"Is that so?"

"You're the sun that he orbits around."

"Gosh."

"Why, I wish I could drag you upstairs and put on a big pot of coffee and talk recipes, but I've got two shows to do."

"Some other time would be great."

"Isn't it queer that we both knew each other without even knowin' each other?"

"Yes, a little."

"But that's New York for you. Isn't it sumpin'? I never get over it," Lorna said, squeezing past Maggie in the cramped vestibule. "Bye-bye, Maggie Darling."

"Break a leg, Lorna," Maggie called after her.

Meanwhile, she'd kept the inside door from shutting.

Moments later she was upstairs regarding Reggie's glossy red-painted steel door on the second floor. A blather of television was audible within. She was not particularly surprised that he refused to answer the doorbell, but she was now determined to break his rather cruel and implacable will, and she leaned on the button while she batted on the door with the flat of her hand, crying, "Reggie, open the door right now! It's me!" It was possible to keep at it for only so long without becoming discouraged, and it was with a final lame gesture of disgust that Maggie angrily shoved the doorknob with a torquing motion, only to feel the door yield inward. It had been unlocked all along.

Across the broad loft, with its supernatural tidiness and eclectic mix of English country, Bauhaus, and Santa Fe furniture, Maggie saw Reggie slumped in an overstuffed armchair with the haze of MTV encircling the back of his head like a high-tech halo.

"Reggie?" she called tentatively. The loft, which was divided into areas rather than rooms, was a good forty feet across. A rap video happened to be playing loudly on the TV, a futuristic aural sludge of rusted chains and buckets slamming and grinding together behind a zombie chant of grievance. "The door was open and I let myself in," Maggie said, trying to sound both friendly and authoritative.

When Reggie failed to stir, she advanced across the polished hardwood floor. Her sense of dread accelerated with her heartbeat as she flew around the chair to find him unconscious, with a nearly drained vodka bottle between his legs, a plastic prescription container still gripped in a clammy hand, and a tendril of vomit running down his sweater and across a note on letterhead stationery that was neatly pinned to his chest.

Maggie ran wildly around the loft searching for a telephone. She found a cordless handset charging on its stand on the granite prep island in the kitchen and dialed 911.

"Send an ambulance to 327 Vestry Street in Tribecca at once," she stated clearly. "Someone here has attempted suicide."

"Is it an elevator building, ma'am?"

"No, second-floor walk-up."

"Go down and unlock the ground-floor door. Is the individual breathing?"

"I'm not sure."

"Make sure his air passages are not clogged. We'll be there in ten minutes or less." The dispatcher hung up.

Maggie marveled at the system's efficiency. At least one thing still worked in the United States. She wet a dishtowel and hurried back over to Reggie. He was breathing, she now saw, but shallowly. She wiped the vomit off his face and sweater, removed the note from his sweater, and inserted two fingers into his mouth. No obstructions were evident. By the time she rushed downstairs, the EMTs were hurrying into the vestibule with their equipment. They had Reggie on the stretcher with an airway and a blood pressure cuff inside of thirty seconds.

"His pulse is still strong," the squad chief told Maggie. He was a very dark, small wiry West Indian with a melodic voice. "Can you tell me if the gentleman is insured and if so with whom?"

"I have no idea."

"Oh dear," the chief said. His three associates put the stretcher down.

"Can't we go over this at the hospital?" Maggie asked.

"Well, you see, there's a bit of a problem. Unless we can identify the insurer, we are obliged to take the gentleman to Bellevue. How much do you know about the city hospitals, madam?"

"Can't you take him over to University or Cornell Medical?"

"Ah, I see you understand. There is the matter of the ambulance fee. We must have assurance of payment."

"How much do you charge?"

"There is the dispatch fee of two hundred dollars and the staff fee of fifty dollars per person, plus equipment, bandages, IV drips, what-have-you."

Maggie fished her wallet out of her handbag and began extracting fifty-dollar bills. When she had forked over $450, the EMT chief still stood there as though expecting more.

"You haven't used any bandages or IV drips," she said.

"There is a surcharge on trips after nine P.M."

"How much?"

"Fifty dollars."

Maggie rolled her eyes and gave it to him and then held her wallet open to show that it was empty.

"We are ready to go, madam," the EMT chief said, folding the bills and sliding them into the breast pocket of his white medical jacket. "Will that be University or Cornell Med?"

11
∽ Fluorescent Tedium ∽

They let her ride uptown in the ambulance, but once inside Cornell Med, the doctors made her wait in a room so blindingly lit with fluorescent bulbs that she felt as though she were trapped inside a television set. In the frightful tedium of the claustrophobic room, she excavated Reggie's suicide note from inside her brassiere. It was penned in green ink in a highly formal and artistic block handwriting, and it read:

> To the Finder,
> What you see I have done out of love. A love that fails to adhere. To the one who is my love I bear no curses. You are strong and will survive this petty interruption. I have no other complaints. For instructions as to disposal, et cetera, contact my attorney, Jay Lefkowitz, Esq., 845 Third Ave., and my brother Anthony Chang of Santa Rosa, Calif.
> Farewell all others,
> R. Chang.

The banality and bad composition shocked her. It seemed unworthy of the man she had known. She was angry at herself for having exposed this streak of shallow sentimentality in someone she wished to regard as a deeper person, and it made her wonder if we ever really know anyone. Combined with the atrocious fluorescent lights, reading the note over and over again gave her a pounding headache.

She kept inquiring about Reggie's condition at the nursing station, but they had no updates. After an hour of this, wracked with hunger and with nothing else to divert her but some exceedingly old and grubby women's magazines, she set forth to the hospital cafeteria, where she sat under another powerful bank of fluorescent lights picking at a crusty portion of gray-green vegetable lasagna and a slice of rubbery devil's food cake. Only the pint of milk tasted like real food. When she returned to the ER waiting area, there had been a change of staff and it took the graveyard-shift nurses twenty minutes to even find out what room Reggie Chang had been assigned to. She was permitted to go see him there only after she had persuaded the charge nurse that Reggie was her son.

He was sleeping very peacefully on his back with a glucose drip running into his arm. The nurse, reading Reggie's chart, informed Maggie that his stomach had been pumped. His blood levels of Restoril and alcohol were "within a nonlethal range," and she expected he would be able to go home before lunch the next day. "This was not a serious suicide attempt," she declared with unconcealed disdain as she flipped the chart closed and left the room.

12
ᠳ The Patient ᠳ

As it happened, Reggie woke her up hacking and coughing. Maggie's neck ached from sleeping in the battered Danish modern hospital-issue chair. Dawn light the color of pocket lint gathered outside the window. Their eyes met in an uncomfortable moment of recognition.

"It's you," Reggie croaked.

"Of course it's me."

"Why in the fucking hell did they call *you*?"

"They didn't call me. I found you."

"Oh, God."

"Wasn't that the whole point? To make me feel bad?"

Reggie turned his face away. She could hear him make a pitiful puling sound like a child.

"Well, I do feel bad. I feel terrible. You see, you've succeeded."

"I failed," Reggie blubbered.

"Oh, stop it. They say you didn't take enough of that stuff to kill a rubber duckie." Maggie was shocked by her own vehemence. All the affronts and difficulties of the past few months suddenly welled up in her as a tsunami of anger that now crested and broke over Reggie. "And what's more, that suicide note of yours was practically illiterate!"

Reggie stopped blubbering, returned her gaze stonily, and said, "I'm a visual artist, not a fucking author. I suppose you'd be more satisfied if I left a nice set of silver gelatin prints behind."

"I'll tell you what will satisfy me: if you stop being a baby about this and get back on board with this book shoot. And quit pretending that you even meant to put this world behind you, you big phony. I'm told you took about five pills and the equivalent of a margarita."

"I didn't want to leave a big fucking mess."

"You think dead people make less of mess when they take a smaller overdose? I never heard anything so idiotic."

"Oh, leave me alone. I hate you."

"I won't leave you alone until you swear you'll get back on this shoot. I saved your life. You owe me."

"You didn't save my life. I didn't take enough of that stuff to kill a rubber duck, remember?"

"So then tell me why I spent the whole night in this chair?" Maggie hollered back at him.

"Because you're a fucking saint? How the fuck should I know?"

"No, because you wanted to punish me, you mean-minded little shit."

"I don't have to punish you! It's punishment enough for you to *be* you."

"And to have to rescue all the sad-sack, self-absorbed, mean little shits in the world like you."

"Get out!"

"Get back on the job!"

"I'd rather die."

"You wouldn't know how!"

"That's what you think."

"Oh, fuck you."

"Fuck you and kiss my Chinese ass!"

A nurse fairly burst into the room, a slender and rather attractive, middle-aged African-American woman with a no-nonsense manner and witheringly haughty look of authority that shut up the combatants instantly. She was holding a small plastic garbage bag.

"Just what is all the shouting about in here?" she inquired.

Both Maggie and Reggie merely gawked at her in mortification.

"Do you realize we've got sick people down the hall?" she continued and at once set about removing the IV from Reggie's arm. "You're out of here, mister. Doctor's orders. Here are your clothes," she said, tossing the garbage bag onto the end of the bed. "And you," she said, turning to Maggie with the cold light of contempt burning in her dark and handsome almond eyes, "can wait for him in the lobby."

"Don't wait for me," Reggie said.

"I'll wait."

"Please, don't bother."

"You," the nurse said to Reggie, "shut up and get dressed or I will have you arrested. And you," she said to Maggie, "well I don't care what you do, as long as you get out before I finish counting to ten . . . One, two . . ."

Minutes later, Maggie intercepted Reggie in the lobby.

"I told you not to wait."

"Yeah, well, I gave all the money I had to the goddamned ambulance crew and you are going to goddamned well get a cab and take me to the garage on Eighty-fourth Street where I parked my car."

"How the hell do you know I have any money?"

"Because I took your wallet out of your pants pocket in the ambulance so the orderlies wouldn't rob you in the hospital."

"Jeez, that was pretty good thinking," Reggie observed.

Maggie produced the wallet now—an iguana-skin Julian Vizoon—from her handbag. Reggie took it and peered inside.

"I only have ten bucks," he said.

"Don't sweat it," Maggie said. "That'll get us to the garage. Then I'll drop you downtown in my car."

"Okay, okay," Reggie said. "You win. I'll do the fucking shoot."

Part Eight

An Abominable Ruse

I

⤳ Rising to the Bait ⤳

Maggie turned down the driveway of Kettle Hill Farm as Walter Fayerwether's little blond cookie was driving out in their Volvo—just another minor irritant that barely registered, like a single grain of salt in the open wound that Maggie's life had become. At quarter to nine in the morning, the crickets seemed to be shrieking in the gardens. The sun glared menacingly above the tree line to the east out of an unnaturally brilliant blue sky. The house proved to be unpopulated. Lindy, of course, was not on the premises, nor Hooper or Quinona the maid or Nina.

Nina! The thought of commencing a search for another culinary assistant nauseated Maggie, evoking the spiritual equivalent of a stench like tripe boiled with cabbage (a strange, old-world favorite of her grandma Elsie's). Meanwhile, it unnerved Maggie to realize she had no idea what day it was. Was this the next stage in a life unraveling? It wasn't until she entered the kitchen to study the wall-mounted catering manifest that she discovered it was Friday. To her vast relief, the manifest showed no jobs until the coming Wednesday—a luncheon for the Fairfield County League of Women Voters, seventy-five heads, count 'em, a horror, no, an impossibility without Nina and at least two "shiftlings," as they called the ever changing cast of part-timers. In a panic, she called Nina at home once again, and this time the message said, "Hi, Nina here. Well, actually *not* here. I will be in Spain and Morocco until June fourth. Leave a message. Get back to you then. Bye."

Why, the message sounded . . . blithe! Gone off on a lark! Was this aggression by other means? Was the very blitheness of the message intended to wound her? Maggie wondered, and was further proof needed that Nina had left her employ? It was too, too depressing. Maggie rummaged halfheartedly through the huge Rolodex there on the butcher-block counter. For all the hundreds of cards in it—including many employees past and present—there was nobody she could really depend upon, in the Nina sense of rock-ribbed professional reliability. Each name greeted her with a little stab of anguish as she recalled some special area of inadequacy—too slow, too sloppy, too mouthy, too clumsy, too lacking in imagination, too starstruck. Nina had none of those failings, and now she was gone. Lost! Maggie slumped. The thought of planning a menu or even a shopping list for the League luncheon heaped her with despair. As the emotion rapidly morphed into more familiar terror, she lunged for the telephone and punched out a number.

"Why, Harold," she said, trying to sound nonchalant.

"Is that you, Maggie?" Harold Hamish said. "I was but momentarily out the door."

"Really? Where to?"

"Vermont. Remember? The green drake hatch."

"Yes. That funny little fly with a name like a duck's."

"Precisely."

"I thought you'd be relieved to hear that Reggie Chang is going to shoot those photos for the book after all."

"That's grand news. I'm very relieved, indeed. What did it take?— no, forget I asked. I'm just glad to hear we're on track again. Bully and hip hip hooray and all that."

"So, you're going up to the country, are you?"

"I am. Did you care to join me?"

"As a matter of fact, I was thinking about it."

"Really?" he sounded very surprised. "Think no more before you change your mind. Just pack a bag. I'll come by and get you in an hour."

"It's been a hideous week, Harold. A perfect horror."

"Let's see if we can make up for it, then, with a rousing Green Mountain adventure. I'll be along in an hour or so. Be prepared to depart at once."

"You're my knight in shining armor."

2
ᕽ A Glandular Exchange ᕽ

She stuffed a Vuitton weekender with North Woods togs and then assembled a tote bag of potables and comestibles—two each Matrot Meursault, Pouilly-Fuissé, and one really splendid 1988 Criots-Batard-Montrachet. For eats she packed a fat wedge of buttery St. Andre, a tin of foie gras, boxes of oat and water biscuits, a jar of her own chowchow pickle, a pound of prosciutto, a perfectly ripe muskmelon, some green tomatoes from the garden, a jar of toffee-covered cashews, and several big bars of Lindt bittersweet chocolate. She luxuriated in the tub for a while, sloughing off all the grime of the hospital ward, and then threw on a boxy red checkered sleeveless jumper that made her feel sixteen and a half. Just as she clipped a swag of her silvery gold hair in a tortoiseshell barrette, there was Harold down in the driveway, standing beside his restored 1965 crimson Morgan Plus Four Plus with the top down and neatly secured under the leather bonnet, leaning on the horn like one of the high school boys who used to call on her thirty years ago.

By some coincidence, Walter Fayerwether ambled through the arbor from the rose garden just as she settled into the passenger compartment. He wore a strange look on his craggy, scholarly face, a look that might have signified . . . amusement! It rather confused Maggie, but in her exhaustion this morning everything seemed a little off.

"Oh, Mr. Fayerwether," she said, unnerved by both his sudden appearance and his demeanor. "I'm going away for the weekend."

"That's nice," he said, grinning it seemed.

"Anything we need to talk about before I go?" she asked.

"I don't think so."

"Well, then. Everything in hand?"

"You have a good time and don't worry about anything here," he assured her. It was only then that she realized Fayerwether was grinning at Harold, who was beaming incandescently back at him, as though he'd won a trophy in some athletic contest. It didn't occur to Maggie that the prize might be herself, but the visual exchange between the two of them smacked of some recondite male glandular process and seemed potentially hazardous to bystanders. To put an end to it, she formally introduced the two men to each other. They shook hands in the guarded manner of males who recognize their mutual types and who had encountered those same types in many settings many times before in preparatory schools, college fraternities, country clubs, and corporate offices. Maggie couldn't help noticing that the Morgan's beige leather seats gave off a wonderful scent of commanding British masculinity. She buttoned a cotton sweater over her sleeveless dress as the men exchanged meaningless pleasantries about the beauty of the weather and the excellent condition of Harold's vintage car.

"You take good care of her," Fayerwether said as Harold swung into position behind the wheel. Maggie rather liked the sound of that and the way Fayerwether gazed after her as the agile little car swung around the parking circle. Harold seemed very eager to get under way and the wheels kicked up little rooster tails of loose gravel as they turned out of the drive.

3
ᑦ Enchantment ᑦ

The combination of extraordinary fatigue, warm spring sun, and the drone of the engine put Maggie to sleep just south of Hartford as they motored north up Interstate 91, and she didn't wake up until they pulled off the highway at Windsor, Vermont.

"Where are we?" she said, stretching up into the gorgeous afternoon sunshine.

"We're nearly there."

"How long have I been dozing?"

"A couple of hours."

"Oh dear! I hope you weren't bored stiff."

"I have an active fantasy life, thank you," he said, cutting a humorous glance her way.

"Well, it was sweet of you to let me sleep."

They picked up eggs, butter, lemons, potatoes, coffee, and other common larder items at a battered little country store in the crossroads hamlet of New Caliban. A short way down the county road they turned down a gravel lane, which soon joined the course of a rugged brook.

"Catamount Creek," Harold explained. "It's a little feeder that runs into the Otterkill River. Full of wild brookies."

"How marvelous," Maggie said.

"I think you're going to like it here."

They motored another mile, passing only one human artifact, an abandoned and decayed Federal period farmhouse once surrounded by tillage and pastures but now nearly swallowed up in second-growth hardwoods. Where the lane finally dead-ended stood a handsome wooden building of weathered gray board and batten with Gothic windows to each side of a bright red door. The sashes, shutters, and trim were also red.

"Here we are," Harold said.

Maggie pronounced it adorable.

"It was a schoolhouse long ago," Harold said. "Odd now, isn't it, to think there were ever enough children living around here?"

"What a different people we were then," Maggie said. "My God . . ."

Harold fussed with two locks and threw open the door. Downstairs, a sort of kitchen and sitting area flowed into each other. Against the wall opposite the spartan galley stood a fieldstone fireplace flanked by shelves of books from floor to ceiling. A stuffed owl that uncannily resembled Harold perched on the mantel.

"Somebody else did it over back in 1970," Harold explained. "Unspeakable materials. Dropped ceilings. Fake pine paneling. Shag carpets. The downstairs was all chopped up into dreary little cells. Dismal doesn't come close to describing it. It was like a provincial police barracks in Romania. But we saw the glimmering potential and we gutted it down to the timber frame."

A set of French doors now occupied the rear wall and led out to a deck that overlooked the Otterkill. A long wooden farmhouse table was deployed at the room's center with a fly-tying station set up at the end nearest the afternoon light.

Toward the front of the house, stairs raked so steeply as to appear ladderlike rose up to a couple of small bedrooms with a bath sandwiched between them. Harold climbed up behind Maggie, toting her bag and admiring her rear. The guest room, painted stark white, was furnished with nothing more than an iron frame bed, an oak nightstand with a kerosene lamp, and an edition of William Bartram's *Travels in Georgia and Florida, 1773–74.* The extreme simplicity appealed to Maggie. Here was a wonderfully clarifying place, she thought, a place to reorganize and reenergize the battered spirit. Here was a room in which one might actually be able to think!

"So peaceful and lovely," she observed.

"We've got mice," Harold said.

"I'm not afraid of mice."

The modest bathroom contained an ancient claw-footed tub. Harold had rigged a five-gallon military jerrican lengthwise from the rafters. Six inches beneath it he'd hung an old two-burner propane camping stove. There was a long copper supply pipe soldered into the top of the can. The pipe terminated in a showerhead cobbled out of the spout of an ancient watering can, and there was a brass petcock valve just behind the showerhead for turning it on and off. Light for the whole room was supplied by twin kerosene wall sconces above a chipped and ancient pedestal sink.

"If you want a shower, you have to light the fire twenty minutes beforehand," Harold explained. "Any longer and you're liable to get a scalding. It's primitive but effective."

"Enchanting," Maggie sighed. "I may never go back to the real world."

"Yeah," he agreed with a sardonic gleam in his eye. "Let's you and me chuck it all and stay here forever."

4
⌇ At the Vise ⌇

Maggie overcame the restlessness of arrival by organizing the food supplies and acquainting herself with the kitchen. The equipment was barely adequate—a pitiful assortment of cast-off pans and cheap aluminum pots picked from tag sales, she supposed. Tableware ranged from pewter to Lucite. She was overcome by a desire to bake cornbread and scared up the necessary implements and ingredients while Harold settled in at the end of the great table and commenced tying trout flies.

She kept an eye on him as she prepared the simple batter. It looked like surgery. He secured the tiny fishhooks in a little vise, wrapped bits of fur around the shanks, and wound feather hackles over the fur. When the batter was in the oven Maggie settled into a chair beside him to watch.

"Hope I don't make you nervous," she said.

"Not at all."

"Is it hard to learn?"

"Takes quite a bit of practice. Like cooking well or sewing well, I'd imagine."

"Would you teach me how?"

"No," Harold said. "There are only so many things in the world a person *should* be good at. I feel a professional obligation to protect you from spreading yourself too thin. You can be the cook and everything else. Let me be the flytier in here."

"Oh, all right. But will you show me how to handle the rod and all?"

"You betcha."

"If I were a trout I'd go after that little morsel you're making there."

"Would you?"

"It looks . . . scrumptious."

"Then you'd be caught, you know."

"And I'd die in a panful of bubbling sweet butter," she said. "Pure heaven."

"Of course, I'd have to eat you, then," Harold said and hastened to add, "Say, would you mind fetching me a Scotch? I've literally got my hands full here."

5
⇜ The One-Rod Method ⇝

When Harold had tied about a dozen flies and they'd both knocked back two Scotches, it was time to fish.

"We take one rod tonight," Harold said as he donned a very complicated-looking vest with dozens of bulging pockets. "It's too prime out there tonight for instruction. Just pay attention to what I'm doing. Tomorrow morning you'll get a rod too."

Maggie put on the decrepit pair of sneakers Harold gave her for wading in the river. She felt like a clown. He also insisted that she put on a sweater, though it was a warm evening. The sun had dipped into the treetops and a gold-tinted twilight was under way that would persist for a good hour.

They waded through some emerald bracken along the riverbank to the water's edge and Maggie followed Harold into the stream. It was like leaving one world behind and plunging into an entirely different one. The water was shockingly cold, though not much more than calf deep. When she'd caught her breath, Maggie was glad Harold had made her wear a sweater. The footing was good on the stream's gravel bottom. The current made a slight burbling sound and left a trail of bubbles where it swirled around her bare legs. The golden air was full of bobbing motes. Among them but less numerous were the large, fluffy mayflies winging up into the forest canopy.

"The green drakes are out," Harold said.

Cedar waxwings swooped across the tunnel-like stream corridor picking them delicately out of the air. Sometimes they'd hang suspended in place for a moment like large hummingbirds, feeding on more than one bug at a swoop.

"Beautiful," Maggie said, goggling at the spectacle of it all. The Scotch in her bloodstream was casting an additional patina over the scene.

"Stay on my left," Harold whispered.

She followed him upstream.

He halted at the tail of a riffled pool and began manually stripping line off his reel, very businesslike. The reel emitted an insectile screech with every pull. Then, he was whipping the supple rod back and forth until the heavy line was in the air in a big loop, going forward and back, rhythmically. At every back-cast he yanked more line off the reel until the loop was flying out a good fifteen yards. Finally, he hurled the loop forward until all the line paid out. The leader unrolled like a red carpet and deposited the fly at the head of the pool like a little foreign dignitary landing in a new country. The fly bobbled swiftly downstream in the surface tension, its cream-colored hackle and light deer-hair wings making it easy to track against the dark water. A liquid hump swelled behind it and then there was a little splash, like a mousetrap springing just under the surface. The rod tip jerked visibly.

"Got one?"

"Yeah."

He stripped in the line with his left hand dragging the fish closer until, with a deft motion, he reached down into the water and brought up a smallish trout, holding its lower jaw between his thumb and forefinger.

"A tiddler," he remarked.

"A what?"

"We throw back anything under twelve inches."

"Well, of course," Maggie said.

"Did you watch what I was doing."

"Oh, yes. It looks rather difficult."

"It is. You'll find out tomorrow."

Harold tossed the little trout back into the stream and it streaked under a rock. They moved forward skirting the edge of the pool to get to the next riffle ahead. There Harold laid out a cast just to the side of a piano-size rock. In fact, the fly bounced off the rock's face before it landed in the water with a little plop.

"Did you do that on purpose?" Maggie asked.

"Of course."

The fly jiggered gaily down the current for a few seconds. Then the water exploded under it and the reel whined as a much larger trout ran off upstream with the fly. Harold slowed down the run by palming the spool until the line stopped paying out. The rod tip darted at the water as the fish chugged around. When it broke water about thirty feet away trying to throw the hook, it looked like an airborne wriggling gold ingot. Then the line went slack for a while as the fish drifted with the current. Harold appeared to anticipate the move and took in the slack until the rod tip was darting again. The fish ran upstream twice more, and the third time it floated down on the current, exhausted, Harold slipped the fatal net under it.

"Now, this is a fish," he said, fastidiously extracting the hook with a surgical hemostat.

The fish had jewel-like red spots on its side and a bright yellow belly. It gasped and tried futilely to wriggle free from Harold's grip. When the hook was out, he took the trout up in both hands and, in a motion that seemed well practiced, bent back the trout's head until its spine snapped. Maggie recoiled.

"What did you just do?"

"I killed it quickly and mercifully," he said.

"Good Lord . . ."

"You understand we intend to catch our supper?"

"Yes, but . . ."

"Therefore, we have to kill them."

"I know, but . . ."

"It's either this or they suffocate slowly in the creel. Which would you prefer?"

"Quick and merciful," Maggie glumly agreed.

"It's not as though you were a vegetarian."

"No."

"Nature is red in fang and claw, my dear."

"Sure. I'll be okay."

Harold seemed satisfied. He nodded slightly and made a barely audible harrumphing sound. Then he swiftly had a knife out and slit the trout's belly from its anal vent to its throat. He tore out the gills and tossed them aside, pulled the viscera loose from the body cavity, and squeezed the trout's fibrous stomach so that a paste of partly digested insects came out of it like black toothpaste from a tube.

"What in God's name are you doing now?"

"I'm examining the stomach contents to see what kind of bugs it's been eating."

"Oh."

"It's been feasting on these drakes, all right. Ants, too. I try to get the guts and the gills out as soon as possible. Spoils the meat otherwise."

He pulled some ferns off the nearby bank, lined the bottom of his wicker creel with them like bedding in a casket, and slipped in the gutted fish. He appeared to admire it a moment before closing the lid. Then he took a silver flask from one of the innumerable pockets of his fishing vest and presented it to Maggie.

"Drink?"

"Yes. I think so." She unscrewed the top and took a stiff slug.

"Nature red in fang and claw," he repeated jovially and took a swallow himself.

Harold lost a trout in the next pool and threw back another tiddler in the one after. By now Maggie had recovered her emotions and, influenced by the slug of Scotch, regained an interest in what Harold was doing.

"Can I try a cast?"

"I told you, tomorrow."

"Aw come on. Don't be so rigid."

"All right," Harold said. "Go ahead and try." He handed Maggie the rod.

"I've been watching you very carefully."

"Uh-huh. And what if you actually hook a fish?"

"I'll, uh . . . take care of it."

Harold gestured toward the riffle ahead and said, "Have at her, pal." He moved gingerly around to Maggie's left to get out of the way of her casting arm.

"Gosh, this rod's light as a feather," she noted.

"You're holding a thousand bucks worth of graphite."

"Golly!"

"And if you break it, you have to buy me a new one."

She shot him a worried glance.

"Just kidding. It's practically indestructible."

Maggie prepared to imitate what she'd seen Harold do. The rod felt altogether alien in her grip, though Harold had made the procedure seem so simple and straightforward. It is fair to say that she did not come close to approximating the correct method of casting. She immediately snagged the fly in an overhanging willow branch some twenty feet behind her.

"Oops," she said.

"Not as easy as you thought, is it?"

"No. You were right. It's rather difficult."

"Takes practice."

She sheepishly handed the rod back to Harold. He had to break off the leader and reattach all the terminal tackle—tappet, blood knot, and everything. It took a good ten minutes, during which Maggie sat on a rock, like a wood nymph being punished by the river god. On his second cast to the riffle ahead, just above a downed log, Harold hooked on to a fourteen-incher. And that was all they needed for supper.

6
∽ A Long Trip to a Strange Land ∽

They set a table on the deck overlooking the river. Maggie fried some green tomatoes to accompany the two trout, which she sautéed in olive oil with shreds of prosciutto. A creamy red pepper and cabbage slaw completed the picture. By the time she brought their plates outside, a few mauve streaks of underlit cloud lurking in the treetops were all that remained of the eventful day. A warm darkness enveloped the river. The green lights of fireflies flickered festively above the bracken. Harold lit a kerosene lantern for the table, pulled the cork from the Pouilly-Fuissé, and filled their glasses. They were both so ravenous that they ate silently in sheer animal introspection for several minutes.

"Sorry if I was tough on you down there," Harold said at length, as he spread butter thickly over a square of cornbread, wielding his knife as though he meant to physically subdue it. "I get into this ridiculous he-man mode around woods and water."

"No, you were right," Maggie admitted. "How many times have I slipped a fish into a hot pan without thinking that somebody had to take its life? One ought to be more . . . *responsible*! Oh, I'm really so glad I came, you dear man."

The *dear man* made Harold blink.

"I savor each day here," he said, "knowing how few there are left."

She lifted a forkful of fish without eating, ingesting his remark instead.

"Why summer's barely begun," she said. "I don't think it even officially starts until the twenty-first of the month."

"The man in the bright nightgown doesn't go by the calendar."

"Who?"

"The Grim Reaper," Harold said. "Death."

"I'm sorry," Maggie said, putting down her fork. "This is a bit abstruse for me. Did you say death?"

"I did."

"Don't be morbid, dear."

"Isn't it death that gives life its savor?"

"I suppose."

"Those mayflies we saw on the river live but a single night in their adult form. That brief one-night life they spend seeking a mate. They don't even eat—"

"Now, that *is* dreary," Maggie interjected, her mouth full of slaw.

"In fact they're no longer equipped with the organs of digestion. They're just little flying sex machines. At dawn, having achieved their reproductive destiny, they drop exhausted onto the film of the water, their little wings outstretched like miniature angels. And there the trout gobble away all trace of their existence."

"You make it sound so . . . operatic."

"Imagine your whole life crammed into a single night! The intensity of it!"

"I prefer dragging it out. There's the change of seasons, for instance."

"Still, Maggie, you must consider that we're not going to live forever."

"I refuse to dwell on it. There's too much to be done in the here and now. A lovely dinner to eat, for instance." She wielded her fork again and stabbed a piece of fried tomato.

"Sometimes one has no choice."

"Certainly you have a choice. A person's attention really is limited and life is a matter of what we pay attention to."

"A diagnosis changes all that," Harold said, quaffing his wine and refilling his glass.

"You're being awfully enigmatic," she said, finishing her wine, too, as if bracing herself for some blow. "A diagnosis of what."

Harold refilled her glass before he uttered the word: "Cancer."

"Cancer?" Maggie said. "Who? You?"

Harold, rather than answering verbally, merely cocked his head in reply, as though he had received an award and extreme modesty were in order.

"Wait a minute," Maggie said. "You're saying you've got cancer?"

Harold nodded.

"What kind?"

His eyes went glassy as if some rogue memory had momentarily distracted him. Then they refocused on her. "Pancreas," he said.

"Oh, God," Maggie said, pushing her plate forward." You don't look . . . ill."

"It's a subversive little bastard," Harold said gloomily.

"How long have you . . . had it?"

"Something came up on the blood test in a routine checkup last month. I was sent to an oncologist—horrible-sounding word, isn't it? Oncologist. It reeks of angst and misery. Yeccchhh. Anyway, he gave it to me pretty straight. Frankly, I don't know how a fellow can do that, what, ten, twenty times a day, without becoming an alcoholic."

"Do what?" Maggie said weakly.

"Tell people it's checkout time."

"I don't know what to say."

"Nothing *to* say. Let's drink to life."

He raised his glass as though to make a toast.

Maggie gazed into her lap as tears pooled in her eyes.

"Don't start," Harold said.

She began to blubber uncontrollably.

"Cut that out, right now, Maggie Darling."

But there was no ordering the emotions around. The human heart is not an underling in an office. Maggie cried exuberantly for several minutes while Harold finished his trout, his slaw, his tomatoes, and slathered another piece of cornbread with butter.

"How can you just sit there, eating?" Maggie finally said, blowing her nose in the paper napkin.

"What do you think I should do? Run around and holler? Volunteer for clinical experiments? Fly off to Lourdes?"

"It's so unfair."

"I wouldn't even say that. I've had sixty-one good years. That's more than Babe Ruth and Mozart. Never had to go to war. Enjoyed life in a great city. Ran a fine company. Knew a lot of interesting people. It would be indecent to whine."

"Can't anything be done?"

"Not a goddamned thing. This thing I've got is one of the deadliest there is."

"Then what *are* you going to do?"

"I'm going to follow my normal routines until I get too sick to carry on. Then it's off to a friendly little hospice run by monks over in Montpelier. I've scoped it all out. Helluva smooth way to go."

"You talk about this as though you were planning a vacation."

"Well, what is it but a long trip to a strange land? Say, what's for dessert?"

"Do you expect others to act normal around you? As if this ghastly thing weren't happening?"

Harold sighed. "No, I suppose I have to let you get over the shock. But if you're really interested in my well-being, I'd encourage you to normalize as soon as possible. For instance, tell me, what's for dessert?"

"Some lovely St. Andre and ripe pears."

"Nothing for the old sweet tooth?"

"There's chocolate bars."

"Oh, goody. I'll fetch the cognac."

7
⤳ Glory Days ⤳

Maggie proceeded to get rather drunk. Harold began reminiscing about the old times and old friends, about what it was like to come to New York as a young man in 1961, the year when Mantle and Maris were at Yankee Stadium, and Jack Kennedy was in the White House, and real writers hung out at P. J. Clarke's on Third Avenue, and Norman Mailer turned up at all the parties along with Ken Tynan and Gay Talese, and occasionally someone as legendary as Auden would blow into a Greenwich Village apartment, and "La Vie en Rose" always played at their favorite little French place with the stuffed pheasants in the window off Sheridan Square—what *was* its name?—and the Met was free in those days, and a bottle of good Scotch was six bucks and a rib-eye steak $4.95, and you could get a splendid apartment with a working fireplace on East Sixty-third Street for two hundred simoleons, and people still got married and had their wedding parties at the University Club, and the fabulous Ernie Kovacs did that utterly insane half-hour TV show on Thursday nights, and there were no sniveling guitar pluckers cluttering up Easthampton, and remember Checker cabs . . . !

This was the renowned Harold Hamish charm they wrote about in *Vanity Fair* and *PW*. He glowed like a hearth. The night was warm and soft. The cognac, a Kelt Amiral, was outstanding, the chocolate kept Maggie reasonably alert, and she quite enjoyed hearing about that bygone world of America at its supreme imperial moment before everything went to hell. But, of course, the ghastly backdrop of Harold's illness remained with them, like a terrible beast of prey waiting beyond the glow of a campfire. It was exhausting simply to be reminded of it. So, when he paused at the conclusion of some anecdote about the extraordinary drinking exploits of one Malachy McCourt, a Manhattan bar owner, Maggie begged Harold to excuse her for bed.

"You've been sweet to listen to such a prating old windbag," he said.

"I love the old stories," she said and came around the table to give him a good-night hug. There was a wonderful smell in his clothes, a masculine scent of juniper and exertion. He kissed her more than once in the tender spot beside her ear and held her tightly in his arms just a moment longer than she felt was wise. Then, with a twinge of regret or guilt, she wasn't sure which, she left him on the deck and went up to bed.

8
⟲ The Sonata ⟳

She read Bartram's *Travels* for a while. It was lovely reading by the light of the oil lamp. The room smelled reassuringly like camp when she was a girl: pine straw, old blankets, unpainted wood. Harold remained out on the deck for while, drinking, she supposed. Then he clomped around downstairs putting things away. Finally, she heard his footfalls on the creaking stairs. For an electric moment, she held her breath wondering if he might come into her room and what on earth she would do if he did. But then she heard his door open and shut and his bedsprings creak as he shifted this way and that and then silence. Maggie didn't know whether to feel grateful or cheated.

She awoke sometime later in the darkness to feel him in her bed pressing up against her back spoon-wise, a large hand cupping her shoulder. Oddly, her first thought was, This is not Kenneth. She feigned sleep a few moments longer, trying to think tactically. In fact, the sensation of the large warm presence behind her, and her own mammalian response to it, quite hampered her thinking. Moreover, her head felt uncomfortably hollow from all the drinking, like a cored winter squash. Harold buried his nose behind her ear and kissed her as he had earlier. A tremendous chemical rush quickened the nerve endings throughout her body and urged her to surrender to sheer sensation. Harold moved his hand strategically to her hip, pausing to caress it before moving on to the complicated topography of her right breast, exploring the nipple at its eminence and emitting a little groan of longing to which Maggie could not help but reply in kind. Moments later, she had swiveled around so they were face-to-face, lips-to-lips, and hips-to-hips until she opened to him like a great night-blooming flower. She made love with him without a word being spoken.

He was powerful and deliberate. In his lovemaking he had the quality of a master musician playing a sonata on a rare and valuable instrument, sure yet careful, and he displayed that paradoxical stamina of the older man who can soldier stolidly through a long and elaborate piece of music, never flagging, without reaching the highest pitch of emotional intensity too soon. In their heavings and pantings she lost track of time and gave herself to him repeatedly, each time thinking, strangely, that the very galvanic power of her pleasure might infuse him with enough vitality to battle and perhaps even vanquish the molecular monster that threatened his existence. Finally, she felt him release himself with a plangent sob, and they both sank wordlessly spent into a cool, pine-scented oblivion.

9
⤳ The Proposal ⤳

The same odd thought visited her upon awakening: this is not Kenneth . . . She quickly amended it, telling herself, But it is dear, dear Harold, and rolled over to find him yet engrossed in slumber. A trapezoid of morning sunlight glowed on the wall opposite the window. Quarreling blue jays made shadows in it like Balinese puppets. So, Maggie reflected, they had crossed the frontier of friendship and professional fellowship into the uncharted territory of conjugality. In light of his illness, was it a tragic error or a kind of mutual gift that transcended ego if not time? What would they do now? Pretend to have a future together? Or was this perhaps nature's way of telling her not to try to plan everything, to let go, to give up the perpetual struggle to control persons and events? For what could one do in the face of such a fatal diagnosis? Perhaps Harold was right to submit to the inevitable as gracefully as possible. He stirred and opened his eyes.

"Why it's you, Maggie Darling, my dream girl."

"You're very sweet."

"I've hungered for you like a mad dog for years—"

"You concealed it nicely."

"—waiting for you to ditch that reprobate husband of yours."

She looked away, their nearly futureless fate glaring at her like the trapezoid of sunlight on the wall. It was something of a relief to her that he drew her close to him again and commenced to perform a feat of stimulation that made her forget the train of doubts and regrets that rushed so obstreperously down the main track of her mind. Then he was upon her like the night before, a magnificently subtle engine generating heat and sparks. He made love, she thought, the way a prisoner on death row might take his very last meal, in desperate delectation. When the act reached its gratifying denouement, she could only wonder what perverse power of manners or psychology had kept her out of Harold's arms all these years until now, when it was nearly too late. The idea reamed her with sadness, yet she dared not express it.

"Say, I'm so hungry I could eat this book," Harold declared, hoisting the Bartram. "How about some breakfast."

Yes, breakfast, Maggie thought. Her sadness dissolved as she began to imagine the many ways to feed Harold magnificently and defeat the beast of illness that lurked inside him.

She ended up making pancakes because Harold asked for them—though he called them, winningly, "flapcakes." There was plenty of real maple syrup on hand. This was Vermont, after all, where they sold the stuff in gas stations. While rashers of thick-cut cob-smoked bacon sputtered in a cast-iron pan, and the espresso pot heated on a back burner, and Maggie attended the delicate assembly of the cornmeal and buckwheat batter, Harold sat at the end of the great table tying caddis flies for the day's fishing. Mozart filled the house with brilliance. The day could not have been more perfect. Soon, she presented his stack of buckwheat and corn flapcakes with a garnish of cranesbill geranium. There was something in Harold's grateful smile that made her want to give herself to him carnally right there, and on a wild impulse she ducked under the table and serviced him in the continental style before he tucked into his all-American breakfast.

"My God, but you are a great artist, Maggie," he said when she resurfaced.

"I want so desperately to make you happy."

"Then marry me."

She felt a sensation in her brain equivalent to tripping on a dark woodland path.

"Harold, dear, there's the divorce. It could take months."

"What's a few months?"

Maggie blinked more than once, unable to reply.

"Oh, I see what you're thinking," he said, slashing his pancakes this way and that so as to reduce the whole stack to bite-size shreds. "Well, I've got a bit of good news."

"What's that?"

"I'm not really ill."

"You're not ill?"

"I'm as healthy as a Brahman bull."

"Is this what they mean by the denial stage?"

"Denial? Pish posh."

"Really?"

"Really."

"Wait a minute. You're saying you're okay?"

"Yes. Aren't we lucky?"

"What about the . . . the oncologist?"

"A literary embroidery."

"Oh?"

"Maggie, the plain truth is, I don't have cancer. I just said that to, uh, break the ice."

"Why you perfect pig," she said, seizing his plate and flinging the contents all over his face and chest.

She was packed and out the door in under one minute. What a lovely day to walk down a country road, she kept telling herself, lest she go to pieces. A minute or so later she heard Harold putter up beside her in the Morgan.

"Aren't we overreacting a little here?" he ventured.

"You don't exist, except as a ghost of a pig."

"Oh, Maggie . . ."

She marched straight ahead, lips sealed.

"You're blowing this all out of proportion," he said, wearing his desperation rather visibly now.

No reply.

"Am I to think that you were only interested in me because you thought I was dying?"

The stone wall.

"Get in the car, Maggie."

She quickened her step.

"You don't even know where you're walking. It's miles to anywhere."

She advanced undeterred.

"You goddamned willful bitch!"

He swerved ahead into her path, cutting her off. She stopped marching. He leaped out of the car, slamming the door, and hurried around it to confront her bodily. She thought he looked rather ridiculous out on the road in his silk Japanese bathrobe.

"Get in the car, Maggie," he growled.

Though something about his costume may have inspired her subconsciously, Maggie was quite untutored in the martial arts; perhaps his bobbing Adam's apple just presented an irresistible target. She didn't even feel as though she struck it very hard, but the blow produced immediate and impressive results. Harold crumpled beside the right front fender and began making a peculiar and unpleasant noise as of steam escaping an old clogged pipe. Pitiful as he was, it took a moment for Maggie to decide not to attend to him. Instead, she went around to the driver's side, tossed her bag into the passenger seat, and threw the tight little gear shift into first while acquainting herself with the brake and clutch positions.

"Aaaarrggghhh . . ." Harold said. She peeled out, raising a plume of gravel and dust that obscured him until she rounded a bend and his croaking was subsumed by the rich country verdure.

∽ Part Nine ∾

Penultimate Disasters

I

⤳ The State of the Nation ⤳

"... so I ditched the car in Windsor and found a kid at the gas station who was willing to drive me home for a hundred dollars and expenses," Maggie said, digging into her smoked duck salad with a *chilpotle* lime dressing. Christy Chauvin gazed across the table with a sly smile that seemed to signify approval. Maggie had unloaded in minute detail not only the sordid saga of her night in the country with Harold Hamish but also the unfortunate amorous incidents with Swann and Reggie that had preceded this latest debacle. The lunchtime crowd at Tontine, on Columbus Avenue and Eighty-first Street, could not help stealing glances at their table, even though Christy wore nothing more provocative than a V-necked J. Crew T-shirt and jeans and Maggie was virtually hiding inside an Hermes scarf. "He was a nice boy," Maggie added of the young Vermonter, "but when we passed Hartford he asked me if it was New York City."

"Couldn't read, huh?"

"I didn't ask but it was pretty obvious. The exit signs for Hartford were as big as the side of a barn. Can you imagine?"

"You'd be surprised how many Americans can't read," Christy said. "I work with Literacy Volunteers. It's an enormous scandal, a kind of national dirty secret."

"Fifty years ago everybody could read. Domestic servants. Hotel bellboys. Grease monkeys. My Grandma Elsie read Thackeray out loud to us on the front porch on summer nights—and she spent the first half of her life in Czechoslovakia."

"Some of the adults I tutor actually graduate from high school as functional illiterates. They can't read their diplomas," Christy said.

"How is that possible?"

"Nobody gets left back anymore. It's called social promotion."

"What will become of us?"

"We may forfeit our democratic institutions," Christy said, addressing her scallop, arugula, and Peruvian blue potato napoleon. "We'll become a crazy quilt of bickering regions inhabited by morons and governed by scoundrels. California will secede first, then the Pacific Northwest, the old South, eventually the Great Lakes states will go their own way, and so on."

"Good gracious. You mean the end of the United States?"

"Well, yes."

"What about the . . . uh . . . the national defense?"

"We'll have more to worry about from the yahoos in North Carolina than the Islamofascist suicide bombers," Christy said. "I just wrote a piece for *Commentary* about this. I can fax you a copy if you like."

"The end of America," Maggie mumbled introspectively. She had lost her appetite. Would there still be a Fourth of July? she wondered. And what about Thanksgiving? "I'll miss it horribly," she declared.

"Civilizations rise and fall," Christy said, reaching for a square of Tontine's signature shallot focaccia. "History is merciless."

"And I thought men were a problem."

"Well, they are. They just aren't the *only* problem."

Maggie silently watched Christy eat for a while.

"Now that you know what a hash I've made of my love life," Maggie said, "would you mind my asking how you manage yours?"

"I'm a virgin," Christy replied at once, guilelessly.

Maggie gagged on her Pellegrino water, and some of it worked up through her nostrils. The ensuing coughing spasm gave the other diners another excuse to stare at their table.

"You're putting me on," she eventually croaked.

"I'm quite serious," Christy said.

"Excuse me for appearing astonished, but how is that even possible in your line of work?"

"Simple determination."

Maggie leaned over and whispered. "Are you telling me you've never had sex?"

"I've . . . touched myself. Everybody does."

"I mean with another person. Weren't you going with that Arlie Hodge, the movie star?"

"We dated a few times."

"You didn't sleep together?"

"We did some smooching."

"And you were never tempted to go all the way?"

"Of course I was. I was tortured by it."

"But you never gave in?"

"Well, no."

"Why?"

"Because I knew he could never be my husband."

Maggie was having such a hard time processing this information that her eyebrows appeared to be at war with each other.

"You are an even more remarkable person than I thought," was all she could finally say.

"I suppose I must seem like a freak."

"What did you tell Arlie?"

"I told him he just wasn't the one."

"How did he take it?"

"He cried."

"Oh, God, how mortifying."

"He's a nice boy. That's why I was attracted to him in the first place."

"Well, then, what was wrong with him?"

"There were no books in his apartment. He promised to get some if I would sleep with him, and that's when I knew it was hopeless."

"I see what you mean."

"Oh, Maggie. What I've told you is terribly personal. I hope I can depend on you to keep it confidential."

"I will. My word of honor."

"Word of honor," Christy mused. "How strange to hear another woman say that."

"Maybe I'm a freak, too," Maggie said. "I can tell this is the beginning of a beautiful friendship."

2
⤳ A Close Encounter ⤳

They were saying good-bye in the heat out on Columbus when a beige panel truck pulled up with a *skreek* of rubber and double-parked in front of Tontine's crimson canopy. Six furtive figures wearing camouflage jumpsuits and ski masks hopped out of the van's side door and hurried toward the restaurant. One of the figures collided with Maggie and spun her around as though they were performing a clumsy ballroom dance move from the 1940s. For a moment their eyes interlocked, and Maggie was sure she had seen the brown-flecked hazel irises somewhere before. It was as though they belonged to a former lover, someone with whom she had known the most powerful intimacy. The figure made a strange gerbil-like *gleeping* sound that was also vaguely familiar. Then he roughly disengaged himself and followed the others inside. Maggie was still caught up in the bewilderment of the encounter when she realized that the camo-clad figures had been carrying firearms.

She grabbed Christy's hand and ran uptown on Columbus. At Eighty-second Street, with Christy in tow, Maggie ducked inside a shop that specialized in expensive acrylic decor: clocks, pepper mills, photo frames, telephones, and the like.

"Call the police," Maggie shrieked to a clerk with an arresting pink hairdo, who looked like a piece of fluorescent plastic decor herself. "They're robbing Tontine!"

The clerk lunged for a phone, dialed 911, and, enunciating very clearly and calmly, reported the robbery in progress. Maggie was impressed. It was the kind of grace under pressure she prized in her own kitchen employees.

"You're not from here, are you?" Maggie observed.

"Salisbury, Maryland," said the girl, who couldn't have been over twenty-five. "It's real different down there."

"Do you cook, by any chance?"

"I make the best smothered chicken on the Upper West Side, if I do say so myself," the girl replied. "And a darn good chess pie."

Maggie was thrilled. "Let's talk later," she said, extracting a card from her handbag. "The pink hair has got to go, though."

"Whatever . . ." the girl said with a shrug.

"Hey, they're coming out," Christy reported from the door.

The three women peered down the avenue and saw the masked figures briskly exit the restaurant with their boxy machine guns and sacks of loot. Moments later their beige van swerved out into southbound traffic and vanished.

Maggie and Christy hurried back down to the scene. The police cruisers skidded up a good seven minutes later. Half of Tontine's patrons had spilled out onto the sidewalk. They percolated with that same odd mixture of giddy excitement and indignation Maggie had observed after the Four Seasons robbery months earlier.

"I saw the getaway car," she volunteered to a cadaverous-looking detective.

"That's nice," the cop said.

"It was a beige van."

"Super."

"You don't even care."

"Lady, we know this bunch. They use a different vehicle on every job. All stolen right before and ditched right after. Next time, do me a favor and shoot out the tires."

3
⤳ The Fence ⤳

The Crumpled Coverlet was an overpriced antiques salon in New Canaan owned by a vicious old queen named Robert Twelvetrees who lived to spread vile, if often truthful, gossip about the sundry celebrities who populated Fairfield County, Connecticut. Maggie happened to stop in there because it was next door to a bakery that produced a particularly sinful large, hazelnut-studded, brownielike cookie called "the Brown Death" (which Maggie permitted herself to devour only when in a state of horrible anxiety). And, because she could hardly bear the prospect of returning to Kettle Hill Farm to the usual avalanche of messages, obligations, requests, responsibilities, and painful memories that awaited her there, she desperately sought any excuse to delay her arrival.

Maggie was therefore dawdling in the center room of the Crumpled Coverlet, finishing the last morsel of her cookie—with Mr. Twelvetrees buzzing in her ear like a large horsefly, emitting hurtful tidbits about this person and that person, and about who was divorcing whom—when she spied a familiar ruby ewer amid a display of other cut-glass objects atop a perfectly dreadful ormolu buffet. She seized the ewer and examined it closely.

Twelvetrees said, ". . . and I hear Eva Mosley is getting ready to dispatch the mister now—"

"Where did you hear that?" Maggie spun around angrily. "Eva Mosley happens to be a friend of mine."

"Well, whu, whu," Mr. Twelvetrees waffled in embarrassment, "she's a friend of mine, too, at least a customer, a very good customer, I should say, and—"

"And where did you acquire this object?" Maggie asked, thrusting the ewer into the proprietor's face.

"I, uh, came by it recently."

"This belongs to me," Maggie declared.

"Perhaps you have one like it—"

"No, I used to have one like it, but it disappeared about a month ago, and this is the very same one."

"Whu . . . whu . . . whu . . ."

"How did you get your mitts on this?"

"Look hear, Mrs. Darling."

"Don't you 'look here' *me*, buster. Receiving stolen goods is a crime in this state."

"What proof do you have that this ever belonged to you?"

"If you look on the bottom you will see the initials *M. D.* inscribed in the glass. Look."

She tilted the base just beneath his half-glasses so he could see. The initials were boldly visible. Twelvetrees read them and flinched.

"It could be a coincidence," he said, wilting.

"I put those initials there with my diamond wedding ring the very day I bought it at a rummage sale in Maine. Now, how did you get your hands on it?"

"Someone brought it in," Twelvetrees confessed. "I bought it fair and square."

"Who?"

"It's hard to remember. People come in here all day long."

"A man or woman?"

"A . . . a . . . a woman. Yes, a woman."

"What'd she look like?"

"Let me think . . ." he said. Little glistening beads of perspiration sprouted on his forehead. ". . . Uh, your age perhaps, medium height, short brown hair, rather scrawny—"

"Lindy!" Maggie yelped.

"Linty? No, I wouldn't say she was linty . . ."

"Oh, God . . ." Maggie cried, clutching the ewer to her stomach. "How much did you pay her for this?"

"I dunno. Perhaps a hundred."

"You slimy bastard."

"She seemed a p-p-perfectly respectable person. There was nothing linty about—"

"You know goddamn well what this object is worth, you chiseling creep."

"I'm in business, Mrs. Darling. The whole idea is to buy low and sell higher."

"What else have you bought from her?"

"Oh, a few little things now and again," Twelvetrees said. His hands trembled as his confidence ebbed away to nothing. "She was always as nice as pie."

Maggie now advanced until Twelvetrees's back was up against a Queen Anne bonnet-top highboy. He attempted desperately to loosen his cravat, as though to improve the airway.

"Did you buy a Lincoln and Foss coffee urn from her?"

"No! Well, I'm not sure. Perhaps—"

"How about a Canton Rose Medallion porcelain punch bowl?"

"Maybe. I don't recall—"

"Twelve Newell Harding fiddle-pattern soup spoons?"

"Soup spoons? We get scads of spoons—"

"A silver Revere porringer?" Maggie was beginning to shriek. Twelvetrees slumped and cringed before her.

"It's all a blur—" he cried.

"A Sunderland pink luster butter dish in the shape of a pig?"

"Stop—"

"A pair of Pennsylvania chalkware squirrel salters!"

"No more! No more!"

She had reduced him to little more than a damp quivering blob of cotton-covered protoplasm whimpering on the floor.

"Why you're nothing more than a common fence," she said.

"Mercy! Please!" he blubbered. "Don't call the police. You can have them all back. At no charge."

"Okay, I'll give you until noon to deliver my treasures, or you can contemplate spending your golden years in the state penitentiary at Deep River."

"Oh, God!"

"Stop caterwauling. Did you hear me?"

"Yes, yes, your things."

"And if any of them have been sold, you will pay the full appraisal price."

"Of course, full price."

"Don't bother getting up. I'll find my own way out."

4
⤙ Heartbreak ⤚

It was evening when she finally returned home. Walter Fayerwether evidently had left for the day. Shadows were long in the garden, endowing it with that buttery light that photographs so well. The beds and bowers had never looked so beautifully kept, even by the late and lamented Bob DiPietro. The garden was the one thing in her life these days that Maggie could recognize as maintaining its excellence and integrity. The house itself was empty . . . desolate. Maggie realized in a rush of emotion that the house had assumed the character of an adversary, an *enemy,* a thing to be feared and avoided. In the same instant she also saw what a personal tragedy this represented, for the house was the very polestar of her universe, and without it everything familiar would fly into a chaos. These personal griefs reverberated in her mind with Christy Chauvin's prophecies about the fate of the United States like a particularly discordant symphony by Stockhausen, nearly overwhelming Maggie with anxiety and depression.

As usual, she sought relief through activity, specifically in the painful matter of what to do about Lindy. For the first time in weeks, Maggie entered the guest room occupied by her erstwhile best friend. She was astonished to find that Lindy had transformed 264 square feet of perfect Shaker austerity into something that resembled a South Florida convenience store after a hurricane. Empty take-out food caskets, microwavable plastic casseroles, and pizza boxes lay strewn about everywhere along with candy bar wrappers, taco chip bags, cupcake packets, soda cans, chocolate milk cartons, and Styrofoam coffee cups—

not to mention moldy fragments of the food itself deliquescing into the rug. Soiled clothes lay in heaps. There were strange dried splashes of various liquids on the walls The bed was not just unmade but wildly disheveled, dirty, and stained, as though gladiatorial contests had taken place upon it, and the sheets stank. Literally hundreds of strange, tiny empty glass tubes were scattered around the floor—they crunched under-foot—and it took Maggie several moments to understand that these articles might have something to do with drug use. A larger glass tube on the bureau top looked like an instrument for the smoking of such illegal substances. The bathroom was unspeakable, the toilet unflushed for God knew how long, the shower curtain torn from half its rings, and something that resembled dried vomit in the tub. She wanted to set fire to the whole repulsive mess, but inasmuch as it was connected to the rest of the house, that was out of the question. Instead, she dole-fully fetched a roll of plastic garbage bags from the pantry downstairs and returned to begin the odious job of filling them with trash and Lindy's belongings (not necessarily distinguishable from the trash). This act of purification she performed with tears streaming down her cheeks and an ache in her chest that felt palpably like physical heartbreak.

She had actually managed to clear a considerable amount of de-bris when she realized that the task of truly rehabilitating the room would have to be completed by professional carters, fumigators, and painting contractors. Then, of course, there was the horrible prospect of telling Lindy to her face that she could no longer live at Kettle Hill Farm. That confrontation suddenly presented itself as Maggie heard a vehicle out in the driveway and doors opening downstairs and a clat-tering from the vicinity of the kitchen. She took a deep breath and set forth to dismiss her old friend from the household.

But it was Hooper, not Lindy who had turned up. He had a bag of groceries on the center island and stood downlit in a brilliant pool of halogen track lighting like a tragedian on a classical stage. They re-garded each other warily for a moment from across the large, compli-cated room.

"Your aunt Lindy's been stealing from us," Maggie said.

Hooper heaved a sigh but said nothing.

"I'll have to kick her out now," Maggie added gloomily.

"What did she steal?"

"Silver. Other stuff. Little treasures."

"I'm real sorry, Mom."

"It's breaking my heart."

"Is she here?" Hooper asked.

"No. Of course not."

"Then you don't have to kick her out right now."

"Well, it's as much as done. She's a drug addict, you know."

"I know she's . . . got problems," Hooper said, and as though to dispel a deeper inquiry into his personal conduct in the matter, he remarked, "This whole country is screwed up." He then began to unpack the grocery bag with strangely strenuous concentration. He had always been a physically deliberate boy, careful in his movements, but he performed this particular task as though he were a sapper disarming a bomb.

"What's with the groceries?" Maggie asked.

"I thought I'd make supper for us," Hooper said.

"That's an interesting idea. What's the occasion?"

"A farewell supper."

"Farewell to whom? This thing with Lindy is no cause for celebration."

"No. Me. I'm going away, Mom."

Maggie felt another little stab to the heart, though she knew perfectly well that it was mere maternal reflex. For practical purposes, the nest was already empty. She crossed the darkened space to the center island.

"What's for supper, then?" she asked.

"Smoked duck salad," he said, looking down at the various deli packets and little heads of endive and radicchio.

"Oh . . . ?"

"With a lime *chilpotle* dressing."

"You don't say?" Maggie exclaimed. "I had the very same dish this afternoon at . . ."

He finally looked up and their eyes met. There were the brown-flecked hazel irises she knew so intimately. A steely shiver ran down her spine. Time felt stretched out between them, an awful crevice in reality into which one could accidentally fall and disappear forever.

"Wait a minnute. I don't even want to ask," Maggie said.

"Don't then, Mom. Don't ask."

"It *was* you."

"Don't ask, Mom."

"I'm *saying*, not asking."

"Don't even say it."

"Do you know what kind of trouble you might be in?"

"All you need to know is that I'm leaving the country. I'm leaving all this insanity behind me for a while. No one will ever have to find out I was involved. Please, let's not talk about it."

It took a mighty effort for Maggie to drop it.

"All right, then," she finally said. "How about a drink. I could use one."

"Sure," he said.

Maggie fetched a bottle of unbelievably expensive 1974 Margeaux that she'd been saving for some celebration. Now that all her prospects and her only child's future seemed utterly hopeless, there seemed no reason to put off drinking it. She decanted it into a glass pitcher for a hasty aeration and then filled two crystal goblets. What a splendid wine, she thought, sloshing a sip over her teeth and palate. It left a tingly afterglow on her tongue. Big, lusty, and dark, it seized her senses like an animus out of the best erotic dream.

"Shall we make supper together?" she asked.

"Okay," Hooper agreed.

5
∽ Family Matters ∾

They worked silently. Maggie sliced the duck breasts and fanned them over the washed lettuces. Hooper, who had absorbed many of his famous mother's teachings by osmosis, simmered a dried *chilpotle* pepper in an inch of white vermouth until the essential smoky flavor was extracted. Meanwhile, he made a lime juice and olive oil mayonnaise in the food processor. When the vermouth was reduced to about a tablespoon of syrup, he discarded the brown *chilpotle* pod and combined the sepia liquid with the mayonnaise. Maggie garnished the two salad plates with a tangle of the thinnest raw Vidalia onion rings and a sprinkling of scarlet pomegranate seeds. She lit the four-taper candelabra on the farm table and they sat down to their supper of duck salad, a fresh baguette, and the superb red wine.

"This is somewhat better than Tontine's, I'd say," Maggie remarked.

Hooper only nodded.

"Better bread, for one thing. Where *are* you going, then?"

"France."

"When are you leaving?"

"Tomorrow."

"What'll you do there?"

"I want to paint and draw for a while."

"When did you take up art?"

"I'm taking it up now."

"Are you serious?"

"Yes, Mom. Don't look so shocked."

"I had no idea."

"Gauguin worked in a bank until he was thirty-five."

"You don't work in a bank."

"What I've been doing is just as pointless."

"I just never knew you were that interested in art."

"Maybe there's a lot you don't know about me."

"Apparently there is," Maggie retorted, and regrettably so, because Hooper clammed up again. She refilled their wineglasses and they
both addressed their plates sullenly. "What are you going to use for
money?" she ventured after a while.

"I have money," Hooper said.

"Did your father give you money?"

Hooper smiled for the first time since he'd entered the house
that night.

"What's so funny?" Maggie asked.

"I think Dad's broke," he said.

"You think that's funny?"

"Actually, yes, I do. Imagine Dad with no money. It's hysterical."

"Where did you hear this?"

"The gossip guy at MTV heard it from a guy at *Forbes*. *Forbes* is
going to run a piece about how Dad ruined himself."

"Isn't that lovely . . ."

"Well, you had your turn in *People,* Mom."

Maggie stifled an impulse to reach across the table and smack him
on the head.

"What happened to me is hardly comparable," was all she could
say in her defense. "I hardly ruined myself."

"I just don't think anybody in this family is in a position to cast
stones," Hooper said. When Maggie looked at him now, she had the
strange impression that she was seeing another sovereign adult. Her little
boy had vanished. "Anyway, you're doing all right financially, aren't
you, Mom, with all your books and business ventures?"

"How much do you need for this trip?"

"I'm not hitting you up for money," Hooper said. "I just want to make sure that you're okay, since Dad's tanked."

"Oh?" she said, a little nonplussed by his solicitude. "Gosh. Well, I'll be okay."

"You could always sell the house," Hooper said.

Maggie almost choked on a piece of duck. He suddenly looked like a boy again, callow, naive.

"What makes you think I'd ever sell this house?"

"I'm not saying you should. I'm just saying you could if you had to, that's all."

"I'm *not* selling this house," Maggie insisted nevertheless.

"Fine. Don't. You shouldn't."

"I can't believe you said that."

"Forget I said that, Mom. Okay? I know you love this place."

"Europe's very expensive these days, you know," she said with mounting anxiety. "The dollar doesn't go very far."

"I'll be all right," Hooper said. "I've got . . . resources."

"From robbing all those restaurants?" she blurted out.

"No," he said almost inaudibly.

"How'd you get it, then? From a minimum-wage internship at MTV?"

He glared across the table like a rabbit caught in headlights. "I told you not to ask."

"But I'm asking anyway. Just explain it to me so I don't think the whole world has gone mad."

"If I talk to you about this, will you promise not to ever mention it again, to me or anybody else?"

"Yes."

"All right," he said. "Go ahead and ask me whatever you want to."

She worked her thumb along the fine edge of her wine goblet.

"Those boys you robbed with—they were the boys in the band, weren't they? The ones who were here the night I returned from Venice?"

"Yes. Chill Az Def."

"You said they were making a fortune with their recordings."

"Yes. They're all millionaires."

"Then why on earth rob restaurants?"

"To *keep it real,* be genuine, authentic," Hooper said. "To *represent.* To live up to their public image. I know it sounds absurd, but they're actually pretty nice, normal guys when you get to know them."

"And they find it necessary to steal from defenseless people?"

"It's just theater, Mom. You of all people should understand that."

She tried to understand. She really did.

"The world *has* gone mad," she eventually said with resignation.

"This country certainly has," Hooper said. "That's why I'm leaving."

That was when Maggie started to blubber, right there at the table over the remains of her duck salad with *chilpotle* lime dressing. Hooper came around to her side and tried to comfort her. Indeed, she allowed him to shelter her in his arms, thinking all the while that her baby would be a fugitive from justice in a foreign land and that, unless he was rather lucky, the law would sooner or later pluck him from hiding and subject him to the grossest imaginable indignities and terrors.

"Look, Mom, I only went out with them on two jobs. This one today and Aureole months ago."

"Why?"

"To feel what it was like."

"Oh, dearest one," Maggie wept.

"Nobody got hurt. Nobody got caught. They'll never implicate me, even if they get caught. I helped make them stars by getting their video on MTV. They owe me everything."

"Oh, my darling Hooper. The world *has* gone absolutely mad."

6

∽ Always Room for More Madness ∽

She went to bed not long after that with a raging headache and a heart that felt like a sash weight and CNN *Headline News* playing lowly in the background to keep her company until she slid down the slippery slope of dreams. She was asleep, therefore, when CNN returned to the top of their news cycle at half past midnight, and she was dreaming something not quite coherent about a mountain of chocolate ganache when the newscaster led off the broadcast with a story about the decapitation of supermodel Christy Chauvin by an apparently deranged homeless man while returning to her apartment at Central Park West and Seventy-seventh Street.

∽ Part Ten ∽

Climactic

I

ᔕ The Burden of Memory ᔕ

She woke up to the thunk of yet another car door shutting, unaware that it was the taxicab bearing Hooper to the Westport Train Station and ultimately to Kennedy Airport. A note scrawled on a sheet of her own letterhead lay on the carpet in the hall right outside her bedroom door:

> Dear Mom,
>
> I couldn't face a tearful farewell so I am leaving early for the city and will catch a cab to the airport. Don't worry about me. Everything will work out just fine. I'll let you know how I am doing when I get settled somewhere (not sure whether France will work out or not). Everything is going to be all right, though. You'll see. I love you.
>
> Your son,
Hooper
>
> PS Am just leaving the Saab here. Don't sell it. I shall return!

She loved the "your son" part, as though there were another Hooper with whom this one might be confused. It almost made her forget for a moment the gravity of his situation. A mental film clip of an Easter egg lawn party, 1988, suddenly played across the cinema of her mind: little Hooper in his first blazer and tie, one shirttail out, of course, grass stains on the knees of his linen trousers, and her friends' little girl children in their white dresses, perfect little ladies except for the ice-cream smudges around their mouths that gave them an antic look of angels playing minstrels. Wasn't 1988 the year of cilantro and gravlax? Was that the same spring she discovered natural herbal dyes for the Easter eggs? Lovely mauves, pale gray-greens, straw yellow, and true indigo? The past was becoming cluttered like an attic that needed a thorough cleaning.

Her new constant companion, Monsieur le Anomie—a foreign gentleman in a dark suit who could be glimpsed (and then partially so) at the peripheral margins of vision—took his place at her side, right there in the upstairs hallway, and threatened to overwhelm Maggie with his eager solicitude. A deep instinct told her that the best way to shake him would be to immerse herself in some kind of purposeful activity, even if it felt at first as though she were going through the motions. Motion itself, she well knew, often magically transposed itself into purpose. Thank God for the upcoming Fairfield County League of Women Voters board of directors luncheon, she now recalled, only three days away!

She hurriedly navigated the gloomy, unpopulated hallway and stairs down to the kitchen. There she checked the catering manifest on the wall for a head count: thirteen hungry Women Voters board members. (Nevermind the ominous numerology, she paused to reflect; this was no time for side trips into the occult.) She could easily handle lunch for thirteen without assistance. It would be like the early days when she did it all herself—if not exactly fun then at least absorbing. In any case, the prospect of being saved from madness and despair by the challenges of cookery gave her sufficient reason to live for more than another twenty minutes. A menu took shape in her mind even as she put Johann Christian Bach on the stereo, switched off the monitor on the telephone answering machine, and made a pot of inky Irish tea. She even compelled herself to eat a ginger scone for energy and mental acuity, being a strong believer in, if lately not much of a practitioner of, breakfast.

She took her tea to the window. The sky outside was extraordinarily dark for a June morning. Gray-yellow clouds raced over the treetops like malicious wraiths hurrying to bring woe to the virtuous yeomen of southwestern Connecticut. The warm mug of tea clutched between her hands offered the only comforting counterpoint to these doomful intimations. Beneath this portentous sky, Walter Fayerwether just then stepped into view in the allée between the rose garden and the brick wall of espaliered plums. His crew of four followed and assembled around him. Fayerwether's blue denim shirt, buff khakis, and silver hair glowed against the darker background of green foliage. He stood with military aplomb, clipboard in hand, like a bomber pilot in a World War II movie, briefing the boys about their morning mission. The sight of him, so obviously capable, dedicated, and reliable both reassured and unnerved Maggie to such a confounding degree that she couldn't bear to gaze at him another moment. She therefore turned away from the window and fled into the alternate universe of cooking.

There were pâtés to make: a layered tricolor vegetarian affair constructed of beet, kale, and carrot—bound with white bean puree, gelatin, and egg—and a sturdy pork, duck, truffle, and prune composition she had first encountered in that wonderful little market street, the rue de Buci in St. Severin (the Eighth Arrondissement), that time she and Kenneth took the fast train from Paris to Lyon and brought the most extravagant picnic along (including, she now remembered with uncanny precision, a fantastic bottle of 1974 Château Lafitte). By the time she spooned the forcemeat into the prepared pans, draped with strips of Flag Harbor organic peppered Virginia bacon, her spirits had begun to lift. If M. Anomie was still in the room, then he was off in a corner absorbed in an activity of his own—perhaps a crossword puzzle titled "Hopeless Diphthongs."

2

↬ Just Gossip ↫

There were, next, the individual capon and chanterelle pies to prepare, including the laborious puff pastry caps for each ramekin. She had just finished the velouté when the doorbell sounded. It was Robert Twelvetrees, as promised. He had several cardboard cartons stacked beside the welcome mat.

"Thank you for coming," she said, feeling some regret over her treatment of him the day before, and hoping to palliate his obvious humiliation.

"Oh, I'm pleased and honored to be of service, madame," Twelvetrees retorted with unctuous, smiling sarcasm, and Maggie was at once sorry she had even attempted to be nice to the malicious old queen. "Ahem," he said, clearing his throat theatrically. "I've made every effort to account for each piece. Here's the list and the prices I paid to the, er, lady in question." He presented the document with a sinister flourish, reminiscent of Basil Rathbone playing Sir Guy of Gisborne.

"Is this all you paid?" Maggie said, gaping at the bill. The total came to $1,150.

"I should have thought you'd be pleased," Twelvetrees said.

"I'm shocked that you paid so little for all this. My ruby ewer alone was worth a thousand."

"I can revise the tally upward if it will make you happy, Mrs. Darling."

She squinted at him with loathing and wonder. "Wait here." She returned minutes later with a yellow bank check. The sight of it seemed to perk up Twelvetrees.

"I trust that there will be no further . . . uh, ramifications," he averred. "All this talk of the *authorities* and so forth makes a fellow feel less than entirely at ease."

"I just wanted my stuff back," Maggie told him wearily.

"Well then," he said, shifting swiftly into a cheerful gossiping mode while pocketing the check, "how about that fashion model?"

"Huh? What about whom?"

"The model who lost her head."

"Models are always losing their heads," Maggie said with eroding patience.

"No, this one really lost hers. And apparently it was quite a doozy. I guess you haven't seen today's papers."

"Actually, I haven't."

"Oh," Twelvetrees said, shifting into storytelling mode, "well, she was literally beheaded by a homeless man with a sword."

"A sword?" Maggie yelped, her stomach clenching.

"Yes, an 1861 U.S. Army dragoon's saber, to be precise. Said so in the *Post*. On Seventy-seventh Street right in front of that sunken entrance to the Museum of Natural History. He was a known character in the neighborhood. Fond of military garb, apparently. Called himself the 'Emperor of the New Age.'"

"Sounds like a lunatic."

"Oh, certifiable. He'd been hospitalized more than once. But you know how that works. Garbage in, garbage out. Anyway, he up and kills this poor young girl, carries the head three blocks to a sushi bar on Amsterdam Avenue in broad daylight, and sets it right there on a chair next to him. Can you imagine?"

"No. It's too horrible."

"And he just sits there with this head, as prim as a schoolboy, until the fellows in blue show up. What is this world coming to, Mrs. Darling?"

"I wish I knew," she said with the utmost sincerity. "Please just go now, will you?"

"Oh, of course, must mind the store," Twelvetrees said, his ability to deflect disgust seemingly boundless. "May I just say how lovely your home is and—"

"Say that but no more, please. I beg you."

"Ciao then . . ."

3
⤙ Seeing Red ⤚

When she returned to the kitchen, the genoise for her petits fours had cooled sufficiently to receive the requisite jam fillings and ganache icings. The operation took a good hour, and when completed, M. Anomie once again slid into view, glowering seductively from the pantry door. To keep him at bay, Maggie slapped together a brie sandwich, made more strong tea, and retreated to her safe, intimate, beloved sewing room upstairs.

There was the matter of Harold Hamish to be faced—their professional relationship beyond reclamation, she assumed. She was quite prepared to buy her way out of Trice and Wanker's contract for *Keeping House* by simply returning the rather enormous advance, but would they let go? Unfortunately, her agent Joyce Munger was not answering her cell phone (meaning, most likely, that she was at that moment enjoying an amorous interlude in the Sherry-Netherland Hotel with her lover of several months, Dr. Nathan Toth, Ph.D., the phenomenally successful author of *The Thirteen Sacred By-Laws of Successful Relationships* and *Everyman's Guide to Marital Fidelity*—the slut.

Why, Maggie despaired, did everyone have to confide in her? Why was there no one to whom she, Maggie, could turn? Of course, that very instant she realized such a figure *had* entered her life in the person of Christy Chauvin, whose telephone number she now dialed at once.

With each ring of the phone, Maggie's pulse quickened. Was she crying on Christy's shoulder too much? Would Christy think she was an emotional basket case? A pain in the ass who—

On the fifth ring the phone was picked up.

"Christy . . . ?"

"No," a man's voice replied.

"Excuse me? Is this 879-9673?"

"Yes it is."

"Well, who's *this*?"

"This is Lieutenant Pfeister."

"Excuse me. Did you say this is 879-9673?"

"Yes."

"Well, where is Christy Chauvin?"

"Who is this?"

"What does that matter?" Maggie retorted. "And where is Christy?"

"Are you a family member?"

"No, I'm a friend."

There was a pause on the line, a kind of peculiar aural chasm above which Maggie felt suspended, like an experienced acrobat who has just slipped and discovers to her great surprise that she is about to fall a long way.

"Miss Chauvin is dead," Lieutenant Pfeister said.

"What!?"

"I'm sorry," Pfeister said.

"When? How?"

"I'm sorry, ma'am. We're trying to keep this line open for family members—"

Maggie didn't so much reply as let out an animal-like howl of grief.

"—it's all in the papers if you really want to know—"

Maggie flung the cordless phone across the room, as though it were a piece of fruit suddenly discovered to harbor a disgusting infestation of moth larvae. It bounced off a framed watercolor of Vita Sackville-West's white garden at Sissinghurst, breaking the glass. Maggie sat on the edge of her wingchair shuddering with loss and horror. Somewhere outside the dubious security of the little windowless room, a commotion seemed to rise, but Maggie could barely distinguish it from the commotion in her heart. A tsunami of terror swept through her veins and it was suddenly hard to breathe, as though the Atlantic had somehow inundated lower Connecticut, sweeping everything into a maelstrom. Thinking she was about to drown, Maggie bolted out of the suffocating room, raced downstairs, and fled out the front door.

4
ᔕ The Storm ᔕ

A fierce and abnormal wind out of the southeast swept so violently through the trees that the pale undersides of their leaves now turned up against the turbulent, darkling sky like the little white faces of lost souls crying for heaven. Maggie struggled up the lanes of the orchard toward the rose garden, the world itself seeming to come apart all around her. Her mental boundaries felt as though they were dissolving. She could hardly tell anymore what she was running from or where she was running to—only that existence itself had become wholly fearsome, detestable, and indistinguishable from her tortured self. She could not even hear herself bawling in the din. The wind's velocity increased, bowed the trees, and made them groan. Then, things began to fly past her: branches torn off trunks, a blue tarpaulin, a squawking chicken, a peach basket. Something hit her in the back of the head and she went down like a hundred-pound sack of potting soil in the cold grass. What had at first seemed mere blunt force turned into sharp pain. She tasted dirt in her mouth. Then she felt herself virtually lifted, spinning, and carried—not on her own feet and not upright—an interminable distance and then dropped on a hard wooden floor in a very dark place. Something clapped and set the roaring world apart from her. Then someone was cradling her from behind.

"Don't hurt me," she heard herself say, thinking her own words very strange, even under these bewildering circumstances.

"It's only me," a voice said above the roaring.

"Kenneth?" she asked, stiffening.

"No, Walter."

She yielded to his cradling embrace. He was warm and sinewy and smelled of clean earth. He was like something that had risen out of the very ground to hold her tethered to the planet against this terrible revolt of the earth's elements. She recognized now that they were on the floor of the potting shed, braced in a corner among some old hardwood tomato stakes. When it seemed impossible that the wind could roar more loudly, an even greater and deeper tumult mounted behind it, not so much an atmospheric noise anymore but a tremendous basso vibration, as of tectonic forces cleaving the bedrock deep below Fairfield County. Then a fusillade of hailstones pelted the tin roof. She covered her ears and fairly burrowed under Walter's arm. The little building shuddered. Its single window shattered with a barely audible ping. As an immense dark force rocked the little building, they bounced up and down on the bucking floor. Then all thought and sensation was subsumed in the sheer brute energies of nature. Locked in an embrace of resignation, they retreated into the personal citadels of their own mumbled prayers as the world seemed to pitch and yaw around them.

Maggie had lost all sense of time, but eventually the commotion ceased, the vibration stopped, the rat-a-tat-tat on the roof ended, the roaring died down and became a thin, forlorn, empty whistling wind. The sound of her own blubbering alerted her to the fact of her survival. She peeled herself warily out of Walter's arms.

"What *was* that?" she asked breathlessly.

"I think it was a tornado," Walter said. He was shivering, though it was not particularly cold.

"This is Connecticut," Maggie said. "We don't get tornadoes here."

"The weather's not what it used to be," Walter said, laughing in release of his own terror as though at a quip from the *Old Farmer's Almanac*.

"I don't remember coming in—how did I get here?" Maggie asked.

"You were lying in the grass."

"Oh, yes, something hit me!" She reached for her head. "Ooooh."

"Let me see."

"Here. Back of the head."

"That's quite a goose egg."

"Stuff was flying all around. I've never seen anything like it."

"It was goddamn scary, wasn't it?" he said. "Wooooo . . . !"

"Thank you for . . . rescuing me, Walter," Maggie said. A tender emotion so strangely incongruous with the day's violent events stole through her like a warm cleansing current. "Walter . . ." she repeated to herself quietly as though practicing the sound.

"Yes?"

"I've never called you that before."

"No, you haven't."

"We've been so very . . . formal."

"You seemed to want it that way."

"Not really," she said.

They exchanged fraught glances.

"Let me help you up," he said.

"Is it all right then, for us to be just plain Walter and Maggie?" she asked. He had gotten off the floor and offered a sinewy hand to hoist her up.

"It's funny," he said. "My daughter refers to you as Maggie all the time. She's a great admirer of yours."

"I didn't know you had a daughter."

"You've seen her a dozen times."

"Huh?"

"The gal who picks me up every day. In the Volvo?"

"That's your daughter?"

"Yes."

It was Maggie's turn to laugh. The laughter poured out of her as though a ferment of wishing and dreading corked in an enormous vessel had finally burst out as a sweet froth of hilarity. "What's her name?" she asked.

"Sarah Jane," he said. "She's too shy to meet you."

"Shy?" Maggie gasped incredulously.

"She worships the loam in your perennial beds."

Maggie recalled the many instances when she'd seen Walter with the girl and stewed in preconscious resentment. "She's a very attractive young woman."

"You think so?"

"Obviously."

"I'm her father. Of course I think she's gorgeous. You know how fathers are."

The image of her own father, Frank, flashed intensely through her memory, a snapshot of him out of the 1960s as a younger man than Walter. He'd been trying to grow sideburns in an attempt to look "with it," as he always so embarrassingly said. The sideburns had lasted perhaps a year. By then, the family had broken up and Maggie was only seeing him on the occasional Saturday. He would drive into the city from Pennsylvania and take her to a different restaurant each time. He was a marvelously adventurous eater.

"I am such an ass," Maggie mumbled, emerging painfully from the interior arcade of memories. "All this time I thought she was your girlfriend."

Walter grinned. "Well, she thinks God's a woman and you're it," he said.

Somewhere outside a rooster shrieked. Through the paneless window in the distance they could see the storm clouds breaking up and shafts of sunlight beginning to penetrate the gloom.

"What do you say we have a look around outside?" Walter suggested.

"Quite right," she said, having a hard time taking her eyes off his. "Let's."

5
⮌ Debris ⮌

They emerged blinking from the potting shed. Broken branches lay strewn about everywhere. A rose arbor had blown clear over. The blue tarp had lodged in the crotch of the great white oak tree outside the north end of the ballroom. The house was still there, apparently intact, its roof in place. But as they made their way past the fern garden and the nuttery, Maggie could see that the intense storm had carved a path of devastation across the northwest corner of the property. At least three ancient maples along Kettle Hill Road had been savaged, uprooted, and toppled. The henhouse lay literally flattened and several birds stood dazed outside it like trailer park people in TV news footage of someplace like Arkansas. A beloved *Magnolia grandiflora,* the herald of spring at Kettle Hill Farm, tilted at a strange angle from partial uprooting, and many of its enormous shiny leaves had been stripped off. Her lovingly cultivated collection of rosemary topiaries on the terrace above the swimming pool was strewn about the flagstones, their terra-cotta pots smashed, and the pool itself looked like minestrone, there was so much vegetative flotsam in it. Maggie resumed weeping.

"Could have been a lot worse," Walter observed.

"I suppose . . ."

They continued up through the vegetable beds. The rest of the crew was up there, standing around dazed like the chickens.

"You guys all right?" Walter hailed them.

"It was a twister, a goddamn twister!" cried Chad, an earnest towhead of nineteen with aspirations to become a wildlife ecologist someday. "Just like in the movies!"

"I actually prayed for the first time in my life," said Ben, the youngest son of a boat-building family from Mystic, who was going to law school, nights, at UConn.

The hail had torn perfect bullet holes through the large rhubarb leaves. The first lettuce crop, nearly ready for the table, lay pummeled and shredded in its black earth bed. The sugar snap peas were ripped from their hemp supports. A marble sundial she'd found in Newport had toppled on the bluestone footpath and cracked into several pieces. Maggie gave up trying to compose a mental inventory of all the damage.

"I need a drink," she said.

"I understand," Walter said awkwardly.

"Don't take that the wrong way."

"No, I could use one myself."

"Okay then, let's go to the house. I've seen enough."

6
⤺ A Cry for Help ⤺

Maggie filled two pony glasses with Armagnac and resumed weeping again right there in the kitchen. She emitted a high, thin, hopeless keening noise.

"The world is coming to an end," she said.

"We'll have this place back to normal in two days," Walter said. "Just watch."

"You don't understand," Maggie bawled, and she proceeded to not altogether coherently relate all the catastrophes of recent months, not in strict chronological order, beginning with the murder of Christy Chauvin and weaving in the failure of her marriage, the unraveling of her professional life, the loss of her trusted colleagues, the criminal dalliances of her son, the sordid goings-on in her household, and even vaguely alluding to the botches and disasters of her love life.

". . . and now I've completely humiliated myself by telling you all this," she concluded, burying her face in a kitchen towel.

Before Walter could even respond, the phone rang. Maggie looked up from her towel, flinched, and regarded it with the utmost suspicion. It rang a second time and then a third.

"That could be Sarah," Walter said. "You know, the storm and all."

"You answer it then," Maggie replied breathlessly.

"Maggie Darling's house," he said with a sort of plain, cheerful assurance. "Let me see if she's in." He covered the mouthpiece with his broad suntanned hand. "Are you in?"

"Who is it?" she mouthed the words.

"Who's calling?" he inquired. "It's Lindy," he said, lowering the phone. A barrage of harsh squawking issued from the handset.

Maggie lunged for it.

"I could kill you," she said.

"I only borrowed it, okay?" Lindy protested.

"Borrowed it! You sold it!"

"How could I sell it? I'm talking on it."

"Talking on what?"

"Your cell phone. I borrowed it."

"My cell phone?"

"Yeah, from your car."

"Oh, Lindy, you've become so wicked. You sold all my little treasures."

"This isn't the time, Maggie," Lindy replied. Her voice was suddenly ragged and pitiful, a haunted cry from an abyss.

"Where are you?"

"Not sure. Oh, I know I've been bad. You gotta get me out of here." There was some commotion in the background. Glass breaking, unintelligible cries, a profane objurgation, a groan. "I'm in hell, baby."

"Where are you?"

"Hartford, I think. That fucker Julio got me so fucked up."

"Julio . . . ?"

"He split on me."

A woman shrieked in the background

"Lindy, who are these people—?"

"Oh, Maggie, don't ask, don't start with a million questions. He loved me for who I am, okay. He didn't give a shit about Hollywood, or Smith College, or Great Neck or white people or black people or whatever."

"So, why doesn't he bring you home?"

"I told you, he split. Besides, I have no home," she whimpered.

"Of course you have, despite everything."

"Anyway, he's out of the picture—hey, get the fuck away from me, asshole—!" Sounds of a scuffle, a thump, a cry of pain.

"Lindy!"

"I'm here, babe."

"What is going on in there?"

"Fucking crackheads."

"You're with crackheads?"

"I'm in hell, Maggie, hell. Don't you understand?" More bawling.

"Lindy! Lindy, this place you're in—"

"A shitty hole in a shitty neighborhood in a shitty city."

"What does the building look like? So we can find you!"

"It used to be a Masonic temple, I think," Lindy said, suddenly giggling. "Greenish roof. Big brick monstrosity. There's a park out there. Oh, I don't know. I'm so fucked up, baby. You gotta help."

"Lindy, Lindy, listen to me. Call the police and—"

"Are you crazy? I can't call the police!"

"Why not?"

"These are, like, my friends."

"Your friends!"

"Well, not my friends. But—ah, forget it."

"Wait, wait, Lindy—"

"I'll just fucking die here, okay? Bye, Maggie."

Click.

"I can't believe it," Maggie muttered. "She hung up on me."

"Who was that?"

"My college roommate. You've seen her around here, I'm sure. Dark hair. Very slender. Has a different boyfriend every week."

"Uh-huh. I've seen her."

"She's been staying with me. Lots of personal problems. Her husband—it's a long story. Too long." Maggie fidgeted, turning this way, now that way, as if wondering where to move first.

"And you say she's with crackheads?"

"Apparently so. Oh, Walter, we've got to go rescue her!"

"Hadn't we better call the police?"

"Right! The police! Of course! *We'll* call the police!"

Maggie pulled herself together and got back on the horn at once. With all the spiffy new computerized directory assistance programs, it took a quarter of an hour to get the number for the Hartford police; this number directed her to another computerized labyrinth of menu choices operated by the police themselves, which routed her ultimately to the limbo of perpetual *hold,* a virtual place of no return that was audially wallpapered with festive salsa Muzak in the manner of the late Tito Puente.

"I can't believe this country of ours," Maggie moaned and slammed the phone down.

"Just dial 911."

She did, and she was soon speaking to a real, live Westport policeman.

"Hello!" Maggie said. "God, I'm so grateful to have a live human being on the line."

"What can we do for you?"

"A friend of mine, a close friend . . . well, I got a call a little while ago . . . she's . . . I think she's stuck in a crack house in Hartford."

"Stuck?"

"Unable to leave."

"Is that what she said?"

"In so many words."

"Have you called the Hartford police?"

"I got lost in their phone system. It's a computer."

"Hartford is not our jurisdiction, ma'am."

"Sure. But I thought you might know how to get through to them. Don't you have two-way radios?"

"And what was it you wanted us to ask them to do?"

"To help my friend."

"Do you know where this alleged crack house is?"

"Not exactly. No."

"No address?"

"It used to be a Masonic temple, we're told. There's a green roof . . . a park."

"Is there a street and a number?"

"Well, no."

"Do you know how many crack houses there are in the city of Hartford?"

"Could there be more than a couple?"

The policeman laughed out loud.

Maggie's spirits flagged again. She wanted to smash the phone against her own head.

"Can't you help us?"

"I can't call Hartford and tell them that somebody from Fairfield County is patronizing one of their fine crack houses."

"No, of course not."

"And you don't have an address?"

"No."

"Ma'am," the policeman said. "We've got kind of a situation here and I've got to keep these lines open—"

"Did that storm do a lot of damage in Westport?"

"What storm?"

"We had a terrible storm in West Rumford. A tornado, we think."

"You don't say."

"Oh, it was frightful."

"Well, alls we had was some thunder 'n' lightning. Right now, we've got a gunman pinned down off the Merritt Parkway at Hoyt Swamp."

"The sniper!"

"We don't know if it's the same guy. I'm going to hang up now, ma'am. Whatever you do, I advise you to stay off the Merritt today. Looks like this bird is dug in with plenty of ammo. Bye now."

"Bye . . ."

Maggie indulged in no more than a minute of pure despair, savoring its hollow contours and jagged surfaces. Then she looked up and locked eyes fiercely with Walter, and the two of them spoke the same words simultaneously, with the same grim determination.

"I guess we'll have to do it ourselves," they said, scouring each other's faces and marveling at the revealed synchronicity of their intentions.

7
⤙ The Searchers ⤚

Maggie slapped together two pâté and sourdough bread sandwiches, and they left directly in the Toyota Land Cruiser. Her head still throbbed so Walter drove. Everything about the afternoon seemed several degrees out of kilter. The fractious weather produced a strange ponderous light that seemed to weigh down upon the landscape like a bad destiny. The landscape itself sprawled awkwardly along the enormous highway in a panorama of doom, a wilderness of gigantic discount stores, free parking, and screaming signs that left the mind wounded and exhausted. The Connecticut of the old *New Yorker* cartoons and the Bing Crosby movies had been displaced by a diseased, surreal terrain of glowering plastic and heat-trapping asphalt, an endless, hopeless, futureless automobile slum.

Soon, they reached the ragged edge of Hartford and passed the famous blue Islamic-style dome of the abandoned Colt firearms factory along the elevated freeway near the river. American history looked like it had been carjacked, beaten up, and left for dead here. From a mile away, a cluster of the city's late-twentieth-century glass office towers gleamed with false promise. At that distance the mirrored slabs might be regarded by the simpleminded as interesting monumental sculptures of an exuberant age. One could not so easily perceive the downtown office vacancy rate of over 75 percent, the foreclosed commercial mortgages held by banks teetering on the brink of insolvency and run by anxious fiduciaries contemplating one-way plane tickets to obscure Caribbean pseudonations—as opposed, say, to arrest, trial, and five years in the federal slammer at Lewisburg.

The off-ramp dumped them onto a surface street where the dereliction of the city became palpable. In all directions the business district stood eerily empty on this weekday afternoon, an ordinary business day, as though a plague were apocalyptically burning cell by cell through the ranks of grandiose office towers.

A couple of blocks south of the old gold-domed state capitol, they entered a district of empty redbrick factories on narrow, treeless streets. Here, the industrial revolution looked like a tragic swindle, all the former riches of the empire reduced to a multitude of vacant rooms in dreary worn-out brick behemoths, the machinery long ago sold off for scrap. Here and there along the street they could see the ghosts of ordinary twentieth-century commercial life: rusted Coca-Cola signs denoting bygone lunchrooms, tavern windows boarded up with delaminating plywood. Even the few remaining trash cans in the alleys were empty. A solitary wino, superfluous here in his failure, lurched along the sidewalk emitting a lonesome wail.

"What has happened to our country?" Maggie marveled almost reverently.

"I'm fresh out of easy answers," Walter said, and she was rather grateful for his diffidence.

The adjoining residential neighborhoods looked as though some supernatural rot, a kind of civilizational leprosy, had infected them, producing a desolation more potent than war. This was a blight from which recovery of any kind seemed unlikely, a form of demoralization that cut across the boundaries of living personalities and mere material things, rendering all hope of regeneration permanently moot—the coming attractions of a dead planet.

They methodically crisscrossed the town in the big car. A few streets showed signs of life but of a Hobbesian order: skulking figures drinking out of paper bags in decrepit doorways; a child straddling a broken bicycle, pretending to ride; a woman in red hot-pants crying against a lamppost; a young man beating a broken refrigerator with a length of chain. At one point, crossing Farmington Avenue, they came upon a familiar icon, a large, dark, Victorian house opulently decorated and in oddly good condition. A plaque posted on the sidewalk read MARK TWAIN RESIDENCE.

"My God," Walter groaned. "Imagine what he'd think."

"It's too sad to imagine," Maggie said, thinking nonetheless of that famous photo of Clemens resplendent in a sealskin coat and matching hat at the height of his fortunes, setting forth in the family sleigh with his wife, Olivia, and their three pretty little girls, Susy, Clara, and Jean, for a Yuletide sermon by the Reverend Joe Twitchell to be followed by punch and cakes (and, for the men, whiskey) at Mrs. Stowe's house. This was the Hartford of another planet, not just of another time. "I can't bear to think about it," she muttered.

Remarkably, it was within five blocks of that landmark, on a street named Bovington, that Maggie experienced a jolt of recognition. For there, between a burnt-out wooden triple-decker and a one-story concrete block box that had most recently (seventeen years prior) functioned as a wig shop, they came upon a once proud Italianate brick heap with a green copper verdigris roof. Just under the gable could be seen the carved stone insignia of the Masonic brotherhood. Across the street lay a wretched little square, its few trees scarred and spray-painted, its pavements broken, its benches seatless and backless, and its little central oasis of grass long ago trampled and littered with glass shards, cans, and rusty supermarket carts.

"Wait," Maggie said urgently. "This is it!"

Walter pulled up to the curb. Across the street an old Pontiac Grand Am sat on tireless hubs. The driver's door was missing and all the remaining windows had been smashed. A man and a woman came out the front door and, after carefully glancing up and down the street, furtively scuttled away like a couple of insects.

"So," Walter said, "you think she's in there?"

"Yes. I do. It's just what she described. The little park. Everything."

"Maybe you should stay here in the car while I check it out."

"No way," Maggie retorted. "I'm coming with you."

The heat of the afternoon shocked them when they stepped out of the air-conditioned Toyota. The hard surfaces of the city seemed to amplify the heat. Walter opened the back hatch and rummaged there, quickly finding an umbrella.

"What's that for?"

"In case someone gets smart with us."

8

ᕮ The Very Maw of Evil ᕭ

The interior of the place was designed like a branch bank in hell. It was a high-ceilinged vestibule of perhaps ten by ten feet. At center, a single bare bulb dangled from the end of a long frayed cord. Opposite the entrance stood a kind of teller's station, a steel slot set into a concrete block wall that was rather sloppily constructed, as though by inept amateur masons. The wall itself was decorated with graffiti as well as black, brown, tan, yellow, and fuchsia splashes and smudges suggesting the intentional discharge of various bodily wastes against it. On an adjacent wall—also shoddy cement block—was a steel door, much dented, scratched, and scribbled on. The room stank ferociously. They were unsure how to proceed.

Just then, a customer shambled through the door behind them, a twitchy scarecrow of a man dressed in ragged sporting togs, a man with the physiognomy of youth but the physical mannerisms of old age.

"You coppin'?" he asked them.

"No," Maggie replied. "Why don't you go ahead of us."

The customer regarded them askance, as if politeness was but a dimly remembered, highly suspect convention of another lifetime. When he limped up to the slot in the wall, they observed the transaction at a remove.

"Yo, gimme two blue ice rock," the scarecrow said.

"Ain't got no blue ice," the slot said.

"Gimme a half-crank, den."

"Ain't got no half-crank."

"What the fuck you got den, muthafucker?"

"Got moon rocks."

"Yo, man, dat shit is cut all to shit."

"Dat's de shit we got."

"You muthafuckers sellin' shitty-ass shit."

"You want de shit or not, muthafucker?"

"'Ite, gimme some."

"How much."

"Two dime."

Scarecrow placed a tube of rolled-up bills in the slot. Seconds later, a wooden tongue rather like a pizza paddle protruded from the slot. Two vials containing crack cocaine lay inserted in a groove on it.

"Yo," Scarecrow said into the slot, "I gotta pipe up here."

"You go pipe up yo' sorry ass somewheres else."

"I ain't got no pipe."

"You sell dat, too?"

"No, I sat on de muthafucker."

"You a sorry-ass nigga."

"Yo, come on, man. Lemme in."

"Las' time you peed in de corner."

"Naw, wasn't me. Dat was Slo Mo."

"Dey said it was you."

"Yo, man, fuck dat shit. I seen de muthafucker do it. He inside? I kick his muthafuckin' ass. Come on, man. Buzz me in."

"'Ite. But soon's you high, git de fuck out."

"Yeah, yeah. 'Ite."

The door buzzer went off with such startling loudness that Maggie and Walter both leaped back a step. The scarecrow man skulked into the dimness within. The heavy door slammed shut resoundingly behind him.

"We have to get in," Maggie whispered. "Lindy's back in there somewhere."

"We'll have to buy drugs."

"I suppose so. Here." Maggie extracted a twenty-dollar bill from her wallet.

"No, this one's on me," Walter said. He took a deep breath and proceeded up to the slot.

"Let me have two dimes of those moon rocks," he said.

"Ain't got moon rocks," the slot said.

"Didn't you just—?"

"We out."

"What have you got?"

"Who the fuck you is, white boy?"

"Working man."

"Oh yeah? Why you don't jess make yourself a gin and tonic?" Laughter emanated from the slot, intimating more than one vendor within.

"Lookit, I need some shit," Walter said. "Help me out."

"Dis shit is too nasty for bridge-and-tunnel mo'fuckers."

"We'll take our chances," Walter said and pushed the twenty through the slot.

"I guess a man's gotta do what he gotta do," the slot said. Anon, the wooden paddle emerged with two vials of crack cocaine. Walter pocketed them.

"Buzz us in," he added.

"I don't think so."

"We have to pipe up."

"What are you, crazy, mo'fucker? Dis place is fulla crackheads."

"That's all right. We're used to it."

"Where you-all's from?"

"Westport."

"How come you don't go to yo' own white-ass country club pipe house down there?"

"Because we're here and I need a smoke."

"You a determined muthafucker."

"You don't know the half of it."

"Cost you another twenty, first-time club membership fee."

"Whatever." Walter peeled another twenty out of his wallet and passed it through the slot.

"One more thing. No peein' on de flo."

"Sure thing," Walter said.

The buzzer went off like a Klaxon. He and Maggie stole into the dimness like two innocent children entering an amusement park house of horrors.

Inside, an elaborate old oak staircase, barely lit by a small grimy glass window, corkscrewed up one flight. Mammals of different orders had been using it as a urinal for a long time. They followed the stairway to an enormous, dim room, some forty by fifty feet, the entire footprint of the building. It was the former Masonic lodge, proper, even in its heyday a spookish Gothic chamber for secret ceremonies. The wainscoting had been ripped out. The windows were boarded over. Here and there, low-wattage blue bulbs burned in old wall fixtures, casting an aura of perpetual nighttime through the huge room. Despite the high ceiling, the air was extraordinarily hot, thick, and close, more like a fluid than a gas. Faces appeared sucking on glass pipes in the flare of butane lighters. Old reeking mattresses were deployed across the floor in no particular pattern. Many were occupied singly by ragged persons who looked like shipwrecked mariners riding pieces of flotsam. Some mattresses held groups of three, four, or five individuals sharing a pipe, resembling a scene Maggie recalled from some bygone collegiate bash of the hippie years. More than one sexual performance could be glimpsed through the murk.

They made their way around the room, eliciting a few hostile glances from the still-sentient. In the farthermost corner, in a pool of darkness most remote from any light source, they came upon a shrunken, wasted, but recognizable figure seated on a pallet of filthy foam rubber and bundled in a stinking polyester quilt.

"Oh, dear God, it's her, it's Lindy!" Maggie said, seizing Walter's arm.

At the mention of her name, the wraithlike figure of her old friend and college roommate, who had been staring bug-eyed into fetid space, turned her sunken visage upward in an expression that seemed equally an appeal and an accusation.

"How'd you find me?" she asked raspily.

"You said a Mason's lodge, a green roof, a park. Give me your hand—"

"Wait! How'd you get in here?"

"It doesn't matter. We're here to bring you home. Can you get up by yourself—"

"Did you cop?"

"Yes, we had to buy drugs to get in here," Walter said.

"Who the fuck is he?" Lindy asked Maggie.

"He's my gardener."

"Oh, yeah? You plowing a furrow there, pal?" Lindy said, but her gallows laughter quickly degenerated into a coughing spasm. "I'm sick," she said.

"I know. We're here to help you."

"Then give me some of what you copped."

Maggie and Walter swapped a fretful glance. Walter then reached into his pocket and proffered the two little glass vials.

"All right!" Lindy exclaimed, grabbing them greedily.

"Lindy, this stuff is crack cocaine."

"Duh, really?" Lindy said. She allowed the filthy quilt to fall from her shoulders. She was apparently naked from the waist up. Her ribs showed above two rather flattened, deflated breasts. A dark contusion spread amoebalike between her left clavicle and armpit. With trembling hands she opened one vial and tapped out the rock into the bowl of a glass pipe. Then, with a strange manic precision for someone so obviously ill, she fired up a butane lighter and lit the rock, inhaling the smoke hungrily. "Oh, yeah," she said, exhaling a cloud of acrid chemical smoke. "All right."

"Okay, honey. Give me your hands."

"You got anymore?" Lindy asked, exhaling a huge volume of blue smoke.

"Yes," Walter said.

"Can I have it?"

"No, you can have it later," Maggie said. "For now come with us."

"But I don't want to come with you, okay?"

"Oh, Lindy, honey—"

"Gimme that other rock."

"But you can't stay here."

"Says who?"

"Lindy, dearest, look at this place. It's a disgusting hole."

"I hadn't noticed."

"Obviously your judgment's impaired from all these drugs. Walter, help me get her up."

"Get your hands off me, motherfucker," Lindy screeched, her vocal energy incongruent with her wasted appearance.

"We're taking you to a hospital."

"Get the fuck offa me!"

"Please don't be like this."

"I am like this. This is what I am!"

As she resisted and fought, Maggie and Walter failed to hear the figures stealing up behind them.

"What de fuck you think you doin'?" a familiar voice upbraided them. Maggie and Walter dropped the bag of filthy quilting and bones that was Lindy and turned to see the owner of that voice. He was of an age, physical size, and heft that might have qualified him for defensive line of an NCAA Division One football team—had not other vocational opportunities presented themselves. He was accompanied by a young man half a foot shorter but equally hefty, who sported a bit of nylon stocking headgear that made him look futuristically androidal. "Do you know what you fuckin' with?" the tall one asked.

"Excuse me," Walter replied manfully. "This person is a friend. We've really got to get her out of here."

"Dis'ere is T-Bone's Hollywoot bitch."

"Give T-Bone our regrets," Walter said. As he stooped to retrieve the uncooperative Lindy, the tall figure reached down and, with a hand about the size of a squash racket, slapped the side of Walter's head. Walter struck back with his umbrella, but it was as though he had swatted a bronze statue. Their large adversary snapped the umbrella in half like a twig and flung the pieces off into the darkness—where one bit apparently landed on someone, provoking cries of outrage.

"Y'alls paid but only one special membership. Deys two you come in," the tall one said.

"We'll leave as soon as we can get our friend up," Maggie retorted, her voice quavering but loud.

"You leavin' now, bitch, 'cause we kickin' yo' asses out."

Maggie and Walter were then pulled, shoved, kicked, pushed, dragged, and rolled across the dim, hot, stinking room, past bloodshot eyes wide with hilarity and toothless, raw-gummed smiles, to the stairway and finally back into the entry vestibule, where they came to a halt side by side on the floor against the wall like a couple of rag dolls.

"Are you all right?" Walter gasped to Maggie, clutching her as if to fend off more expected blows.

"I'm all right," she breathed back.

Their attackers loomed over them, glowering. Several jittery crackheads just in from the streets hovered in the background.

"Dat yo' big-ass Toyota outside?" the tall one said.

"Yes," Maggie said.

"Gimme de keys."

Maggie glanced fretfully at Walter.

"It's just a car," Walter told her.

Maggie dug the keys out of the patch pocket of her sundress and reluctantly handed them over.

"Lemme see yo' wallet, dickbrain."

Walter extracted it from his back pocket. The shorter one grabbed it, swiped all the bills and credit cards, and tossed it back.

"You know, we jess tryna run a muthafuckin' bidness here," the tall one said. "You and yo' bitch get de fuck out and don't even think about comin' back."

"Yeah," said the shorter one.

"Are you letting us go?" Maggie asked, rather astounded.

"No, we kicking you out. We don't have time to kill you." He turned to his colleague. "Yo, git dat ride off de street." Then back to Maggie and Walter. "Y'alls git de fuck out my sight, now, 'fo' I change my mind."

Moments later, they were out blinking on the sun-blasted sidewalk, watching the Toyota disappear around the corner.

"What do we do now?" Maggie asked, growing teary again.

"Go to the police," Walter said.

9
⤳ The Fortress ⤳

They found the Fourth Ward precinct house a mere nine blocks from the crack establishment on Bovington Street. It was a one-story industrial box plopped in a parking lot in a neighborhood that had suffered the ravages of "urban renewal" back in the sixties. The building presented windowless facades on all four sides, lending it the look of a science-fiction fortification. The main entrance was a mere hole in the wall. Its flat roof was decorated against casual ingress with coils of razor wire.

The entry vestibule of the precinct station was only marginally more hospitable than that of the crack house. There was no graffiti. It stank of disinfectant rather than urine. The cinder-block room was lighted with fluorescent fixtures and contained a half dozen blow-molded plastic chairs. There were two pay phones and a soda machine against the wall. Like the crack house, business was conducted through a relatively small, fortified aperture, in this case a bulletproof glass window, behind which operated the intake office. A young, male officer with a very short forehead and beetling dark eyebrows that came together at the center, giving him the look of a cookie jar, sat at a counter behind the bulletproof window.

"Our friend is trapped in a crack house on Bovington Street," Maggie told him. "We tried to remove her, but they threw us out."

"You're lucky they threw you out," the officer remarked. His voice came over a little loudspeaker in the wall above the aperture. He sounded as though he were talking through a tin can on a string.

"Sure, but she's still in there," Maggie insisted.

The officer took Lindy's name, age, physical description, et cetera, and said, "Okay, then. Thank you very much."

"What are you going to do?" Maggie asked.

"We'll let you know when she turns up."

"But she could turn up dead."

"Wait a minute, Officer," Walter said, inserting himself before the window, "this gal's life is in danger. She's all drugged up. You've got to get her out."

"Yeah," Maggie said. "You've got to send some men into this place."

"How did she get in there?"

"Someone brought her there."

"Who?"

"I don't know. Some dreadful man."

"And where's this man."

"Who the hell knows. He's a . . . criminal."

"Is he forcing her to do the drugs?"

"Perhaps at first. I don't know. It doesn't matter. She's a slave to the crack now."

"That's how they all get," the officer said.

"She has to be saved from herself," Maggie explained.

"They all do," the officer said.

"Lookit, do you know this house we're talking about?" Walter said.

"Well, there's a lot of these places over there. They come and go. They burn up. Open up elsewhere. Like mushrooms after the rain."

"We'll be happy to lead you directly there," Walter said.

"Sir," the officer said, looking straight through the thick glass, "we don't *storm* crack houses. This is not the Marine Corps."

"You can go in there, though, can't you? With a bunch of guys."

The officer laughed. "Do you know what kind of weapons these characters have?"

"Obviously they have guns."

"That's right. Only theirs are automatic. They fire bullets the way a garden hose sprays water. We don't have that kind of firepower. And if we did, the public wouldn't let us use it."

"Wait a minute," Walter said. "You're telling me that you don't even bother trying to control these places?"

"I wouldn't put it that way."

"How would you put it?"

"We don't believe in committing suicide."

"So you just let these hellholes go about their business?"

"Like I said, we ain't the marines."

"May I speak to your supervisor?" Maggie interjected. "Is there a lieutenant or a captain on the premises?"

"Yeah. He'll tell you the same thing."

In a matter of minutes, a certain Lieutenant Muybridge came to the window. An athletic, somewhat horse-faced man with sleepless eyes and a defeated demeanor, Muybridge told them pretty much the same thing.

"The bottom line here, then, is that you won't do anything," Walter summarized.

"We'll call the building inspector," Muybridge said.

"And what does that accomplish?" Walter asked.

"He determines if the place is in compliance with health and fire codes, and if it's not, he issues a summons."

"And what does that lead to?"

"In a week to ten days it could result in a revocation of certificate of occupancy."

"So, we have to wait about two weeks for you to kick people out of that hellhole."

"Actually, we don't handle evictions. That would be the city health and fire safety commissioner's office."

"But if you guys, the police, won't even go into these places, why would the safety and health people go in there?"

"The truth is, they don't."

"Then this is all just bullshit."

"There's no need to use foul language, sir."

"All right. All right. But it does nothing to solve the immediate problem of our friend, who is being held prisoner in this crack den on Bovington Street."

"No. I suppose not," Muybridge said with a sigh. "But it does show the importance of personal responsibility and healthy lifestyle choices."

"Cowards!" Maggie screamed, unable to control herself any longer. "Craven bastards! Worms! Pussies!"

"Sir, tell your wife that we don't tolerate abusive behavior here. This station is our home. You wouldn't want us to come into your home and holler vulgarities, would you?"

"You haven't heard the end of this, Lieutenant," Walter said. "There's still an attorney general's office in the state of Connecticut and we're going to complain long and loud."

"There's a pay phone over there. Feel free to call them. They'll tell you the same thing. We follow established procedure here. We don't invade secured drug depots with SWAT teams. We're not cowboys. It's that simple."

"Wait!" Maggie cried. "I have an idea."

Both Walter and Lieutenant Muybridge looked at her with anticipation. She hurried across the room to the phone and dialed New York City on her calling card number.

10
⟆ The Cavalry ⟅

"Lawrence Hayward," she told the receptionist. "Maggie Darling calling."
 The Merlin of the Markets picked up a moment later.
 "Oh, Maggie, I'm so terribly sorry," he began.
 "Excuse me . . . ?" she said, instantly taken aback.
 "You mean you haven't heard?"
 "Heard? What?"
 "About Kenneth."
 "What about him?"
 "Why, he was picked up this afternoon for sniping cars along the
Merritt Parkway."
 There ensued a stunned pause. With different personalities in
the same circumstances, the interlude might have been filled by such
pungent exclamations as "Fuck me gently with a chain saw!" or "Holy
jumping weeping Jesus on the cross!" but in this case there was only
shocked silence.
 "Hello, Maggie? Are you there?"
 "Yes," she fairly croaked, having become worn down to a nubbin
by cumulative disaster.
 "Awful sorry to break the news," Hayward said.
 "Well . . ."
 "Is there anything I can do for you, Maggie?"
 "Actually, yes."
 "What?"

"You can send a small troop of heavily armed mercenaries to Hartford, Connecticut, as soon as possible and help rescue my friend Lindy—you remember Lindy, don't you?"

"Yeah, sure. Skinny brunette. We had dinner one time at your place."

"That's right."

"You say she needs to be rescued?"

"Yes, she does."

"From what?"

"A crack house."

"Crack? As in drugs?"

"Yes."

"Well, I'll be. How'd she get mixed up in that?"

"Don't ask."

"When you say 'troop,' what did you have in mind, Maggie?"

"Oh, say, twenty guys with machine guns."

There was another pause, this time at Hayward's end.

"I can do that," he eventually said.

"Great."

"You want 'em right away?"

"The sooner the better."

"Where are you now?"

"Police station somewhere in Hartford."

"They're useless sonsabitches, aren't they?"

"You said it."

"Do you know the address there?"

"No. Wait a second." Maggie hollered at the intake window. "Walter, ask the lieutenant for the address of this place."

"Right," Walter said and conferred with Muybridge. "It's 2009 Charity Street," he reported.

Maggie relayed it to Hayward. "Say, how will you ever find us?"

"Global positioning, dear. I could pin the tail on a donkey with it ten thousand miles from my desk."

"No kidding?"

"It's a brave new world of consumer electronics, Maggie. Say, anyplace we might put down a helicopter there?"

"Oh, there's acres of parking around the building."

"Swell. Give me an hour and a half."

"Okay. That would be about seven-fifteen P.M."

"Roger," Hayward said.

"Lawrence, are you really serious?"

"Oh, absolutely."

"You're going to show up here in an hour and a half in a helicopter with a gang of armed thugs?"

"Thugs is a little . . . indelicate. Call them highly trained counterterrorist specialists. And you can bet we'll be there on the dot. You just sit tight."

"Okay, then."

"Say, Maggie. When you rang I was just on my way to a terrific new discovery. Unigatzsu, on Greene Street. Little hole in the wall. Heard of it?"

"No."

"You wouldn't believe what they do with abalone."

"The stuff is hell to work with. You've got to beat the devil out of it with a mallet."

"Really? Mine was as tender as milk-fed veal."

"Some people have the knack."

"Well, thank God for that," Hayward said. "See you in a little while."

Maggie told Lieutenant Muybridge and Walter that the cavalry was coming, so to speak. Muybridge was amused. He told them to go ahead and have a seat, make themselves comfortable "until zero hour, ha ha"—while he surreptitiously flipped some Rolodex cards on the intake desk to find the phone number of the psychiatric unit at Hartford General.

11
⇜ The Op ⇝

Imagine the surprise of all the officers and staff present in the Fourth Ward station house when, at precisely 7:13 P.M. the *whupwhupwhup* of helicopter rotor blades became audible through the building's concrete walls. Maggie and Walter rushed outside to see the huge Sikorsky touch down mere yards from Lieutenant Muybridge's very own five-year-old Geo Prizm coupe. Policemen of all ranks debouched the dreary building and went to the parking lot to gawk.

Hayward was first to hit the ground, wearing a flak jacket over his gray Brooks Brothers business suit and also a baseball cap bearing the logo of Cleansweep Military Technology Services—an eagle clutching a broom and a dustpan in its talons—a company he had picked up at a fire sale in March. Behind him, the aircraft disgorged twenty-two "peace associates" (PAs), as the company called its employees, armed with fully automatic AMT-Harlan 9mm carbines, twelve-gauge magazine-feed British Rackley "street sweeper" riot guns, concussion grenades, armor-piercing rockets, tear gas canisters, and enough ammunition to put down a medium-size insurrection in an average Third World capital city—which was a close approximation of what Hartford, Connecticut, had become.

The police would not hear of lending any of their vehicles for the operation. There was brief discussion about calling taxicabs, but in the end it was decided that the PAs (and everyone else) could more easily walk the nine blocks to their objective on Bovington.

The men were led by their team leader, Howard "Howie the Hawk" Kaplan, veteran of the U.S. Special Forces with bravery citations from the pacification op in Streltzy, Serbia, back in the nineties. Through the ruined streets they went, past the hibachis of the homeless and the disintegrating houses of the powerless, the moneyless, the hopeless, the fatherless, the feckless, the reckless, and the aimless—all stepping outdoors, blinking, into the harsh, hot evening sunlight as Hartfordites of a bygone epoch might have watched the passing of a circus parade—making their way in close order like an occupying army across town toward the former Masonic lodge on Bovington.

Once there, the "overtake operation" took a total of thirty-eight seconds from entry to Team Leader Kaplan's declaration of "Site secured." From out on the sidewalk, a few mere pops were heard. Then silence. Then the building came alive as maundering crackheads poured out the front door like roaches fleeing the exterminator's toxic wand.

"There's some slumber bunnies upstairs," Agent Kaplan reported, "case you want to ID the hostage."

"Huh?" Maggie said. She was so overwhelmed by the dazzling efficiency of it all that it took her a moment to realize that he was referring to Lindy, the object of the operation. She marshaled her wits and crying "Lindy!" hurried inside. Among the crack house staff being rounded up at gunpoint was the shorter of the two who had thrown them out earlier in the afternoon. His wrists were bound with plastic twisty-cuffs.

"That fellow took our car!" Walter exclaimed.

"Did you take their car?" Agent Kaplan interrogated the man.

"Yo, wussup wid dis. You ain't no po-lice."

"That's true," Agent Kaplan said. "So when I put the muzzle of this nine between your little buns and pull the trigger, you won't be able to call it police brutality. Think you can remember where that car is now?"

"Yeah."

He was led off with three PAs to find it. At the same time, his taller colleague was carried out of the building horizontally in a latex bag on a stretcher.

Meanwhile, Maggie had ascended to the Masonic sanctum above. Flashlights cut through the dense, fetid air like knives through dirty gelatin. One addict kneeled on all fours vomiting onto the floor. The lights revealed another lying where she had been strangled hours earlier by the man with whom she had conceived a child that would never enter this world. A few others were too weak or too drunk-stoned-smacked-and-cracked to move. Then there was Lindy.

She lay in her stinking quilt panting and spasming, the result of one last speedball of the poorest quality, more methadrine and animal tranquilizer than true crank, with some toilet cleanser tossed in for good measure.

"Oh, dearest one." Maggie fell at her side, ignoring the stench. "Just hang on. Hang on to life. We're here now."

Lindy tried to speak, but the sounds were not really words, and frothy bubbles were forming on her lips.

"She could go into arrest any moment," said one Agent Grimsby, who had been a medic in the Kazakhstan airport hostage incident of the previous summer in which nine U.S. Marines had been gassed.

"Okay, let's get a stretcher up here, pronto," said Hayward, who knelt beside Maggie and held her shoulders. In less than a minute six agents were carrying Lindy double-time up Bovington Street, back toward the waiting helicopter in the police parking lot. Then, suddenly, magically, they were aloft, swinging up, up over the wounded city, up over the golden dome of the state house, over the empty factories and the forgotten lives, and all that forsaken Yankee heritage, up and away, until the tattered cityscape and its asteroid belt of malls and parking lots gave way to soft green woods and a tender patchwork of summer fields and pastures. As they rose higher in the sky, the temperature dropped until it was actually chilly in the shuddering barn of the huge chopper's cabin. Walter held the saline bag of Lindy's hydration IV. As the revivifying fluid entered her struggling cells, she tried to speak again. This time, words came out. Maggie had to hold her ears to Lindy's cracked, peeling lips to hear through the horrible machine hubbub of the aircraft.

"I'm f-f-f-freezing," Lindy said.

"We'll be at the hospital real soon," Maggie assured her and pulled the Mylar emergency blanket up around Lindy's ears.

"Rem-m-m-m-member that first week of . . . s-s-s-s-school?"
Lindy said.

"I do, dearest. Like it was yesterday."

"You . . . you b-b-b-baked a b-b-b-birthday cake for . . . for
K-K-K-Katie Spofford in my . . . my . . . my toaster oven?"

"Yes, I remember, Lindy. It was a lady cake."

"L-l-l-lady cake," Lindy repeated. A smile played across her face,
momentarily erasing all the sickness and agony of recent months. "I
th-th-th-thought, this chick is a p-p-p-perfect fucking angel. The
f-f-f-future seemed im-m-m-mense. I r-r-r-remember what it was like
to want . . . want . . . to l-l-l-live."

"You're going to live. You're already getting better."

"B-b-b-but I don't want to."

"Don't say that."

"It's t-t-t-too fucking d-d-d-difficult."

"It only seems that way because you're unhappy."

"No. No, you don't understand. Th-th-th-this is the secret of life.
I s-s-s-see it now. Some p-p-p-people are good at it. You're g-g-g-good
at it. I'm just t-t-t-taking up space with m-m-m-my stupid p-p-p-
problems."

"You'll get over them. You can be happy. I swear."

"No. I'm n-n-n-no fucking g-g-g-good at this. Y-y-y-you live for
me, Maggie."

Tears ran down her face and dripped onto Lindy's.

"Tell you w-w-w-what."

"What, dearest Lindy?"

"I'll g-g-g-go up to . . . to heaven and t-t-t-turn down the sheets
for you. It's the . . . the least I c-c-can do to . . . to repay all your . . .
k-k-k-kindness." Suddenly, Lindy's mouth drew into a rictus and her
eyes bulged. A great spasmic shudder rocked her and a strange rattling
noise issued from deep within.

"Oh, Lindy," Maggie howled. Walter put down the saline bag
and came around the stretcher to take Maggie in his arms. She resisted
for a moment and then yielded, feeling as she sank against his strong,
dense frame like a small furry animal who had come home to a famil-

iar place beneath a great sheltering oak tree after a terrifying journey in a strange land.

Agent Grimsby muscled in to attempt CPR, but Lindy failed to respond, did not come back, would not come back.

"It's a damn shame," Hayward reflected, turning to watch the astounding spires of Manhattan appear at the horizon in the syrupy summer twilight. "Funny, though," he continued, speaking to no one in particular, "I have a lot of hope for mankind. Didn't used to but I do now, despite all I've seen, all I know. A strange feeling has come over me lately. I'm convinced that a new day is at hand. We won't all get there, but some of us will. Those of us who would be saved have to save ourselves. If I ever wrote a book—and I just might do it—that would be the moral of the story. It would also be nice if everybody lived happily ever after. Who knows? This is a mysterious universe. Anything's possible. Even happiness."

Epilogue
᭡ Noel ᭡

The winter solstice of that year brought viewers of the Family TV Cable Network "A Maggie Darling Christmas," taped in the ballroom of the house at Kettle Hill Farm on a snowy night that could not have been more perfectly New England. Public opinion had swung back Maggie's way at the end of this *annus horribilis*. On the eve of jury selection for the Merritt Parkway sniper trial, it was announced that defendant Kenneth Darling had signed a deal with Apex Communications—parent company of Trice and Wanker Publishers—for a tell-all book about his twenty-year-marriage to the goddess of hearth and home. He hated to do it, Connie McQuillan reported in *People* magazine, but there was no other way to cover his lawyers' fees. (Ms. McQuillan, incidentally, was not among the 214 guests invited to the taping of "A Maggie Darling Christmas," nor for all Christmases to come so long as there is a Christmas.)

It happened that Maggie had seen a Xerox copy of Kenneth's book proposal—she still had friends in the employ of Trice and Wanker, though it was no longer her publisher—and it was a pitifully composed semiliterate pack of lies involving stock pornographic fantasies of the most puerile kind and wild accusations of Maggie's infidelity with everyone from Mr. Steve Eddy of Hollywood, California, to the vice president of the United States. In fact, it was such a meretricious bundle of self-evident absurdity that Maggie deemed it beneath her dignity to even bring suit against her former husband, who, in any case, stood to forfeit his life on the alter of justice for the deliberate murder of twelve Connecticut citizens.

Besides the scurrilous Ms. McQuillan and the dastardly Kenneth, a number of other personalities present at the previous Christmas Feast for Two Hundred either could not come or were not invited to return. Frederick Swann was in London preparing for the December 25 opening of *Starvation,* Franz Tesla's $165 million vampire epic. The stakes were so high that Basilisk Pictures had to sink $40 million into advertising and promotion alone. The showbiz grapevine had it that the movie was an unspeakable abortion. Swann himself was said to have shown promise as an actor but had forsworn any future roles because of the hardships of life on a movie set—all that waiting around, the fussing of the makeup artists, the gaffers' never-ending technical boo-boos, the extreme boredom of it all, not to mention the travail of dealing with such monsters of egotism as Tesla. Swann told *Rolling Stone* magazine that he was happier singing his "little ditties," as he called them, and playing a benefit concert once a year for Her Majesty.

Harold Hamish would not have been invited to the party taping even if he had not suffered the misfortune of being clipped in the groin by the mirror of a speeding gypsy cab in front of St. Patrick's Cathedral the week after Thanksgiving. In any case, he could watch "A Maggie Darling Christmas" on TV, if inclined, from his hospital bed at Columbia Presbyterian, where he was still recovering from penile reattachment surgery.

Leonard Moile would have been invited, but an aortic embolism intervened in September of the year and his ashes had since been scattered around the kelp-carpeted rocks of his beloved summerhouse in Bar Harbor.

Fedo Prado, of the New York City Ballet, was prevented from attending by the AIDS virus. Lucius Milstein had taken his own life (asphyxiation by oven à la Sylvia Plath) after being described as "an arrant fraud" in the *New Yorker*'s coverage of the Whitney Biennial. Milstein had long been considered mentally unstable and had threatened to kill himself so many times before that even his art dealer laughed at his continual threats. The morning after his body was found in his West Broadway loft, the price of his fraudulent paintings quadrupled.

Of course, Maggie's mother, Irene, and stepfather, Charlie, were not there because Maggie detested them—guilty as this made her feel.

Nina Stegman had returned to the fold, no longer as an employee but as a dear friend who was now the proprietor of a fabulously successful seafood restaurant, Nautilus, on the sound in Fairfield. And where would she be found this evening, in the hour of pre-party culinary-preparation panic? But, of course: in the kitchen, helping to mount the angels on their savory horsebacks and test the hams and taste the plum puddings and whisk the hard sauce and generally to lend a hand to Rosie Bly, the formerly pink-haired, former Columbus Avenue shop clerk who had so impressed Maggie with her poise and self-possession that she had given her a chance to run the Kettle Hill Farm kitchen. Rosie had proven herself magnificently in the months that followed Lindy Hagan's tragic departure from this world.

With regard to Lindy, there was the matter of Buddy Hagan, lately of Hollywood, California: upon learning that he was, in fact, HIV-negative, he had moved to a Benedictine monastery in Novato, taken the vows, given away his house, his Mercedes, his cell phone, and everything except his Montblanc Diplomat pen, and had rededicated his life to the service of Christ and mankind.

Lawrence Hayward was fully a hundred pounds heavier than he was at Christmas a year ago.

Not invited under any circumstances, and no longer present in this world of sin, either (but of some account to this narrative), were members of the Businessmen's Lunch Posse, aka the entertainers Chill Az Def. They had been gunned down in an ambush laid jointly by the FBI, DEA, and ATF, who, having received a tip about an upcoming caper at Bouley Bakery on Halloween Day, had arranged to pose as customers and staff in an attempt to entrap the bandits. In the course of the operation, Murphy's law had asserted itself, resulting in the death of one ATF agent and all members of the posse. The rights to their life stories were purchased by the Disney Corporation, which planned to make an animated feature and a line of children's action figures based on their "hip-hop Robin Hood" exploits. Their sudden demise—and the secrets that died with them—permitted Hooper Darling to return from exile in Rome, where he had settled in a garret behind the Piazza Navona and spent half the year sketching the classical orders and antiquities in preparation for the architecture program at Notre Dame.

Having been home for a month now, Hooper was therefore on hand for the Christmas festivities this enchanted evening and was very much occupied by the alluring Sarah Jane Fayerwether, who had become a production assistant for Maggie Darling's newest venture, the *Maggie Darling Way,* a monthly magazine of recipes, domestic crafts, and gardening that was an instant runaway hit at the airport newsstands, with a circulation of just under one million after four months of operation. Hooper and Sarah Jane made a lovely picture, full of vitality, promise, beauty, and gravitas. Something equally felicitous could be said for Sarah Jane's father, Walter Fayerwether, and Hooper's mom, Maggie Darling, only the picture of them was not a figurative but a literal one—composed and shot this holiday evening by Reggie Chang as they stood hand in hand beside the glowing hearth in the music room, in those magically fraught moments of anticipation when everything that could possibly be looked after had been looked after, before the first guests arrived.

By Columbus Day, Walter had given up the pretense of keeping a domicile of his own and moved into the mistress's house (and bedchamber) at Kettle Hill Farm. He still supervised the gardens, but he was now Maggie's business manager as well, and it was he who held chief responsibility for organizing the new magazine and hiring its staff, negotiating the twenty-six-weeks-per-year Wednesday feature appearance of Maggie Darling on *Good Morning America* (at a cozy $3.4 million a year), and licensing the Maggie Darling line of kitchenware to Neiman Marcus and the signature apparel line to the Gap. The divorce from Kenneth would be granted around Valentine's Day, whether he was sentenced to lethal injection or not, and there were intimations around Kettle Hill Farm of an upcoming nuptial event in the springtime.

The state of the nation early in the twenty-first century could be described as precarious but holding. The Pacific Northwest had not yet seceded, despite the best efforts of the radical ecologists. Boston was the hot new city. San Francisco's stock was decidedly down after another earthquake (moderate: 5.1 on the Richter scale). Los Angeles was a hopeless ethnic war zone. The Biscayne aquifer was drowning in salt water as the ocean's level rose with global warming; Florida's coast would soon be uninhabitable. Atlanta was choking on its car traffic. The Hanta virus replaced AIDS as the most lethal contagious disease in the U.S., with severe outbreaks in Las Vegas, Phoenix, and Albuquerque. The Miss America Pageant was discontinued. The New York Yankees were sold to Madonna and took up residence in a brand-new ballpark on 125th Street. The St. Louis Rams moved to Salt Lake City. The cuisine of the decade was Tibetan ("Chinese done by the Scots," quipped Maureen Dowd in the *Times*).

More than this it would be unfair to reveal, except to say that the human race's indefatigable resilience allowed us, even in the most trying of times, to carry forward the difficult enterprise of civilization.